MONA AWAD was born in Montreal and now lives in the USA. A graduate of York University in Toronto, her debut novel, *13 Ways of Looking at a Fat Girl*, won the 2016 Amazon Best First Novel Award, the Colorado Book Award and was shortlisted for the Giller Prize and the Arab American Book Award. Her writing has appeared in *McSweeney's, TIME magazine, Electric Literature, VICE, The Walrus* and elsewhere.

Also by Mona Awad

13 Ways of Looking at a Fat Girl

Mona Awad

Bunny

First published in the UK in 2019 by Head of Zeus Ltd
This paperback edition first published in the UK in 2020 by Head of Zeus Ltd

19

A catalogue record for this book is available from the British Library.

ISBN (PB): 9781788545440
ISBN (E): 9781788545457

Typeset by Adrian McLaughlin

Printed and bound in Great Britain by
CPI Group (UK) Ltd, Croydon CRO 4YY

Head of Zeus Ltd
5–8 Hardwick Street
London EC1R 4RG

WWW.HEADOFZEUS.COM

For Jess

Contents

Part One

I

We call them Bunnies because that is what they call each other. Seriously. Bunny.

Example:

Hi, Bunny!

Hi, Bunny!

What did you do last night, Bunny?

I hung out with you, Bunny. Remember, Bunny?

That's right, Bunny, you hung out with me and it was the best time I ever had.

Bunny, I love you.

I love you, *Bunny.*

And then they hug each other so hard I think their chests are going to implode. I would even secretly hope for it from where I sat, stood, leaned, in the opposite corner of the lecture hall, department lounge, auditorium, bearing witness to four grown women—my academic peers—cooingly strangle each other hello. Or good-bye. Or *just because you're so amazing, Bunny.* How fiercely they gripped each other's pink-and-white bodies, forming a hot little circle of such rib-crushing love and understanding it took my breath away. And then the nuzzling of ski-jump noses, peach fuzzy cheeks. Temples pressed against temples in a way that made me think of the labial rubbing of the bonobo or the telepathy of beautiful, murderous children in horror films. All eight of their eyes shut tight as if this collective asphyxiation were a kind of religious bliss. All four of their glossy mouths making squealing sounds of monstrous love that hurt my face.

I love you, Bunny.

I quietly prayed for the hug implosion all year last year. That their ardent squeezing might cause the flesh to ooze from the sleeves, neckholes, and A-line hems of their cupcake dresses like so much inane frosting. That they would get tangled in each other's *Game of Thrones* hair, choked by the ornate braids they were forever braiding into each other's heart-shaped little heads. That they would choke on each other's blandly grassy perfume.

Never happened. Not once.

They always came apart from these embraces intact and unwounded despite the ill will that poured forth from my staring eyes like so much comic-book-villain venom. Smiling at one another. Swinging clasped hands. Skins aglow with affection and belonging as though they'd just been hydrated by the purest of mountain streams.

Bunny, I love you.

Completely immune to the disdain of their fellow graduate student. Me. Samantha Heather Mackey. Who is not a Bunny. Who will never be a Bunny.

I pour myself and Ava more free champagne in the far corner of the tented green, where I lean against a white Doric pillar bedecked with billowing tulle. September. Warren University. The Narrative Arts department's annual welcome back *Demitasse,* because this school is too Ivy and New England to call a party a party. Behold the tiger-lily-heavy centerpieces. Behold the Christmas-lit white gauze floating everywhere like so many ghosts. Behold the pewter trays of salmon pinwheels, duck-liver crostini topped with little sugared orchids. Behold the white people in black discussing grants they earned to translate poets no one reads from the French. Behold the lavish tent under which the overeducated mingle, well versed in every art but the one of conversation. Smilingly oblivious to the fact that they are in the mouth of hell. Or as Ava and I call it, the Lair of Cthulhu. Cthulhu is a giant squid monster invented by a horror writer who went insane and died here. And you know what, it makes sense. Because you can feel it when you're walking down the streets beyond the Warren Bubble that this town is a wrong town. Something not quite right about the houses, the trees, the light. Bring this up and most people just look at you. But not Ava. Ava says, *My god, yes. The town, the houses, the trees, the light—it's all fucked.*

I stand here, I sway here, full of tepid sparkling and animal livers and whatever hard alcohol Ava keeps pouring from her Drink Me flask into my plastic cup. "What's in this again?" I ask.

"Just drink it," she says.

I observe from behind borrowed sunglasses as the women whom I must call my colleagues reunite after a summer spent apart in various trying locales such as remote tropical islands, the south of France, the Hamptons. I watch their fervent little bodies lunge for each other in something like rapture. Nails the color of natural poisons digging into each other's forearms with the force of what I keep telling myself is feigned, surely feigned, affection. Shiny lips parting to call each other by their communal pet name.

"Jesus, are they for real?" Ava whispers in my ear now. She has never seen them up close. Didn't believe me when I first told her about them last year. Said, *There is no way grown women act like that. You're making this up, Smackie.* Over the summer, I started to think I had too. It is a relief in some ways to see them now, if only to confirm I am not insane.

"Yes," I say. "Too real."

I watch her survey them through her fishnet veil, her David Bowie eyes filled with horror and boredom, her mouth an unimpressed red line.

"Can we go now?"

"I can't leave yet," I say, my eyes still on them. They've pulled apart from one another at last, their twee dresses not even rumpled. Their shiny heads of hair not even disturbed. Their skins glowing with health insurance as they all crouch down in unison to collectively coo at a professor's ever jumping shih tzu.

"*Why?*"

"I told you, I have to make an appearance."

Ava looks at me, slipping drunkenly down the pillar. I have said hello to no one. Not the poets who are their own fresh, grunty hell. Not the new incoming fiction writers who are laughing awkwardly by the shrimp tower. Not even Benjamin, the friendly administrator to whom I usually cling at these sorts of functions, helping him dollop quivering offal onto dried bits of toast. Not my Workshop leader from last spring, Fosco, or any other member of the esteemed faculty. *And how was your summer, Sarah? And how's the thesis coming, Sasha?* Asked with polite indifference. Getting my name wrong always. Whatever response I offer—an earnest confession of my own imminent failure, a bald-faced lie that sets my face aflame—will elicit the same knowing nod, the same world-weary smile, a delivery of platitudes about the Process being elusive, the Work being a difficult mistress. *Trust, Sasha. Patience, Sarah. Sometimes you have to walk away, Serena. Sometimes, Stephanie, you have to seize the bull by the horns.* This will be followed by the recounting of a similar creative crisis/breakthrough they experienced while on a now-defunct residency in remote Greece, Brittany, Estonia. During which I will nod and dig my fingernails into my upper-arm flesh.

And obviously I haven't talked to the Lion. Even though he's here, of course. Somewhere. I saw him earlier out of the corner of my eye, more maned and tattooed than ever, pouring himself a glass of red wine at the open bar. Though he didn't look up, I felt him see me. And then I felt him see me see him see me and keep pouring. I haven't seen him since then so much as sensed him in my nape hair. When we first arrived, Ava felt he must be nearby *because look, the sky just darkened out of nowhere.*

This evening, all I have done in terms of socializing is half smile at the one the Bunnies call Psycho Jonah, my social equivalent among the poets, who is standing alone by the punch, smiling beatifically in his own antidepressant-fueled fever dream.

Ava sighs and lights a cigarette with one of the many tea lights that dot our table. She looks back at the Bunnies, who are now stroking each other's arms with their small, small hands. "I miss you, Bunny," they say to each other in their fake little girl voices, even though they are standing right fucking next to each other, and I can taste the hate in their hearts like iron on my tongue.

"I miss *you,* Bunny. This summer was so hard without you. I barely wrote a word, I was so, so sad. Let's never ever part again, please?"

Ava laughs out loud at this. Actually laughs. Throws her feathery head back. Doesn't bother to cover her mouth with her gloved hand. It's a delicious, raucous sound. Ringing in the air like the evening's missing music.

"*Shhhhh,*" I hiss at her. But it's already done.

The laughter causes the one I call the Duchess to turn her head of long, silver faery-witch locks in our direction. She looks at us. First at Ava. Then at me. Then at Ava again. She is surprised, perhaps, to see that for once I'm not alone, that I have a friend. Ava meets her look with wide-open eyes the way I do in my dream stares. Ava's gaze is formidable and European. She continues to smoke and sip my champagne without breaking eye contact. She once told me about a staring contest she had with a gypsy she met on a metro in Paris. The woman was staring at her, so Ava stared back—the two of them aiming their gazes at each other like guns—all the way across the City of Lights. Just looking at each other from opposite shores of the rattling train. Eventually Ava took off her earrings, still not taking her eyes off the woman. Why? Because her assumption at that point, of course, was that the two of them would fight to the death. But when the train pulled into the last stop on the line, the woman just stood to exit, and when she did so, she even held back the sliding doors politely, so Ava could go first.

What's the lesson here, Smackie?

Don't jump to conclusions?

Never lower your gaze first.

The Duchess, in turning toward us, causes a ripple effect of turning among the other Bunnies. First Cupcake looks over. Then Creepy Doll with her tiger eyes. Then Vignette with her lovely Victorian skull face, her stoner mouth wide open. They each look at Ava, then at me, in turn, scanning down from our heads to our feet, their eyes taking us in like little mouths sipping strange drinks. As they do, their noses twitch, their eight eyes do not blink, but stare and stare. Then they look back at the Duchess and lean in to each other, their lip-glossed mouths forming whispery words.

Ava squeezes my arm, hard.

The Duchess turns and arches an eyebrow at us. She raises a hand up. Is there an invisible gun in it? No. It's an empty, open hand. With which she then waves. At me. With something like a smile on her face. *Hi,* her mouth says.

My hand shoots up of its own accord before I can even stop myself. I'm waving and waving and waving. *Hi,* I'm saying with my mouth, even though no sound comes out.

Then the rest of the Bunnies hold up a hand and wave too.

We're all waving at one another from across the great shores of the tented green.

Except Ava. She continues to smoke and stare at them like they're a four-headed beast. When at last I lower my hand, I turn to her. She's looking at me like I'm something worse than a stranger.

2

The next day, I find the invitation in my school mailbox, expertly folded into a white origami swan. One of them must have slipped it in between the experimental poetry journals and the postcard-size ads for faculty readings, a Romanian documentary, and a one-woman play about the town being The Body and The Body being the town. I came here early, in the off-hours, to see if my monthly stipend check had arrived. No check. I tip the rest of my mail into the recycling bin, then stare at the swan, upon which one of them has drawn a rudimentary face with magenta ink. Two bleeding dots for eyes—one on either side of its very sharp beak, which, with the help of some dimples and inky lipstick—appear to be smiling at me. On one of its wings, the words *Open Me* ☺

Samantha Heather Mackey,
YOU are cordially invited to . . .

SMUT SALON

When: The Blue Hour ☺
Where: You know where ☺
Bring: Yourself, please ☺

I stare at the loopy, shimmering font, the little hearts one of them (had to be Cupcake, or possibly Creepy Doll?) has drawn around my name. I feel myself start to sweat though it's freezing in this hallway. Mistake. Has to be. No way in hell they would ever invite me to Smut Salon. That was their own private Bunny thing, like Touching Tuesdays or binge-watching *The Bachelorette* or making little woodland creatures out of marzipan. Something they'd talk about in low voices all last year, while we were waiting for Workshop to begin.

Smut Salon last night was SO crazy oh my god.

I drank WAY too much last night at Smut Salon.

I was thinking that for next Smut Salon we should . . .

And then they'd cup each other's ears and whisper the rest.

I scan the invitation again. Impossible that it's for me. But it has my name on it and everything. *Samantha Heather Mackey* flanked by bloated hearts. At the sight of my name rendered in those loops, I feel a weird and shameful swelling in my heart. I recall them waving last night. First the Duchess, then the other Bunnies. How I waved and waved back so adamantly.

It'll be just us five again in Workshop this semester. Which starts tomorrow. I'd been dreading it all summer. Just me and them in a room with no visible escape routes for two hours and twenty minutes. Every week for thirteen weeks. I imagined it would be much like last year. Me on one side of the table and them on the other, sitting in a huglike huddle, becoming one body with four heads the more I narrowed my eyes. The Duchess reading aloud from a diamond-etched pane of glass while the Bunnies closed their eyes as if hearing an actual aria.

Holding hands while they praised each other's stories. *Can I have five thousand more pages of this, please? Can I just say I loved living in your lines and that's where I want to live now forever?* Petting each other absently while they discussed the weekly reading. Suddenly erupting with laughter at an inside joke, a laughter in which I never participated because I was never in on the joke, which they never explained because they were too busy laughing. *Sorry, Samantha,* they might say between gasps, *you weren't there.* No, I might agree, I wasn't. It could go on for several minutes, this laughter. They would shake with it, grow teary-eyed, grip each other's wrists and shoulders in the throes of it while I sat on the other side of the table, watching them or a nothing space between their heads. Meanwhile, Fosco observed us all, saying nothing. I started coming to class later and later. And by the end, I didn't come at all. *Where's Samantha?* I imagined Fosco asking. *We have no idea.* Shrugs of their sweatered shoulders. Helpless smiles.

But maybe they're actually trying to include me this year? Maybe this invitation is a gesture of kindness? Or it might be a joke. Of course it's a joke. I picture a pair of small-fingered hands folding the swan at a grand oak desk that looks out onto a view of canopied trees. A balmy grin biting on itself with small white teeth.

"Bitches," I say very quietly in the hall.

"Hey, Sam."

I jump. Jonah. Standing beside me, leafing through his mailbox, smiling his *Eternal Sunshine of the Spotless Mind* smile.

"Jonah, you scared me."

"Sorry, Sam." He really looks sorry. "Hey, who were you talking to just now?"

"No one. Just me. I talk to myself sometimes."

"Me too." He grins. "All the time." Soup-bowl haircut. An unzipped parka that he never takes off. Underneath he's wearing a T-shirt featuring a kitten playing keyboards in outer space. Jonah's a recovering addict who is so saturated with meds that he speaks as though his voice is tunneling through sludge. He's the best poet in the Program by far. Also the friendliest, the most generous with cigarettes. I don't quite know why he's so reviled by his fellow poets—apart from a couple of mixed-genre classes, poets and fiction writers tend to be siloed from one another both academically and socially. But I've seen Jonah trailing behind his cohort on the street, sitting in the far corner of class in Workshop, smilingly staring into space while they eviscerate him with their feedback. I know what this feels like, of course. The difference is, Jonah doesn't seem to care. He appears to be more or less content to remain adrift and immune in his poetry cloud.

"What are you up to, Sam?"

"Oh, just looking for my stipend check."

"Oh, hey, me too." He looks ecstatic. "I need it so much. I bought all these books and records and then I pretty much had to live on pasta for the rest of the month. Do you ever do that?"

"Yeah." I don't do that. I can't afford to. I stiffen a little.

"Hey, do you think you'll go to this?" He holds up the play postcard.

"No," I snap. Then I feel bad. I add, "I sort of hate plays, Jonah."

"Oh. Me too, mostly. Hey, I saw you at the party last night. I had an extra smoke waiting for you in the alley but you never showed."

"Yeah. I left early."

"Oh." He nods in a dreamy, knowing way. I've basically gotten to know Jonah over shared cigarettes in the alleys, corners, and back porches of the various department parties and functions I'm trying to dodge. I'll be sneaking out the door, desperate to escape, and I'll find him out there in the dark cold, shivering and smoking by the dumpster. *Hey, Samantha.* That's how I learned that, like me, he's the only one in his cohort who didn't come from a renowned undergraduate program. That he too applied to what we are continually told is one of the most exclusive, selective, hard-to-get-into MFA programs in the country on a lark, thinking No Way in Hell.

Isn't it a trip to be here? he said to me on the back porch at one of the first parties.

Yeah, I slurred, my eyes on the Bunnies, already in the midst of one of their communal, eyes-shut-tight, boa-constricting embraces, even though they'd only just met.

It's sort of like a dream, Jonah continued. *I keep thinking when will I wake up, you know? Like maybe I should ask someone to punch me.*

You mean pinch you?

A pinch wouldn't wake me up from this. And if it did, I'd be back in Fairbanks, living in my dad's basement. Where would you be if I punched you, Samantha?

Staring at the brick wall of my life from behind a cash

register in the intermountain West, I thought. Writing myself elsewhere in the evenings.

Mordor, I told Jonah.

We better not punch each other then, I guess, he said, grinning at me.

"So how's your writing going, Sam? Did you *take advantage of the summer*?" He smiles. He's making fun of our Mixed-Genre Workshop leader last spring, Halstrom, who kept telling us we *must not let the summer pass us by*. Because this year, the final year, in which we're all expected to produce a complete manuscript by April, would go by oh so quickly, we wouldn't believe it. Literally in the blink of an eye, all of this—he gestured with his manicured hand to the stale classroom air around us, the fake pillars, the unlit fireplace, the cavelike walls—would be gone. I watched the Bunnies shiver and give each other a group hug with only their eyes. The poets brace themselves for imminent, overeducated poverty.

"I pretty much wasted it," Jonah says. "I mean, I wrote like two volumes of poems but they're terrible so I'm back to square one. I'll bet you wrote like crazy this summer, though."

I think of the summer, my days spent gazing at dust motes from behind the Warren music library information kiosk, my nights on Ava's roof, drinking and tangoing ourselves into oblivion. Sometimes I'd stare at a blank page, a pencil held limply in my hand. Sometimes I'd draw eyes on the page. Scribble the words *what am I doing here? what am I doing here?* over and over. Mostly I just stared at the wall. The page and the wall were one and the same to me all summer.

"I don't know about *like crazy*. . . ."

"I still remember that piece you brought into Workshop last year. You know, the one everybody hated?"

"Yeah, Jonah, I remember." The horrified faces. Heads slightly bowed.

"I still think about it. I mean, it was pretty hard to forget. It was so . . ."

"Mean?" I offer. "*Willfully twisted*? *Aggressively dark*? I know, I think that was pretty much the consensus."

"No! I mean yes, it was mean and twisted and dark and it actually scared the living shit out of me for weeks. But I loved all that. I love how mean and twisted and dark it is." He beams at me. "Who ever thought going to an aquarium could be so treacherous and horrifying, you know?"

"Yeah."

"But if you really think about it, it kind of is."

"Thanks, Jonah. I liked your piece that everyone hated too."

"Really? I was going to scrap it but—"

"Don't do that, that's what they *want*." I say this more intensely, more bitterly than I intend.

Jonah looks confused. "What?"

"Nothing. I should probably go. Late for class." I'm not late for class. There is no class now. But I imagine Ava waiting for me outside by the bench, giving undergraduates her death stare. *Hurry the fuck up, Smackie*.

"Oh, okay. Hey, Sam, can I read more of your stuff sometime? I kind of dig it. I mean, I really dig it. I was actually kind of jonesing for it after I read it, you know?"

"Um—I guess so. Sure."

"Cool. Maybe we could hang out sometime and . . ."

Down the corridor, behind Jonah, I hear the elevator ding and my stomach flips. Because I know before the doors even open who it will be. I know even before I see his tall, sleek frame exit the doors, whistling. Mane a carefully cultivated chaos. Arms inked with watchful crows. The Lion. Approaching us. Wearing his usual obscure noise band T-shirt. One of the bands we used to talk about back when we used to talk. He carries with him the scent of the green tea he used to brew for us in his office, which he would ceremoniously stir, then pour into mud-colored, handleless cups. *How's the writing, Samantha?* he might ask in his deep Scottish lilt.

Now I see his leonine face fall slightly at the sight of students with whom he must fraternize. Ask about their summers. Their writing. Did they get their stipend checks okay? And then there's the fact that I'm one of the students. Makes it much more difficult. But he smiles. Of course he does. It's his job.

"Hello, Jonah. Samantha." Definite voice drop when he said my name, though he tries to make it sound cool, even-keeled. Small, subtle nod of his maned head.

I watch him busy himself at his own cubby, which is full to exploding with letters and books. Humming a little. Taking his time.

"Samantha, are you okay?" Jonah says.

I should just walk over there like I've imagined doing how many times, tap him on the shoulder and say, *Look, can we just talk?* He'll look surprised, perhaps. Caught off guard. *Talk?*

he'll say, his gaze sliding from side to side, assessing routes of escape. As if it's a highly suspicious activity I'm proposing. Illicit. *I'm afraid I can't talk now, Samantha. But perhaps you could come by during my office hours?*

Or perhaps he'll play dumb. Look at me with a chillingly neutral expression, revealing nothing. *Sure, Samantha. What's up?* Meeting my eyes like *go ahead, absolutely, please, talk.*

"Samantha?"

And then what? And then I could just cut to the chase and say, *I don't understand what happened between us exactly, but can it just not be weird anymore?* But my fear is that he'll look at me like I'm insane. Weird? Happened? Between us? *Samantha, I'm sorry but I really have no idea what you're talking about, I'm afraid.* And he won't look afraid at all.

But now when I see him standing there, humming, checking his own mail slowly, smiling to himself, my body goes rigid with—I really don't know what, but I have to go.

"Samantha, wait—" Jonah says.

"I'm really late for class now."

The Lion looks up from his mail. He probably knows that I am not late for anything. That there is no class right now. That I'm running from him like a scared little bitch. What's the prey of a lion again?

"Oh, okay. Have a good class, Samantha." And then Jonah waves and waves and waves at me and I'm reminded of myself, last night, waving, my hand high over my head.

3

Before I leave to meet Ava, I shove the invitation in my pocket. She said she would wait for me outside the Center for Narrative Arts, sending check vibes. *Because I'm not going in there, Smackie. Sorry. You know why.* I nodded solemnly. *Yes.* Even though the truth is I don't really know why, apart from the fact that she's militantly anti-Warren and feels it's full of entitled pricks. Also that it's killing my soul/creativity. She knows firsthand because she went to the art school right next door which is almost as famous and elite as Warren, and it nearly killed hers. But she didn't let it. She dropped out before they killed her soul. Fuck that. Fuck *them.* Now she works in the basement of the nature lab down the hill, shelving dead bugs. Every single dead bug gets its own tiny glass drawer. It's kind of nice. And infinitely better for her spiritual and creative well-being than hanging around the fake poor and fashionably deranged, aka the art school student body.

The only thing Ava enjoys about Warren is raiding the dumpsters behind the undergraduate dorms and fucking with student campus tours. From time to time we'll even get drunk on a bench by the infamous flying-hare statue and wait for a drove of would-be students and their parents to pass by. The mothers always look around the campus like extremely interested buyers, their jeweled hands rubbing the backs of their fawnlike spawn as if to say: *This could be yours, this could be yours.* The future students gaze hungrily or with proprietary ease at a campus green that shimmers like their own skin, perhaps imagining their lavishly appointed dorms or the school orgies they've heard about, which Ava says are only attended by the very lame and unexcitingly naked. Not imagining, I'm sure, the very real possibility of being beheaded on their way home one night from a student bar. Or else beaten with crowbars by the roving gangs that stalk the campus and its surrounding area. Because the violence of this place, existing as it does in the fragile heart of seething poverty, doesn't exactly feature in the script of the Warren campus tour, which is always led by some undergraduate tool in designer sportswear who is quite expert at shouting cozy factoids about statue erection and chandeliers while walking backward. Hence Ava's pointed disruption.

Warren was founded in 1775 and over here—

Blah, blah, BLAH, finishes Ava on the bench beside me. *What he's not telling you is that there are people right here on campus who will chop your head off,* she shouts to the mothers, who look at her, appalled. *That's right. With an ax! Like this.* And then she'll stand up and take a step toward them with an invisible ax over her shoulder and one or some or all of them will scream.

Though I'm horrified, I laugh until I cry every time.

Now that bench has actually become our unofficial meeting place. It's where she should be sitting at this moment, glaring at the passing students, drawing what she calls *the monstrous truth* in her sketchbook, as is her wont.

At the sight of the empty bench, I panic. All my lonely days last year swell up in my heart and my vision goes swimmy. Then I feel my right arm being grabbed and I am blindsided by a waft of familiar scent. Two hands swathed in fishnet mesh cover my eyes.

"Boo!" she whispers into my ear.

Though I know who it is, I act surprised. Gasp.

Raucous laughter. She claps her hands. "Jesus Christ, you're easy," she says.

"I know. Where did you go?" I ask.

"Two idiots were having a discussion about Virginia Woolf with such orchestrated earnestness, I had to move. What the hell took you so long, anyway? You were gone for like five years."

I remember the invitation in my pocket, the swan beak poking my stomach flesh as we speak. "I talked to Jonah for a bit."

"The dreamy poet boy who wants to fuck you?"

"He does not."

"It's ridiculous how much he does."

"He called me dark, twisted, and mean."

"How sweet. He's in love."

"Can we not talk about this?"

She looks at me. "Something else happened. Tell me."

"Nothing. Just. I had a run-in. Near run-in. With . . . you know."

Ava nods. She knows, of course. "Did you *talk*?"

"I couldn't. You know. Face him. After, you know, everything . . ." I trail off because she's staring at me intently. I can't tell if she's disappointed in me or angry at him.

"You should really consider setting his office on fire," she says at last, and smiles. "For a second I thought you got kidnapped by those bonobos."

"Bunnies," I say, feeling myself flush. Recalling those smiley faces on the invitation. All those hand-drawn hearts.

"Whatever. I was worried."

She shivers at the view of the grand trees, as if they're not trees at all but something truly vile, like all the rosy-blond light that seems to forever bathe the campus is about to punch her in the face like a terrible fist of rich. She looks at it all with disgust—the tall old buildings, the ornately spiked gates, the endless stretch of carefully manicured perfumed green teeming with bright-eyed squirrels and rabbits, the students walking here and there, discussing Derrida and their nose jobs, their hair kissed by a September light so golden and perfect it's as though they'd paid the sun to beam down on them in just that way. I am not immune to the beauty. All year last year I took lots of pictures of campus—*click, click, click* with my cracked, ancient phone during every season, at different times of the day, in all kinds of light—that I don't look at anymore and which I sent to no one. A placarded bench between two weeping trees. A two-hundred-year-old bell tower. A fireplace you could stand up in like the one in *Citizen Kane*. There's a selfie of me I took in that fireplace. There's one Ava and I took by the fireplace together, temple to temple, not smiling, as is our way. Her arm is around me, swathed in holey lace. There's one of just Ava. Because of the way she's standing before the flames, she looks like a witch being burned at the stake.

Now, she puts a hand on my cheek, gives me a small smile. "Can we get the hell out of here, please? You know I only come here for you."

I don't say anything to Ava about the Bunny invitation all day. Instead, we celebrate what she continually called my final day of freedom by going to the monster diner where she draws and I write. Supposedly. I just sat there with my notebook open, watching her draw. Then the zoo to say hello to the Moon Bear in his pit. Then out for Vietnamese iced coffees at the sketchy place we like downtown, where I almost got shot.

"You did *not* almost get shot, Smackie. Jesus Christ. That was a car backing up or something," she said when I brought it up.

"Yes, I did."

"You need to get out more."

"I get out. I'm out with you, aren't I?"

Now we're back at her place drinking the sangria she made that's so strong I'm pretty sure it's poison. It's that time of evening she calls the hour between the dog and the wolf. A time that actually makes this sorry swath of New England beautiful, the sky ablaze with a sunset the color of flamingos. We're on her sagging roof, listening to Argentine tango music to drown out the roaring Mexican music next door. We're practicing tango, like we did all summer, taking turns being Diego for each other. Diego is an imaginary panther-footed man we dream will one day come into our lives and whisk us off our very large feet. He has the smoldery, dangerously mesmeric looks of Rudolph Valentino but with the trustworthy eye crinkle of Paul Newman, the smiling insanity and very long torso of Lux Interior of The Cramps, but with the swoon-inducing earnestness of Jacques Brel. Diego wears white suits or black Cuban shirts patterned with orange flames. He bakes bread for us in the morning. He cuts fresh flowers and leaves them in jars all over our apartment. He does not write poetry, but he reads it for fun. He has a pied-à-terre in Paris, a mansion in Buenos Aires. Most importantly, he tangos like a dream. I'm Diego right now for Ava, which means I'm leading and she can close her eyes.

The Bunny invitation is still ticking in my pocket like a little bomb.

R u coming tonite? ☺ one of them texted earlier this afternoon.

"I can't dream that you're Diego if you keep dancing like an engineering nerd, Smackie. Panther-footed grace, remember?"

"Sorry."

"What's with you tonight?"

"Nothing."

"You seem distracted."

I should just text *Sorry, sick* ☹ and be done with it. Because I shouldn't go. Because even being in their vicinity, hearing their childish voices from the other side of the room, hurts my teeth. And yet the sun has set. And I have yet to say no. Probably they don't want me to come anyway. Probably they did it just to be nice. Nice? No. Not nice, exactly. So they can say, *Well at least we tried. She's the one who didn't show.*

See, Bunny? I told you she wouldn't come. This is how she wants it. She wants it like this.

Why, though? Creepy Doll will ask. She'll be wearing the cat ears they stuck on her head last Halloween that she has yet to take off.

I told you, Cupcake will say, petting her. *She's a freak.*

Oh, you're so funny, Bunny. I love you.

I love you, *Bunny.*

"Okay," Ava says, "let's stop."

"Why?"

"You're obviously not into this tonight."

"No, no, I am," I lie. "I am."

"What's going on with you?"

It's now 6:30. I have to decide. I shouldn't go. I just won't go.

"I might have to go out tonight," I say.

She raises an eyebrow. Understandably. In all the days that have passed since we first met last spring, I've never had other plans.

"This thing at school," I say.

"Didn't we just go to one the other day?"

"This is another one."

She looks at me. "You're not sick of me, are you?"

"No. Never." I say it fervently because it's true.

"You can tell me, you know. I'm not going to cry or anything."

I pull the invitation out of my pocket and hand it to her.

She doesn't touch it, just looks at it.

"It's probably from Caroline," I say. "Cupcake?" I clarify, realizing I've never shared their actual names with her.

She blinks at me, expressionless.

"The blond one with the perfectly undertucked bob and the pearls and the blue orchid corsage on her wrist? You said she looked like a Twinkie. Or a child of the corn going to prom?"

"They *all* look like Twinkies to me, Smackie: fake-sweet, squidgy, unsurprising packaging. I'll bet the ink on this thing is scratch-and-sniff," she says, snatching the invitation from me, scratching at the *cordially,* and holding it up to her nose. "When did you get this thing anyway?"

"It was in my school mailbox this morning."

"So that's why you've been weird all day."

"I just don't know how to respond. I feel like if I don't . . ."

"Here," she says, and pulls out her Zippo and holds it at the corner of the shimmery invite.

"Wait," I say. "What are you doing?"

"You're not actually thinking of going to this party for dorks, are you?"

"No."

"So," she holds the lighter up to the invitation again, this time even closer, and looks at me. It starts to crackle.

"Wait, wait, *wait*."

"*What?*"

"It's just. Well, Workshop starts tomorrow."

"So?"

"So it's just going to be me and them again in class this semester. Just us five."

"And?"

"I'm just thinking of how not to be rude. When I say no. I mean, I'm going to say no, obviously. It's just . . . you know, these are the women in my department, my . . . you know . . . peers."

"Whom you call Cuntscapades."

"I just have to figure out the right wording. So they don't think I hate them."

She stares at me. "But Smackie, you *do* hate them."

I look at her through my bangs, which she has encouraged me to grow over my eyes. Makes you look punk, she says. I look at her different-colored eyes, her bleached and feathery hair that is the antithesis of Bunny hair, cut asymmetrically and shaved in places, her fishnet veil that she wears like a threshold to be crossed only if you dare. And here's what I realize: she would never wear mittens shaped like kittens or a dress with a Peter Pan collar. She would never say, *Love your dress,* if she fucking hated your dress. She would never say, *How are you?* if she didn't care how you were. She would never eat a lavender cupcake that tasted like perfume or wear a perfume that made her smell like a cupcake. She would never wear lip balm for cosmetic purposes. She would never wear it unless her lips were seriously, seriously cracked. And even if they were, she'd still put Lady Danger on them, which is the name of her lipstick, this bright blue-red that looks surreally beautiful on her but when I tried it on once made me look insane. Her perfume smells like rain and smoke and her eye makeup scares small children and she wears pumps even though she's at least two inches taller than I am and I'm a freak. Why? Because life is shorter than we are, she says, so why beat around the bush?

"I *do* hate them," I say quietly. "So I *should* just say no. I mean . . . what do you think I should do?"

A faint smell of garbage rises up with the heat of the end of the day. I stare at her for a while, but her face is absolutely deadpan. She lights a cigarette. I gaze down at my legs in their bland, black jeans.

After what feels like an unbearably long time, in which a wind swooshes through her sycamore, a gusty wind that takes my breath away briefly, that reminds me that we're near the ocean even though I've never seen it—but the Bunnies have, of course, because one of them has a Mercedes SUV and they drive there on the weekends and take pictures of themselves in Esther Williams–style swimsuits, laughingly wading together into the white crashing waves with arms linked—Ava says, "You should go if you want to go."

"What? I *don't* want to go."

"But you also don't want to be rude, right? These are the women in your department."

She stares at me until I lower my eyes.

"Look, you don't know what it's like to be in class with them. To be in Workshop with them. Maybe they're trying to make an effort this year. You know, to be nice or something."

She snorts.

"I'm serious. And if I snub them, they'll . . ."

"What? Tell me what they can possibly do."

I think about last year. How they would look down at each story I submitted like it was a baby that just gave them the finger, and then side-eye each other for a long time.

It's very . . . angry, they'd say at last.

Yes. Abrasive. For my taste?

Exactly. Sort of in love with its own outsiderness? Its own narrative of grittiness? Of course, that could *just be me.* (Small smile of deference.) *Still. I* do *wish it would open itself up a bit more.*

"Look, I'll go for like an hour," I say. "Tops. Just to make an appearance."

"Whatever."

"I'll text you pictures of their apartment so you can see how hideously twee it is."

She nods. "Sure."

"You could come along if you want," I offer lamely.

"Don't sweat it, Smackie. You couldn't pay me all the money in the world to attend that little soiree. Speaking of which, you oughtn't dally. Better hop along."

"I'll be back soon. Like later tonight even. Anyway, I'll text you."

She says nothing, just frowns into the book she's cracked open, like the book made a face at her, stuck out its tongue.

"Hey," I think I hear her say as I'm starting to climb down the ladder from her roof, but when I look up, she isn't looking at me. She's still staring at her book. The wind picks up again, stirring the pages, turning them this way and that, but she keeps reading like she hasn't lost her place at all.

4

How long have I been standing here, outside her front door, staring at the tuliplike flower she drew next to the brass bell and the loopy letters that comprise her real name? Long enough for the sky to grow darker. The street to smell sweeter. The shadows to get thin and grow teeth. I can hear well-schooled female laughter drifting from an upstairs window. I shift my weight from right to left. Turn back. Not too late to turn back and watch the family of raccoons make their way down Ava's drainpipe, as they do each evening. Cheer on the little one who is always afraid to go down. *Come on, little one,* Ava and I always say, raising our drinks to him. *Be brave. Be bold.*

Her neighborhood is obscenely beautiful. I cannot help but observe this as I stand on her marbled steps, flanked by stone griffins, beaks open in midscreech. A line of stately houses, a canopy of grandly bowing trees. Just a block from campus, off a poshly quaint street lined with bistros that offer champagne by the glass, cafés that make the cortadas with the ornate foam art that all the faculty drink, shops selling cold-pressed juice and organic dog treats. Unlike my street, which smells of sad man piss, hers smells of autumn leaves.

As I stand here, my finger poised over the bell, the laughter morphs into hellion squeals. Four distinct shrieks. I hit the bell, not because I want to but because it's getting cold out here and this town, even in Cupcake's neighborhood, is ridiculously dangerous after a certain hour. I don't need to look up to feel the fact of four heads suddenly appearing in the upstairs window, flanked by billowing white curtains. Four heads full of white, orthodontically enhanced teeth. Hair so shiny it will blind you to look at it directly, like an eclipse. My phone buzzes with a text from an unknown number, the emoticon of a monkey with its hands over its eyes. I think: *I should go, I should go, I should go.* But I stay right where I am. I wait. I wait so long the sky gets darker still. The sweet smell of the street acquires a tang of rot. Leaves from a nearby luxury tree fall and I count them falling. One. Two. Three.

5

I am staring into the eyes of the one I call Cupcake. Because she looks like a cupcake. Dresses like a cupcake. Gives off a scent of baked lemony sugar. Pretty in a way that reminds you of frosting flourishes. Not the forest green and electric blue horrors in the supermarket, but the pastel kind that is used at weddings or tasteful Easter gatherings. She looks so much like a cupcake that when I first met her at orientation, I had a very real desire to eat her. Bite deeply into her white shoulder. Dig a fork in her cheek. Tonight, she wears a dress of cerulean blue patterned with sinuous white clouds and one of her many matchy cardigans. Blond hair freshly flat-ironed. Lips shiny but colorless because *lipstick is for whores, Bunny*, I have heard her say and I really couldn't tell if she was joking or dead serious. Glinty pearls around her neck that she never takes off. She'll often gently tug on them in Workshop while reading aloud from her work—the most recent iteration of which was postfeminist dialogues between herself and various kitchen implements.

I think she's going to greet me like she usually does, like I'm an unfortunate patch of gray sky from which she should soon take cover, or a tall, mildly disease-ridden tree—it is so sad and creepy about my bare and unseemly branches. Normally if she and I catch sight of one another in the halls or around campus, she'll draw her Christopher Robin cardigan closer, clutch her books tightly to her chest as though, tut, tut! Looks like rain. *Oh, hi, Samantha,* she'll say, looking around at anything like it might be a buoy that will save her from the fact of me standing right in front of her. A telephone pole in the distance. A gnat only she can see. Frankly, I don't know what I did to get on the wrong side of Cupcake. Perhaps she sensed my hunger when we first met and has understandably kept her distance.

But tonight, Cupcake smiles at me. Her pink-and-white face lights up. "Samantha, *hi!*" As if she's actually delighted to see me. I'm a jewel-colored cardigan. I'm a first edition of *The Bell Jar.* I'm a marzipan squirrel. I'm a hairdresser who knows exactly, exactly, how to handle her carefully undertucked bob of golden hair.

"*So* glad you could make it. Bunnies! Look who's here! She came!"

She takes my hand—actually takes my hand—and leads me into her giant living room, which is what I pictured and not what I pictured. Lots of soft, lush, cushiony fabrics. Ceilings that stretch up and up and up. A white fireplace in which she was has placed a vase full of delicate pink blossoms. They're all sitting around a candlelit coffee table as though they've been kept waiting for a guest. Creepy Doll, aka Kira. Vignette, aka

Victoria. And of course, the Duchess, who in another life is merely Eleanor. On my way over, I'd envisioned various nightmare scenarios of what awaited me. I feared they might be naked, reclined on whimsical furniture out of *Alice in Wonderland*. Or else in pastel lingerie, using Anaïs Nin erotica as fans. Massaging each other to the music of Stereolab. Obscure yet erudite porn projected on some massive screen. Reading sex manifestos from the seventies using pastel dildos as mics. A tiered tray of erotically themed cupcakes, I had no idea. But instead, they're just sitting in a circle like it's Workshop, wearing their usual clothes, notebooks clutched in their laps like purses. Normally when I enter Workshop, they give me tightfisted Hi's, little upward jerks of their lips, making me feel, as I take my seat, like a portentous fog has somehow settled into the room. But this time they're all looking at me and smiling like I'm the actual sun. Smiling with the whole of their mouths and eyes.

"Samantha!" Creepy Doll gasps. "You're here. We thought you got *lost* or something."

Lost? I look into the amber eyes of the one I call Creepy Doll. Because she reminds me of the creepy dolls I used to want when I was little, with their saucer eyes and their velvet dresses, their Shirley Temple curls of blood-red hair and their Cupid's-bow lips molded into little pink oh!'s of wonder at the world. Writes fairy tales about girl demons, wolf princes, the cozy phantasmagoria of her native New Hampshire. Collects antique typewriters, each of which she claims has its own unique "ghost energy" that she channels into her stories as she types, head tilted back, eyes closed. She is the literal doll-pet of the other Bunnies. Sits curled in their skirted laps like a cat. Purrs when they pet her, makes hissing sounds when they stop. Her voice is the feathery baby voice of children in horror films. I have heard that same voice go down about five octaves when she thinks she is alone, become deep as a well. Out of all of them, she is the first to usually extend a social hand to me in the form of a random troll emoji, or a last-minute invite to places they already are.

Hi Samantha, We're having bento boxes. You're welcome to join ☺

She's also the only Bunny who attempts to talk to me at social functions. She'll come up to me and ask me questions like little digging hooks and while I'm answering, she'll nod and murmur *cool* while her eyes flit from side to side. Like she is a child who has dared herself to knock on Boo Radley's door, and now that he's opened it she isn't sure what to do, should she run?

Now, though, her golden eyes gleam goodwill. By far the most obscenely beautiful of them all, the most strangely sexy. Still wearing the leopard print cat ears that her fellow Bunnies drunkenly plonked onto her head last Halloween (I saw the pictures on FB). A black dress patterned with white ghosts that have what appear to be blobs of blood for eyes. Surely she knows I didn't get lost. They saw me standing outside the front door for a good fifteen minutes.

I feel my ears get hot. My lip begins to twitch. "Um. No. I—"

"Bunny, we didn't *really* think that," Vignette cuts in. She is seated in a chaise longue to the left of the Duchess, under a lamp shaped like a swan's neck, the light of which illuminates her auburn tresses. Vignette, their sexy punk. The bluntest of the Bunnies. Her dainty dress countered by combat boots, unbrushed hair, a half-open mouth that never closes. Her cloudy gray eyes full of *fuck you*. Writes for shock value. Existential vignettes about Disney princesses engaged in blood orgies, feral girl-women crawling around on all fours at the bottom of Beckettian wells of the mind, munching Barbie doll parts. Looks stoned most of the time, as if she is perpetually enveloped in opium smoke. She was apparently a ballerina in another life, before she went off the rails, discovered conceptual art and slouching. Despite her translucent, blue-veined beauty that reminds Ava of skulls and me of the Victorians, she didn't always dress like prettified confection. When I met her at our very first Narrative Arts welcome reception, saw another girl in jeans and plaid with a plastic cup of wine in her hand, which she was holding like she'd never held a cup before, I thought maybe she and I would be friends. I went up to her at a party once when she was alone, when she hadn't yet been sucked into Bunnydom. Hi, I said. Hi, she said. And she looked at me like she was so grateful. We had a stammering conversation, which I prolonged by pretending to love Pilates. Soon we were just nodding our heads at one another, taking quicker, larger sips of our drinks, mumbling about how cold we heard New England winters could be. Then she excused herself to go to the bathroom. Since then, whenever we wind up together in a corner of a party she'll look around like she's trapped. All the doors in her face will close one by one. But right now, she's looking at me the way she did that day when I first approached her, her face saying *Come in, Come in.*

"We did wonder if she got lost for a minute," Creepy Doll insists.

"*You* wondered," Vignette says, putting her delicate hand on Creepy Doll's. "*We* just wondered if she was going to show. But here she is." She looks at me. "Here you are, Samantha." She gives me a half smile.

"Yes," Creepy Doll says. "Here you are."

They both look over at the Duchess, who is sitting on a loveseat upholstered in a soft plush velvet. Her head cocked to one side. Her long silver locks eerily luminous, swept up here and there, with what appear to be birds of paradise. She's wearing a white bell-sleeved smock trimmed with lace as though she is a graven image of a C-list moon goddess or one of those watchful-looking egrets I saw in the weeping willows at the zoo. The intricate lacework and the woven fabric reek of large amounts of money spent in a store that also sells crystals.

She's staring at me with a neutral expression of infinite patience, the same expression she wears whenever I speak in Workshop. Of all of them, her prose is the most inaccessible and cryptic, etched on panes of glass using a dagger-shaped diamond she wears around her neck. She calls them *proems*. If forced to say something about her work in class, I'll describe it as jewel-like and enigmatic. And she'll look at me like she knows I'm lying. Like she's my therapist, and I'm trying to pull a fast one on her, which she'd expected, but *come on, Samantha, let's get, you know, serious here*. Like she knows I think I'm better than everyone else. Like my stammering shyness, my headphones, my dark, unassuming clothes, my politeness are all well and good but she can see through it, *yes, Samantha,* and what she sees, what it's masking, is a very deep hate, a very deep rage, a very deep social bruise, *what happened there, Samantha?* Like she knows that I have nicknamed them all and, well, *how sad, really.* But being a moon goddess, a more highly evolved artist, a being full of nothing but love and tropical shore (though she is Upper West Side via Charleston), she's going to tolerate it, love me from a distance all the same, wish me well on my stunted little path where I clutch my rage close like a book or a pet rat. *We are all on our own paths after all, aren't we?*

My lip is twitching so violently I feel like I need to run out of the room. I contemplate it. I won't even look for a door, I'll just run and tear a hole through the wall.

Then she suddenly smiles at me, and it's like an embrace.

"Samantha," she says, "we're *so* glad you could make it after all."

The Bunnies nod on either side of her. I can feel Cupcake nodding at my side. *Yes, so glad. So glad,* their faces say. *So.*

"Can I take your coat?" Cupcake offers. I turn to her. She's looking at me so hopefully. So willing to take a coat I'm not wearing, I almost want to give her my skin. I feel my chest going red in fiery patches.

"Um."

"She's not wearing a coat, *Bunny,*" Vignette observes from her invisible opium cloud, still looking at me with her conspiratorial half smile.

They all break out into laughter. Cupcake claps a hand over her mouth and looks at me aghast. Like I'm something worse than naked and she only realized it now. I feel terribly hot. Sweat drips down my back.

"I'm sorry," are the words that come out of my mouth before I can stop them.

"Why are *you* apologizing, Samantha?" Creepy Doll says, her breathy voice full of demonic emoticons flanked by winking smileys.

"Why?" I repeat.

They're all looking at me. *Yes, why?*

I become light-headed, painfully aware of the fact that I'm still standing and they're all sitting in a snug circle. There is nowhere to sit except a heart-shaped ottoman between Creepy Doll and Vignette, which I presume is for their feet. Should I wait until they ask me to sit down? Should I—

"Samantha," the Duchess says, opening her arms. "Come. Sit." She pats the space beside her on the loveseat. The others look at Cupcake, who is looking at that space like it was hers until I got there. She turns to look at me as though she's just been smacked across the face. Then she smiles. "Yes, Samantha," she says, "sit, please."

"I can sit here," I offer, gesturing to the ottoman.

"No, Samantha, sit on the couch," Cupcake says. "You absolutely should. You're *so* tall."

"Like Alice on mushrooms," Creepy Doll says.

"Or Gilgamesh," Vignette observes from her reclined position on the chaise. "Or the Tower of Babel."

"But in the *best* way."

I make my way over to the Duchess. I've never sat near her before. She opens her arms and hugs me, her airy embrace all fragrant hair and frail bones and elegant fabric. A smell like flowers and burning. When she pulls away, she is smiling intimately, as though we've just been through something words cannot express. Her long-fingered hands are gripping my arms. She's looking at me like I'm her favorite special-needs child.

"Samantha," she says, taking my hands, "we're *so* glad you could make it after all. How about a drink? We came up with a cocktail just for you."

"For me?" Something breaks in me. That strange heart swell I felt when I first saw my name on the swan's wing. Not believing it could be for me. Could it be for me?

They all nod. *Yes, Samantha. For you.*

"Here, taste," Creepy Doll says, offering me her drink. I stare at the bile-green concoction in which what looks like a small black turd floats. I want to ask what's in it, but this seems rude, somehow. When they're all still smiling at me like this.

They watch me take the proffered glass. *Why are you being nice to me?* I want to shout. *Why, why, why, why?* Instead, I smile back. Bring the drink to my lips. As it hits my tongue, I wince.

"Well?"

"Isn't it *so* you?" Creepy Doll says.

It is a mouthful of dark acid, with something deeply, unrelentingly bitter in the finish that causes my eyes to tear and my lips to pucker. I cough despite myself, while they watch.

"It's a little intense, huh?"

"Kind of hard to take it straight like that, right?"

"I could sweeten it a little, maybe? Maybe that's all it really needs."

They look so genuinely concerned.

"No, this is fine, really."

"Are you sure?"

"Yes. It's great." I take another sip of the terrible drink, try not to grimace.

They all smile except for the Duchess.

"Samantha," she says, resting her hand on my knee, squeezing. "*Lies* aren't allowed in Smut Salon. This is a night of Absolute Truth." I look down at her lacy white lap where a pane of glass sits, poking out of a rabbit-fur case. There appear to be words etched on the glass. I feel a lick of fear in my gut.

"I love it," I say. "I do. I—"

They laugh. *What's so fucking funny?* I want to say. But I don't. I laugh with them. Ha. Haha. Hahaha.

"Oh, Samantha, we're *so* glad you're here," the Duchess says.

"Me too," I say. The mystery liquor is in my toes. Making little prissy flowers open all through me. Like the ones blooming in her fake fireplace. Like the freesia on the coffee table. Like the tulips that I now observe are stenciled all over her impossibly high pastel-colored walls. There's a ceiling up there somewhere, from which a mysterious rosy-golden light shines down on all of us.

I open my mouth and apologies tumble out. I'm so sorry I kept them waiting. I hope I didn't keep them waiting? Did I? I—

"*Don't* even worry about it, Samantha. We were honestly just getting started."

I notice a self-conscious arrangement of books on her hexagon-shaped coffee table, which is lit here and there with tea lights: The collected Byron and Keats. Some Sade. Barthes's *Erotisme. Wuthering Heights.* Ovid's *Metamorphosis.* And, surprise, surprise, a book by the Lion. His infamously horrific and debauched novel, a fever dream about a sociopathic Scotsman who engages in deeply philosophical acts of homicide against women has been reverently placed atop an anthology of Russian fairy tales. I flush at the sight of his name on the cover, at the cover itself. When the Duchess sees me eyeing it, she tucks the book discreetly under the pile.

How much they think they know about what transpired between the Lion and me last year is anyone's guess. Probably they think I fucked him. Maybe it's even the reason they kept their distance from me. Or maybe he and I got close because they kept me at a distance, I don't know. All last fall in Workshop, they'd side-eye each other if he praised my stories. Because surely they'd seen me leave class with him, walked past us chatting together in the hall, observed us exchanging books and vinyl. Caught us sitting together in cafés or in the basement of the Irish pub, having a drink, another drink, *one more for the road, why not?* They'd noticed him walk over and talk to me at department functions, sit beside me at readings. Then, in the winter semester, they might have observed how quite suddenly all of this stopped—that he no longer sat next to me at readings or talked to me at parties or met me off campus. And then, of course, in spring, on the night of the end-of-year party, they definitely observed me drunk in the passenger seat of his Subaru.

I imagined they imagined wild things. *Probably he ties her up like in his sick stories and she loves it because of her sick stories.* I want to defend myself against these unspoken accusations, against the microaggressive manner in which the Duchess now smilingly straightens the stack of books though it doesn't need straightening.

You think you know, I want to say to them. *You think you know but you don't.*

But know what, exactly? What is there to really know? Sometimes when I tell myself or Ava the story, it grows teeth and it's something. Definitely something. Other times, it comes apart in my hands like air. But if I remember all the right details. If I tell them in the right order. If I pause in the right places, trail off in the right places . . .

The Duchess smiles at me as she rearranges the other items on the table—a Ziploc bag full of short brown sticks, some dried flower petals. No dildos in sight.

"Samantha," she says gently. "Have you *never* been to a Smut Salon before?"

You never invited me, is what I want to say. Instead I look at the smiling pink plastic pony standing in the middle of the coffee table like a sacrificial lamb. "Um. I don't think so. Was I supposed to bring something or. . . ? Are there rules?"

"You'll be *fine,*" Cupcake says, swatting my question away like a fly. "Just follow our lead. Really this is just meant to be a night of inspiration for us. As artists, you know?"

"To awaken our creativity," Creepy Doll says. "To open our hearts."

"To be perverse," Vignette adds.

"*Bunny*. Anyway, Samantha, you'll see," the Duchess says. "Caroline was actually just about to start us off, weren't you, Bunny?"

Cupcake nods gravely and sets down her cocktail.

"Lower the lights, please, Kira," she says to Creepy Doll, who jumps from her seat.

Suddenly we're in semidarkness. The only light in the room comes from a few tea lights and the shine in their hair. Cupcake rises up off the floor. Clears her throat. Reaches for the Ziploc bag full of what I now realize are cinnamon sticks. She pulls one out and holds it in front of her like a candle. She sniffs it fervently. Her eyes closed tight.

Then she begins.

"If I were a cinnamon peeler," she begins in a quavering voice, "I would ride your bed . . ."

As she recites the Ondaatje poem, she begins to shave the stick with long, tender strokes. Earth-colored dust falls onto the table. I look around. They're all listening intently, nodding solemnly. The Duchess has her eyes closed. Creepy Doll is absently petting the fluffy pink tail of the pony. Vignette is staring straight ahead with her mouth open. Not sure what to do, I just sit there, clutching my drink, watching Cupcake shave and recite with increasingly fast, fevered strokes. Her head is thrown back and she looks ecstatic. A little breathless. The whole time she recites, the Duchess holds my hand firmly, as if she's seeing me through a birth. An unholy laugh rises in my throat but I hold it in.

When she's finished, they're all silent for a minute. Solemn. As if they've just heard a prayer.

At last Creepy Doll whispers, "Oh my god. *So* erotic."

"Hot," Vignette says.

The Duchess nods. "I absolutely love the way the erotic is rendered as a tactile, olfactory experience. Every time you read that poem, Bunny, it seems to possess you."

They're all looking at me, I realize now, with expectation. I'm supposed to say something.

"So great," I murmur, but it rings false, so I add, "I love the cinnamon peels."

"I was going to do just the powder or serve cinnamon cookies, but then I was like no, bark. It has to be bark."

"You also didn't want to disrupt the purity of cinnamon," the Duchess observes.

"Exactly," Cupcake says, as though the Duchess has articulated a truth she's been trying to pin down for years.

The Duchess breathes in deeply, then exhales slowly with eyes closed, the way my old therapist did. The one my father sent me to when I was a teenager, after my mother died. The one with the intricately knotted scarves. I'd lie to her. *Do you hear voices? Yes. See demonic entities? All the time. Now Samantha, tell me, why do you think the dream means you're going to die a fiery death imminently?*

The Duchess says, "Kira, your turn, Bunny."

They go, one after the other. Creepy Doll reads an erotic

version of "Little Red Riding Hood" while donning a red cloak, Vignette reads a chapter from Marguerite Duras's *The Lover* while Cupcake passes out Vietnamese spring rolls, and at last the Duchess removes her pane of glass from its rabbit-fur case, and begins to read aloud a very oblique and circuitous passage of theory she has etched from Julia Kristeva about the nature of the erotic.

After each of them is done, they all sigh collectively, as if post-orgasm. I sigh with them. At this point in the evening, I've downed a few Samantha cocktails as well as several Light and Sunnies, a sky-colored drink they invented that is the inverse of a Dark and Stormy. I'm swaying in my seat. The Duchess keeps patting my hand. The pink pony winks at me with its sparkly eyes fringed with enviable lashes. *Great, so great,* I'm murmuring. *This is fun, this is fun, this is fun. It is fun,* I tell myself. It really is. It's not stupid or lame. I clap along with them, and they all smile at me as if I'm a many-headed beast who is at last letting them put bows in its tentacles, braid its mange.

We're so glad you're here, Samantha, they say, again and again.

"I'm glad too," I say. And I mean it more each time. I'm saying it fiercely into each of their four pairs of eyes. To the freesia on the mantle. To the pastel cushions. To the winking pony on the table to whom I now raise my glass that never seems to empty. *I'm glad too.*

Every now and then I think of Ava, her burst of laughter erupting in my head like a dangerous firework. She would not even be able to sit in this room, for what Smurf chair would accommodate her height? Wearing her stolen clothes, her ripped tights, biting on her lip behind her fishnet veil, dropping ash onto the shaggy carpet shaped like a heart, filling the room with her rain and smoke. Her blue eye and brown eye boring holes into their faces. *Lame,* her face would say. *Lame, lame, lame.*

"What did you say, Samantha?"

"Nothing." *Shut up,* I tell Ava, swaying. *These are the women in my department. These are my peers.*

Women? Try children, Smackie. Try grown women who act like little girls.

They're graduate students, I argue back.

Exactly. Hiding from life in the most coddling, insular, and self-aggrandizing way.

But I see the Duchess has slipped her diamond proem back into its rabbit-fur case. She's looking at me. They all are. "Well, Samantha, it's *your* turn now."

I look at them, surrounding me in a semicircle, their hair the same shiny nonshade in this light.

"My turn? But. I didn't bring anything."

"So *tell* us something, then—"

"Something smutty, obviously."

"Like we just did," Creepy Doll says, her red cloak still on her shoulders.

The Duchess rests her hand lightly on my shoulder. "I bet you have a *ton* of smutty stories, Samantha."

"A whole other dirty, mysterious life."

"What? I don't—"

"Of course you do."

They've become a many-legged blob in the darkness. Eight eyes staring at me with such expectation. *Spill. Spill.*

"No, really I—"

"Come *on*, Samantha." Their eyes become slits. Their smiles tighten. They look at me like they know I have a burning slutty secret I am willfully withholding. Like I'm denying them entry into my whorish vagina and it's a real problem. *This is why you're not part of things, Samantha. It's not us, it's you. Don't you see that? You're the one who isn't willing to put yourself out there and share.*

I look at the green, bitter drink on the table that they made in my honor. Then at the stack of books on the table, his name imprinted on one of the spines.

"We never fucked, if that's what you're thinking," I whisper.

"What was that, Samantha?"

"Nothing." I stare down at my lap, my mind a great, blazing blank. "I really don't know what to tell you. I'm sorry."

"Well you have to tell us *something*, Samantha. It's the rules."

Rules? But you didn't tell me anything smutty!

I look at the Duchess, who nods sadly like she is so sorry but yes, these are the rules. *We can't break them even though we invented them.*

"What if I read a poem or a passage from one of your books?" I offer, reaching toward the stack. *Like you guys did,* I don't add.

They don't answer. Vignette yawns luxuriously. Cupcake coughs behind her fist. I watch as they all pick at invisible lint on their clothes, pointedly sip the sky-blue dregs of their Light and Sunnies while avoiding my eyes.

I want to explain. Tell them that whatever gave them the

impression that I have this "dirty mysterious life"—seeing me with Ava? the Lion? my "sick" stories?—was surely misleading. I have no dirty mysterious life. I have no life. *If only you knew how empty and boring my hours were last year. Maybe I should just go.*

Instead I say, "I guess I could tell you about the time I died with Rob Valencia."

They look up at me now. *Well?*

I take a breath, then a swallow of Samantha. I wince again at the bitter taste, but it goes down easily. Velvety. Almost sweet.

"Rob Valencia was a guy from my high school," I begin. "A couple of years older than I was. I thought he was the hottest man I ever saw." So far this is all true.

"Who did he look like?" Cupcake prompts.

I think about Rob Valencia. Taller and broader than the school hallway, or so it seemed to me then. Small dark eyes like liquid smoke. His prematurely balding head of brown curls. His pale, thin-lipped smile that made me pant-y with fathomless lust.

"Zeus," I say at last.

"The Greek *god?*"

I nod. "But seventeen. And he liked to wear vintage suits. He oozed charisma like . . . ooze."

They all lean in. "What made him sexy, Samantha?"

"Sexy?" I repeat. They're looking at me, waiting.

"Not one particular thing, really. It was more . . . complex, you know? Sort of like an . . . animal magnetism."

I see they're all staring at me now like wide-eyed little girls. *Tell us, Samantha.*

I tell them how he was old-school Spanish Catholic and his

family slaughtered goats in the backyard. So he always smelled sort of biblical. Like incense and roasted flesh.

"That's hot," Vignette says.

"And then there was his voice," I say. "He had one of those deep, serene, all-knowing voices like a documentary narrator. Like any moment he could tell you a fact about a penguin or the war and you'd believe him. It was soothing. But sexy too. Like a tongue was being dragged up your inner thigh every time he said hi."

They're hanging on my every word. There is no more lint to pick. Ever.

"But the best, the hottest thing about Rob Valencia . . . ," I say, pausing to drink, "was dying with him."

"Tell us, Samantha."

I tell them how long I'd loved him from afar. Then I played his wife in the school play. How, because it was a murder mystery, we both got murdered two thirds of the way through by electrocution. In the scene, we were holding hands, and then he was supposed to plug a lamp into a wall, at which point we were to convulse and die.

"Hot," Vignette says.

I tell them how we got to die together over and over. How every Monday and Wednesday afternoon for three months during rehearsal and then for the five nights of our performance and once for a final matinee, I died with Rob Valencia. How we would hold hands and shake and tremble and fall together to the stage in a heap. How we'd lie there while everyone pretended to scream and accuse each other of our murders.

How we'd lie there until the stage got swallowed in darkness and then, only then, would we get up. How I hated it when we had to get up.

"Of course you did," they all murmur. Except the Duchess. She says nothing. Just sips her drink and stares straight ahead.

I tell them how erotic it was to be lying next to him on stage and to feel him trying to be so absolutely still and failing, his chest rising and falling beside me, his panting breath on my face, his roasted goat and incense smell filling my lungs. Sometimes we'd fall to the floor in a tangle and our bodies would touch. Sometimes we'd fall a few feet apart from each other and he would be close but so far away. Both were erotic in different ways.

"It was like fucking," I say, taking a sip of my drink. "But way more intense, you know? Cosmic."

Cupcake and Creepy Doll are nodding. *Yes. Of course. Cosmic. So very.*

"So you never *actually* fucked him?" Vignette says.

I look at the Duchess, who just stares at me, blinking. Her lovely dark blue eyes seeing the truth, *which is not so interesting, so dark, so gritty, after all, is it, Samantha? Which is sad and sort of humdrum pathetic, huh?* An unfortunately shaped virgin's paperback fantasy, a tenuous castle made of air.

I never fucked Rob. He wasn't in lust, let alone love, with me, even though height-wise we were perfect for one another. Even though I knew he saw through my ravaged skin and lank hair into my very soul. Even though we loved similar music, similar books—he too had read Dante's *Inferno* by candlelight,

I was certain. Even though I knew he knew there were worlds in me. One time, he pity-danced with me to "Slave to Love" at the cast party. But that was it. He was in love with Alyssa Fisher, who played Véronique, his French mistress. He took her to prom. Waved at me from the dance floor. *Hey, Samantha.*

But who wants to hear that story?

I look at these women now, their skins glowing a little in the dark, gazing at me with such dreamy expectation, and even—is it admiration? All but the Duchess. For a brief moment, I think she can see me moping on the outskirts of the dance floor in my regrettable Goodwill dress with the fire-breathing dragon on it, watching Rob and Alyssa slow dance to some song I told myself I hated anyway, wishing for a *Carrie*-like catastrophe to mitigate my broken heart, my teenage scorn.

So instead I tell them how, on the last night that we died together, just after the curtain came down but before the lights went up, he held out his hand in the darkness and led me to the woodlot behind the school. There, among the bare-branched quivering aspens, Rob Valencia ravaged me like a wolf. I describe the crunching of the many-colored leaves beneath us. How I stared up at the gray sky while he performed miracles with his mouth. How I sank my hands into the muddy earth as I orgasmed. How it was so intense, the mind-body-spirit connection we experienced in that woodlot as a result of dying together all those months, that, well, we never spoke to each other again. When we were dying it was like we were fucking. But when we fucked it was like we were dying. For real. And after that . . .

"After that, what?" Cupcake prompts, breathless.

"After that, we were simply past language," I say.

Silence.

"Hot," Vignette says at last, raising a glass.

"So hot," Cupcake says.

"*So*," Creepy Doll adds.

I smile. Yes. It was hot, wasn't it? I feel a small surge of shameful pride. They liked my story. I like that they liked my story. I blush and take another sip of Me, which is not bitter at all anymore. It's perfect.

"But also quite . . . sad, Samantha," the Duchess says, looking at me with her cocked head, her probing Zen face, a sudden warmth and concern spreading over her features like a rash. "He broke your heart, didn't he?"

I nod. My lip quivers. Begins to twitch violently again.

They're looking at me with such kindness. "It's okay, Samantha."

Tears fill my eyes. Real ones.

The Duchess puts her hand on mine and squeezes. "Let's get you another drink."

6

I wake up with my face mashed into my sagging mattress, still in my clothes from the night before. There's a red cloak on my shoulders, a smell of cinnamon, baked lemony sugar, all the twee things of this world rising from my own flesh, hovering in the stale air around me.

How I got back here I do not remember. I recall headlights. A twitching pink nose. Long gray-brown ears. The black gleaming bead of an animal eye. A sky-colored cocktail the size of my head being refilled and refilled by a girl with a rabbit face. *A cocktail just for you, Samantha,* said the rabbit girl, pouring. *Thank you,* I said. *Thank you all.* And I drank and drank of the cup. And I told them—what did I tell them? All I remember is them nodding. Smiling. *Yes. Tell us, Samantha.*

How much did I invent in the end? Probably a lot.

Why do you lie so much? And about the weirdest little things? my mother always asked me.

I don't know, I always said. But I did know. It was very simple. Because it was a better story.

I stare up at my cracked ceiling. The water stains that look like jaw-baring beasts seem to have spread since the last time I was here. The yellow light fixture has filled with more moth carcasses, so now there is more moth than light. The towers of books stacked against the walls are all in various stages of collapse, and the walls themselves, thin and piss colored, which are all that separate me from a perverted giant on one side and a sallow-faced girl on the other, appear to have crept even closer together. The black vinyl curtains, which came with the apartment and which a previous tenant seems to have stabbed multiple times, are open, revealing a view of chipped brick.

I haven't been back home since I met Ava. *Don't live here,* she said, standing in my single room which she was much too tall for, which she made seem impossibly sad and small with her height. *I don't want to think of you living here.*

It's not so bad, I told her. Far better than my first apartment in town, a tiny blue room in the cat-piss-infused basement of a sadly unhinged Dutchman who claimed to teach at Warren, but who I quickly found out was just a self-appointed, slightly horny philosopher in desperate search of a pliant pupil. Better too than my car, where I was forced to live briefly when the Dutchman wouldn't give my deposit back after I proved to be so "unteachable," and our stipends didn't kick in until October. Or the undergraduate dorm I squatted in for a short time after a faculty member caught me sleeping in my car. When I locked eyes with him through my bug-streaked windshield, I cursed myself for parking on such a leafy, luxurious street, where even the dogs in the yards glowed with money. It only took a few weeks of living among the truly, absurdly rich in their incongruous prison dorms for me to decide to sell my car, and that's when I found this place. A single room on the west side, which

I really thought was just fine even though it didn't quite pass my suicide visualization test. Could I picture shooting myself here? Definitely I could. Hanging myself? Sure. Some nights, I could even see the noose swinging from the light fixture on the ceiling. But I figured with a few well-placed posters, I might mute the sound of my own future death cry that would sometimes flood my ears upon entering this single room with galley kitchen. Perhaps even write my masterpiece. Or at the very least, Think Great Thoughts, Dream Big Dreams like full worlds you could wander. I did none of these things here. What I did here was seethe about petty things. Count the moth deaths. Think of money.

It's really not so bad, I told Ava. *Anyway, this is the only place I can afford to live in without roommates. I can't get work done with roommates, I told you.*

But she was already packing my things. *You're coming home with me.*

Now the place is pretty much empty, apart from some books and a pine desk I found on the street, which I never worked at anyway. And the mattress, of course, upon which I now lie, the weight of the red cloak heavy on my shoulders. There's a spiky flower in my fist. *Here,* I remember the Duchess saying as she pulled it from her silver hair. *For you, Samantha.* Their coos of sympathy are still in my ears. Their finger pads still wiping tears from my cheeks. Because I did cry. Why did I cry again? What did I tell them? Their little hands patting my knees, shoulders, hands. *Tell us another story, Samantha. Another. How erotic. How gritty. How brilliant.*

That's when I see it perched on the outside sill of my window. Looking in, looking right at me, or so it seems. Twitching its nose. Slitty eyes black and shiny and peering right at me through the smudged glass. Floppy ears hanging on either side of its face like little-girl braids.

I scream until the sallow girl next door thumps the wall with her fist.

Everything from the night before comes back to me. How I told them about Rob Valencia. How we drank some more. At which point the room began to sway like it was dancing, the pastel furniture began to change shape. Their shadows on the wall seemed to stretch. Their hair grew shinier and longer, their eyes red, and I did not know which small hand belonged to which pink-and-white body, which coo came from which glossy mouth, which fingers were getting tangled in my hair. And then a voice like warm fur, her balmy lips very close to my ear.

Go outside and bring us a bunny, Samantha.

I remember looking at them all, sitting equidistant from me, mouths closed like purse clasps.

What?

You heard us, the Duchess said.

It's actually really easy, Samantha.

Super easy.

There are like a ton of them on campus, haven't you noticed?

Why? I asked.

It's a dare, Vignette said.

How we round off every Smut Salon, Cupcake added.

I couldn't tell if they were joking. Were they joking?

We never joke about bunnies, Bunny.

Bunny, did they just call me Bunny?

Yes, Bunny.

I dimly recall protesting a little about the darkness, about the lateness of the hour, about the danger of going out at this time of night in the streets. I slurringly cited the recent, horrific news—the girl getting raped on her way back to the dorm, the boy who got clubbed on his way home from the lab just the other night. And then those rumors of actual decapitation, had they heard those rumors?

We're not asking you to go to the lab, Samantha. Just right outside.

Never mind, Samantha, the Duchess cut in. *It's fine. It is getting late. You're right, you should probably be getting home.*

No, wait, I said.

Me in Creepy Doll's red-riding-hood cloak, drunkenly circling the damp front lawn outside while they watched from an upstairs window for I don't know how long.

I still don't remember how I got home. Did I walk? Take the bus? Flashes come back to me. Waiting for the bus on her fancy street, staring at the glittering sidewalks. Thinking every sound was a machete-wielding maniac. Readying myself to tell him, *I am not rich. I am not one of Them. Do not judge a woman by her red cloak soft as tiger pelt. There is nothing in these pockets but lint.*

That's when I heard the rustle. The sound of definitely disturbed leaves. Crunched on. A shadow getting longer. Two shadows. Three. Four. Seven. Emerging from the bushes.

I closed my eyes. Waited for the inevitable to fall upon me.

Waited for the blade to strike my neck. Please be quick. I said hi to my mother in heaven, who I'd be joining soon. She shook her head at me: *You're an idiot for going out after dark to hang out with these cunts. You deserve your fate,* she said. *But yes, see you soon. It's nice here. There are all manner of purple flowers, there is the shade of great weeping trees, there are golden-green leaves rustling in the breeze and a late August light falls over everything.* Not in her voice, but Ava's. Then it was Ava's face I saw. Then nothing. No club to my skull. No blade at my throat. On my neck nothing but a fall breeze, very much of this world. And then into my lap, something leapt. Small. Heavy. Soft. I looked down to find it gazing up at me with its shiny black eyes.

See? hissed a voice from an upstairs window.

I lifted my gaze just in time to see a light go on then off. When I looked back down, my lap was empty.

Is that what happened? Is that what I saw? There is simply no way that is what happened. There is simply no way that is what I saw or heard. *No,* I tell the bunny now sitting on my sill. *There is no way.*

Now, I watch it leap off, leaving my barred window empty, the view of a brick wall and New England sky in all the bleakness of midmorning. The mist in my brain clears. Ava. I check my phone to see if she texted.

Nothing but a troll emoji from Creepy Doll, followed by a tulip and an open-armed ghost. And then, from an unknown number: *Did you make it home okay, girl?* And then from another unknown number: *See you in class tomorrow* ☺

Class. Our first Workshop. I'll go to the diner on my way

there. Where Ava and I always go in the morning. Where she drinks her spiked gunpowder tea and draws the world as a series of zombies. Her sky is full of lightning. Her sun has teeth. She gives all the spoiled Warren girls gills, fangs, wings. She sets the frat boys on fire. While she does this, I stare at New England. Sometimes I write. Sometimes I just stare.

7

It has been so long since I walked to school from my apartment that I've forgotten how to get there. I get lost. I don't see Ava anywhere. The air is alive with crackly fall and the murmurings of mad people. This place is so beautiful you find it hard to believe that it's overrun with the insane and the desperate and the lonely. That wildly violent assault happens almost daily. Rape, clubbings, stabbings, and shootings as common as finding pink champagne by the glass on bistro menus. That rumors of random decapitations are on the rise. One day, you might see a perfectly respectable-looking man walking down the street across from you in the slanting fall sunlight and you might think I am mistaken about this place. It's not an insane and violent place after all. It's not a wrong place. It's a place where people walk at a leisurely pace in the slanting sunshine. It's a town named after a godly gesture of gratitude and fate. Then a small wind comes and the man's coat blows open like the wings of a bat spreading. And when he comes closer you see that he's talking to himself, this man. Not only talking to himself, no. He's arguing profusely. His face is red. His features are warped with rage. All the veins in his neck are pulsing and thick and full to bursting with blood.

And that's when you start to notice all the abandoned houses, the spiderwebs of smashed glass in storefronts, the busted windshields, a ripped, empty purse lying on the sidewalk. You see all that and you remember, that's right, I'm in Sketch City. I'm in the Lair of Cthulhu.

I walk toward what I think is the school, getting lost again and again until at last the moldering, vacant storefronts switch to juice bars and dog salons and I glimpse the Ivy Bubble. The towers upon which Ava and I have sat like gargoyles. Everyone on the street suddenly goes from looking like an extra in a zombie movie to the star of a French New Wave film.

Workshop is held in what is called the Cave, but is really just a black-box theater in the basement of the Narrative Arts Center. No visible doors, no windows, and of course, no clocks. Only dark, damp walls that evoke the womb. I enter late and apologize under my breath—no sign of Ava at the diner, which was empty but for one red-faced man hunched at the counter, hissing at his plate. The Bunnies, seeing me come in, smile like librarians, then look away. They do not look hung over. At all. They are seated in their usual huddle on one side of the hollow square arrangement of tables, leaving the other three sides open to me. My stomach sinks a little to see this. But what did I expect anyway? For them to suddenly embrace me?

Cold dread in my chest. Fluttery hummingbird heart.

I look at them—my gaze a question—but they're blinking thoughtfully through their designer reading eyewear at our teacher, Ursula, whom they have christened KareKare, *because she cares so, so much.* I call her Fosco, after the villain in the Gothic novel *The Woman in White.* I don't know why. I suppose there is just something about her gravitas, her voice like a thick mist, her long, ever gesturing white hands and her saccadic violet eyes that suggests she has distressed maidens in her basement, human livers in her fridge, that she baby talks to pet mice, attends the opera in a box seat, clapping lightly from the shadows. *My god, yes,* Ava said when she saw her. *My god.*

"Samantha," Fosco calls in her usual booming voice as the heavy double doors clang shut behind me. "So glad you could join us."

They all watch me walk toward the stage at the center of the room, where they're all seated as though they're in a play. In what Fosco likes to call the "Hermeneutic Circle," aka a "Safe Space" in which to bravely bare our souls to one another in the form of cryptic word art. Evoke our alchemical experiences and experiments. *In which our work will perform the Body and the Body shall perform our work.* Whatever that means. Even after a year at Warren, I'm still not totally sure. The school is known for its highly experimental approach to narrative. Hence no windows or clocks in the Cave. Because we cannot, we will not, be slaves to the time-space continuum aka plot. And yet she knows I'm late.

"We were worried," Fosco says, tapping her bare wrist as though there is a watch there. It's always unclear to me if Fosco is using the royal we or if she is referring to herself and the Bunnies.

"Worried?" I repeat.

"That something happened to you, weren't we?"

She looks around at all the Bunnies for confirmation. They nod, their dewy faces turned toward her as though toward a goddess shrine. She was our Workshop leader last spring and though we were supposed to work with the Lion again this fall, they fought to have KareKare come back again. *Because she just gets us more. Also, she is just so like a wondrous bear. A care bear! A karekare!*

Yes, KareKare, they nod now. *Worried. Very. Oh so concerned.*

"Sorry," I say. "I got . . ."

"Lost?" Creepy Doll fills in. Her tiger eyes betray nothing, but her Cupid's-bow lips curl into a slight smile. *I draped my red-riding-hood cloak on your shuddering shoulders while you drunk-cried. Remember?*

"Lost," Fosco repeats, her rich voice reverberating in the theater. When she repeats the word, the lilt in her tone suggests its aptness in my case. *Perhaps, Samantha, you are lost in more ways than one?*

She smiles at me now with her silvery-rose lips. Her hermetic silence filling the air like so much machine-generated fog. There are people who come to Warren just to breathe the same incense-choked air as Fosco. Rabid fangirls who have her name tattooed to the inside of their wrists, the smalls of their backs, their winglike shoulder blades. Who clutch her fiercely experimental novels to their chests like witchy talismans, murmuring passages as though they were prayers, incantations. *Because she is so mystical, so maternal, so wise.* I am not one of them. When I observe Fosco in her iridescent smock that calls to mind New Age priestesses, her hands performing vaguely gynecological gestures over stories that I'm certain she's just now speed-reading for the first time, her rose lips spouting cryptic feedback which she'll punctuate now and then with her infamously ever pregnant pause, I cannot be one of them.

And yet I am not entirely immune to the occult probing of her eyes contemplating my face now like it's a lost cause.

"I'm sorry." I feel myself flush.

"It's a confusing building," Cupcake says, not looking at me. I watch her absently run a finger along her pearls, her blond bob glowing beneath the lights. Today she's wearing a dress patterned with patches of green grass. Green cardigan to match. I recall her fervently shaving the cinnamon stick with her golden head tilted back, pearled throat of soft blue veins exposed in open-mouthed ecstasy, and a sudden, violent urge to hug her briefly courses down my arms, making my fingers twitch. She's never stood up for me before.

"I *still* get lost on campus," Creepy Doll adds. "All the time."

"Really, Kira?" KareKare says. "*All* the time?"

"Well definitely sometimes. Once for sure I did," she says, glancing at me. *Hi, Bunny.*

I smile at her, awash in gratitude, but she quickly looks away. It's only then I realize I've already walked over to my usual seat, on the opposite side of the square. Habit and muscle memory must have led me there. I hesitate there, my hand on the back of the chair. Maybe I should sit closer to them, maybe it was up to me to sit closer to them? Should I now? I look over, but they're all focused on KareKare.

"Everything okay, Samantha?"

"Fine. Yes. Of course. Sorry."

I take my usual seat. Fosco returns to her speech, which concerns this all-important penultimate semester. Our last semester of Workshop. A time in which we must Dig Deep. Ask the big and scary questions of ourselves. Fully embrace the alchemical experience of Creation before we are released into the wilds of our final term, when we will write our theses independently. As she did last year, she uses a lot of birthing metaphors, which I only half hear in my hungover daze, my vague and fluttering panic. Meanwhile, Fosco's sweatered terrier yips at her heels or else runs idiotic circles around us. She brought it to every class last semester. The Bunnies would coo at the creature for a good fifteen minutes at the start of class while I sat there, pretending to reread whatever random, formally experimental text Fosco had assigned that week, holding the book very close to my face. I'd stare and stare at the dense, unreadable lines while they squealed *So cute! So cute! Oh my god, SO.* Reminding myself what an opportunity it is to be here, that this school opens doors, so many doors, surely it does, doesn't it? That I came here because they give you the most funding, the most time to write, both of which I desperately needed. Neither of which I really had when I was working as a bookstore wench, a waitress, an office wench, a waitress again—the only jobs I could seem to get with my English degree.

Poor Cinderella, Ava says when I tell her this story. *Where are your anthropomorphic mice? Your cinder-encrusted frocks?*

But I did need—

Want, Ava always corrects. *Need, my love, is a whole other story. Also, you're not exactly writing up a storm here, you know.*

It's true that I wrote way more before I came here. Spent my nights after whatever job or jobs I had in a feverish ecstasy of scrawling on whatever surface was at hand. Since I arrived, not so much. A few faltering stories last fall for the Lion when I still lived under that sun. Since then? Some half-formed things, mostly fragments, phrases. Many, many drawings of eyes. That stare at me.

I told you it's crushing your soul.

But how was I to know that was going to happen? I couldn't turn down this opportunity. To go to Warren? I mean, it's *Warren.* The high experimentalism, the parlance, is annoying, sure, but it's worth it.

Is it? Ava always says.

At last, we move on to discussing this week's stories, which Fosco asked each of us to write over the summer by either dragging a talisman of our choice *through ash* or pulling a tarot card from the deck at random, then contemplating it while walking widdershins around a crossroads.

And you wonder why you're blocked, Smackie?

First, Vignette's piece: a series of unpunctuated vignettes about a woman named Z who pukes up soup while thinking nihilistic thoughts, then has anal sex in a trailer. I hate Vignette's pieces. They are dreary word puzzles I'm always too bored and annoyed to solve. Each paragraph is a half smile, half frown, way up its own asshole. Also, they beg questions like: when on her perilous, pirouetting journey from Interlochen to Barnard was she ever in a trailer?

Rich playing poor, Ava would say. *Fake white trash by the over-educated. The worst kind. It happens at art school all the time.*

Fosco is looking down at Vignette's piece the way she normally does, the way she looks at all of their pieces but mine. Like they're fussy, brilliant, but ever-so-slightly retarded babies. What went wrong in the birth canal? She holds a lantern up in the form of a concerned brow. *Well,* she'll announce at last, *what do we think? Thoughts?*

"I'm fascinated by the soup," Cupcake says, as though she is actually fascinated. I notice the urge to hug her has distinctly faded.

"As am I, Caroline," Fosco says. "As am I." She looks back down at the pages.

"I'd just like to believe it more, I guess," the Duchess says, like she's concerned about the prognosis of a disease. "Although I must say, Victoria, it's just always *so* interesting how you engage the Body."

Murmurs of approval all around. Little nods. *Oh, absolutely. I agree. So interesting.*

I record the number 1098 in my notebook. Which is the number of times I've heard "the Body" mentioned since being at Warren. Because at Warren, the Body is all the rage. As though everyone in the academic world has just now discovered that they are vesseled in precarious, fastly decaying houses of bone and flesh and my god, what material. What a wealth of themes and plot! I still don't quite understand what it means to write about The Body with title caps but I always nod like I do. Oh yes, The Body, of course.

Other words I've been keeping track of: *space*, *gesture*, and *perform*.

"I appreciate the uncertainty the piece gestures toward," Creepy Doll says. "I just think she could go further into the dream space. It's so interesting how she performs and reenacts trauma."

I watch Vignette actually take notes about this. As though it's helpful, these insights. Her auburn hair tumbling over one shoulder, an opium cloud surrounding her, even here. As she writes, Cupcake lightly pets her shoulder. *Bunny, I love you.*

"What do you think, Samantha?" Fosco asks me.

That it's a piece of pretentious shit. That it says nothing, gives nothing. That I don't understand it, that probably no one does and no one ever will. That not being understood is a privilege I can't afford. That I can't believe this woman got paid to come here. That I think she should apologize to trees. Spend a whole day on her knees in the forest, looking up at the trembling aspens and oaks and whatever other trees paper is made of with tears in her languid eyes and say, *I'm fucking sorry. I'm sorry that I think I'm so goddamned interesting when it is clear that I am not interesting. Here's what I am: I'm a boring tree murderess.*

But I look at Vignette, at Creepy Doll, at Cupcake, the Duchess. All of them staring at me now with shy smiles.

"I think I'd like to see more of the soup too," I hear myself say.

Eventually we turn to my piece, one of my last completed stories before my block descended. They're silent for a long time. Fosco looks at the piece like she doesn't even know where to begin. No formal experimentation. No character named after a letter of the alphabet. No soup puke nihilism. And a plot of all things, *oh, dear.*

I brace myself for their usual criticisms.

Angry.

Mean.

Distant.

Dark but like not in a good way?

Funny, yes, but almost too funny?

Exactly. It's like what's behind the laughter, you know?

But they're still silent, looking down thoughtfully at the story.

"It's weird," Cupcake says at last. "The *first* time I read it, I have to confess I was quite put off." She wrinkles her nose as though the story has a smell she finds unfavorable.

"Tell us about that, Caroline," Fosco urges.

"Well, it just seemed *so* . . . mean at first."

"And angry," Creepy Doll adds, not looking at me. "And abrasive."

"Dark but like not a good dark," Vignette says.

"And just way too invested in its own outsiderness."

"Exactly. It really keeps the reader at a distance at first. But then . . ."

"But then?" Fosco prompts.

"I don't know. On the second read, I sort of like all of that now. The angsty grittiness, the adolescent rawness. It's . . . compelling."

She looks at me from across the room, tilting her golden head to one side.

"More vulnerable than I expected. Almost desperate."

"Sad," Vignette says.

"But in the *best* way," Creepy Doll adds.

"I mean, I still think it could definitely open itself up a bit more. . . . "

"A *lot* more."

"And it could definitely use more . . . bounce?" Vignette says, looking at the Duchess, who has said nothing up to this point.

"We want *more*, I guess is what we're saying, Samantha," the Duchess says. Hands braided over my pages, looking not at me but at Fosco, who nods with motherly gravitas.

"Does that make sense?"

8

Ava. All week I don't see her. I walk by her house: dark. I pass by the diner: Ava-less. I go to the bowels of the nature lab where she's usually to be found sitting among the drawers of dead bugs or else in the basement library shelving what she calls the True Corpses. *Because books are dead, Smackie, didn't you know? Because almost no one comes down here but you.* I turn on the humming light in every aisle, but she is not smoking and reading among the tall dark stacks. I call her name until a man sitting at a desk nearby turns and frowns at me. Can I *help* you?

She isn't sitting on the dumpster behind the undergrad dorms, legs swinging, fists full of Warren spoils. She isn't at the anarchy bookstore, browsing through the new acquisitions. She isn't sitting on the domed roof of the science building like a glam rock gargoyle.

I go back to the park bench by the pond where I usually meet her. The bench is empty. I gaze at the pond's still surface, the tree leaves winking and shivering around me in the afternoon light. Even before Ava, I used to come here by myself. To feel less lonely. To write, though I never did. I'd just sit here with an untouched coffee beside me, a notebook in my lap, a pen in my lax hand, watching a lone swan turn circles in the sludgy water. For hours I'd do this. I'd come here after class, with the insular laughter of the Bunnies still ringing in my ears. Or before class, bracing myself to go, *just go, this is fucking ridiculous, what are you afraid of anyway?* On weekends, telling myself I enjoyed this break, I was glad for this time alone with no plans, never any plans, it was good for my work, absolutely. I did love the quiet. How there was never anyone here. Except the swan, of course. Turning and turning its lonely circles. Or else just drifting there. And then, one morning, one terrible-wonderful morning, there was Ava. Sitting on the bench like she'd always been there. Asking me for a light I didn't know I had.

But now, there's no swan on the water.

No Ava either.

All I see are the people she hates and the golden light she hates more falling upon buildings she wants to set fire to.

And bunnies.

So many bunnies. I do not believe my eyes. But they are there. Possibly they were always there. Hopping across the green. Dashing across my path and disappearing into a cluster of bushes. Tripping me up on the winding campus paths like so many soft, heavy stones. Each time I see one, I feel a little lash of fear and excitement in my gut. I recall the soft but heavy magic of the animal in my lap that night. Me drunkenly staring down into its twitching, leporine face. An upstairs window turning on, then off. Their little-girl voices warm and peltlike in my ears.

See how easy, Samantha? We told you.

★

Every day they dog me, little furred shadows. One afternoon on the bench, I look up from my reading to find one, two, four bunnies. Sort of surrounding me in a little fuzzy circle like I'm their leader, about to give a speech. I even find myself opening my mouth. Then I close it again. Get up and leave. Walk hurriedly away toward the library. *Don't follow me. Okay?*

A couple of Wes Anderson–type girls stare at me through their hipster frames. Little silky French shifts with an understated pattern. Little smirks to match. Because I'm a grown woman talking to rabbits. I remember the man I saw on my walk to school, screaming at a tree. *What did it ever do to you?* I wanted to ask him. Now I'm not so sure it's a fair question.

"*Don't* follow me!" I hiss at the rabbits under my breath.

"Samantha?" Jonah in his parka, cigarette burning between his fingers. Wheat-colored hair in his eyes. Grinning at me like I'm Christmas.

"Hey, Jonah. Sorry I was—"

"Hey, were you just talking to those rabbits?"

"No."

"It's cool if you were. Sometimes I talk to things too." He nods as if to reassure me. "And they are staring at you pretty hard. Weird."

"They are?" Even though I know they are.

"Oh yeah. Definitely. Wow. I've never seen anything like that before. It's almost like they want to talk to you or something. Are you freaked out by it?"

"No," I lie.

"You shouldn't be. One time in Alaska, this bear followed me home from a bar and we ended up talking for a long time. He was telling me all these things. I guess because he knew I was a poet and he needed someone, you know, to tell his story."

We look back at the rabbits, who are still looking at me.

"Maybe you're part rabbit and you don't know it." He smiles at me. "Hey, you want to go for a drink or something? I just got out of class. We could go to the ale house?"

"I thought you didn't drink."

"Yeah. But I could watch you drink? I like doing that."

Over his shoulder, I look at the bunnies. They are fucking staring at me.

"I can't right now, Jonah. I'm sorry. Maybe some other time, though, okay?"

I rush off and nearly trip on a shaggy gray one crossing the road. It gets hit by a car that doesn't even break and I scream.

"Hi, Samantha," the Bunnies say now whenever they see me on campus. They smile at me like I'm a boy they might like, they're not sure yet. Wave at me from across the green where they sit in their little cluster. *Hello. Hi. Hey. Bonjour, Samantha.* They attempt to make awkward small talk. Ask me how my week is going. Vignette's half smile waxes to three quarters. Cupcake shyly offers me a cupcake. Tells me she likes my dress even though I am not wearing a dress. I am never wearing a dress. But I say, *Thanks. I like yours too.* Creepy Doll gives me a sharp, glittering black rock. *For your altar, Bunny. You do have an altar, right?* I don't, but I just smile as if to say, yes, I do, thanks so much for this. Twice in class, the Duchess reaches out and puts her hand on my wrist. Says my name with a voice like a lacy embrace.

They do not mention Smut Salon except to say, *That was super fun. Wasn't it?*

Yeah, I say. *It was.* It's only when I say this that I realize I'm not lying. It's true.

It was fun, I repeat.

I want to ask them, *Did you really ask me to hunt a bunny? Did a bunny leap into my lap?*

I want to tell them, *You know, rabbits are following me now.*

We should do it again sometime, Creepy Doll says shyly, like they're asking me on a second date.

9

All week, I go home alone to the apartment where Ava pronounced I should not live. I eat the generic-brand cans of chili I bought last fall in anticipation of a hurricane that turned out to be nothing but a light and dismal rain. I pour the several-months-old bottle of wine in my fridge that tastes like acidic needles into a souvenir mug featuring the Falls of Falling, my hometown, and drink.

Probably you have visited the Falls of Falling. For like an hour, a half day, a day and night tops, you parked in event parking, even though there is no event there but water. You stood against the railing for a selfie or a family photo, the Falls roaring behind you, donning shorts you'll later regret, trying to smile or maybe really smiling as the water sprays your legs and arms and hair with endless mist. Maybe afterward, you took that boat ride called Under the Falls, where you don't actually go under the Falls because that would literally kill you, wearing one of those thin yellow slickers that fails to keep you from being drenched to the bone, because I wasn't there to tell you it's not worth it. I was in downtown Falling, a place no one goes but the people of Falling, likely in my teacher's office getting in trouble for the stories I submitted instead of math homework, or in my mother's hair salon writing them, or in my room or on the branches of the thin trees outside dreaming myself elsewhere.

Probably you didn't go to downtown Falling but maybe you went so far as to make a day of it on the cheesy main drag by the water—toured the lame arcades, got lost in the mirror maze I was too tall for by the age of nine, sampled the "ice cream of the future," had a surf-and-turf dinner at a restaurant shaped like a ship. Cut into a dry steak by its porthole windows under a net full of fake fish, enjoying the music of Heart, which is everywhere, as though piped into the mist-filled air. If you happened to be there around Halloween, you might have gone to the live-action haunted house, where a man in a hockey mask comes out of a meat locker and chases you around black-as-pitch tunnels with a fake chain saw. From 1985 to 1992, this man was my father. Maybe you dropped some pennies at the casino, where he later worked, climbing his way up the ladder from waiter to manager.

But I doubt you did any of those things unless you have a mullet or a deep sense of irony.

Likely you left Falling after the waterfall selfie and didn't look back. Maybe on the way out you bought an overpriced shot glass, or a mug like this one. Or a magnet with a Falls pic better than the ones you took. Perhaps it's getting struck by a rainbow. *I'm Falling for You.* My mom gave me one that said that once, as a joke. I took it with me everywhere. Put it on every fridge I've ever had since, even this one. This summer I gave it to Ava, who put it on her fridge.

Our fridge, she said.

I drink more needle wine. Listen to the perverted giant next door laughing at a sitcom but never along with the laugh track. I wonder how he lives in that small, low-ceilinged room when he is larger than any human. The cheap black rubber boots he leaves outside his chipped front door could club a seal. Above me, the Ever-Practicing Opera Singer sings songs from a D-list opera. She sounds like a schizophrenic songbird gone off the rails. I keep my curtains shut lest Flasher Man is sitting on my fire escape again, waiting with bated breath to show me his glittered junk. Always naked despite the chill of the evening. Cock in hand, clouding up the glass with his breath, staring at me or not, I never keep the curtains open long enough to find out. Also, whenever I open them now, there is that same bunny sitting there on the sill like he never left. Staring at me.

I finish off the wine and attempt to write. I must write, I have to write. Writing is why I'm here. I stare at my open notebook, blank for all but one badly drawn eye. A few swirls. The words *I don't know* scratched over and over again. Surrounded by limp flowers.

I long for my first writing office, the waiting area of the hair salon where my mother worked when I was a child. I wrote with such feverish abandon on that sagging couch between the dusty Buddha and the dustier fake flowers, beneath framed photos of women smiling under impossibly, painfully elaborate arrangements of hair. Clients would sit in waiting area chairs nearby, pretending to read magazines but all the while regarding me askance, a lanky child in a Swamp Thing T-shirt clutching her mermaid journal close, staring at them through bangs I barely ever let my mother cut. I was afraid she'd gouge out my eyes.

Whatcha workin' on there? they might ask me.

Uncovering your secret shame, I thought.

Don't mind my daughter, my mother would say as she led them to a chair, tilted their heads back into a wash sink where they'd immediately close their eyes. I'd watch them sit caped in their swivel chairs, looking straight ahead into the mirror like they were contending with their faces for the first time. They'd say things—addressing her or their own reflection, I could never tell. Things I couldn't catch over the sound of *The Best of Heart* and the drone of hair dryers that I would try desperately to guess at.

I am actually a lizard person.

I commune with aliens in the evenings, that's why I need my hair like this.

There is a squirrel in the park who is a man who is my lover. The dye job is for him.

Tonight I shall jump headfirst into the falls with my new permed extensions flying beautifully behind me.

She'd nod or laugh as she took a brush, a pair of scissors, a razor, a hot iron to their slightly bowed heads full of clips, wrapped their wet locks one by one into little squares of tin-foil, then made them sit under what I believed, at the time, to be brain-sucking head ovens. There they'd contentedly cook, flipping through magazines.

Sometimes my mother wouldn't lead the man or woman to

a swivel chair, but to a small, dimly lit treatment room down the hall. The sounds emanating from behind that closed door were the source of all my early horror stories. I heard barklike screams, grunts. Nervous laughter. Softer screams too, almost like sighs. Other loud nonverbal sounds that I didn't understand, that scared and puzzled and thrilled me. I expected clients to emerge from this room with scorched faces, gills cut deep into their cheeks, horns hammered into their heads. But when they came out, nothing looked different about them at all, except their faces were slightly flushed.

A waxing room, she never told me, but then I never asked.

The fevered stories I wrote in the hair salon were all rip-offs of the thriller and horror paperbacks she devoured on breaks and in the evenings, which I read on the sly. I based the characters on her clients, my classmates, teachers who distressed me.

Let me see, she'd say, seeing me writing in the evening.

It's not ready, I'd say, even though it absolutely was.

Your daughter submitted this to the essay-writing contest and I have to say we are quite concerned by the content, never mind that it isn't an essay, my teacher later informed my mother.

Oh, please, my mother said. *Samantha's scared of her own shadow. She just has a vivid imagination. What kid doesn't?* Though I knew she was worried. My increasingly horrific and fantastic version of events. Telling her all manner of lies in answer to questions like *So how was school?* instead of whatever boring thing really happened. Disappearing into my room or into the thin cluster of trees behind our apartment complex with my mermaid notebook. *What are you doing in there*, my mother would say through the crack in the bedroom door, as if I wasn't in a room in her apartment, but a distant place, far from her reach, where I'd decided to live instead of here.

I don't have those hair salon novels anymore. I like to think they were swallowed up in the Falls after she died. In my memory, those years remain my most prolific writing period although I've never really not written, never not had another world of my own making to escape to, never known how to be in this world without most of my soul dreaming up and living in another. Until I came here.

Sometimes it's good to take a break, the Lion said to me last January, whisking his tea. *Focus on other things. Read. Be a guest in other worlds. Perhaps you're growing. Evolving. Trust, Samantha. Patience.*

We were meeting in his office to discuss why I hadn't turned in any new writing. At that point, our friendship had already fallen away. We were still meeting, but only every couple of weeks or so now, and only in his office and only with the door open. I never asked why he no longer emailed me playlists in the middle of the night or asked me to drink Scotch with him in the middle of the day, and he never explained.

Nothing at all to be ashamed of, he said. Tight smile.

I guess I just don't understand what happened, I said, squinting, the sunlight from his window backlighting him and blinding me. *To me, I mean. I used to write all the time. And now . . .*

These things have their own ebbs and flows, he said, and looked pointedly at his watch.

And then I felt insane. Like I'd imagined his warmth, our closeness.

Bullshit, Ava said. *I bet he cooled off because of the bonobos. I bet they saw you guys getting friendly and got their sugar whiskers in a twist. Started a rumor and he freaked out like a little pussy-man. He's not a lion, he's a lemming.*

I told myself to get a grip, focus on my writing, forget about him. He wasn't even our Workshop leader anymore, just my thesis advisor. What did he really owe me beyond an occasional email check-in? On paper, absolutely nothing.

Fuck him. You have me now.

I look at my phone. Nothing from Ava. Look back at my mostly blank page but all I see is the Lion's face in his office that day.

You're thinking about it too much, Samantha. Really.

Maybe. So should we meet next week then? I asked him.

Why don't we hold off for now. Not a question. *Just send me something when you're ready.*

I haven't sent him anything since then. I was planning to before the summer hit, but then the spring party happened. If things had been awkward between us before, they were impossible after that.

Theoretically I should have checked in with him a couple of times over the summer. I definitely should have checked in this week, sent work toward my thesis, updates on my progress. But I haven't reached out and he hasn't either. I can't bear the idea of facing him now. And there's nothing but a bunch of eyes and sad flowers and *I don't knows* to give him anyway.

⋆

I close my empty notebook. Shower in my graying tub. Brush my teeth in the chipped sink, avoiding my reflection in the rusty little mirror. Instead I stare at the cracked yellow tiles above the ancient toilet that the one man I slept with here said reminded him of a navy ship. I was rich once. Briefly. After my mother died. When, as a morose thirteen-year-old, I went to live with my nomadic father, following him across the country as he chased one vivid dream of wealth after another that only he could see. I never understood what it was he did for a living, exactly. *Talk shit,* my mother once said, drunk. My father called it real estate development, *business opportunities here and abroad, Samantha, having vision, eyes to see.* A chain of resorts in South America. A spa on the Black Sea. He just needed investors, people who saw what he saw, people who believed. Then he found them—a Middle Eastern prince or two, some big-thinking Bulgarians, a slew of Texans—and overnight, our life changed.

It lasted only a few years, his good fortune, my glimpse into what I imagine to be the Bunny life. Spring breaks and summers spent in centrally located hotels that were once castles. Spa treatments that involved sea kelp. Sinks deep as oceans. Mattresses like dreams. Tall windows that looked onto manicured parks, rolling hills, crashing waves. Everything in that other life was stretched and gleaming and perfumed. Each room had a temperature I could control with the turn of a little dial. I should have felt like God. Instead I forgot that I had ever been poor. It grew so normal so quickly, that life. In my memory of this time, I sit looking bored out the window onto the most beautiful, serene stretch of the world left to look at, not even seeing it. Wearing a string of pearls that, the first time they were clasped around my neck, felt like strangling but after a week felt like nothing at all.

So you were a Bunny, Ava said from behind her cloud of smoke, when I told her.

I was not.

You so were. She narrowed her eyes and pointed her cigarette at me. *It all makes sense now.*

What does?

She stared at me until I looked away.

You're too crushed and obsessed about being poor to have always been poor, she said, leaning back in her chair like she should know.

I looked at her in her blue dragon kimono, so perfectly worn and ripped you'd think she'd planned it. Reclining in the red velvet chair we lifted off someone's curb on trash day. Her red-painted toes poking out of the holes in her fishnet tights like candy. The light from her stolen lamp buzzing over her feathery head like a flickering motel sign. Sipping champagne from a wide-mouthed flute. Where does she get it? *Never mind. Places.* Ava never seems to worry about money. Yet somehow her apartment is like a movie of arty poverty in Paris. Run-down but chicly so.

You're better off, Ava said. *You are, Smackie. You could use a few rips in your soul's kimono. Seriously. A little fall never hurt anyone, you know? Also, you need to learn to kill your own spiders.* Referring to my spiders-in-the-bathtub problem, which she was taking care of for me. *Just don't go crazy on the violins. Don't trade one kind of blindness for another.*

Yeah, I said. *Wait. What's that supposed to mean?*

But she just sipped her champagne.

Now I text her *I miss you*. I text her *Everything okay?* I text her *Did I do something wrong?* And then I text her *Whatever I did, I'm sorry*. I text her *There is a giant spider in my bathroom*. Because probably there is.

Nothing.

Then one morning, six mornings later, I wake up from a terrible dream in which my hands are full of blood and white feathers. I get a text. Two texts. Three texts! Four texts!!! I'm so excited, I lunge for the phone, but it isn't from Ava.

Troll emoji. Tulip. Open-armed ghost.

And then *Hey girl. Just wanted to let you know we're having a party tonight.*

And then *If you want to join.*

And then ☺

Beside the word *tonight*, she's put the emoji of a dancing girl in a red dress.

Then I remember: Tango class. Tonight. That's where I will find Ava. That is where she'll be.

I will tell her I am so sorry. I will tell her *never leave me again*.

10

The tango class we go to is downtown, in a walk-up studio that looks out onto dead trees and sketch street. It's called Tango Palace, even though all it is is a low-ceilinged room strung with mostly nonworking lights. The class is taught by a brusque, beautiful Polish woman in strappy black and a grave-looking man in a suit who always seems covered in an incongruous amount of sweat.

They bark at us when we do poorly. Put us on the spot. *You! What are you doing? I don't know,* I always say, going red. But mostly I do well with shame.

The students are mainly locals as well as some engineering nerds from Warren who are using this as an opportunity to socialize. There is never any sign of the mythical Diego, which is why Ava and I keep coming back, apart from the sheer pleasure of dancing, though we are truly terrible (I am truly terrible). We dance with each other because that is better than dancing with the office types and the engineering nerds. We wait for Diego.

There's no way she would miss tonight.

But when I arrive at the studio, there's no sign of her. Not in the small circle of students clustered around the couple, who are already in the midst of showing us tonight's combination. Not on the bench outside smoking, not standing in a corner plotting the social apocalypse.

The music starts and I'm about to leave because she isn't here and I didn't pay attention to the new move anyway. But the engineering student to my right has turned to me with an awkward smile. I am the person to his left, am I not? I am. We dance.

I'm terrible. I can't follow. That's the downside of only dancing with Ava. We don't really do the follow-lead thing, we just close our eyes and sort of go with it. I step on his feet. He is polite about it but visibly frustrated. I am apologetic, but not overly so because I am distracted. Where is she? Why isn't she here?

And that's when I see her, standing a little outside the circle of dancing pairs. Not looking at me at all. Pretending that she is actually interested in learning these moves, in observing everyone's feet. I try to catch her eye, but it won't be caught. When at last I see her looking at something close to my direction, I smile. But she looks past me, through me. A guy asks her to dance, and I watch her accept.

"Hey," the man I'm dancing with says. "Ow."

"Sorry."

During break she walks out of class quickly. I follow her out there, into the dark street. Ava! At first it's all black, but then my eyes adjust to the dark and I see her silhouette in a cloud of smoke, under the Tango Palace sign.

I run over to her. "Ava!!!"

"Hey," she says. Smiles. Like everything is normal. Like she hasn't been ignoring me for the past two weeks. Like it isn't weird that we came here separately for the first time in months. Just you know, *Hey. S'up.*

I want to say, *What the fuck? Where the hell have you been? Why did you disappear on me?* But she's looking at me so normally that all I can say is, "Hey. How have you been?"

She shrugs. "Okay. You know. Life among the dead bugs and book corpses. You?"

I look at her face through her fishnet veil. Is she pissed? I can't tell because it's hard to see her expression in the dark. I shrug, smile, but feel my lip jerk to one side.

"Okay. Stressful. School and all."

She nods at the moon, who would never be stressed out by dumb things like school. I wish she would look at me.

"I missed you." I say it with feeling. Too much feeling. "I tried to text. I thought maybe you left town or something."

"Nope, still here. Well, there was that really brief stint with Diego in Paris. He got me this coat."

"It's nice." I say it before I even look at her coat but now that I do, I realize it is a nice coat, a very nice coat, and I've never seen her in it before. Probably another spoil from the Warren dumpster but no, it looks too new. It's got a fur collar. "Is that real fur?"

"Rabbit." She blows smoke coolly out of her nostrils like a dragon. "He skinned it himself. Don't look so appalled, Smackie. That's what they do in Europe. Anyway, it had a good life before he shot it. Lots of tall grass and hopping in the Bois de Boulogne or whatever."

She grins at me, her eyes shining. "Oh, how was your little sex party thing, by the way?"

"Okay."

"Cool."

"I mean, it was super lame," I add. "I don't think I'll be doing that again. Ever."

She looks at me. "You're allowed to have fun without me, you know."

"I know," I say. "But I really didn't. At all."

She looks at me until I look away.

Silence.

When I look back at her, she's staring up at the moon, smiling serenely at it like the moon is her new best friend, it's telling her the most gorgeous things in the world, it would never betray her for some dumb cunts. I could never compare. I shouldn't try.

"I really missed you this week. I thought maybe you were upset with me."

"Why would you think that?"

"I don't know."

"Because you went to that lame party?"

When she says it aloud like that, it sounds utterly stupid. "No. I don't know. Maybe," I say.

She laughs and shakes her head. "Don't be an idiot."

She turns back toward the moon. "Unlike your new friends, I'm a *grown* woman."

"I know."

"I have my own devices." She looks down the street as though she's waiting for a taxi that will arrive and whisk her away any minute now. The street is dark, empty, aside from a few scared-looking undergrads walking quickly down the sidewalk, huddled together, their coiffed heads bent, purse logos shimmering in the dark. Probably venturing toward the one cool bar downtown.

The tango music swells up again.

"We'd better go back inside," she says and moves to walk in.

"I'm sorry I went," I blurt out. "I would much rather have hung out with you." It's the truth. It's so the truth I can't even look at her.

"Do you want me to be mad at you? Is that it?"

"No," I say.

"Because I will be. Samantha, how dare you."

"Ava."

"Why oh why did you desert me for three hours?"

"Stop it."

"Do you know I almost died? In fact," she turns to look at me, "I am dead."

"Don't."

"Oh yes. I'm a ghost now, Samantha. I died of a broken heart. I died of grief. It's in the autopsy. And it's all your fault. My tombstone reads, Friend Deserted for Evening. I didn't invite you to the funeral because I figured you wouldn't care."

"Ava, please stop—"

She moves in closer. Cups her hands around my face. Her

hands are cold and soft and strong through the mesh gloves that grate my skin. She smells like wet leaf, firewood, and green tea. Her hair is platinum feathers brushing my cheeks. Her eyes are runny and scary with makeup, both the brown one and the blue one boring into my skull. We're swaying slightly like we're about to dance.

I remember how the first time we came to class, we were late and all the men had been taken. So the teacher said, *You two, pair up! Take turns leading.*

Are you leading or am I? I asked Ava.

Whatever, she said. *We can both lead.*

Okay, I said, not knowing what to do. So I sort of followed and led at the same time. She was looking right at me sort of dreamily, happily, like *what bliss, what fun, isn't it?* but I didn't know where to look, so I kept my eyes on a peacock feather earring dangling from her left ear. It felt a little like holding a dream.

I'm staring at that feather now though this doesn't feel like a dream.

"Samantha," she says now, "I don't *care,* okay? I really don't. You want to go to a pretentious party and fraternize with bonobos, I honestly give zero fucks. I don't care what you do or where you go, okay?"

I feel my breath being knocked out of me. "Okay," I say.

She looks at me.

Tears are suddenly running down my face.

"Smackie," she says softly.

But I'm walking away, stumbling then running. Even though

the night scares me. Even though I hear her calling my name as I walk off into the night. I hear her calling me back, but I don't turn around. I want to show her I'm not scared. I'm not scared of the weird man who is suddenly coming toward me, screaming *LONELY I'M SO LONELY!* I can walk away into the night alone. Without her. With very quick steps. With galloping steps. I feel my phone buzz in my pocket. I pull it out, thinking it's her. She's saying, *Come back.* She's saying she didn't mean it. Instead, on the screen is a text from a number I vaguely recognize. Words flanked by tulips and open-armed ghosts.

U coming 2nite? :D

11

Samantha," Cupcake says, pressing her palms into my cheeks so hard she almost breaks my face. "If we braided your hair, would you kill us?"

She's wearing a Peter Pan collar dress she tells me she ordered off the internet called All She Wants To Do Is Prance. A peachy-nude lip balm, which I am drunk enough on Bunny punch to let her smear onto my lips with her little perfumed finger. We're in Creepy Doll's living room, which is all done up with high-school-dance-style party decorations. Crepe paper dangling in ornate arrangements from the ceiling. A tower of mini cupcakes and a backlit bowl of bright punch on a nearby table swaddled in white gauze. Kate Bush roaring from every speaker. *Wuthering wuthering wuthering heights.* A mirror ball turning slowly above their Arthurian-inspired updos.

They answered the door wearing pastel dresses that bell out into gauzy blobs. Corsages on their wrists. Because it's Prom Night, didn't I know? And the theme is These Dreams. *All the graduate students do it, Samantha. It's a thing, didn't you know? Also, we wanted an excuse to wear these,* they say, holding up their white-gloved hands and wriggling their fingers. *We didn't tell you, Samantha, because if we told you, well—*

"We didn't think you'd come."

"But you did come."

"And we're so glad."

"The problem is you're not dressed."

Can we dress you? they ask me, leading me by the hand into the bedroom. *Also, there's this hair we saw on the internet that would look so good with your face oh my god. Do you mind? Don't kill us.*

I think of Sissy Spacek covered in pig's blood as I watch Creepy Doll go through her closet to find the dress that, according to her, I'll love so much I'll want to have its dress babies. I look around her bedroom—the walls lined with her many typewriters, her various prints of fairy-tale wolves and mythical creatures, an altar that is billowing a strange-smelling smoke. I drink more punch. Think, *This is nice, isn't it?* Their hands pawing through my hair, twisting it into faux medieval configurations. *Don't be so stuck up and dour, Samantha,* I tell myself. *Don't be suspicious. They're probably just being nice. This is their way. You should be nice too.*

"Thanks for this," I say, as I watch Cupcake in the mirror, drunkenly twisting my hair into an updo quite like theirs. *Fucked-up dos,* my mother called them, the favorite of prom monstresses and bridezillas, the bane of her existence—and mine, for she'd sometimes practice on me in the evenings. The salon clients who requested them were nothing like the Bunnies, of course—they were much poorer, had no knowledge of Latin, abject theory, or the lute—but on their faces the same palpable desire for some kind of impossible transformation that embarrassed me to behold, that always made me look away. That is, to my horror, on my own face now.

"No worries, girl. We're glad you came."

Creepy Doll looks at Cupcake braiding my hair in the mirror and smiles. I notice her red hair has been twisted into a viselike knot on top of her head and affixed with a ribbon. What I can see of her scalp is bright pink.

"So tell us about your prom, Samantha," Creepy Doll says. "Did you hate it?" She makes an anticipatory *ew* face that welcomes me to make my own.

"We picture you hating it."

"Or being way too cool for it."

"I didn't hate it." I loathed it with my whole soul.

"Did you have a date?" Cupcake asks me, tugging so hard on my hair, a tear slides down my cheek.

"I went with my best friend at the time." Alice. A lazy-eyed goth girl with whom I used to skip school to go read horror novels at the library. Alice showed up at my door wearing a skull-and-roses ball gown and her Day of the Dead tiara. I wore a floor-length black silk halter dress with a fire-breathing dragon on it that I thought was oh so cutting edge when I first came upon it at Goodwill. But when I put it on that night, saw my shoulders bared, the flames coiled around my cleavage, it made me feel weirdly shy. All night, I folded my arms over the dragon's forked tongue in profound embarrassment. Ava would have rocked it, of course. Thrown her shoulders back. Added spiked heels. A Lady Danger lip. A cigarette holder I'd never have the balls to wield. I think of Ava standing in the dark outside the tango class. *Smackie. I'm sorry. Come back.* Didn't she say come back?

"Oh," Cupcake says. "That's cool but kind of sad?"

"What about that hot boy you told us about?" Creepy Doll asks. "The one you were hardcore obsessed with in high school? The one you died with all the time? Was he for real?"

I stare at her little heart-shaped inquiring face. "He was more like a composite," I lie.

"Oh. He felt so real. What was his name again? Rob something?"

I want to snatch the name, a name I wrote in all kinds of ink in every notebook I owned from grade ten through twelve, from her little bow of a mouth.

"Rob Valentino?" she says.

"Valencia," corrects Cupcake. "We totally stalked you on the internet."

"We hope that isn't creepy," Creepy Doll says.

"No." Of course it's fucking creepy. The four of them huddled around a screen, drinking champagne and eating mini cupcakes, scrutinizing what photos of me they can find. Not many, thankfully.

Through the open door, I can see the Duchess and Vignette in the living room, dancing and laughing with four conspicuously handsome young men. The men stare intently at me with vacant eyes the blue-green of glacial lakes.

"Kira, shut the door, will you? I need to concentrate on this hair." I feel Cupcake gently running her fingers through my hair as though I'm a skittish horse she wants to groom.

Part of me wants to swat her hand away. Instead, I close my eyes.

"Is it the same Rob Valencia you're friends with on FB?" Creepy Doll asks me as she goes to shut the door. "The prematurely balding one?"

"Yeah." He hardly ever posts. When he does, it's disappointing. A song I don't love celebrating the arrival of Friday. A picture of a cocktail also celebrating the arrival of Friday. A picture of him and other businessy-looking people at a table groaning with tapas. He appears to be in some sort of sales but I don't look too closely. He's had the same profile pic forever. Him in front of some Spanish church steps, shirt collar open, looking as tall as he does in my dreams.

"Well," Cupcake says, massaging the back of my neck a little, "he does look a little like Zeus."

"Samantha," Creepy Doll says, putting her hand on my wrist, "I'm sure Rob really wanted to go to prom with you."

"Of course he did. He was probably just super intimidated." Now she's pulling on my hair again. Tying it into what feels like elaborate knots.

"Like we were last year," Creepy Doll adds.

"You were?" I gasp through the pain.

I think about last year. Them looking at me from opposite shores of the room during functions. All of us waiting outside the Cave before Workshop for the Lion to come and unlock the door. They always sat on the floor in the hallway waiting, slumped against the wall as though they didn't have the energy to stand, their legs had given way, surrounding the grandfather clock like dolls someone forgot to put away. Smiling at each other. Chatting softly about the night before using so many GRE words. Falling silent when I approached. Looking up, up, up at me, I was so tall. In my jeans and a T-shirt featuring some jaw-bearing animal. If they thought I was wearing that to intimidate them, they were not wrong. Sometimes one of them—usually Cupcake or Creepy Doll—would say something to me while the Duchess and Vignette exchanged looks.

I like your bag, Samantha, Creepy Doll might say. *Where did you get it?*

I didn't know how to take that. How could she possibly like my bag?

Just this place. In a basement.

Oh. Cool.

I like your earrings, Cupcake might say. Even if I wasn't wearing earrings.

What was I supposed to say? So I just stared at her.

What did you do last night, Samantha?

Was this a trick question?

Cool, they'd say to whatever platitude I mumbled in reply. Then they'd all nod and look at one another.

"Totally," Creepy Doll says now. "We still are a little bit. You're so . . . Anyway, he's probably been fantasizing about you all these years."

"He totally has. That's a given." Cupcake's tugging and twisting my hair so hard my skull feels like it's on fire. Every scalp nerve screaming.

"Maybe he's dead now because of you. Can you imagine?"

"He is not *dead*, Kira. Stop trying to make everything into one of your ghost stories. He's probably just utterly heartbroken because his life is ruined. But I'll bet if he were here right now, he would be like, *Samantha, oh my god, darling Samantha, dance with me. Have my babies, please.*" She turns my screaming head around so that I'm facing the mirror again. In it is a woman I do not recognize. Her bangs have been pinned back. Her hair is the hair of queens from fantasy lands. There are tears in her eyes from the pain.

"Oh my god, amazing," Cupcake says with a sharp intake of breath. "I'm amazing. What do you think?" She isn't asking me, she's asking Creepy Doll.

Creepy Doll looks at me, her trussed-up head tilted to one side. "I think that if Rob Valencia were here right now he would die. Especially if you wear this." She hands me a dress patterned all over with little beheaded girls with blond beehive hairdos, their smiling heads floating next to their decapitated bodies. "Marie Antoinettes," she says.

They lead me into the living room, where the Duchess and Vignette are on the makeshift dance floor, being turned round and round by their handsome dates. Not at all like the sad students that swarm the tango class. No masturbatory sheen to their faces. No dingy shirts. No look of naked hunger in their glacial lake eyes. The Duchess presses a hand to her corsaged heart at the sight of me. Vignette just grins.

"Perfect?" Cupcake prompts.

"So perfect," they say.

"Samantha," the Duchess says, taking my hands, like I'm infirm, "we have a surprise for you."

I have a vision of maggots exploding from a shiny, be-ribboned box.

"What sort of surprise?"

They all look at each other and smile.

"Make yourself comfortable and we'll be right back, okay?"

"Wait, what's—"

"Our friends will entertain you. Hugo, Beowulf, Blake, Lars, this is Samantha. *Samantha,*" the Duchess repeats loudly as if talking to someone who is nearly deaf or foreign or five.

"Samantha," they all repeat in eerie unison. They stand there blinking at me, while the Bunnies disappear through a door to the right of Creepy Doll's bedroom in a cluster of giggles.

We stand there for a while, me and these men. The room is spinning. Kate Bush is still singing "Wuthering Heights." How long is this song anyway? The disco ball turns uselessly above our heads. I take some huge sips of punch. Look more closely at them. Beowulf looks like a young Marlon Brando, the other three vaguely like actors from teen TV. They're all wearing dark blue suits. They're staring at my hair like it's a volcano that could erupt at any moment.

"So do you guys go to Warren?" I ask, downing the rest of my punch.

They look at each other. One of them, Lars I think, coughs in my face.

Then, Beowulf says wistfully, "Your beauty is nuanced and labyrinthine like a sentence by Proust."

I laugh, but Beowulf looks dead serious. He raises his glass to me. I notice his punch is in a plastic sippy cup. That he's wearing black leather gloves.

"Melanie Shingler is a whore compared to you," says the boy next to him. Blake. "Pigeon-toed. Bad eyeliner. I couldn't see it then because I was a fool but I have since developed my perception."

He too solemnly raises his sippy cup to me. He's also wearing black leather gloves, I see. They all are.

Suddenly, I hear screams coming from above.

"Jesus. What was that?"

"Samantha," Beowulf says. "Tell us about you, Samantha."

"Samantha, tell us everything, Samantha."

"Samantha, we want to listen."

"Samantha," says Blake, taking my hands in his hands, "we're dying to know." He really does look like he's dying. Maybe he's drunk.

From upstairs, I hear more screams.

"Don't you guys hear that?"

They look at one another. Genuine confusion troubles their brows. "Hear?"

"That screaming?!"

"Your beauty is like screaming, Samantha," says Beowulf, touching my face. He strokes it with his gloved hand, like my skin is the most delicate pet.

The lights go off. Then on. A rustling. A thud. Then silence.

The sound of heeled footsteps clambering down the stairs. Beowulf's hand drops and Blake crushes his sippy cup in his fist.

They emerge from the side door and swarm into the living room like a plague of hair and pastel taffeta. "Hey, girl," they say. They look vaguely disheveled. Creepy Doll's cat ears are askew on her head and she's clutching Cupcake's arm like she's lost in the woods except this isn't the woods it's her own living room. Cupcake's glove has a little dark blotch on it. Her skin has a pink glow, as though she's just been masturbating.

"Where were you guys?"

Vignette grabs a handful of chips, shoves them into her mouth, and crunches. Stares at me with her lovely, fuck-you eyes. "Surprise," she says.

"We can't tell you," Cupcake explains like she's her translator.

"I thought I heard screams."

"That was *me*," Creepy Doll says. "Sometimes I scream." I watch her sloppily pour more punch into my glass, then into hers. "It's sort of a disorder."

They look restless. Excited. I notice they're all staring at the front door.

"What's going on?" I ask.

"Nothing, nothing," this from Cupcake, who's white-knuckling her own corsaged wrist, her eyes on the front door.

A knock, knock at the door.

They look at each other. At last the Duchess says, "You

should get that, Samantha. I believe you have a guest." She looks at me like I'm a sick kid and she's a nurse about to give me the biggest lollipop I've ever seen.

"Here," she says. "I'll come with you."

She stands up, holds out her hand to me, and smiles. It's the nicest she's ever looked at me. For a minute she reminds me of Ava.

I take her hand, which feels like a cool, thin skipping stone, and we walk to the door.

"Open it," she says, gesturing toward the door as though it's a present.

"What's going on?"

"Just answer the door, Samantha. Trust us this time, okay?" Her face says *it's about time you trusted us.* Her face says that has been the problem thus far. Me. My lack of trust.

I open the door.

"Samantha Heather Mackey," he says.

My heart explodes. I'd scream but I've lost my voice. Run but my legs are all swimmy. He's the same. Sort of balding. Small eyes, which I described in the last diary I ever owned that had a lock as smoky. Tall and broad in his dark blue suit. Is it the same suit he was wearing that night? The night I didn't even stay for four songs? Watched him dance with Alyssa Fisher while I ate a hard roll two tables away with Alice. The last man whose name I'd write in a notebook. Again and again and again with loopy hope.

"Rob Valencia."

"Samantha Heather Mackey," he says again. "Hello."

"Oh my god. What are you doing here?"

He looks at the Duchess.

"We called him," she says, looking at him and nodding. "We hope you're not mad, Samantha. We called him and when he found out you were going to be here, he came right over. Didn't you?"

Rob's nodding now too. He takes my hand in his and I notice he's also wearing black leather gloves.

"I came right over, Samantha," he says, squeezing my hand.

Rob Valencia is squeezing my hand. This is on a giant marquee in my mind. Flashing and flashing and flashing.

"I can't believe you're here."

"Believe it, Samantha," the Duchess says.

"What are you doing here?" I hear myself say again.

Rob Valencia looks at the Duchess again.

"You're in town on business, aren't you?" the Duchess says.

"I'm in town on business," Rob says. "I'm a businessman now, Samantha. I travel and I'm very successful."

"Serendipitous," the Duchess sighs, looking at me. "Isn't it?"

Rob nods.

"I'll leave you two alone," the Duchess whispers, patting us both on the back, patting my shoulder a little. Then she walks away.

Rob Valencia is still squeezing my hand in the doorway. "Samantha, I would like to come in," he says. "Will you let me in, Samantha?

⋆

I am sitting with Rob Valencia in Creepy Doll's living room. A mirror off to one side which I consult from time to time confirms this. That Rob Valencia is not a mirage. He is actually here. Sitting beside me on the loveseat. A thing of flesh in a suit. Looking vaguely like Zeus. I have consumed more punch. I have forgotten that I am a twenty-five-year-old woman. The heart Rob Valencia holds in his hand is a seventeen-year-old heart, warped and badly drawn with purple ink. It is Samantha Heather Mackey's seventeen-year-old idea of her heart. And it has Rob Valencia's name drawn inside in jagged, bleedy letters.

"I can't believe you're here," I hear myself say in a voice that does not sound like my voice. It is a voice filled with twinkly stars, with overly lashed cartoon eyes.

He smiles at me. The eye crinkle that made me rabid with lust as a teenager. I never cared that Rob Valencia was balding at sixteen and I'll tell you why. Rob Valencia had charisma. And at six foot four he is the only man in the universe who ever made me feel short.

"It surprises you," he says, grinning.

"Yes," I say, swaying a little from the Bunny punch. "Very much. I can't believe it."

"Believe, Samantha," he says. "Please. It makes sex faster."

Sex faster? "I—"

He puts his leather finger to my lips. "*Shhh,*" he says. "*Shhh, shhh.* Samantha, I must say something. There is something missing from my life that has been missing since that night seven years ago when I went to the dance with that slut whose name I do not even remember because she is that inconsequential to me."

"Alyssa Fisher," I offer.

"Alyssa Whatever," Rob says. He sighs and clutches my hand tighter. "Do you know, Samantha, I do not even masturbate to the memory of fucking her in the mermaid limo?"

I shake my head.

"It's truth," he says.

He pours us some punch, which I drink down in two seconds. "Do you know what I do masturbate to, Samantha?

I shake my head, my body a swell of pinprickly lights. Because it cannot be. Because surely it isn't—

"Dying with you, Samantha. Three months of rehearsal. Five nights of performance and one matinee. It remains the most erotic time of my life."

Rob Valencia looks at me with eyes I don't remember being so smoky. Electricity courses through me. Down my arms and legs. Butterflies hatch in my gut and go flying out, flapping their wings furiously in my chest. My intricately noosed hair is going to burst into flames.

"Really?" I whisper.

"Yes, Samantha. In fact the whole time I was dancing in Alyssa Whatever's unmagical arms, the whole time I was fucking other women in various venues, but mostly my car, I was still thinking this is not at all erotic at all. And how much infinitely better, how much infinitely hotter it would be to die by electrocution with Samantha Heather Mackey. Because we died like we were fucking, didn't we, Samantha?"

I nod yes. Oh, yes.

He takes my hands again and I shiver.

"Samantha, I found your treelike height erotic and I enjoyed your bleak dress sense more than I can say. All day, I wanted to tongue the little skull pin you wore on your boob. Yet I did not. You intimidated me because you were so . . ."

"*What?*" I whisper.

"Formidable. Angry. Scary-angry. You refused to turn that frown upside down. You scared us all year, Samantha Heather Mackey. But we knew the truth too."

"We? What do you—"

"That you were just a lonely girl. That you were a sad girl."

He reaches up and holds my face lightly, tenderly, between his gloved hands. Gazes at me so tenderly with his eyes of smoke. Rob Valencia's eyes of smoke.

"Weren't you, Samantha?"

I cry a little. Probably it's just the punch. I cry into Rob Valencia's boulderlike shoulder, which smells just like it did seven years ago when he was lying there beside me on the saw-dusty stage. His smell of seventeen-year-old-boy sweat, roasted animal, church incense. And something else now too, like some sort of muffin mix.

"Samantha," he says, "there is no need at all for eye water."

"What?"

"Ultimately we find you vulnerable and desperate but compellingly so."

The Duchess, who suddenly appears in the periphery, slides

a clear box toward him on the table. There's a flower inside. A corsage. It looks like an orchid. White and shimmery and with a little purple mouth full of pale pink veins.

He opens it and holds the flower in his palm like a baby bird. He looks down at it hungrily. For a second, I think he's going to eat it.

Then the Duchess comes by and pats him on his massive shoulder, and he takes my hand and fastens the flower onto my wrist. The music changes to a song I know so well, though I've forgotten the name.

"Samantha," he says standing, "will you dance with us?"

Dancing with Rob is not at all like dancing with Diego. His football-player chest. His broad shoulders. His large, sure hands going up and down my back like I'm not six feet tall at all but a mere wisp of a thing. Everything about him feels solid as bricks or stale bread. So different from Ava. Her hands of mesh. Her airy frame. Her feathery white-blond hair grazing my shoulder. Her smell of fallen leaf and firewood not at all like the smoky synthetic sugar, the burnt animal scent emanating from the flesh of Rob Valencia.

Over his shoulder I observe the other Bunnies dancing with their dates. Their eyes are closed—except for the Duchess, who's looking right at me. When we lock eyes, she winks. I smile at her. The beautiful room is spinning. The open windows are letting in a gentle fall breeze, making the silky curtains swell.

I close my eyes and hear a voice in my ear, like a cupped whisper, female, velvety, that says, *Float, float, isn't this nice?*

"Isn't this nice, Samantha?" he says.

So nice. Except the burning sugar smell is getting stronger. I look up at Rob. No. He's Rob Valencia. I'm dancing with Rob Valencia. In the flesh.

I think of Ava out there in the dark, smoking on her roof, or maybe reading in her red velvet chair, but the thought seems very far away. She's in silhouette. I can't see her face.

That's when I hear the chewing sound. Like excited teething punctuated by little grunts.

I open my eyes. I see Cupcake and her TV boy, dancing. Her head against his shoulder, her eyes closed, her lips parted and blissful. He's chewing on her peach spaghetti strap. His eyes are open but vacant. When he sees me watching, the strap drops from his mouth. Then he picks it back up again and starts chewing. His eyes have a glazed, contented look to them.

I look away, toward Creepy Doll. I see her date is doing the same thing. Except it's a fallen rope of her hair he's chewing.

When I turn to look at the Duchess, her head resting against Beowulf's shoulder, I see Beowulf is gnawing on her pearls. The Duchess appears oblivious.

And Vignette. Vignette is sitting in the window seat in the corner like a drunk music-box ballerina, drinking a beer, while her boy lies in her lap, chewing on her crinoline.

Then I feel it. The mouth at my wrist. Rob Valencia is hunched over my hand, his teeth full of orchid. For a moment, he just looks at me like a dog caught eating a shoe.

Then he starts up again.

I try to pull away, but he grabs hard at my wrist and starts munching on the corsage with a vengeance.

"Jesus, stop it! What are you doing?!"

But he keeps chewing, harder and harder. His eyes narrow into dark little slits.

"I said STOP." I slap him on the cheek. Harder than I wanted to. The sound is louder than I expected, a sharp crack.

The music stops. Everyone stops dancing and looks at me. Rob stares at me, shocked. He touches his cheek with his gloved hand. His eyes cloud. His nose starts to twitch. His mouth full of chewed-up bits of flowers opens to say—

"Look, I'm sorry," I cut in. "I didn't mean—"

"Abrasive," he says, stroking his cheek. "Angry. Invested in her own outsiderness. Gritty, oh so gritty."

"What? What are you talking about?"

Then his eyes suddenly fill with hate.

"You think you're better than us, Samantha. Well, you're fucking not."

"What?"

He takes my face between his hands and hisses, spitting flowers and foam from his mouth.

"We tried to braid your hair, you didn't let us braid it. We invited you to things, you wouldn't come. We asked you to come out for bento boxes and you said, *No, no, I'm too busy and important and better than you are for bento boxes.* But you don't remember. All you remember is Samantha Heather Mackey is the victim. Samantha Heather Mackey is in pain. Samantha

Heather Mackey's heart is on fire with all the feelings she thinks only she can feel."

The burnt sugary smell is overwhelming now. I think of a squid releasing ink. I try to release myself from his grip. That's when he starts screaming. He just opens his mouth and screams and screams, looking right at me like I'm the most horrifying thing he's ever seen.

Then all the men start screaming. Just stand there shrieking at the ceiling. The noise is deafening. I cover my ears with my hands. Watch as the Bunnies attempt to *shhh* them to no end.

They pull Rob away and try to lead him to a door, not the front door, but the door that leads to the attic. But he's too worked up to go. Shaking his head. Screaming his head off. Even though my ears are covered, I can hear every word.

"Samantha Heather Mackey thinks her stories are so fucking great! Samantha Heather Mackey doesn't say it but she thinks she's too good for the whole fucking world! Samantha Heather Mackey acts poor but why then does she behave like a princess? Samantha Heather Mackey slept with her professor! Sucked him off! For preferential treatment! There is no way in hell that Samantha Heather Mackey can be that tall, she wears stilts! Samantha Heather Mackey wears stilts so she can look down on us! Oh, ho, ho, ho she loves every fucking second of that!! Samantha Heather Mackey thinks we have everything under the sun, that we sleep on a bed of gold, and meanwhile she sleeps on a bed of dirt. That she has nothing, nothing, and she thinks this makes her deep. It doesn't make you deep, Samantha Heather Mackey, it just makes you rumpled and it makes you smell of old potatoes. Samantha Heather Mackey thinks she understands everything, but she fails to understand the depths of the human heart. She fails to understand the depths of our heart. Our heart our heart our heart! We've read *Jane Eyre* too, you cunt, and we've read *The Waves*, and when we read it, you know, we wept for minutes."

Then he starts weeping.

I think *Go now. Go fucking now*, but in the spinning, swaying room, I find I can't move, I'm transfixed by Rob Valencia's rage. His hissing, spitting rage. His tears. By the sight of the Bunnies gently shushing him. The terrible suffocating smell of muffins on fire. It all feels like a terrible play. Maybe it will end with Rob Valencia and me twitching on the floor. I almost want to laugh. A hysterical laugh comes out of me like a cough.

That's when Rob Valencia's head explodes. Literally explodes. Blood and brains all over me, the walls. Blood all over the Bunnies and their whimpering boys. Bits of skull falling on the hardwood floor like hail. His headless, suited body remains standing before me. Then it collapses to the floor.

I hear my own scream stretching my face.

Something drops at my feet. An ear. Rob Valencia's ear.

I fall to the earth. I fall and fall and fall. It's a long way down to the blood- and skull-splattered floor. And in the background, the song that was so familiar is still playing, the song my seventeen-year-old heart knows so well yet the name escaped me, becomes one I finally recognize as "Slave to Love."

12

I wake in a bed that isn't my own. Open my eyes to a poster of a woman, a famous English actress, hugging a man dressed like a pirate in a whirlpool of smoke. She is clinging to him for dear life, her head thrown back in ecstasy. Beside the poster is a corkboard full of photos of a smiling, redheaded girl with her family, her friends. She is posing on a stone beach, she's in the midst of a fecund vineyard, she is standing atop a mountain, in every photo the same happy, sane expression. She looks familiar, very familiar, and yet I cannot put the face to a name.

I turn toward a window that looks out onto leaves that are gold and green. I am filled with an inexplicable peace. I observe the events of the night before from a great, cloudlike height. I observe too that the bed is neither too hard nor too soft. It's a perfect bed. Just right. Goldilocks could set up shop here forever. Masturbate. I picture Goldilocks brazenly masturbating in this bed while the Three Bears watch. She is daring them with her slitty eyes to tell her to stop. The Bears are too polite to say anything. I laugh at what a picture that makes. Ha. Hahaha. The comforter smells of a luxury detergent, like real fucking pines. I could be in a forest. My bed is a bed of moss.

"Bunny?" I turn and see a woman sitting on the edge of the bed.

I smile. "Ava," I say. "Oh, Ava. Thank god you're here."

"Who's Ava?"

The figure dissolves before my eyes, morphing into a grown woman with cat ears on her head. My soul screams and goes howling out of the room. My heart slides down to the floor and weeps. But I stay right here, in her bed, her small, cool hand stroking my face.

"I'm Kira," she keeps saying, because I keep shaking my head, no, no. She isn't Kira. That's not her name. It's something else. What is it again?

"Kira."

Tears are falling down my cheeks, they must be, because my face is wet. Last night is replaying itself in small bits like the arty video collages Fosco sometimes projects onto the black walls of the Cave, sequenced to be generative, to inspire us toward some great creative epiphany. The hissing, spitting head of Rob Valencia, my seventeen-year-old love. The blood splatter on the walls. Someone's blotched white glove. A boy's mouth full of orchid. The pink, veiny mouth of that flower, pursed like it's ready for a kiss. I'm watching it all from a cottony cloud. I whimper.

"Shhh," she says. She hands me a giant glass patterned with smiling watermelons and two pills the color of Easter eggs. "Take these, Bunny," she says.

I look down at the pills she's cupping in her small palm. They look like Tic Tacs.

"What are they?"

"They'll help. Trust us."

I take them. Wash them down with whatever sugary liquid is in the smiling watermelon glass. Lemonade, I realize. Pink lemonade. She watches me drink it down.

"You okay, Bunny?" she says in a voice that isn't at all little girlish, but deep. Like a normal young woman. A normal, anxious-looking woman who's looking at me like I'm about to spontaneously combust.

"Yes." I'm in my forest of pines. I'm in my perfect hijacked bed with my golden locks all around me. I look out the window again at the golden green leaves.

"Rob Valencia," I tell the leaves. "His head exploded."

When I say this, I realize how funny it is. A high, shrieking laugh comes out of me. It won't stop.

She smacks me, hard. Just like that, I'm silenced. Then she strokes my cheek softly. "That's what you think you saw, okay?"

Saw. I think of the silver, toothy blade that cuts things. Trees. Women. Cartoon animals. Skull hail. Brain rain. A severed, still-smoking ear.

"Saw," I say. "I saw. I saw, I saw, I saw, I saw, I—"

She smacks me again, harder this time.

"Things aren't always what they seem, are they?" I look at her cat ears. Her golden, pleading eyes. The smiling watermelons in my fist wink at me. The toothy blade of saw dissolves into silvery, light-kissed waters. I float on their buoyant waves.

"Bunny," she says, "I think you should have lunch with us today. After Workshop. Are you free?"

I try to think of something I have to do. Something I could say that wouldn't be a lie. Some essential person I have to see. But I can't find her in my brain now. Every shape in there is dark, indiscernible. Like someone turned out the light. All I see are the bright leaves before me. "Yes, I'm free."

"We're going to be late for class," she says, getting up. "You can take SafeRide with me."

"SafeRide," I repeat. The university's car service for when we don't feel safe walking home from campus. I look out at the sunny day. "But it's daytime."

She shrugs. "Better safe than sorry."

I think of Rob Valencia's head. The blood on the wall. I scream but all that comes out of me is a soft sigh.

"You have to get ready now. I laid out a dress for you because the one you were wearing is . . . anyway, there's that one," she gestures toward a blue bit of floof draped over her chair.

I look at the dress. It's got kittens licking ice cream cones all over it. The kittens are wearing slightly askew crowns.

"Okay," I say.

"I left you some coffee too. Oh and you should probably put these on," she says, picking up a pair of sunglasses with heart-shaped frames from her dresser and tossing them onto the bed. "Those pills will make you sensitive to light."

She walks out of the room, leaves me clutching the smiling watermelon glass, the heart-shaped lenses in my lap. A stuffed frog prince on her nightstand gazes at me with something like happy horror. *Samantha, oh, Samantha, whatever will you do?*

⋆

In the SafeRide van, I sit beside Kira while she chats with the lady driver, Elaine. Elaine says she's glad we girls called, with this recent violence, we need to be careful, and Kira is saying, "We will, I know, SO awful." And then she changes the subject to the weather. "Such a lovely day for October, isn't it?" Like no one at all exploded. Like there isn't blood and skull splatter on her living room walls.

And the weirdest thing is there isn't. When I walked into her living room just now, everything was shining and regular. No evidence of Rob Valencia's demise, no These Dreams detritus. Just her books neatly lining the shelves, her walls full of prints of bored nymphs gazing into glass waters out of which mermen are emerging. All surfaces gleaming, the hardwood floors pristine. And Kira at the front door in her red bell coat tapping her Mary Janed foot, waiting for me. *Let's get a move on, Bunny.*

I tug at Kira's coat now and she turns to me. "What?"

"I haven't done the reading," I tell her. "For class." My voice sounds eerily alien to me, like it belongs to this other woman who's strapped in a van beside a homicidal lunatic. I want to tell this woman to run away. Unlock the van and run. But she is calm. She stays in her seat. She looks out the window with her hands in her lap like a couple of dead fish. Palm trees sway in her voice when she speaks. "I haven't done the reading," I hear her repeat.

"Bunny, who ever does the reading? Seriously. Hang on, Caroline's having a dress crisis."

I look at her texting away. Wearing one of her darkly adorable dresses. Pentacle glinting around her neck. She's clutching her notebook and the bullshit book Fosco assigned.

"You did the reading," I say.

She shrugs. "Only because I was bored one night," she says. I can picture her in her living room in a flouncy forest-colored dress patterned with sly-eyed foxes. Doing the reading while putting out the fires of Caroline's constant texts. Always, always doing the reading. The truth is, if you go to Warren, no matter what is going on in your personal life—hair trouble, existential malaise, ax murder—you do the reading.

"What's it about?" I ask her, pointing at the book.

"Hard to say. It doesn't really have a narrative spine, you know?"

"She'll call on me, though. She always calls on me," I whisper.

"Who?"

"Fosco."

She looks confused.

"Ursula."

"You mean KareKare?" she says. Her tiger eyes light up. "Oh my god, I LOVE KareKare SO much I want her to have all my babies. Probably they would be mermaids. Look, if she calls on you, we'll back you up, Bunny," she says, patting my folded together hands. "Just chill, k?"

"K."

I look out the window. I see green leaves, I see boy blood, green leaves, boy blood. Ava. I see Ava. Standing by the road under a tree, watching this van go by. "Ava! Stop the car," I shout, but it comes out a whisper. Kira and the driver don't even hear me. I check my phone to see if she texted.

She hasn't texted. I send her a single question mark like an SOS.

In the Cave, they're super kind to me. They all sit around me so close, so close. Not on the other side of the square, but in the chairs immediately next to me. They call me Bunny. I've forgotten all their names, but they help me remember. The edible-looking girl with the golden bob is Caroline. The blunt, veiny, pretty one who looks like another century is Victoria. And then the one who is their queen, who resembles evil Icelandic royalty but who is gazing at me so very kindly today, is Eleanor. *That's right, Eleanor*, she says, taking my hand and squeezing it like I'm recovering from a near-death experience.

They say terribly kind things about my story, another bottom-drawer one I wrote a while ago, then polished up in a panic. Numbered the pages and even stapled them together, it seems. They are now all looking thoughtfully at these pages, making small murmurs of appreciation.

"This is great, Samantha."

"Wow, just wow."

"Frankly, I'm blown away."

"So."

"I mean. What a fascinating commentary on the social politics of . . ." I hear music that drowns out their voices. A strange swell of dreamy, Henry Mancini violins like I'm in an old movie.

"So true."

They liken me to Woolf, to Borges, their praise as lavish as their handbags. Gone are the inanities I have witnessed among them outside this room. The hair braiding. The organ-crushing hugs. I almost feel as if I dreamed their cooing, their Bunnyness.

Now it is the girl with the golden bob's turn to be Workshopped. Caroline. I find myself saying very kind things about her story about a girl who is having a vague love affair with a mist that only she can see. "This is wonderful, Caroline," I say. And her name feels strange in my mouth, but lovely too, like a new kind of candy. *Caroline, how original. What insight, Caroline. Caroline, what poetic phrasing.*

"And what did you think of the reading, Samantha?" Fosco asks me when we—very suddenly it seems to me—switch to discussing the reading.

I look down at the book cover, which features an art-house photo of a girl who looks pleased that her hair is on fire. I flip through and find nothing but blocks of text, unpunctuated. I look back up at Fosco, who is looking at me with the certain knowledge that I did not do the reading. Briefly, I picture her head exploding.

"Fosco," I say softly. "I actually haven't—"

"You were telling me earlier that you thought this book gestured toward a complex paradigm of female desires," the girl named Eleanor interjects, not looking at me. "That it languages the circumnavigation of the hermeneutical circle. And I think

Samantha's piece is clearly talking to that piece. You must have taken inspiration from it. . . ."

Fosco nods. "Eleanor, that's very true. Samantha," she says, turning her grand head toward me. "I'm very impressed by your piece this week. You've been doing a lot of emotional growth, lately, *that's* clear."

They all nod at me and smile.

I stare at Fosco through my heart-shaped frames. Because of the tint of the shades, she appears to be dark pink. They all do.

"Clear." I nod. "I'm so glad." I bite into the mini cupcake Caroline offered me at the start of class. *For the hangover,* she said, shyly offering up the ornate confection in the cupped bowl of her small, pink hands.

13

We're at the café they love where you can get everything in miniature. Mini sodas. Mini burgers. Mini poutines. Mini cupcakes. How often have I pictured them eating here together? Clinking mini cocktails. Talking about me, maybe. *Who fucking cares if they are?* Ava would say. *Seriously.*

They're not looking at their cupcake-shaped menus, which I know they know by heart. Instead they're looking at me. Four pairs of eyes watching me as I scan the menu. Every item on it is a dark pink headless body to my eyes, but the haze of drugs is clearing, is beginning to clear, is clearing imminently. And I have questions. I want answers. I open my mouth to ask—

"Samantha," Caroline says, "we want to talk to you about last night."

She's wearing a dress patterned with little Bunsen burners, her Christopher Robin cardigan, her hair in a French twist. I touch my own head, find the elaborate knots she tied still there. How strange that I don't even feel them anymore.

"I don't feel them anymore," I say softly, clutching my cupcake menu close.

"Feel what?" Victoria asks.

"My hairs," I whisper.

They look at each other.

"Samantha, we want to talk to you about what happened last night."

"What happened," I repeat.

"About what you saw."

Saw. I recall once more the wobbly blade with the winking teeth.

"About what you *think* you saw," Caroline says. "Samantha," she starts again, "last night didn't exactly go the way we hoped."

"I hope you know that, Bunny," Kira says.

I look down at the menu. Mini churros. Mini chicken and waffles. Mini sweet-potato fries with mini aioli. "Rob Valencia exploded," I hear myself say as though I am commenting on the weather. Going to rain later. Ho hum.

Caroline sighs and blows her shiny blond bangs out of her eyes.

"He didn't *explode.*"

"Well, he sort of did," Kira says. "And he didn't. I don't know what I'm saying. Never mind."

"He did NOT explode," Caroline says.

"He totally didn't, Bunny."

"That's just what you think you saw," Victoria says.

I stare at Victoria's pretty skull face, the skin shimmery like white orchids. Her fuck-you eyes bored but also amused. *Oh, Bunny*. She's holding a flute full of fizzy pink water upon which I am now drifting, thrashing a little to keep afloat. Inside, a spiked red thing bobs, bleeding red into the pink waters. My heart or the heart of Rob Valencia? I recall the blood splatter on the walls. How at the sight of Rob's head blowing up, Victoria's face remained composed, more annoyed than shocked. She might have even rolled her eyes.

"What did I see?"

They look at the silver-haired one who is named Eleanor, who is sitting with her bonelike hands braided over a mini basket of mini breadsticks she is not touching.

"Samantha," she says dreamily, "may I just say that I've always loved your work?"

"You do?"

She keeps her dreamy cobalt gaze on me.

"So much. I'm a real fan."

"Really?"

"Are you kidding? Your . . . grittiness. Your salt of the earthiness. All that brooding, dark-night-of-the-soul melodrama. Just wonderful. I mean . . . jarring at times, don't get me wrong. Over the top. Willfully provocative. But the talent is undeniable. And your voice adds so much to the collective."

"A stiffness, so to speak," Victoria adds.

I look at them all nodding at me—their hair bright as the sunny sky right before me.

"Thank you," I say.

"Which is why I was so *saddened* to hear that you're having some difficulty writing lately. That you're . . . blocked."

Now they look away. Avoid my gaze. The sunny sky vanishes and I'm alone in the rain, in the shadows. I imagine the Lion telling them, whispering it to them. See him stirring his tea, saying not unkindly, *There's no shame in it. It happens to the best of us.*

"What? Who told you?"

"Samantha," Eleanor says, shaking her head, patting my hand, "we could *sense* it. It's so obvious."

I shake and shake my head. "I'm not. I wasn't. I'm writing all the time." But my tears that fall and fall betray me.

Kira hands me a handkerchief patterned with rainbows. They wait while I blow.

"Samantha," Eleanor continues, "there's no shame in it. You're an artist. We all are. Our desires, our needs, what makes us thrive and flourish as artists—"

"As *women*."

"Exactly. Is a complex and delicate thing, isn't it? Nuanced and immense."

I nod.

"Here is your desire," Eleanor says. She looks at Caroline, who pulls a pink plastic pony from her purse and places it on the raised cupcake stand in the middle of the table.

I gaze up at its long, pink plastic body in the center of the stand. Emblazoned with hearts. Frozen in midprance. Its large, ever-smiling eyes full of sparkles.

"Pinkie Pie," I whisper.

"And here is the world," Eleanor says, looking at Kira, who pulls what looks like a small plastic square of latticework from her purse.

A fence. A toy fence.

She places the tiny fence in front of Pinkie Pie.

"You see how the situation is dire?"

"Dismal is the word we use."

"Stifling."

We gaze at Pinkie Pie. Fenced in and alone on her elevated perch, empty of all but crumb dust. The table so far below.

"It's no wonder you're blocked, Bunny."

"Samantha, we're undertaking a project that addresses this issue."

"A sort of . . . collaboration."

"Oh," I say. "Like a novel? Or a short story?"

They smile. *Oh, Samantha. So behind the times. Sitting alone in the dark at her prehistoric desk. Clutching her little blunt pencil oh so tightly!*

"No, no, no. Not a novel, Bunny."

"Which is no longer novel, you know."

"Such a tired form."

"Flaccid. Limp."

"What we're doing is far more . . ."

"Innovative."

"Experimental."

"Performance based."

"Intertextual."

"*So* intertextual."

"Basically: a hybrid."

A hybrid. That most obscure of academic beasts. What you call something when you just don't know what you're doing anymore. "A hybrid. So, combining genres?"

They smile that *tsk-tsk* smile again. Shake their heads.

"Samantha, we're at *Warren*. The most experimental, ground-breaking writing school in the country. This goes way beyond *genre*. It subverts the whole concept of genre."

"And gender narratives."

"And the patriarchy of language."

"Not to mention the whole writing medium."

"It basically fucks the writing medium, Samantha. Which is dead anyway, you know?"

"Exactly. This is about *the Body*. Performing the Body. The Body performing in all its nuanced viscerality."

"The Body fucking," Victoria adds.

Eleanor gives her a dark look. Then she looks at me with a smile like glass breaking.

They're waiting, I see, for a response from me.

"Great. That all sounds so great. So—I'm sorry—what is it that you're doing? Exactly?"

They look at each other again. *Samantha. We always forget that she attended a state school for undergrad. The first in her family to even go to college. Maybe even high school? We always forget that. That's okay, Bunny. Let's break it down for her. Let's use smaller words.*

"Samantha, we're female artists. Right?"

"Right."

"So do you *really* want to be a passenger in someone else's narrative?"

They all look at me, waiting. There is a right answer to this question. *Think, think, think.*

"No?"

Smiles break over their faces like golden sunshine through frowny clouds.

"Of course you don't."

"You want to be empowered."

"You want creative agency."

"You want agency, *period*. Control."

"Over your art."

"Over your life, Bunny."

"*All* aspects of your life—physical, emotional, mental, spiritual . . . even—"

"You want to fuck, not *be* fucked," Victoria says.

"Samantha," Eleanor intones, "is this making sense?"

I stare at them all through Kira's pink heart-shaped glasses. This is how she must see the world all the time. I look at their dark pink faces, so suddenly grave. I should call the police. I should run to Mexico.

"Totally."

"Wonderful. Because we think you're ready."

"Ready?"

"To join us."

"For what?"

"What else? Workshop."

"But we just had Workshop," I say.

They look at each other.

"We should just show her," one of them says, Victoria I think, through a mouth full of mini fries.

"I don't know, you guys," Kira says. "She's already had a pretty rough day." She pats my hand. "Haven't you, Bunny?"

"And is she ready for it?"

"She's ready for it," Eleanor says.

I look down at my phone. No response from Ava. I feel my heart sink deeper into pink waters. Where the haze was starting to clear, it's now grown thick. I'm deep in the eye of the smiling watermelon.

"Show me," I say.

14

Kira's attic. A dollhouse room you have to climb a winding staircase to reach. Steepled ceiling covered in a cloudy sky mural they tell me they painted together last year. The clouds swirly and white like a child's idea of heaven, the blue of the sky shot through with a big bright arch of five-color rainbow. I observe the rainbow through the eyeholes of the rabbit mask they've just slipped over my face. *Why a mask?* I asked. *Trust us,* they said. I notice the curtains on the dormer windows are charred on the bottom, like they've been through multiple fires. In the corner of the room, I see a fire extinguisher. In another corner, an ax. *An ax? What's—*

"You'll see, Bunny, you'll see," they say, leading me by the hand to a white wicker chair in the corner. "Just sit here for now, k?"

Despite their myriad scented candles, the room is thick with the smell of something I can't put my finger on. Something that reminds me of when my old cat Lucifer used to bite the heads off the mice he would find in the basement where I lived and leave the rodent corpses under my futon for me to find days later. Lucifer died shortly after I got accepted into Warren. A *total omen,* Ava said.

Ava. I should—

"You should just chill for now, Bunny. Here. This is for if you freak out," Caroline says, placing a bucket beside me. "I mean, I doubt you will, given all you've seen, your life experience."

My life experience?

"Samantha won't freak out," Eleanor says. "She's been around the block."

She smiles at me. Block. Butcher block. A knife being sharpened by a troll emoji.

Through the rabbit eyeholes, I watch her organizing something in the center of the room. A Fosco-esque display. A large book open and bloodied in the center with what looks like dark red nail polish. A toy bride lies in the middle of the nail polish blood. Beside her is a large box draped in a red velvet cloth.

"What is that?"

"You'll see. Just don't freak out, Bunny."

"She might freak out."

"I still freak out."

"Just don't freak out the boy—I mean, the hybrid."

"What boy?" I ask.

"When it comes into the room, be welcoming, okay?" Caroline says. "Say hi. *Smile*. Smiling is important."

I look at her lips shiny and thick with so much gloss. There's a wavering quality to her voice, like a car swerving down a dangerous road.

I nod. "Hi. Smiling."

"Good." She hands me more Tic Tacs.

What are these again?

"Just a little something to take the edge off."

"And you could really use something to take the edge off, couldn't you?"

"We all could."

"We all do."

I picture a cliff. My hands gripping. I look down at the tiny blue pills in my palm.

"Trust, Bunny, remember?"

Yes. Of course I remember. *Trust.*

I swallow. My hands ungrip the cliff. *Trust.* I will not fall, I will float. Up into their high blue sky full of fluffy clouds and rainbows. Up, up, up into the pink mist and the laughing light.

Meanwhile, down below they look like they're getting ready for some sort of party. Eleanor is working on her bloody toy-bride installation. Victoria's crouched over a sound system. Kira is sharpening the ax with a small black stone, glaring at Caroline, who is sitting on the floor talking softly to the red velvet box.

"Sometimes I don't understand why we have to keep doing Workshop at my place," Kira whispers to her ax.

"Bunny," Caroline says, her arms wrapped around the box, "are you going to make us go through this again? We've already said. One, your aunt is a firewoman. Two, you have an attic. Also, this apartment has an energy mine doesn't. 'Cause it's old."

"I wish *mine* had this energy," Eleanor says. She pets Kira's shoulder, her white lace bell sleeve fanning out like an egret's wing. She looks around the blue room, smiling like it's all too beautiful.

"Did you put the suit in the hallway, Bunny?" Eleanor asks. Her voice has a weird echo in my brain. *Hallway-way-way. Bunny-ny-ny.*

"No," Kira says, shaking her head slowly a thousand times. "Was I supposed to?"

"Well. Last time he came out naked, he freaked Caroline out, remember?"

Who came out naked?

"It wasn't that he was naked, it's that he was oozy," Caroline says. "It was the ooze."

"Ooze is hot," Victoria says from her corner, where she is slouched in a chaise longue of the most voluptuous brocade. "I say more ooze."

Caroline reaches over and tenderly brushes the delicate, auburn curls from her veiny forehead, her languid eyes. "You're gross, Bunny."

Eleanor puts her lacy arm on Caroline's shoulder, and Caroline rests her cheek against it, closing her eyes like Eleanor's forearm is Xanadu.

"I love you," she says.

"I love *you*," Eleanor says.

I watch them hug each other for a good ten years.

Kira watches too, looking at a loss. "I just wish someone had told me this was going to be my job earlier, that's all."

"It's not like it's that *hard*, Bunny," Caroline says, her head still on Eleanor's shoulder. "You just put some clothes in the hallway, big deal."

"It's not about that, it's just why do I have to provide the space *and* the suit? I don't see why it has to be my job." When no one responds, she adds, "Besides, maybe this time he'll come in a suit. We're getting better at this."

Better? Better at what?

"I *like* when they come out naked," Victoria says from her chaise, which now appears to be floating up off the ground.

"Who's 'they'?" I hear myself say from the corner.

They ignore me.

"What about the film? Music?" Caroline asks.

Victoria holds up a remote control like a gun. A TV in the corner comes on and a black-and-white film starts playing. A man and a woman, arm in arm, walking smiling circles around a fountain. She clicks again and speakers I can't see suddenly flood the room with "La Vie en Rose."

Now they gather around the box, beside the bride in her bloody book. Caroline removes the fabric to reveal a bunny, twitching his nose and flopping his ears in a cute way. *Aww*, says a whispery little-girl voice inside me. *Bunny wunny, see?! Aww.*

"Awww, he's SO CUTE," Kira says. "Look at his wittle pink nose!"

"Don't!" Caroline says. "Remember, we're not supposed to talk about how cute the bunny is."

Kira looks like she's about to cry, but only presses her lips together and nods. I nod too.

"He is pretty cute," Caroline says.

Yes.

"So cute."

So.

"Look at his ears."

"Look at his eyes. He looks so excited. Like he knows."

Knows what??

"Can't we at least say good-bye?"

Good-bye? Why good-bye?

"Bye-bye, bunny."

They all wave at it sadly. I wave too even though I don't understand *why are we waving again?*

"Okay," Kira says, "well, shall we start?"

They put their aprons on, tie them, like they're about to bake a cake. *Oh! Can I bake too?*

"Here, Bunny, you better wear this," Kira says, handing me an apron that says No Bitchin in My Kitchen.

Yay! Yay! Wait. What are we making again?

"Are we making cake things?" I ask.

Caroline puts her finger to her lips. "*Shh.* No talking at this point," she says.

"Are we *sure* we want to let her into Workshop?" Victoria's looking at me dully.

There is so much I want to say to this injustice, but when my mouth moves to say the pointed slappy words of retort, all that comes out is happy drool.

"Bunny," Eleanor says. "Remember . . ." She looks at me, then cups her hands over Victoria's ear and whispers. All I can make out in the whisper is "she" again and again. *She she she she.* It sounds like a meany wind blowing through trees.

Victoria looks at me and half smiles. "Fine," she says. "She can stay."

Yay! Yay, yay, yay, yay, yay. "Stay for what?"

They don't answer me. Instead, they put on rabbit-head masks just like the one they slipped on my face. Complete with ears, whiskers. Slitty eyeholes through which their eyes peer out.

"What kind of boy are we trying for today?" one of the Bunny faces asks, without moving its happy lips.

"Boy?" another Bunny exclaims. "Bunny, we've had this conversation. We don't refer to them by such binary labels as *boy.*" I can tell she's making a grossed-out face behind the smiling rabbit mask face as she spits the word. *Boy.* It's a dumb toy or a thin soup.

"Sorry. What are we supposed to call them again?" Bunny looks at Bunny inquiringly. Her eyes wide and open and innocent, fringed by fake glittery lashes.

"What *aren't* they? Intertextual spaces. Fruitions. Hybrids."

"I thought we were calling them Drafts."

"Can we get a move on, please? I'm borny."

I watch them move closer together, forming a tighter ring. I watch them hold hands. A swell of hot longing rises in me like a red wave. *Wait. Me too in the circle. Me, me.* I hold my own hands in the corner and try to make myself into a circle.

"Bunny, stop moving over there."

I am quiet as rainbows. I am still as trees. I watch them close their so pretty eyes. I close mine too but somehow I can still see. The room is creepy-serious, quieter than even my rainbow quiet.

They begin to chant some indiscernible words. It makes the pony in me clap its hooves and dance.

I think the windows are going to break, the ceiling fan is going to come crashing down on their heads, but nothing happens for a long time. The film plays. Edith sings. The toy bride lies in her pool of fake book blood.

They stare at the bunny twitching his ears in the middle of the room.

One of them coughs from behind her cheap bunny mask with its plump pink cheeks like the bunny is wearing blush. Another one sighs. Lame. It starts to feel lame. Like when my best friend Alice and I sat around a Ouija board we made ourselves, using my protractor as a planchette. We sat there for hours until my mother knocked on the door. *Give it up, girls,* she said.

Then the light goes out. A wind comes. The curtains catch fire. The bunny explodes.

I don't realize I'm screaming until Kira slaps my face. It renders me silent, but I can feel my mouth still stretched open into a giant O. And something is shaking violently right in my lap covered in blood. My hands. Covered in blood too. Not just blood. Bits. Wet, quivery, and sticking to my clothes, my skin. I want to run, to scream, but I can only sit there. My mouth open and trying to smile.

The Bunny girls are covered in blood and bits too. Covered from shining hair to shining shoes. But not screaming, not even moving. Silent like they're waiting for something. One of them looks at her watch.

A knock on the door. *Uh-oh! Who could that be?*

They look at each other through their eyeholes.

"Kira," Caroline says.

"What?! But I got it last time," Kira says.

No one says anything. I keep my lips shut tight tight.

"I don't see why I always have to get it," Kira says. "It's like the suit. I don't understand."

They're all looking at Eleanor for confirmation, backup, a decision, but through the eyeholes of her white rabbit mask, I can see she's got her eyes closed like she's in a Zen place. Victoria has lifted her mask off her face. She's chewing her gum like nothing out of the ordinary happened, like she isn't covered in rabbit guts.

"*Fine.* I'll get it," Caroline says, standing up. She takes off her bunny mask and her apron. Smooths down her dress. Looks in the blood-splattered mirror and tosses her impossibly shiny hair so that all the strands sway and dance like laughing light. *She is such magic,* says the prancing pink pony in me. *Isn't she just, Samantha? Yes,* I whisper, from where I am watching high, high up in the rainbow sky where the Tic Tacs have carried me. Edgeless and floating and looking down at Kira, who reaches for the ax in the corner. She doesn't look at it. Just lightly rests a hand on it, while keeping her eyes on the door.

"After this we should go to Pinkberry," she says to the door.

Victoria and Eleanor nod slowly. I'm nodding too. *Oh yes. Pinkberry, lovely.*

Then Caroline comes in, leading a beautiful man by the hand like he's a chimp. He walks a little like one too, I observe smilingly, through the Tic Tac clouds. Stooped. His arms a little longer than his torso. But he's beautiful, apart from a severe harelip that sits like a botched bow on his present of a face. He's wearing a dark blue suit and a pale blue shirt the same shade as his eyes. I notice the black leather gloves on his hands.

My mouth makes a gasping sound. *My god. My god, my god, my—*

"Everyone," Cupcake announces, "this is Odysseus."

"Hello," the others murmur. I feel my own mouth moving too, exactly in sync with their shiny ones.

"Odysseus was just telling me how much he enjoys Fellini films and the novels of Proust. He's also terribly well versed in Barthes's *Erotisme,* and French is his first language," Caroline says, tugging on his large hand like it's a puppet string. "*N'est-ce pas?*"

He looks at her, then at the rest of us, with his wide blue uncomprehending eyes. He opens his botched mouth. Then he lets out a terrible scream.

They cover their ears. I want to cover mine but I can't find my hands, so I just sit there.

"Kira," Caroline says with her hands clapped over her ears.

Kira ignores her. She's seated with her arms folded, the ax on the floor at her side. Staring straight ahead.

"KIRA," Caroline shouts. "Come *on.*"

"I just feel like someone else should pull their weight for once is all," Kira says.

"FINE," Victoria says and grabs the ax from the floor.

"Venez avec moi," Victoria says soothingly to Odysseus, over his banshee cry. *"Ici, ici, dans la salle de bain."* She takes his hand and drags him to the small bathroom. He follows her, still screaming his head off.

From behind the closed door, we hear more screams.

Don't worry, Bunny, they tell me, patting all my hands, which they found so, so easily. *First Drafts. Part of the Process. Sometimes you have to kill your darlings, you know? In fact, that's what we sometimes call them. Darlings.*

Kill?

Victoria comes out alone. Shutting the door quickly behind her so that I cannot glimpse the bathroom or the boy inside through my eyeholes. Just Victoria. Covered with fresh blood. Covering her mouth with both hands.

"I think I fucked up," she says.

"What do you mean you *fucked* up?" Kira asks.

A creature comes running out of the bathroom howling. An animal man. Furry skinned. Floppy eared. Still wearing his dark blue suit. There's an ax stuck deep in its furry shoulder, blood gushing terribly from the cleaved flesh. I watch him run shrieking past the rainbow under which I sit screaming. And yet all that comes tumbling from my mouth is laughter. Laughter like a laughing brook, my waters sparkling in the sun.

"Use the bucket, Bunny!"

Over my bucket rim, I see Caroline is shaking her head

endlessly, angrily, at Kira, who sighs and rolls her eyes while the shrieking, wounded bunny boy runs frantic circles around them. Kira slowly gets up, walks to the wall. Pulls another ax out from behind a chest of drawers. Walks slowly over to the bunny boy, now collapsed in a crying heap on the floor. Raises the ax high above her head.

I shake my head, I close my eyes.

No.

No, no, no, no, no, no—

A cracking sound that makes my skull thrum. Then a heavy thud. Dragging. A terrible, slow dragging. A door closing shut.

When I open my eyes, Kira is leaning against the closed bathroom door, gripping the ax loosely in her tiny hand. She is covered in shining blood like the toy bride sitting in the book. She looks smaller than I've ever seen her. Her pale dollface is solemn.

"You guys, I can't keep doing this. I'm going to start having nightmares, seriously."

Caroline nods, hugs her while she cries a little.

"It's your gift, Bunny. You're wonderfully brave. I love you."

"I love you, Bunny."

I watch them all hug each other, covered in rabbit guts. Their pink bodies framed by my own rabbit eyes. It's sweet, I think. They're nice people.

Finally, Eleanor lets herself out of the huddle.

"Okay," she says. "Thoughts? Responses?"

"I think next time we try for more verisimilitude. I didn't

believe the French thing. Perhaps it's a quick fix. A question of adding something simple, like a scarf."

"I'd like to see more complexity—more Hamlet-esque brooding. But also more cockiness. But also more pride?"

"I'd like to see more animal magnetism."

"Animal magnetism? But we were going for French. Again, we have to think of verisimilitude here."

"In terms of viscerality, I'm not really connecting to the height. I understand we want to go for realism, but I still think we could push that a little more? Even a few inches would help."

"Speaking of which, his cock better work this time. Is all I'm saying."

Silence.

"We should bring Samantha into this conversation. Since she's here anyway."

They all turn to look at me.

"Samantha, any thoughts?"

They smile encouragingly as they wait now for my words. As though I have words they want. They want me. Their bloody faces regarding me so kindly, so openly, that I know this is a friendship moment. All I have to do is give my words. What words, though? *You know the words, Samantha,* and their eyes shine and shine at me like the smiling eyes of Pinkie Pie on her perch. So many sparkles I am blinded.

"Scarves. I love scarves," I tell them.

⋆

Three bunny explosions later, in which the ax gets bloodier and bloodier, the air becoming thick with the scent of dead bunny and boy, Odysseus IV is before us. A sandy blond. Scarved. Slight harelip.

"*Bonjour,*" we say. "Hello."

Odysseus IV looks deeply into each of our eyes. Smiles at us with his twisted lips.

"Tell me everything," he says.

And suddenly, I'm lost in his eyes the blue of food coloring. My blood sparkles. My heart is bliss. A song I used to hate that I loved surround-sounds my soul. It is a song about nightmares dressed as daydreams, about trading your soul for a kiss. I think *not this song, never this song,* but my soul is already singing along, riding its swells like an ocean wave, shimmering.

Kira pats my back, the handle of the bloodied ax still in her little fist.

"Welcome to Workshop, Bunny."

Part Two

15

We huddle-hug on the velvety green among the cherry blossom trees. We link arms. We close our eyes the better to feel each other's bodies. We form a hot little circle of love and understanding. We press our faces into our faces, our cheeks against our cheeks, our eyelashes tickling our skins like little hummingbird wings, like Bunny nose twitches.

Oh, Bunny, I love you.

I love you, Bunny.

We cannot say how long we have been here, hugging like this. Because it is that time of day where we thank each other for breathing. Post-Workshop hug time. A hug to take away all of our owies. The ones that come with sharing your story aka soul in a classroom setting. Though today we really don't need one. We were so brilliant in the Cave today. We were such bright, shining lights. We were so the daughters of Woolf, you should have seen us. In fact, halfway through the class we had to put on sunglasses to shield our eyes from how bright our stars were. We told each other, Bunny, *you are so brilliant, you are so famous in waiting, can we have your autograph now please?*

KareKare did say some not nice things about our stories, though.

We are too pretty, she said. We need to be rougher, rawer. She looked at our heart's blood in the form of four double-spaced pages in carefully chosen fonts and she said: *Where? Where is the heart? Where is the heat?*

Also, we need to get *down in the muck* more. We nodded. We took notes with our multicolored pens into our Moleskines, our Clairefontaines, our Rhodias. We pretended to look thoughtful, narrowed our eyes. Meanwhile we were thinking: *What does this mean, muck?* We pictured an awful swamp overseen by a god of nightmares. *Is KareKare a god of nightmares?*

She was not entirely convinced either about our desire to write on rose petals.

The poets aka the Reptile People pass us huddle-hugging on the green. They are getting out of their own Workshop with their professor, Silky, KareKare's husband, who wants to have sex with us so badly, and has made this known in so many silky, nonverbal ways. The poets are on their way to get beers in the basement bar across the street, which smells of stale kegs and fake cheese. They stare at us with judgy eyes as they pass, grunting nobly in their fake poor clothes. They think we are such stupid girls. The way we hug each other so much. The way we sometimes groom each other at their lame parties by the light of their lame fires, while they roll and roll their eyes until only the whites show. The way we do not want to talk about scansion. The way we do not wish to pretend to be poor, sorry (well, most of us). Or is it our amazingly empathic hive mind that we make by hugging so that we become one of those animals with a brain and heart in each tentacle that connects to a bigger, cosmic heart-brain that is like a shared, all-seeing third eye? Who knows? Who cares? Fuck you, poets. You think you are so smart, so cool with your word art. You have no idea. Can you conjure hybrid spaces? Can you perform the Body and have the Body perform, *literally*? Can you make a Viking masseuse? A pre-TB Keats? A talky Tim Riggins?

Can you make a bunny explode with the combined force of your eight eyes?

Ten, Bunny. Your eyes too.

It is so amazing to see the bunny explode, by the way. We are barely even grossed out anymore. Now we light a cigarette with the guts still in our hair and we lean against Bunny's bloody shoulder and we wait for the knock on the door. It is so amazing when we hear the *knock knock* sound. It is so amazing to see a boy of flesh smiling at us where a bunny used to be. *Hello, Samantha,* he'll say. *Tell me everything.*

Not a boy, *Bunny, remember. A Hybrid. Or a Darling. Or a Draft. We keep telling you.*

It makes us feel a little like God. No, we can't go that far. In fact, we are a little fearful of God right now, if he's out there.

She, Bunny. If She's out there.

Or It. We like to think of It more as an energy.

And don't worry, It would approve.

So approve. Of us.

Because look at what we just did. Look at him.

So what if they all look the same? Like Cape Cod in boy

form. Sometimes like the classic film stars or fairy-tale princes of yesteryear.

So what if they all say the same things? *Tell me everything. Your beauty is like screaming, like Proust, like a Frenchy film complete with sound track. You're a daughter of Woolf.*

So what if anatomically there are some things missing? Essential things. Like hands, genitals. An untwisted mouth. Possibly a soul. Still, it's a good start. We'll get better.

In the meantime, look. He is holding an orchid just for us, which, if we take it from him quickly, he won't eat first. He is brushing our hair. Doing it so tenderly, he doesn't mean to rap the brush handle against our scalp at all. He is painting strange flowers and blobby birds on our fingernails. He is saying we are so beautiful and wild like the black moors of the Brontës, he is saying our talents are as deep as the North Sea. He is saying, *Love your dress.* He is saying, *Pinkberry, would you like some?* He is helping us in the kitchen to make Light and Sunnies or Lady Grey tea, and so what if he is more trouble than he is help? So what if he cries when we say, *Will you fuck us?* So what if he explodes when we say, *Tell me something about you.*

It's amazing, what it promises. We're not bored in the slightest ever, ever. We're blown away.

"Hey, Samantha," a boy with a soup-bowl haircut calls across the quad now, waving. "How are you? Are you still talking to rabbits? Hey, are you okay?"

Amazing. We're all amazing.

We keep hugging until the Reptile People pass us like a

cloud of bad will, until our hearts feel light again, like they are going to burst out of our chests with glee, the way we felt when we made Glitter Viggo or whenever we think of unicorns, until one of us says, *Can we go to Mini, please?*

We go to Mini and we order everything on the menu. Mini fries, mini shakes, mini wings, which are wings from these super-small birds. We know the boy in back who pulls them off their tiny bodies. One of ours that was spared the ax. He doesn't even flinch when he tells us about it even though we are like *ew, ew, ew, stop it!* We forget his name. Maybe Hotspur or Rimbaud VI or was it Jorg?

The ones that don't work out for us for a number of reasons, we let go. Really, it's the best thing for them, Bunny says. The ones who bite, the ones who scream, usually get the ax. Unless Bunny is too tired to put on her apron. Then they go in the basement for a while until Bunny feels like taking a long, long drive. That's when we lead them out the back door at a very dark hour. We drive them out to a field or a warehouse area on the west side and drop them off. Bunny says we're setting them free.

Usually Bunny takes them, because she has the SUV and the strongest emotional constitution. We went with her once. *Keep me company, Bunny!* Bunny said. *And after this we can get drive-thru fries.*

Okay, Bunny, we said.

But it was a not-nice drive. What with the whimpering boys

—the whimpering Hybrids, Bunny—in the trunk whimpering their scrambled words. *Hunt you I will! Everything tell me! Virginia Woolf is not your daughter! I sentence you to a nuanced labyrinth.*

Bunny tried to drown them out by cranking her cherubic harp music, but we could still hear them. *Why do we have to take them so far?* we asked her.

Bunny, we already told you. Otherwise they come back.

Is that really ethical, though, Bunny? To just take them to the other side of town and leave them there? If they're dangerous? If they have nowhere to go?

Ethical? Bunny repeated like she'd never heard the word, even though obviously she had, she is so, so smart. She has been going to the best schools in the world since she was five. She can play the oboe and she can fence and she speaks three dead languages. *Ethical*, Bunny said, like we'd made the word up. Like it was just some silly monster we were trying to make out of our own hair, which she herself lovingly braided for us.

She stared at the windshield. Uh-oh. We upset her. *Don't be upset, Bunny!*

We think of it as art meets life, Bunny. We're putting art into the world. It's like a living interactive installation. You know? But I mean, if you'd rather kill them, you go right ahead, Bunny.

No. That's okay. We can't bring ourselves to brandish an ax just yet, Bunny knows that.

We have nightmares every night as it is, Bunny knows that too. And who is there for us when we wake up? Bunny is.

Shhh, Bunny, Bunny will say, stroking our damp forehead,

our sticky braids. Putting her hand on our heart to stop it from beating. *Take these. They'll help you sleep.*

She turned up the cherubic harp music. Each song is twenty minutes long and meanders like a bitchy cat. The woman's high folksy voice hurts our teeth but we would never tell Bunny this. We said we loved this song. *So much.* But Bunny wasn't listening. Bunny was singing along in her own high voice. Cherubic harp music is her very, very favorite.

Here at Mini they have many cupcakes in mini but they should have more. Why don't they have more? They should have more in mini, more! We tell them how they should have more in mini and they do not seem to make a note of it.

Bunny touches none of it. She is the most upset of all of us about Workshop because of the not-nice things KareKare said about her diamond proems.

Bunny, we say, *what does she know, really?*

Eat, Bunny, we say, *please eat something, please.*

For us?

Because we don't want you to die, Bunny!

We don't want to live in a world without you!

If you died, we would absolutely die too. Please eat, Bunny, please, please, please!

Bunny, we know you sometimes get depressed that your sister is this incredible neurologist in training or whatever and that you have basically lived in her shadow for twenty years reading and seething. But then the day came when you went into your mother's room and dragged her diamond ring across her vanity mirror then along all of the windows in your house, etching messages from the goddess of Wisdom. That was the day a literary star was born, Bunny. That was the day you started giving your special gift of you to the world. Sure your sister saves lives, Bunny, but you save souls with your diamond proems. And how many people can say that?

We watch Bunny touch a mini churro with her delicate fingers. Then we clap our hands as she begins to touch all of it with her mouth. She will not die, not today, and we thank the unicorn goddess to whom we quickly prayed.

We move the conversation to more interesting talk. Like *Who will be our next Boy—we mean Hybrid? Hmm?*

We think about this. It is such fun to brainstorm possibilities with our glitter pens. To take notes upon notes in our leather-bound notebooks with the designer tree paper! To skim the literature and movies and music and myths of the world and take only the cream.

But Bunny says we aren't going deep enough. *We need to go deeper. We need to be rougher, rawer, and richer, like the night.*

Okay, Bunny, we whisper. *Okay.*

We think, think, think.

Bunny takes a sip of her mini French 75 and looks at us, each one of us, over the rim, challenging us. Maybe even daring us. Daring her fellow Bunnies. Which is a little mean but we let it go because *we love you, Bunny*.

"Perhaps some sort of revisionist fairy-tale work?" Bunny suggests. "A subversive play on canonical tropes?"

Which we know is short for Bunny wanting a merman

again. Or another wolf in the woods. Or some pale, sober prince emerging from the briars to climb her hair. Bunny looking down from her tower in a red cloak. Or a dress made of rags. Or a dress made of gold?

But Bunny doesn't like this direction. Bunny thinks the merman/wolf/prince idea is dumb. Child's play. Too heteronormative. We agree. *No, Bunny. We love you, but no.*

"How about a confluence of postcolonialism and literary horror?" suggests Bunny.

Which means she wants a mitigated Dracula again. Not someone who will actually bite her neck and draw blood, but who will maybe drink red cocktails with her in a darkish bar. Speak with a slight but indiscernible accent. Not kill her but sort of look like he's going to all the time—it's just his foreign intensity. Or perhaps a Moorish prince with kohl-lined eyes, familiar with unorthodox hair-braiding techniques and the writings of Sade. An Other but not a so Scary Other that he won't be able to make her tea with the dainty gestures of an anemic Englishman.

We wrinkle our nose at Bunny's suggestion. *We're concerned about the degree of Othering, the Orientalism that you're engaging in, Bunny. We feel you should be more mindful of this.*

"Perhaps then we could draw from film, winkingly indulge in some campy nostalgia," offers Bunny.

This means Bunny wants James Dean again, leaning against a wooden post again. John Cusack in *Say Anything* again, holding up his boom box in the rain again. Marlon Brando again, screaming for Stella in the steamy night again. And Bunny at the French-doored balcony again in a white strapless dress patterned with one-eyed birds again. Sweat beads blooming on her upper lip with every roar of her name. Again.

More nose wrinkles. *Tsk tsk. Reinforcing old narratives, Bunny. Bunny, it's so great you were a failed actress once and that you still want everything to be a scene that is just so. Probably you were so amazing even though they said you weren't pretty or thin enough no matter how much you threw up, but Bunny, what did they know, we think you are so, so beautiful. Still you're not on the stage anymore, Bunny. You have to think bigger, wilder, please.*

"What about if we tried using other animals?" we hear ourselves suggest. "Like instead of bunnies?"

Sudden silence. All mini foods set down. Champagne flutes frozen midsip.

Bunny looks at us like she doesn't understand our words. *Other animals? Instead of?*

"Like *what* other animals, Bunny?"

"Don't know," we say. Suddenly it is very hard to recall any other animal besides Bunny. When we look around in our minds all we see are floppy ears, puffy tails.

"Oh, like what about a wolf?" we say at last. "Or a deer. Or maybe some sort of bird could be interesting. As an experiment."

Bunny looks at us like we are insane. Possibly mutinous.

"Just as an experiment," we say softly, lowering our eyes. "Just wondering can we only use bunnies?"

"Why would we use anything other than bunnies, *Bunny*?"

"Well, then maybe we could try making something other than a boy?" we say, regretting it immediately.

"Bunny, we don't *make boys*, we told you. They're Hybrids."

"Darlings."

"Drafts."

"Also, we don't *make*."

"Okay. Well, maybe—"

Bunny cuts us off, feeling we are missing the point of this exercise. What she means is that we need to go deeper, richer, stranger. Draw from the well of—

"We need a cock that fucking works. I know I do."

Silence falls. We stare at our mini plates. Does Bunny have to be so crude? And yet her point cannot be denied. She has a way of cutting to the chase, it's true. It's why we love her even though it's hard sometimes. It's true that for all our experiments, we have yet to make a Hybrid with working sexual organs. Or hands of actual human flesh.

"Fuck hands," says our crudest, truthiest Bunny. "I want the cock."

"Maybe it's time for Samantha to participate more in the circle," one of us says.

It is so weird for us to hear that name spoken. So familiar but faraway. We perk up our twitchy ears. We haven't led Workshop yet. *Soon, Bunny*, Bunny keeps telling us. *We're actually really excited at what you can bring to us. Given all your gifts, all your life experience.*

But honestly we're afraid of that. Because what if this is Bunny's gift, not ours?

Don't be silly!

"The boys—I mean Hybrids—are getting better just by

having her nearby. Less weird mouths, way less ooze. We're also not getting nearly as many screamy ones lately. Or tails."

"Also, they seem more . . . willful."

"And better in bed. I mean not *in bed,* obviously, but at least they're not so afraid of beds anymore."

"Or maybe we're just getting better," Bunny says. " I think we're also getting better generally speaking."

"I like the ones with tails," says another one of us. "The tails are hot. Can we make me one with a tail, please? Ooh, and a snout. We should have another Broken Boy, I mean Draft party. We haven't had one in ages."

Bunny, you're disgusting, we say. *You're so disgusting oh my god. But we love you anyway, Bunny, like you're our very own sick, alienlike little baby who looks just like a gross old man the way babies can sometimes look to everyone but their mother.*

Bunny makes a face at us. A funny face.

Oh, Bunny, you're so funny.

We say *Bunny is so funny* and we laugh because it's true. She is so funny.

We laugh and we laugh and we laugh and there is a waiter who comes and asks us why are we laughing, Is everything okay? He asks in this so-concerned voice and that is even funnier so we laugh more. Our laughter makes him uncomfortable because he doesn't get it, he's not in on the joke, even though he wants to be, you can tell by his wanting face, which is even funnier to us. We laugh even harder, we grip our barre-toned stomachs so hard we can't breathe. We almost die right there among our mini foods. O*h my god, oh my god, oh my god, so* *funny*. We probably burn at least a thousand calories laughing because it is so, so funny, this joke we are in on about Bunny being funny. Being a funny Bunny.

And now we are hungry again. We are hungry for Pinkberry. *So hungry for it, oh my god. Oh my god, we should go. Is it open?*

It's open, we should go.

We should go. We should go we should go we should go. Can we go?

We can go, Bunny.

Oh my god, how much does Bunny love Pinkberry? She loves it so much she loves it so much she loves it so fucking much oh my god. We are so happy right now, we could hop, we could dance. *Who will dance with us?!*

As we ask this question, a pain seizes us, a memory of a roof. A woman's hand covered in black mesh. A pair of eyes, one blue one brown, like some cool man singer, *what is his name?* For a minute, we can't breathe. She has a name, this woman with the hands of mesh. She held us close once, but never too close. She smelled of something, what did she smell of? Something musk. Something leaf. She had hair like white feathers. What was her name again? Her name was—

We'll dance with you, Bunny.

We dance all the way to the mall. Sometimes on the inside, sometimes on the outside, sometimes both. On the way, there are so many funny things and we laugh at them all. There are so many cute things, also. We can't help but coo and clap our hands at the so-cute things of this world. At the ducks, *oh my god, look at the ducks, so cute*. At the sky, *oh my god, look at the sky, so cute*. At the tall buildings reflecting the sun setting, *look how shiny*

shiny they are. Homeless man *don't look, don't look, don't look, that causes an owie inside. No, do look, it's sad. Makes you think, makes you deep.* Our mothers always said to look hard at the things of this world that are owies on the eyes because they will put more colors in your inner rainbow. One of us does a yoga pose right there on the street, a show-off move where she lifts right into a headstand pose, her legs in the air, balancing on her head and elbows. It is called Crow. We look at her long, slender body, all the ballerina-trained muscles taut in the upper half of this long, slender body, and we remember she nearly flunked out of Interlochen. We remember she has a weird-shaped face and forlorn hair that looks poorly pasted onto her temples. We remember her stories are dumb, she won no prizes at Barnard. Her nose looks semi-smashed onto her face. Her eyes are pretty in some kinds of light, but most of the time they are a drab no color. We remember all of this and then we say, *Oh my god, amazing. You are amazing. Wow. Can we be you,* please?

We are walking down the steeply sloping hill, *la la la,* the hill upon which the towers and bells of Warren shimmer like a wish. Like the corsages we wear on our wrists for Prom Thursdays. As we make our way down the hill, entering the downtown, it's spooky. The air is different here. Humider. Grosser. The sky a dark pink that reminds us of innards, of what happens in the bathroom with the ax with the Darlings who don't make it. We're passing the scary places now. To get to Pinkberry we have to pass some scary places and to get through them you have to think *Pinkberry Pinkberry Pinkberry.* This city is not cute like Pinkie Pie or even scary-cute like a young Marlon Brando. We hold each other close past tattoo parlors and abandoned storefronts. Past the old lady with the spider tattoo on her neck who will be in all of our stories next week. She is waiting for a bus, a grimy bus, we imagine, that takes her to her trash- and raccoon-filled home where she eats quivery things out of jars. *Hold me close, Bunny. Can you hold me close? Closer?* We cannot hold each other close enough somehow, even though we can't breathe because of how tightly, how fiercely we are hanging on to each other, but it still feels like we are not holding anything. We miss something somehow. Like we could hug and hug and hug until our ribs crack and our hearts burst and our lungs collapse and our arms break off and still. We'd still be hugging air. No body.

That's when we feel it, no, smell it. We smell her first. Firewood. Leaf. We're about halfway down the hill when we feel a mesh hand cupped over our face and suddenly we are dragged, dragged, dragged into a nearby alley between the abandoned storefronts.

"Don't fucking scream," a voice whispers in our ear, with a menthol cigarette breath. "Don't fucking breathe."

Out in the street, we hear Bunny calling our name.

"Bunny? Bunny? Bunny, where are you, Bunny? Where did you go?"

"Bunny? Where did she go?"

Here, Bunny! we want to scream through the mesh fingers.

We can hear Bunny turning round and round in her ballerina flats, her brogues, her shiny Mary Janes, her combat bootlets. *Tap tap tap* on the sidewalk. Looking for us.

We're here, Bunny! we want to scream. *In the scary dark! In the creepy alley with god knows how many rats and spiders and killers.* We'd say this but we're afraid to, this perfumed hand around our mouth, the other hand clasped tightly around our pulled-back arms.

We make a noise through her mesh fingers. A noise of protest.

Shhhhh, says the voice, which sounds all hissy and spitty like a snake. If a snake could talk it would sound just like this.

"All right. Let's go," we hear Bunny say. "She'll find us. If she wants to find us, she will."

Then we see Bunny looking down the alleyway, squinting. "Bunny? Are you there?"

"Yes!" we scream.

But the hand grips tighter around our face, muffling the sound.

We watch Bunny give a cursory look down the alleyway before she turns away. Once Bunny has left, a mouth in our ear slowly counts to thirty, then the hands holding us prisoner let go.

We run down the alley to see where they have gone. But the street is empty and oh so dark. Then all at once the streetlights go off. We can't see anything. "Bunny," we whisper. "Where are you?"

The world is blacker than it has ever been. We are lost. We are lost, we are lost, we are—

16

"You're welcome," says a voice behind us. We turn around. We see nothing but a dark, slim shape.

"Who are you?"

"Are you fucking kidding me?" the dark shape says, stepping in closer. Our eyes adjust. A girl. We look at her for a long time, this girl. We are about to open our mouth and scream but something in her face stops us. We know her from somewhere, somewhere before Bunny. Also, we are mesmerized by her ugliness. She is ugly to us because she took us away from Bunny and our good times and also because she is truly very strange looking. That must be on our face somehow because she looks away. Good. It gives us a break. We stare at the bricks behind her in this alley. It is such a scary alley. But she doesn't look scared. Probably because she lives here, with the rats and spiders and killers. Probably—

"Smackie, I've been looking for you everywhere. Where the hell have you been?"

Strange that she calls us that. She seems to think she knows us too.

"Just school," we shrug. "School things. So busy right now oh my god." We look at her. She's making a face that says *What the fuck do you take me for?*

What about you?" we ask. "Where have you been?"

"Looking for you."

"Oh." We picture her in the alleys, opening the trash can lids of the world and peering in. Getting it so wrong. "Why?"

"Because I was worried as hell."

"Don't worry," we say.

"What?"

"Don't worry."

"Smackie, you dropped off the fucking face of the earth for like two months. What's with the dress?"

We look down at our dress. It is covered with kittens who are wearing crowns because they are the kings and queens of this world. It is the blue of the brightest skies, which probably this girl never lived under. You can tell oh you can tell her sky was a heavy one. Always. She wanted it that way. Yes. Sought that out. Some people do.

"It's a pretty dress," we say and we almost swish it a little, but then we don't, we can't in front of this girl. She makes us embarrassed about swishing our dress somehow. Our arms stay stiff at our sides. "Love your dress too," we tell her.

"Liar," she says.

"No," we say, even though we did lie just now. We hate her dress. It's a dark and shredded-looking thing. "Love it," we say.

"You do realize you're in a cult, don't you? You're in a fucking *cult.*"

This word hurts our ears so we cover them and think-sing a song from the latest Disney musical, which is our new favorite musical. Which even though we only saw it recently, we have already watched five hundred times. It is about two sisters who live in a snowy place and one of them goes icy in her soul. It is based on a fairy tale. Now, the fairy tale is dark and stabby like this alley, but in the movie version there is a talking snowman and there are songs we love to sing. We are singing the one now where icy girl is alone on a snowy hill lamenting that she is icy in her heart. She wants to change but she cannot. Because her heart has turned to ice.

"Shut up, Smackie."

It starts to rain. Hard. Because that's the kind of weather that follows this kind of girl. She's so slutty and dark she makes the clouds slutty and dark too. Pregnant with this dirty rain that starts to fall hard on both of us.

"I wish I could have found you earlier," she is saying. "After that night you walked away from me for no reason, I followed you but I lost you. So I waited at your place but you never showed."

Our place? We have a place? A dim image in our brain of a hallway that smells of sewage and boiled things.

"Smackie, look at me."

Why does she keep calling us that? Anyway, we don't want to look at her, this girl. Because she is weird looking, that's why. Because her sky is soaking us to the bone, making our cocoa lemon vanilla moisturizer and our grassy perfume slide off our body in tears, in rivulets, drowning the kitten royalty on our dress. There is something about looking at her that makes us feel like we can't breathe. Not the rib-aching laugh can't breathe that we were can't breathing earlier. Not the those-ducks-are-so-cute can't breathe. This is different. Like there is a terrible sharp pin she stabbed deep into our lungs that is stuck there forever.

"Smackie," she says softly, "look at me." She isn't talking in a snake voice anymore. She sounds like something as familiar as rain on the roof of our old house. Waves outside the motel in Seaside where we used to go with our mother. Wind rushing through leaves in the trees outside our bedroom window, cooling our feverish legs, scoring our dreams.

"Look at me," she says.

Why does she want us to look at her so much? To look at her is scary, like looking at a spider in our perfect white bathtub with the gold feet. Not ours. Bunny's. *Take a bath, Bunny*, Bunny said to us one night after Workshop. *Feel free*. But then we saw a huge spider crawling around in there, its eight legs slipping a little on the polished, gleaming enamel. We wanted so much to take a bath and close our eyes in the warm fragrant forgetting water but we couldn't because of this thing.

"Look at me."

We look at her and our face is a perfumed fist. Ready to smash the spider. Even though we could never kill it. Our way is to get someone else to do this work. To lay a pot over it and walk away for however many days it takes until it dies. But we look at her now. All of this goop we rubbed into our bodies has run, has slid off our skin because of her slut rain. And this time when we look at her, something in us opens. Against our will. I feel it opening. Didn't she kill a spider for me once? Stood in my bathroom with a broom in her fist, while I watched her from the doorway. *I don't see it,* she said. *It's there,* I said. *Keep looking,* I pleaded. *Please, Ava.*

"Ava," I hear myself say now.

She smiles a little, reaches out, takes my hand. Her hand, even though it's covered in mesh, is a solid, familiar thing.

"Come on," she says.

"Where?" I say, though I'm already going.

She doesn't answer. I follow her anyway.

17

I'm sitting across from her at what she says we call the monster diner, in a ripped-up booth pasted all over with duct tape.

"You used to love coming here with me," she tells me.

"I did?" I stare at the creepy customers, cursing into their coffee cups. The cooks with their hairy lip curls and their cheap gold chains. The fish that looks like a shark, swimming around in the cloudy tank by the door.

She follows my gaze. "You loved the shark most. And it's not a shark."

"Is it—"

"Smackie, eat. Or I'll make the shark eat you."

She's ordered me what she claims is my usual. I look down at a not mini plate of what appear to be blobs of yellow pus on brown pits. A chipped mug full of black bile. The pink pony inside me weeps softly.

"What is this?" I ask her.

"Coffee. Eggs on toast."

Is there syrup? Or sprinkles somewhere? I want to ask, but I'm afraid. So I shake my head. *Not hungry right now. Thanks so much, though.* My mouth is dry from sugar consumption. My dress is a cold wet sack. I can't look her in the eye, though I can feel she's looking right at me. My phone keeps buzzing in my drowned kitten lap.

She's telling me all the places she looked for me. Here. The library. The swan pond. Bookstores. Cafés. The zoo. At the zoo, I was always standing too close to the bear pit. Did anyone get mauled recently? How hard she tried to reach me. How she called and called. She must have thrown god knows how many stones at my window. She even climbed my fire escape once and knocked on the smashed glass, and she just saw an empty, made bed. She got to know the naked guy who hangs around my building really well, waiting on my fire escape. They shared a cigarette once. He isn't so bad. He's just a person who needs to be naked after a certain hour. But it's not enough to be in his house and naked. He needs to be seen being naked. Once he's been seen, once he's made someone scream at the fact of his naked body, it's like an itch got scratched and he can go inside and watch game shows.

It was the perverted giant who let her into my building. She went upstairs and sat outside my front door waiting for me to come home, figuring at some point I'd come home, I'd have to, but then I didn't.

I try to picture her sitting on the floor of my foul-smelling, narrow hallway, her very long legs in their ripped-up tights with nowhere to go.

"You really did that?"

She doesn't dignify that with a reply. Tells me how she even went to Warren, inside the actual buildings. *And you know I don't go there.* But she went for me. Called my name in those polished halls. Looking for me. Her friend. Opened the doors to perfumed bathrooms. To classrooms with their own fireplaces. Walked into god knows how many lectures about stem cells and archaeological findings in Egypt, and she called my name there too. Screamed it. No one did anything. Perhaps they thought she was a performance artist.

"I'm sorry," I say. "I'm so sorry."

At first, she thought I was avoiding her because I was mad—even though she had no idea what she could have done to piss me off so much. But as the weeks passed she started to really worry. She was even going to file a missing person's report. She was afraid to go to the police because of some previous unpleasantness. But she was going to do it anyway. Even if they arrested her, she didn't care. She thought maybe I'd been the victim of the Random Decapitators, a supposed band of roving homicidal maniacs. She never really believed they existed. Thought it was just unfounded rumor, an urban legend, an elaborate frat-boy hoax. But when I disappeared, she got worried. That maybe they did exist, that they cut off my head and put it in a locker or something and it was stinking up some marble hallway. That happened here once. It actually did.

"But then I saw you," she says. "Finally."

On the green. Sitting there on the light-splashed grass with the bonobos. I was alive. My head was still on my body. I was fine. Or was I? We were in a circle, the bonobos and I. Doing some of sort of weird huddle hug. The expression on my face was . . .

"What?" I ask, though I don't want to know.

She looks away, embarrassed for me, I guess. I feel a hot swell of something like shame flood my cheeks.

"I almost didn't recognize you. You looked . . . shorter. Also, you were wearing . . ." Her eyes dip down to my prancing kittens. "Anyway."

She says she waved at me. Called my name. I didn't turn around, even though she was sure I'd heard her. Then she screamed "Bunny," for kicks, and I did turn around. We all did.

"You looked right at me. You looked right at me and then you looked away."

I don't remember this. I try to tell her how I don't remember this. "I really don't. I promise. I didn't see you. I must have not seen you."

She just stares at me.

"I'm sorry I worried you. I am. I feel terrible. Really I do." The words fall from my mouth like so many dead leaves. I hear the deadness in them, the crackle. The truth is I feel nothing. It's like I'm looking at her from the opposite end of a very long tunnel, from the very bottom of a deep, dark well. She's peering down at me from way up high and shaking and shaking her head. *What the hell? Why? Why did you fall into there, Samantha? What's wrong with you?*

I don't know, is my only answer. It just . . . happened.

"I guess I got wrapped up," I hear myself say now.

"'*Wrapped up*'? In what, exactly?"

I think about the other evening at Bunny's house with Beowulf VII. We were sitting in the window seat at twilight time, drinking Bunny's best mead. I was drinking mead; Beowulf was sipping appletizer out of a Dixie cup (*actual alcohol upsets them, we've found, Bunny*). How he complimented me endlessly. Took my hand in his black-leather gloved ones and told me I was the shiningest light he'd ever seen, did I know that, Samantha?

Yes. I knew that.

And if I ever needed food, he would hunt for me. Did I know that, Samantha?

Yes. I knew that too.

Tell me everything, Samantha, everything. I'm listening. I really want to hear and see and touch and know you in every way that respects you.

Do you?

Oh, yes, Samantha.

Everything I'm feeling?

Samantha, everything.

I was drunk. I was bored. Beowulf looked like Donald Glover with blue voids for eyes. I stared at his broad but slightly misshapen shoulders, hidden under his Brooks Brothers suit.

I'm feeling like we should get the hell out of here, I whispered to him. *Do some drugs and fuck like rabbits in that patch of woods out there.* At this, his face crumpled and he wept.

Bunny, you have to stop asking them that, Bunny said from the loveseat. She was sitting with her boy, who was bluntly stroking her hair with the back of a brush.

You know it only upsets them, agreed Bunny. Her boy was curled in her lap like a cat. She was dropping bits of freesia into his mouth that he kept failing to catch.

Or the other night when, bored with the compliments, the

tell me everythings, I said to the one we called Big Rig, *No, you tell me something for once!*

Something? I— And then his head exploded.

Or last night, when I tried to peek under Lancelot's black leather gloves to see what the hell was under there. Stumps of flesh? Claws? Hooks? And he bit me. Actually fucking bit me on the shoulder and then the hand. Hard. I screamed and Lancelot screamed and then Bunny grabbed the ax while I covered my eyes and said *don't, don't, please.* And then Bunny had to take me to the hospital because *is the risk of rabies gone after a bunny-to-boy transformation?* We googled and googled, we consulted our fairy-tale and myth anthologies to no avail, and in the end we thought it was best to seek medical treatment just in case, *even though I should just let you die, Bunny, because I told you, haven't I told you so many times to leave the hands alone?* And then all the way there we had to get our stories straight. *My pet rabbit has gone off the rails. I don't know what got into him.* And *Don't forget to cry*, Bunny growled at me, her long silver hair swept up with spiky flowers, her cobalt eyes black with anger, her face and her dress splattered here and there with bits of blood even though she'd worn her axing apron, the one lined with real pearls that said Kitchen Diva in pale pink cursive. I'd ruined her date. *But what sort of date is it, really, Bunny?* I thought. *I mean, if you never even touch hand flesh, let alone fuck? Isn't that more of a Disney ride than a date?* But this I kept to myself even though my mouth was wide open and the mutinous words were on the tip of my tongue, just waiting for my throat sounds to push them out into the air. I stayed silent.

Really I should just let you die, Bunny, Bunny said to me again. And I agreed. Yes. She should have. That she didn't is the most wondrous kindness.

Well. Because I love you, Bunny. Actually. You're actually my favorite.

You're my favorite too, I lied. But in that moment, I meant it. I meant it so much I cried.

And then she took my injured hand and kissed it with her cold, balm-y lips.

Just remember, please, that Creation is a heavy responsibility. And the Work, though necessary, though vital, though cutting edge, is also volatile, dangerous, not at all to be taken lightly.

Yes, Bunny.

And I thought of Chuck E. Cheese. When my father took me there once for my birthday and we watched the mechanical animal band sing. How after they were finished, I tried to ask them questions about their instruments and they just stared at me with their dead eyes and—

"Smackie!" Ava shouts.

"What?"

She grabs the menu and holds it up even though I know she knows everything on it, even though we already have our food. *I'd like some deep fried hare heart, please?* she said to the waitress.

Some what?

I'd like a green tea.

"I'm leaving," she says.

Suddenly I feel all the cold rain on my body. My heart becomes a tight fist in my chest.

"Leaving?"

My phone starts buzzing again.

"You better answer that," she says.

"Wait. What do you mean you're—"

"Answer it. Otherwise they might call the Bunny police on me. Have me arrested. Put me in Bunny jail with all the other not nice people."

"Ava."

"I wonder who my cellmates will be? People who don't coo hard enough at duckies? Cupcake non-enthusiasts? People who prefer their food normal size and are indifferent to sprinkles?" She's blowing smoke rings at me shaped like warped hearts.

"What do you mean you're leaving?"

She looks at me. David Bowie. That's the name of the singer whose eyes her eyes remind me of. "I mean, I'm leaving here," she says. "The Lair of Cthulhu. Sketch City. Whatever you're calling it now. I'm leaving it."

Panic courses through me. *You can't, you can't, you can't.* "When?"

"I don't know yet. Soon." She looks out the window like she could go right now.

"You *can't*!" I shout, and I hear the crack running down the middle of my voice.

"Why can't I?" The look she gives me is challenging.

"Because . . ." Because something very important. Where are the words? My words are far away. The words I need are high and floating in the sky like so many out-of-reach balloons. *I want you to stay. I don't want you to go.* Why can't I pull these words down from the sky?

"*Because?*" she prompts.

“I thought you liked it here,” I say at last, lamely.

She makes a face. “I hate it here. I don’t whine about it the way you do but of course I fucking hate it. Warren leeches off this place like a zombie. I’m tired of being Bunny feed. I’ve actually been thinking about it for a while, if you must know. But I was worried about leaving because . . .”

“Because?”

She looks at me.

“Because of Dolores,” she says at last, smiling fondly at the waitress, whose tired back is to us. She’s in the middle of screaming at a cook. Dolores keeps a knife tucked in her bra, which she’ll whip out at the slightest provocation. There are men who come in here just to see Dolores drive its tip into their unwiped table.

“I didn’t want to leave her here alone with the Warren pricks who treat her like she’s some gritty attraction.”

“You never told me you were thinking about leaving.”

“You’ve been hard to reach lately.” She runs a hand through her feathery platinum hair. I notice a bald spot the size of a coin on the side of her head. At the sight of it, I feel a terrible ache.

“Please don’t go,” I say.

She reaches across the table. For a second I think she’s going to stroke my face, but instead she takes off the heart-shaped sunglasses I forgot I was wearing and puts them on. Two hearts over her eyes. The world goes from dark pink to a gray-white hellscape under grimy diner lights. She’s the only beautiful thing in it.

“What can I do to make you not go?”

But she's looking past me at the front door. "Cover your ears," she says to me.

"Why?"

"Do it."

But before I can bring my hands to my ears, I hear it. Pressing on the sides of my head like little screws being twisted into either temple.

"BUNNY?!?!?!"

They rush over to our table, their shiny eyes wide, their faces warped with concern and relief.

"Bunny, thank GOD!"

"We were looking ALL over for you!"

Caroline. Kira. They look as out of place in the diner as two pieces of Easter confection in the apocalypse. Fawns lost in a forest of fanged shadows. My heart rises and falls at the sight.

"I—"

"We were totally going to call the police."

"Or campus security or something."

"But then Eleanor was like, 'Don't worry about Samantha, it's *Samantha*. She's not like us. She's seen things.' So we didn't." Cupcake looks out the window and waves. I turn and see Eleanor and Victoria are outside, hanging out by Eleanor's SUV, watching us through the cracked glass. *Thank god you're safe,* Eleanor mouths through the window, pressing her hands to her chest. Victoria just stands beside her with her mouth open like a fish, blinking at me.

"But we texted you," Caroline says.

"At *least* a thousand times."

They look at Ava, seeming to notice her for the first time. Her dark clothes, her veil, her mesh-covered fingers gripping a cigarette like she could easily take out an eye with it. And would be happy to. Then they look back at me.

"So what happened anyway?" Caroline says. "You were with us and then you were just . . . *not* with us."

"Like you were . . . *kidnapped* . . . or something?" Kira says. She turns and gives Ava a tight, uncertain smile. "We didn't know."

"We were scared for you, though," Caroline adds.

"So scared," Kira says, sneaking another glance at Ava, who stares back so pointedly, so menacingly, that Kira turns away like she's been slapped.

"What happened, Bunny?" Caroline says.

"Yes, Bunny, what happened?"

Explain this, please.

I become aware once more of the dryness in my throat.

"Well, I—"

"She almost got gored by this giant wolf boy," Ava says, cigarette dangling out of her mouth. "He had these super-white teeth and these fingernail knives like Freddie Krueger."

"*What?* Oh my god!"

"Samantha, is this true???"

"It was terrible," Ava says, kicking me under the table. "She nearly died. Luckily I happened to be in the alley. I pulled her away just in time. Before he raped you. And killed you. Then raped your dead body."

I look at Caroline and Kira, staring at Ava, their mouths wide open. Ava just stares back at them, smoking.

"It was those kittens that set him off," she continues, aiming the cherry of her cigarette at my dress. "He thought they were actual kittens. So he grabbed her thinking, you know, lunch. But then when he realized she was a woman of flesh, that awakened all sorts of other sordid appetites."

They shudder, hold each other, grip each other's hands.

"This is why we should never go downtown," Caroline says.

"At least not to the mall," adds Kira.

"You should definitely shop online from now on," Ava says.

They look at her like she is definitely an Owie. But their eyes say she is something else too. A necklace gleaming in the tall grass that could be a snake. That could be a necklace.

"I've seen you before," Caroline says, narrowing her eyes a little, tilting her head in a dreamy way.

"Have you?"

"At the *Demitasse* at the beginning of the school year. We saw her. Didn't we see her?"

"Yes," Kira says. "We saw you."

They both stare at her with cocked heads, dreamy-curious eyes. Necklace? Snake? Snake-necklace?

Ava just stares back at them like she's in the Paris metro. Any minute now she could take off her earrings and rise to her full, shadow-casting height.

"You're Samantha's friend."

"Samantha, how come you never introduced us?"

"I bite," Ava says, sliding out of the booth. "It's a terrible, voluntary affliction." Standing up, she dwarfs them.

"Where are you going?" I hear myself say.

She takes the sunglasses off and drops them on the table. She looks at them, then at me. "Air," she says. "Just some air."

"Wait, I'll come with you," I say, moving to stand, but they corner me, Caroline plonking down next to me and Kira across, holding my hands tight, patting my damp hair, asking me five million questions at once. *Bunny, are you okay? Did you really get attacked by a wolf boy? Who was he? What did he look like? Oh my god, is this the place where the waitress stabs your table? Are you deeply traumatized? Do you think maybe this experience will feed the Work?*

"Was he hot?" (This from Victoria, who just joined us.)

"Bunny, he was *not* hot, also what kind of question is that to ask her right now?"

"Well, excuse me for not wanting to dwell on scarier stuff like if she thought he was going to decapitate her."

"Oh my god, was he, Samantha?"

"Maybe. I don't know," I say. They ignore me. Their questions no longer directed at me, but each other. I spot Ava through the cracked window. She's standing outside with Eleanor. Talking. Are they talking? I see Eleanor moving her lips like she's speaking. And Ava appears to be listening, her expression cool. I feel my stomach sink, a surge of panic in my chest.

Ava turns away from Eleanor and sees me looking at her.

For a second, we lock eyes.

Then she walks away. Out of the parking lot. *I'm leaving.*

"Ava, wait!"

I climb over Caroline, run out of the booth and out of the diner, through its swinging, clanging door. Outside, there is no sign of her anywhere, no one in the parking lot but vagrants and Eleanor, staring at me with a cocked head, a sympathetic, curious smile.

"Everything okay, Samantha?" she says.

Samantha. When was the last time she ever called me Samantha?

"The girls were worried about you but I said don't worry about Samantha. Give her the time she seems to need to grow."

She's looking at me with such smiling sorrow. *Oh, Bunny. How far away from us you still insist on drifting. Even though I have killed for you now how many times. All the dresses I've given you. All our heart-to-hearts by a fire that kept you warmer than you have been in years. But I understand, of course, that you must have your little outsider moments. And look at us, we let you, even though, well, it upsets us, really. Naturally. It bores us too.*

I hang my head. But I have to ask. "What did you say to Ava?"

I can tell by the hardness in her dark, lovely eyes that *oh you're crossing a line, Bunny*. But she humors me.

"Who?" she asks. Fake confusion followed by fake recollection dawns over her face.

"Oh. You mean your friend. She is your friend, isn't she? Eva? Ada?"

"Ava," I say, and immediately feel like I'm giving her something I shouldn't give her.

"Ava. That's right. Such style. A little dark and over the top for me, of course, but great for what it is. Perfect, really. Exactly what I'd picture." All the sorrow in her expression is making me ill. "How come you never told us about her before, Samantha?" she asks, playing the concerned therapist, leaning forward so that I can smell all the essential oils in which she bathes.

"What did you say to her?" I ask her again more forcefully, surprising myself.

The smiling edges of her mouth go hard, her eyes become little black pits.

You are so, so beautiful, I told her in tears just the other night. Even though in that moment she was not beautiful to me at all, but terrifying. Her silver hair and her so-dark eyes.

"We were talking and then she just walked off."

"She just walked off? Just like that?"

"I did ask her what pets she'd had as a child. Just to make conversation. But I don't know how that could possibly have set her off."

She shrugs. Helpless. *Oh, Samantha, how can I possibly be expected to understand the weirdo ways of you and your gritty ilk?* "She did *seem* like she was in a hurry. I assume she had some other place to go? I didn't ask."

I run across the lot, scan the street for her, but there's nothing there. Dark clouds drifting over weathered houses. Withered people waiting for a bus. *This is a place of despair, Smackie. This is a place of fucking despair.*

I turn to face Eleanor, who has walked out onto the sidewalk and stands watching me, her face awash in a condescending sympathy and something else. Pity? Curiosity? Something that is making my skin crawl.

"Oh, hey. Look. Isn't that your friend Jonah over there?"

"What? Where?"

"There. Hi, Jonah! Hey, come over here! Jonah!" She waves and waves and I follow her gaze to where Jonah's hunched figure leans against a car, smoking, a book open in his other hand.

"Jonah! Jonah!" she calls.

Shhh, I want to say.

But Jonah looks up. He squints and sees Eleanor waving and looks around him, because she can't possibly be waving at him. But she is. He smiles and waves back uncertainly.

"Hey, Jonah, come over here!" Eleanor shouts.

He shoves the book in his pocket and shuffles over. Smiling at Eleanor and me with what I can only describe as undisguised joy.

"Hi, Samantha. Hi, Ellie."

"Jonah," she says, clapping her hands like he's an approaching parade. "It's *so* good to see you."

He looks at her with surprise. *It is? Really?*

"And Samantha was *just* talking about you."

"She was? That's cool, Samantha." He smiles at me, but I can't bring myself to smile back. "I was just thinking about you. I saw you earlier today and tried to say hi but I wasn't sure if you saw me. You seemed sort of busy."

"Yeah."

"I hadn't seen you around in a while. I guess you've been writing and stuff."

"Oh, Samantha's deep into the Work, the Process," Eleanor says. "Aren't you?"

I say nothing.

"Cool. Me too," Jonah says. "Were you guys writing at the diner? I go there to write sometimes too. Everyone in there is so nice. Dolores is always giving me free coffee and stuff. I like the shark a lot too."

"The *shark*?" Eleanor says.

"Yeah, there's this fish in the aquarium that sort of looks like a shark."

"*Wow*. A fish that sort of looks like a shark. *So* interesting. I can't even imagine it. Can you imagine it, Samantha?"

I look at Eleanor, smiling at me so falsely, her hatred of me as clear and deep as the glacial eyes of Beowulf IV. As naked as Jonah's joy. I see it plainly now, just as I saw it before.

Jonah beams at us. He sees nothing, of course. Two girls smiling at one another. It's nice.

"So, Samantha, how's Workshop going?"

"Jonah, it's fine, okay?" I snap. But then I feel guilty, so I add, "I mean, it's a little overwhelming. I'm kind of drowning a bit right now."

I feel Eleanor slipping away beside me.

"Oh, that's too bad, Samantha. I'm sorry."

"It is. Look, I should really—"

"Is it because of those rabbits?"

"What?"

"Earlier this fall, you were talking to those rabbits. Remember, on the green? You looked sort of freaked out."

"The green," I repeat, watching Eleanor and the Bunnies gather and pile into Eleanor's SUV. One of her golden retrievers is barking and wagging his tail happily in the back. *Watch it or they'll turn you into Ryan Gosling.* I try to wave at her to tell her stop, wait, but she just gives me a smiling wink like *I'm leaving you here not because I'm a fucking cunt but because I'm being socially mindful of your chat with the freak boy*.

"I mean, I didn't overhear it or anything," Jonah is saying.

"Overhear what?"

"Your conversation with the rabbits. Was it intense?"

"Yeah. No. I don't know, Jonah." The rain starts falling again, heavily. Ava. She could be anywhere by now.

"I'm sorry but I have to go."

"Wait, Samantha. It's raining pretty hard. Do you need a ride somewhere?"

18

We're in the car he calls the Whale. Jonah is driving about five miles an hour, smoking and smiling beatifically at the windshield. Cranked on the stereo is a weird jazz that consists mainly of horn sounds and squeaks.

"I hope you don't mind this music," he says.

"No." I want to take the CD and throw it out the window, possibly setting it on fire first.

"I love jazz so much," he says.

We've gone to the bus station, the train station, Ava's house (empty), then back to the bus station.

"You leaving town, Samantha?"

"Yeah. I don't know. Maybe."

"Where are you headed?"

"I'm not sure."

"Just being spontaneous? That's cool."

But she wasn't at the bus station or the train station.

"Decided not to leave?" he says, when I return to the car after circling the bus station like a zombie for a second time. I nod at the windshield.

"Cool, Samantha, I'm glad. Well, where to now? You want to get like a tea? I think you could use—"

"Could we just drive around more maybe?"

She can't have gone far in this weather, could she? Then I recall those monsoon nights in June. Us drunk beyond comprehension on the roof. Her staring up at the storm like it was a bright blue sky.

Let's go for a walk, she'd say.

Are you fucking kidding? In this? But she was already gone.

Hours later, I'd wake with her face dripping over mine. Black clothes soaked to her skin.

Morning, Sunshine.

"Sure, Samantha. We can drive around. Like where?"

"Like just all around?" I'm looking out the window but I don't see anything but gray sky, water sploshing the windows.

"Feeling a little wanderlusty, huh?"

"Yeah."

"I get that way too. Sometimes I'll just drive around for hours. I won't have a destination or anything. I used to go to bookstores but I can't go in them anymore because I buy too many books. Last time I went into Ada books, I spent almost a hundred bucks. More than a hundred probably."

"That's nice."

"Yeah, except I was broke after. But it was worth it. I got these amazing poetry books and jazz books. This crazy New Age book called *Moonchild* by this insane guy from 1900. It was crazy. Pretty cool, though."

He's looking at me so I nod. "Sounds cool."

If the storm would just clear I'd be able to see her. What could Eleanor possibly have said to her?

Samantha told me she secretly hates you, by the way.

Samantha has us now. She doesn't need you.

But I can't picture her saying that without teasing her hair and giving the whole scene an eighties movie soundtrack. And why would Ava even care what Eleanor said? She already said she was leaving. I start to feel sick.

"Well, I'm glad you're not leaving, Samantha. Haven't seen you around much this semester. I guess you're been hanging out with Eleanor and them a lot now?"

I see her face, its sharp, dainty bones, the eyes like jeweled pits, and then I remember that she is the Duchess. How could I have called her by any other name? She was looking at me with such hideous . . . what was it? Knowledge. She was looking at me with knowledge. Like she had the most delicious secret morsel on me. So sweet. So creamy, velvety good. *I know you, Bunny.*

"Sort of," I say.

"That's cool," he says. "Sort of weird, though," he adds.

I look at him. "Why?"

"Because you hate them, don't you?"

I feel myself go red.

"I didn't say that."

"Yeah you did," Jonah says. "Remember? We were at the spring party and you and I had a smoke outside. I gave you a cigarette and then you lit the filter, remember? I tried to give you another one but you wanted to smoke that one, which was cool. I guess you were pretty drunk by then. So I asked you how things were going and you said, 'Terrible,' and I said, 'How come, Samantha?' and then you said, 'The girls in my year are Cuntscapades, Jonah.'"

The moment comes back to me now. The terrible smell of burning filter and my own singed hair. The Bunny-induced bile rising in my throat. My drunk heart hammering with whatever mix of drinks I inhaled at that sad excuse of a party. The alley getting weirdly narrower. The night tilting slightly to the left. The rage I felt coursing through my arms at watching them repeatedly congeal into cooing huggy swamps as they bewailed having to part for the summer. Their tipsy proclamations. *I'll miss you, Bunny! Bunny, I'll miss you too! I'll miss you, Bunny! No, Bunny, I'll miss you most.*

Cuntscapades!!!

"I didn't say that," I say, staring at the windshield.

"I'm pretty sure you did. I remember I was sort of surprised, but I thought, Okay. She probably knows because she has to go to more classes with them. But I don't really notice those things. I try not to anyway. They seem nice to me." He turns to me and smiles, so happy in his bubble where everyone is nice. Everyone must mean well. Surely.

"They aren't nice," I suddenly hear myself say. "Actually."

"They're not?"

And I'm about to tell him *they make fun of you all the time. They say you walk around in an Antabuse cloud and the only reason your poetry is any good is because you're so fucked up. They made fun of your sister's outfit when she attended your reading last year.* Actually texted me about it even though they never texted me. *Did you see that hat, girl?* Monkey covering its eyes. Monkey covering its mouth. Laughing crying cat face.

"No," I say turning to him. Looking right at him. "They're not."

"Huh." He raises his eyebrows. "So how come you're friends with them then?"

Yes, Samantha why? This is actually such a fucking good question.

"I—"

Out of the corner of my eye, through the watery windshield, I think I see Ava. Her black leather back walking hurriedly along the sidewalk.

"Jonah, stop!"

I run out into the cold rain the moment he pulls over, slipping on the slippery sidewalk that is fast becoming ice but I run until I've caught up with her. Ava. I tap her on the worn leather shoulder.

A stranger turns to face me.

When I come back he's waiting for me in his car squawking with dissonant sound. I sit in the ripped-up passenger seat with my wet head in my hands.

"Samantha, are you okay?"

"Yes. No."

"Are you looking for drugs?"

"What?"

"First the bus depot, then the train station, then that weird house you went into and then the bus station again? And just now you ran out of the car toward that dealer? Also, you kind of look like you're on something. I mean, I'm not judging if you are, but—"

"This isn't about drugs, Jonah, I promise. I just . . . I lost something."

"Oh no, what did you lose?"

So concerned and well meaning. I can't tell him. Don't have the words or the breath to even begin.

"A book," I tell him.

"I'm sorry, Samantha. Was it like a favorite book? Like one you carried everywhere?"

"Yes."

"Well, how about I take you to a bookstore? Maybe we can find it there."

"It won't be there."

"Are you sure? The bookstores in this town are pretty good because of all the students who come through. We could go to all of them if you want. Just don't let me go in with you, otherwise—"

"I know. You'll buy everything."

He smiles. A smile so kind I almost cry.

"Jonah, I'm sorry, I really am. Making you drive me all around in the rain—"

"I get it, Samantha. Books, they're like old friends. When I was here this summer, I carried four or five with me all the time."

"You were here this summer?"

"Yeah. I mean, I went to visit my uncle in Vancouver for a week, but that was it. I went a bit crazy, I think. I stole a cat."

I laugh. "You stole a cat?"

He smiles at the windshield. His soup-bowl hair is longer, I notice, shaggy around the edges.

"Just for like a day. Three days. For like a week. Then I gave it back. I felt bad. The owners were so nice to me. They wanted to give me money and stuff. I told them, keep your money."

"How come you didn't go back to Alaska?"

"Because if I did I'd drink. Hey, it's snowing."

I look through the windshield. It is snowing. I watch the tiny flakes swim through the air like quick fish. We're by the canal now, and Christmas lights are strung along the bridges, climbing up the streetlights. *You better sit tight,* my father said, through the waterfall of static, when I brought up the holidays on the phone. *But I really want to see you,* I had to repeat, louder and louder until he heard me.

I know. We both know he can't visit me, as he's told me in multiple delicate ways. That he's evading someone—investors, creditors, possibly the authorities, god knows who. I'll never get the full story. Something about partnering with people who raised money for some resort, then disappeared with the funds, leaving him holding the bag. Investors wanted their money back. Some of them were *the kind of people you should never borrow money from,* he said. *Until things simmer down it's probably best if I lay low.*

Well, what if I come there then? I asked him.

Silence. More waterfalls.

It's probably best if you stay put. For now.

But I just want to know you're okay.

I'm fine. But I heard the tremor in his voice. His heavy

breathing. I could picture how gray and worn he was, sitting at the telephone with his endless cigarette. Dogs barking in the background. Roosters cawing.

Is there a friend you can stay with there? he asked me.

Through the windshield, I watch all these people who aren't Ava walk by.

"I was here this summer too," I tell Jonah.

"You were? I wish I'd known. You didn't go visit family or anything?"

The word *family* never fails to make me feel like I've been punched. Conjures an iron gate, tall hedges around a house with lit-up windows, me so embarrassingly obviously outside looking in. Pretending I have people to see, somewhere to go.

"My dad's out of the country on business." I instantly regret my phrasing. Wince before he even asks.

"And your mom?"

And then she's right there in my mind. Cigarette smoking between her fingers. Dark hair aggressively chic. Calling my name from the living room. Encouraging me to join her instead of writing or playing whatever imaginary game I was playing in my room. *Earth to Samantha. Time to come down out of the clouds, please.*

"She's dead."

"Fuck. I'm sorry, Samantha."

"It's okay." It isn't. "It was a while ago."

"How did she die?"

Just running to the store, be right back. The way she said it—so light and quick and already out the door—the familiar roar of

Grace Slick as she started her car, the bright blue of the sky that day, I didn't imagine anything. I didn't imagine anything for once but that she'd be right back.

"Car accident."

"Jesus. How old were you?"

"Thirteen."

"My dad died when I was seventeen. Lung cancer, so we saw it coming. Still, it was rough."

"I'm sorry, Jonah."

"It fucked me up pretty good for a while. That's kind of when I started going off the rails. You know, with drugs and stuff. I mean, I was into them before but after that I kind of lost it, I guess. Like there was no ground anymore, you know?" He smiles at me, sadly.

"Listen, why don't you come over? I could make tea and we could listen to records. Maybe I even have a copy of that book you were looking for. You never told me the title."

"Book?" And then I remember Ava. Out there. Right now in the snow.

"I can't. I have to go. I should probably head out now, actually."

"Okay. Well, I hope you find your book, Samantha. Maybe it will find you. Sometimes, you know, that happens."

My phone buzzes in my lap.

Coming over tonight, Bunny?

And then: *We think we should have a talk.*

A talk. Inside me, something curls and uncurls its fists.

"Actually, Jonah, would you mind driving me somewhere else?"

19

By the time I arrive at Eleanor's, the snow is falling in slow, fat flakes. Fairy-tale flakes. Movie flakes. Perfect flakes falling on her perfect house, its towers, actual towers, shining white and pointy as teeth under a perfect moon. An inch of it on the ground, making her perfect lawn white and shimmery.

"Sweet place," Jonah said when we pulled up. Now, I watch him fishtail down the road and disappear. *They aren't nice actually*, I told Jonah. The knowledge courses through me and makes me braver. Words that came from my own lips. When I walk up to the door, I hold them close. Beyond the door I imagine, no, I *know*, they are whispering about me. That Eleanor has told them things. I don't know what things, but I imagine her leaning forward from her thronelike armchair, them huddled all around. Ready to swallow whatever vile lie or half-truth she feeds them about me like so much cheap candy. Practically panting with the desire to regurgitate little nuggets that validate her claims.

The other day, she didn't seem that into her cupcake. I bet she doesn't even like them.

I think she eats Pinkberry just to please us and it's like, don't do it just to please us, you know?

I'm pretty sure she blew You-Know-Who. That's why he was so into her work last fall.

Guys, you should see her apartment. She lives in a cell. Seriously. Like a cell. It's so dismal. It's so sad. Do we want sadness around us? We're suns, do we want clouds?

I ring the doorbell. I'm here to ask her something, that's all. *What did you say to Ava?*

Remember they hate you. Remember you hate them. I repeat these two things to myself, over and over, like a mantra.

It's then that I hear a faint sound behind me like a branch snapping. I turn, expecting to see a rabbit or a squirrel make a mad dash into the trees. What I see instead makes the hairs stand up on my skin.

A stag. Standing just a few feet away from me in her snowy front yard. Staring right at me, through me, with eyes like liquid smoke.

I stare at his large body gleaming under the moon, his horned shadow darkening the snow-covered lawn, his white-tipped antlers that could pierce me into oblivion. He's beautiful. So beautiful that for a second I forget who or where or why I am. I'm aware of nothing but the racing of my heart.

Probably he just wandered out of the woods behind her house. But his presence, so large and living and wild, turns her blandly picturesque yard, the absurdity of me standing in it, the Bunnies waiting inside, everything, into a dream.

He's looking at me. Really looking at me now.

"Hello, Samantha. Tell me everything," comes a voice from behind me.

Her front door has opened. Standing in it is Orphic French Welder Who Plays Guitar, one of their failed collage experiments from way before my time. He looks, as always, severely depressed. Probably because, like many of their creations, he doesn't know what he is. He is a product of their combined whims. Nothing more. His dark blue suit does not conceal how severely misshapen his body is. His black gloves conceal what look like small paws.

I'm surprised he isn't dead or locked in the basement or out in a field somewhere turning circles, which is often their fate. But sometimes they'll keep the docile, handsome ones and turn them into servants for a while until they tire of them. This one looks a little like a malformed Montgomery Clift.

"Samantha," he says now. "You know I will hunt for you, daughter of Woolf."

"Yes. I know."

Remember, remember the two things.

"Come in, Samantha. Come in."

When I turn back to look for the stag, he's gone.

I follow Orphic French Welder into the living room, where they're all seated in a little circle, flanked by her golden retrievers. They have been talking about me, that's obvious. Their cheeks are plump and pink and shining like they've been eating too much sugar, but actually it's Gossip Glow, the flushed look that comes from throwing another woman under the bus. The room smells of their grassy perfumes and their many organic conditioners. Little flutes before each of them full to the brim with something violet and fizzy. At the bottom of each glass, what looks like an eyeball floats. A lychee.

My heart starts pounding. Two things. Remember the two things.

"Samantha, we're so glad you came."

"Samantha, we've been talking." They side-eye each other.

"And we have something we want to tell you."

Suddenly all my resolve leaves me. *I have something too! I have something. Don't I?*

"What?"

They side-eye each other again.

They're going to tell me I have to go. They're going to expel me from the group. Call their Darlings out of the basement and the locked places and order them to escort me to the oak front door. They'll look at me with their vapid, glittery eyes and with their botched mouths they'll say, *Go*. The dumber ones will just point at the door. And I'll have no choice but to go back out into the Ava-less cold. Face my thin-walled room, sandwiched between the perverted giant and the sallow-faced girl. The desk I've been avoiding.

"What did you want to talk about?" I ask.

"Take a seat."

"Just because you're so tall," Creepy Doll says. "It'll make it less weird if you sit down."

They gesture toward a vacant pouf, extremely low to the ground.

I sit down. I face them. It feels like that first night, ages ago, when they asked me to get a bunny. Ultimatum, I think. They're going to give me an ultimatum. *You can't. You—*

The Duchess smiles at me. "Who wants to tell her?"

"You tell her, Bunny."

"You tell her."

"Should we all tell her?" She makes it sound like a treat.

"We should all tell her."

"Let's count it off, though?"

"Okay! One . . . two . . . three."

What comes out are shouted, indiscernible words, and then a wild eruption of laughter.

"You *guys* . . . let's try one more time, okay?"

"Okay!"

"One, two, three."

It happens again. They laugh and they laugh and they laugh and I sit on my pouf watching them. *Fucking leave. Just leave. Why can't you?* says a woman's voice in my ear. Slightly bullying. Losing patience. Slipping away. Ava's voice. My voice. The hate is bubbling up in my soul and yet I am pinned there by the terrible fear that they will cast me out for good.

The Duchess lays a quieting hand on Cupcake's knee, which creates a domino effect of hush upon them.

"Samantha," the Duchess says after a long pause, "we'd like you to lead Workshop tonight."

"We feel you're ready, Bunny."

"In fact, we can't *wait* to see what you're capable of."

"All that raw energy at work. That imagination." Small, shy smiles all around. Followed by blinky, twinkly-eyed concern at my face, which is doing something, it must be, that I'm not in control of.

"Bunny, what's wrong?"

"Bunny, are you crying?"

"Bunny, don't cry."

"I'm sorry, I just, I thought you were going to say something else, that's all."

"What did you expect us to say?"

"I don't know, I just—" The tears make them go all swimmy and watery. They become one blob of peach-colored flesh wearing a pastel rainbow dress. Her golden dogs stretch into gleaming pillars at their sides.

"Did you expect us to say we were going to throw you out? That we didn't want to be your friend anymore?" asks the blob in a concerned voice.

I look up at the blob. It laughs softly with all its mouths.

"Bunny, this isn't high school."

"This isn't even undergrad, Bunny."

"Or an eighties movie."

"Or even a nineties movie."

"We're all educated adults here."

Behind the blob, I notice another Darling lurking in the corner. He has a wooden spoon in one hand and a hammer in the other. Chefarpenter, because they couldn't decide if he should be a chef or a carpenter. I watch him begin to mix and hammer the air confusedly. He looks at me with his pained, voidlike eyes.

"Here, Bunny," the blob says. It hands me Pinkie Pie, the one they used as a stand-in for their desire—complex and nuanced—that first day at Mini.

I look into its absurdly huge plastic eyes, much too big for its horse face.

"I don't know what to say."

"That's the beauty of being friends with us, Bunny."

"There don't have to be words sometimes."

"You could text us a whale tomorrow afternoon and we'd be like, We know. We'd know exactly what it is you were feeling."

The blob nods its four heads vigorously. Then it rises from its many thrones. It comes toward me awkwardly, almost shyly. It hesitates for a moment. Then it lunges forward and puts all its arms around me. It mashes its many-boobed body into my face so I can't breathe anything but grass and cupcake perfume. Until I am drowning. Suffocated. Full of hate. A desperate desire to escape this saccharine embrace coursing through me. I tell myself I have to fight this—*remember you hate them, remember they hate you*—but all at once I fail. I succumb. I allow the sick need that no degree of revulsion can kill to be picked up out of the cold, wet dark and petted. I melt into it, their hug, allowing, nay, *willing* myself to be crushed. I become one with the blob. Or as close to one as I can become.

"Bunny," one of the mouths says, "get the bunny."

They caught it for me earlier that day, they said. When they remove the red cloth from the cage, I gasp.

"What do you think? Isn't it perfect?"

"We saw it and we were like oh my god, this is *so* Samantha's bunny."

"So cute, but also kind of scary?"

I gaze at the shaggy monstrosity before me. White as snow. Ears and muzzle black. A little black blotch over one red eye like it's wearing an eye patch.

I can't decide if it's beautiful or hideous or just fucking creepy. But they caught it for me. As I stare into its spotted face, I can't help but be touched.

"It's perfect," I repeat. "Thank you."

"We thought you'd think so."

They've lit the scented candles. An incense that seems muskier, spicier, more putrid than the vanilla sticks they usually burn.

"We asked Fern at the magic store what's a good incense to burn if you're more of a bitch."

"Like if you're a bitch in the best way imaginable?"

"Or if you're just a bitch."

"And he didn't even have to think about it, he was like, Oh, here."

No audiovisuals tonight, they tell me, because *surely you don't need those, Samantha. We'd hate to color what you bring to this on your own. We'd hate to get in your creative way.*

I don't know how long we've been sitting here, staring at this creature who has curled himself into a tight, unyielding little ball. His red eyes mock me. His stare mocks me. *Explode. Fucking explode, you little shit.* Caroline yawns discreetly. Victoria yawns openly. Kira looks at her watch and then at each of them and then back at her watch. Eleanor's just watching me.

"I'm sorry," I murmur. "I've never done this before."

"Don't be sorry, girl. It happens. I mean, it's never happened to me."

"Or me."

"Or me. But I'm always paranoid that it's going to?"

Have fun with it, use your intuition, let your imagination loose, they tell me.

"All that raw, angry energy."

"All that dark, complex stuff your stories are so full of."

"She gets the point. I'm borny as fuck over here."

They smile at me. So kindly. *We can't wait to see, Samantha. We can't wait to see what you're capable of.* And it's like someone with a camera is saying, *smile,* and when they say that, your mouth is suddenly frozen. You find you can't move your lips.

Time goes by, I don't know how much. No change. I tell them again *I am so sorry.* And they smile at me again in the most impenetrable way. Disappointment? Impatience? Pleasure?

"Maybe you're overthinking it, Samantha."

"Maybe you need to strip it down."

"Maybe some audiovisual inspiration after all?"

"Maybe just think of men you'd want to fuck," Victoria says. "How about that?"

Some singers and actors flash lamely through my head. I try to go deeper. Think of songs that would make me feel, as I lay in my bed listening, that I was ascending from the cheap sheets toward the ceiling. A wet spring night wafting in. Sweet with dripping green. Rob Valencia's long, lovely shadow passing me in the school hallway, trailing his scent of slaughter and smoke. The Lion stirring his tea. Telling me what, I don't even remember. Because behind him was a window where I could see a sky so wide and purple-yellow and lovely that he could see anytime. Dancing with Diego who never had a face. The smell of rained-on sage. Tendons flexing in a neck. The chiseled, tattooed arms of a fire-eater I saw once in Edinburgh. The way he looked me in the eye when he tipped the flame into his mouth. A one-eyed wolf I became fixated with for a while at the zoo I used to visit as a teenager. If he escaped everything would go horribly wrong but it would be beautiful too. And then I think of the stag I just saw outside. Its eyes like smoke. Probably long disappeared into the trees.

"Samantha?"

But the bunny just sits there. Confirming my worst fears. That I am not like them after all. That I can't do this, I could never do this.

"Maybe we should help her," Caroline offers. But she isn't looking at me, she's looking at Eleanor, who shakes her head slowly. Like *no, no. This is Samantha's catastrophe.*

It dawns on me that perhaps this isn't a gesture of kindness and trust at all, it's a test. Or worse, a way to humiliate me. To show me that they are the ones who have this gift, not me. *Not you, Samantha. Sorry. This ability comes with being us. We inherited it, like our summer houses, our grand pianos, our perfect, nuanced taste.*

"I don't think I can," I say. "I'm sorry."

I look up at them. Are they happy? Angry? Sorry for me? I can't tell. Their smiles twitch slightly. Little sighs of frustration escape them.

"You need to have more confidence, Bunny." I can tell by the way she says it that this is something they've discussed in a perfumed huddle. A cloud of bitchy whispers like tainted pixie dust.

Samantha has no confidence, it's so frustrating.

She doesn't believe in herself. It's like shut up.

I just want to shake her in the nicest way.

Or slap her face.

Or punch her, you know? And be like, I love you. You're amazing.

"You need to focus more."

"Clear your mind."

"Think about your *desire,* Samantha," the Duchess says suddenly, like she's cutting to the chase. "Just think about what you want."

What I want or what you want me to want? It's not that simple.

"It's really that simple, Bunny."

I stare and stare and stare into the red, beady eyes of the bunny. It just sits there, burrowed into itself like a furry little Fuck You.

You have no idea at all, do you? the bunny seems to say to me. *Sad. Very sad, Samantha. To be lost like this. Sad, sad, sad that when someone asks you,* What do you want? *nothing comes to mind but a pair of fists clutching little broken bits.*

I look up; they're all staring at me with their fairy eyes. Fucking with me. They have to be. And yet I feel those eyes all over my soul, plundering whatever pain and want they imagine lives there. That made them keep their distance all year last year. That somehow draws them in now. A pea to put under their twenty mattresses, which they can feel in the night, something from Down There, where they think, where I have somehow given the impression, I live. *Let it out, Bunny. Show us. Or make a fool of yourself trying while we watch.*

"Go on, Samantha."

I close my eyes and see Ava, wandering alone in the snow in scuffed heels. Ava and me dancing on her roof. Who were we dancing with really? Nothing. Each other. Air. My lonely nights. And that's when I realize that whatever pain I have, whatever true want I have that lives under all this greasy, spineless needing to please isn't something I want to give them.

The bunny looks at me. His ears twitch. Then he unfurls suddenly. He looks right at me. He looks right at me with his red rabbit eyes and runs right out of the circle.

Hops is, I guess, more accurate.

Don't be sorry, they tell me. *We know you are.*

"It happens. I mean, it's never happened *before,*" Cupcake says, looking at Creepy Doll.

"But it could happen," Creepy Doll offers. "I mean . . . I guess it could."

"It just did," Vignette says, looking at me like she wants to bludgeon me with her eyes.

They all look over at the Duchess, who says nothing because

her silence says it all. She sips her pale violet cocktail, made for her by Borges Julio Bolano VII. He's put an extra lychee in it, just like she likes.

"What were you thinking about, Samantha?"

"Nothing," I lie. "I just tried to think of what I wanted. Like you guys said."

They look at me. Liar.

"Did you visualize? Did you *focus*? Like we said?"

"Yes. I mean, I tried." I lower my eyes to the perfect floor, the dark cherry wood polished and unscuffed as far as the eye can see.

Vignette gets up. "I'm out," she says. "See y'all tomorrow in class."

We watch her go. Listen to her combat bootlets stomp away down the hall. Then she suddenly stops.

"Oh my god, you guys," she calls from the front door. "Come here."

There, in the shimmery snow, lit up by the moon, are animal prints. They start in the center of the lawn, directly below the window, and make their winding way down her glittering white lawn, circling once around a skinny tree before moving onto the sidewalk and then across the street to the bus shelter.

They're much too big for a bunny, I think, but then I follow Vignette's gaze to the bus shelter. The dark, hunched shape inside.

A boy-shaped shape.

A boy.

My heart starts to thump in my chest.

20

He stands in the far corner of the bus shelter beside a wall of shattered glass. Smoking a cigarette, headphones on. Doesn't look up even though five jacketless girls have just joined him in the shelter, standing in its drippy mouth, staring and staring.

"Well, Samantha?" Creepy Doll whispers, tugging on my sleeve.

The moon's gone behind a cloud, and I can't see his face. Just a wolfish slope to the profile. Dark, disheveled hair. Beaten-up black trench coat. He starts nodding along to the music in his headphones. Honestly, he just looks like a guy waiting for a bus.

"A bus weirdo," Cupcake whispers, staring at him intently.

"A *hot* bus weirdo," Vignette corrects. "Well done, Samantha."

"Look what he's wearing though. He's a Satanist."

"Or an art student? Or a vagrant, maybe," Creepy Doll whispers in her group hug voice.

"He didn't knock on the front door," Cupcake says softly. "They're supposed to *knock*."

"Well, but Samantha's bunny might be different," Creepy Doll says. "Like more . . . I don't know . . . of an asshole? Or something?"

They turn to me, waiting for some kind of pronouncement. *Is he or isn't he? Answer for him, please.* I look at him again. He's completely oblivious to us, or so it seems. His tall, broad frame like a Muir Woods tree. Cheekbones like knives. Something vaguely punk, vaguely murderous about his hair. He seems to be smiling to himself. Is he? Yes, smiling as though the music is telling him a secret. He begins to hum in a rich, low voice.

"I don't know," I say.

"You should say something to him. Just in case."

Even in the dark, he looks like he could absolutely cut our heads right off. His fuck-off vibe is emanating from him like heat.

"Like what?" I hiss.

"I don't know. It's s *your* bunny. Maybe."

"Guys, it's not like he can hear us, fuck," Vignette says in her normal tone of voice. "Watch. HEY, ARE YOU A BOY OR A BUNNY?"

"*Shhh.* Shut up!"

"Excuse me?" The man slides his headphones down to his neck. He's looking right at us now, his face still mostly shrouded in shadow. But I can make out a full, unscarred mouth. Smiling slightly. At something. Us? Maybe us.

I feel the Bunnies push me forward a little.

"Sorry to bother you," I tell the man, who is probably just a man. Maybe a murderer. Probably a decapitator. "We were just looking . . . we lost something."

"A bunny," Cupcake says. "Have you seen one by chance?"

"Hopping by?" Creepy Doll adds.

"Or a boy," Vignette says. The legs of her voice wide open. The others glare at her.

He stares at us, saying nothing. *Can we go before he kills us?* But they've pinned me in place on either side with their sharp shoulder bones.

"You know, a bunny," Creepy Doll continues. "Long ears? Hops around?"

"He *knows* what a bunny is, Bunny," Cupcake says.

"And what a boy is," Vignette says, the legs of her voice spreading even wider.

Oh my god, shut up, I think. *Just fucking shut up and let's leave.*

The man frowns, like he is thinking. His coat falls open to reveal a black T-shirt featuring a skull over a moon-splashed sea.

"A bunny . . . ," he says slowly, looking at me. Deep voice. Like the word tastes surprisingly good in his mouth. Needs salt. But not bad. "Yes. I definitely saw a bunny."

"You did?" Cupcake says eagerly.

Liar, I think.

The smoke coils out of his nostrils like twin snakes.

"Yup. Hopping right across the snow here. Long ears and everything. Went that way." He points down the street.

"Thank you!"

"Until it died tragically," he adds.

"What?"

The man half smiles with his unripped mouth. "Red wolf. Came out of nowhere. Tore the little guy's throat right out. Right before my eyes. So sad." Clearly a fake sad smile, but I can see they're swallowing it whole. He rests his gaze on me. Nothing blue or voidlike about his eyes. I start to feel the back of my neck get prickly and hot.

"Then he dragged him by the neck into those bushes back there."

We stare at the bushes. There are actually small animal prints in the snow. They gasp dramatically like little girls, their grips tightening around my arms like pythons.

"Bad scene," he says.

"How bad?" Vignette says.

He gazes at Vignette dreamily, contemplating her lovely skull face. "Gross," he says softly, making a face. "Like . . . ew."

All around me I feel them nod. *Ew. Yes. So ew.*

"I don't know if you've ever heard a bunny scream?" he says.

They shake their heads. No, they lie. *Never ever.*

"Terrible sound. But it was also sort of . . ." He trails off. I can feel their puppyish blood boiling under their soft-serve skins.

"Beautiful," he finishes, looking so soberly, so intently at them, at us, that I want to burst out laughing even though I'm afraid. Suddenly, I feel them all sigh around me in stereo.

"Beautiful," they repeat.

"I'm sure it was."

"Yes."

"So."

They stare at him with parted lips. Clutching each other's sleeves, and mine. Shifting their weight. Tossing their hair. Running their tongues over their teeth.

The man looks at me. "Yours?" he says.

"Mine?"

"The bunny."

"Oh. Yes."

"*Sort of*," Creepy Doll corrects.

"More like a collaborative effort, really," Cupcake says.

"It was ours," the Duchess says coldly. I realize this is the first time she's spoken. "It was *our* bunny."

"Nature's so cruel," he says. "The wild."

He reaches inside his black coat, and the girls gasp again. *Gun? Knife? Ax?* Cigarette. Lighter. A flash of his wolfish face in the flame. Hands, ungloved and totally human. No claws, no hooks, just flesh. Even though I already knew there was no way in hell, my heart sinks. Failure. I'm a failure.

I turn to go, expecting them to follow me. But they just stand there, watching him smoke in the shadows.

"I'm Caroline."

"Kira."

"Victoria."

"Eleanor."

He looks at me. Well?

"Samantha," I say.

"Samantha," he repeats. I can feel him smiling at me in the dark.

"Can we give you a lift somewhere?" Cupcake offers.

He turns and looks at Cupcake, her dress patterned with unicorns in midleap.

"Because I think it might be too late for a bus," she adds.

Just then, a bus comes around the bend. He straightens up to his full height, and he doesn't even have to say *Excuse me.* When he steps toward the mouth of the shelter, we instantly part like a bland sea. As he passes us, I catch a whiff of something animal and alive. Urgent and vital like blood. Then something like white sage.

"Where are you heading?" I ask him.

He smiles at me. "Home."

"Home," I repeat but it's in stereo. Do I have other mouths? No, we all repeated it.

"Where's home?" one of them asks. Eleanor.

But he puts his headphones back on. Suddenly, I feel the cold, snowy sludge around my toes. I start to shiver. Their grips around my arms go slack as I watch him disappear into the bus. And then I watch the bus disappear into the dark.

21

Last Workshop of the semester. I sit alone again, like before, on the opposite side of the hollow square, trying to bore a hole through the Cave wall with my eyes. I wish for a clock. A window for my brain to jump out of, leaving my body here, a lifeless flesh sack. I stare at Fosco as she speaks her inane words of congratulations on the end of a great semester. There's an unopened packet of cashews on the table. A bottle of mid-priced red wine. *To celebrate our little Circle,* she said. We girls have really *Tapped the Wound.*

I watch her terrier, whose sweater today is Yule themed, turn his yipping circles. *Failure. I'm a failure.*

"What's that, Samantha?"

"Nothing."

She returns to her speech and they keep nodding. *Yes, KareKare. The Wound. The Circle.* They do not look at me. I do not look at them. Last night seems as unspeakable as money or a fart.

Too bad, Samantha, they said to me afterward. *Sometimes you fail. Miserably. Hopelessly. It happens even to the best of us. Well, not to us, it's never happened to us. But it CAN happen. In theory. And that guy! I'm so surprised he didn't rape us. Repeatedly. Or kill us. Or do some sick thing in between? And oh my god, that story he told about the wolf? So weird. Obviously twisted. Probably we shouldn't have told him our names. He won't remember, will he? I mean, it's not like we're traceable or anything? Like he could track us down? Like on Facebook or anything? He's insane, remember? Murderous. Probably he doesn't even have Facebook. I was like a breath away from calling the police the whole time. Or campus safety. Or like, just screaming "rape." You're supposed to yell "fire," though. Because no one comes when you yell "rape," didn't you know that, Bunny?*

What a special group this has been, Fosco is saying now, and from the way she avoids my eyes I know she means them, not me. Warren's first all-female fiction cohort. And the talent so varied, so enormous. The collective energy so distinct. We really dug into the depths of ourselves. We really embraced the Experience. All of us, she says, and again I am not included in the faux magical-maternal embrace of her gaze.

"Ursula," the Duchess says, suddenly clasping the hands of Cupcake and Vignette, who flank her like girl Dobermans, "I think I can speak for all of us when I say that it's been such a privilege to work with *you*. It has really reshaped the way we approach the Work. We've all learned so much."

I watch as they hand her a ficus with a big red bow on the pot, which I did not know they were going to buy her, which I was not asked to chip in for. There's a card too, with a bunny in a Santa hat on it that they've all signed but me. "Oh. When did you arrange this?" I ask.

But my question is drowned in the collective cooing that erupts. Fosco clasps her hand to her smocked chest, as though deeply touched. The Bunnies feign being touched at her feigning being touched. Or *are* they all truly touched? I don't know anymore.

"Oh, my," she says. "You really didn't have to. And on your stipends too."

They're rich for fuck's sake, I want to scream. But I just sit there. My smile is fixed on my face, nailed there, though it jerks under the pins.

"We *wanted* to," the Duchess says.

Fosco is so moved, her silk scarf ripples with the force of her feigned emotion. She repeats that she hopes we enjoy this break. Because the next semester, our final semester before we graduate, will fly by, just as this one did. She hopes we have a firm grasp on our thesis because alas, the collective journey ends here. Next semester we'll be Tapping the Wound all on our own. They all nod knowingly, humbly, dutifully, except for me. This room should have a fucking clock. It's too disorienting. Not to know the time. "Does anyone have the time?" I ask.

They all turn to look at me, acknowledging my presence for the first time. In shock.

"Is there somewhere else you need to *be*, Samantha?" Fosco asks.

"No. I just. Like to know the time, that's all."

"I see." She looks at me like perhaps I should examine that desire. Unpack it. Take it to lunch. Divine it via a tarot card, a rune stone, the mulch of a bitter herb I've chewed and then spit up.

"Well, I personally love not knowing," Vignette says.

"Me too. So much," agrees Creepy Doll.

"So refreshing to enter a space where you can leave the real world behind," adds Eleanor.

"Oh my god, I was *just* going to say that," says Cupcake.

"I find it disorienting," I say.

Silence. A cough. Then, from Fosco, in a voice like she is diffusing an intricate potion, "Disorientation can be a very interesting space to occupy as a writer, Samantha. You should try it as an exercise over the holidays. It could be quite illuminating for you, I think."

Then she turns back to the group. "Write during the break, ladies. But remember to take it easy too. You deserve it. You've worked so very hard. Now have some wine, why don't you?"

They help her pour it into little clear plastic cups, but Fosco and I are the only ones who drink. I am hoping it will warm me—I am somehow still so cold from the night before—but it tastes rancid, cold, thick as blood. I'm about to get up, leave the classroom—class is dismissed, isn't it?—when the Duchess speaks.

"I wonder if we could do a short writing exercise to celebrate our last day," she says. I suddenly grow hot. *No. No, Fosco. Please.*

But Fosco is already frothing at the mouth with pleasure. Such commitment! So keen we are to make every moment of Workshop generative.

"Eleanor. What a marvelous idea. I'm afraid I didn't plan on an exercise but—"

"Oh, well. Too bad," I jump in, about to grab my coat, but then I realize I never took it off.

"Well, *I* actually have an idea for what we could do, if I may." This from Creepy Doll.

I turn to Fosco, hoping she'll interpret this as mutiny, an attempt to one up or dethrone her, but instead she is all charitable ears.

"Tell us, Kira."

"Well, I've been thinking a lot lately about . . . home."

When she says it, the cold evaporates and I suddenly grow flush. I am melting-freezing in the middle of a road of ice slush watching a bus disappear into the dark.

"Since I mean . . . we're all going *home,*" she says. "And since the holidays are really about *home* . . . I wonder if we should spend a few minutes writing about what *home* might *mean.* To each of us. What might *home* mean to Samantha, for example."

"What," I say, but it isn't a question.

"Like, is it a literal place? With an address?"

"Or is it something more . . . elusive?"

"What images does it generate?"

My face and neck burn. Mocking me. They're mocking me.

"For all of us," the Duchess adds magnanimously.

"For each of us," Vignette adds.

Fosco nods gravely. "Interesting," she says, though this exercise is beneath the creative capacities of a twelve-year-old. "Why don't we take a few minutes to meditate on this subject?"

In the course of those minutes, I drink more of the red wine. The burning increases. I am burning now not only up my neck and ears, but all down my body. In my mind, I remove one sweater after another. I watch them all scribble in their notebooks.

Once the minutes are up, I am not at all surprised to hear them say, *I think we should share our work. I think we should read it aloud. Agreed. All of us.*

The last work we'll share as a cohort, as a Circle.

Fosco thinks it's a splendid idea.

I listen to overwritten descriptions of staring deeply into a bonfire on a Costa Rican shore. Of getting pretend-lost in a labyrinthine garden with oh so many nooks and twists. Of being existential in LA, New York, but really, obviously, being rich. And content. And unalone.

"Samantha, your turn."

"Yes, Samantha, I wonder what home means to you."

I look down at my notebook, where I have written *I'll never tell you* a thousand times.

"Samantha?" Fosco prompts.

"I'd prefer not to share mine."

"I'm sorry? What was that?"

"I'D PREFER NOT TO SHARE MINE." My shout bounces off the walls of the Cave. Echoing and echoing.

They gape at me in affected horror. Then smile helplessly at Fosco—*you see?* She looks at me like, indeed, yes, she sees all. *Oh, dear, Samantha. We have quite the long journey ahead of us, don't we?* Her reindeer dog stops yipping. Lifts his floppy ears and looks at me with a cocked head. Almost pityingly.

*

After Workshop, a mandatory end of semester *cookie party*! in the lounge area. Their idea. *Because wouldn't it be so fun? SO fun.* Everyone is in attendance, of course. All the faculty. All the administration. Even the poets have been lured in by the free food.

I hover at the corners, watching everyone crowd around a long table of the Bunnies' baked wares, growing flushed and giddy as they shovel seasonally themed confection into their mouths. Misshapen snowmen made of marshmallows regard me cruelly with their candy eyes. Lemon surprises that surely will not surprise. Spiked rainbow sherbet punch hissing and spitting in the center of them all like a nefarious cauldron. The Bunnies cackling all around it like the witches they really are, I see it so clearly now. Soon they'll start hugging, I realize. And I don't want to be around for that, I—

"Leaving already, Samantha?" asks Benjamin, the department administrator, as I move past him toward the door. Benjamin used to be my friend sort of. At least he'd let me sit and talk to him in his office after receptions and we would eat whatever lesser cheese the faculty left behind. But ever since the barbecue incident, he's been colder with me. It was Benjamin's barbecue. He kindly threw it for all of us Narrative Arts students at the end of our first year. I was supposed to go and I ditched it at the last minute. Because on the day of the barbecue, the Bunnies started an email thread. It was Cupcake, she heard Benjamin say he had a Jacuzzi, should she bring a swimsuit?

You should go naked, Bunny! :D

Ooooh what if we ALL went naked, Bunny? Would Benjamin be pissed??

No way, Benjamin is SUCH a unicorn person! :D

THEN LET'S ALL GO NAKED YAY also what snacks should we bring??? :D

Umm, all the cookie butter please?! ;)

OMG Bunny you are so fucking BRILLIANT also mini chocolate covered peanut butter cups?!?!

SO MUCH YES also pumpkin spice something?!?!?!?!?!?!?

OH MY GOD, PUMPKIN SPICE EVERYTHING!!!!!!!!!!!!!!!!!!!!!!!!!

I watched it grow and grow—their all-caps sentences, their millions of exclamations points, their plague of winks and smileys—like a malevolent vine strangling me. I began to sweat and my heart began to pound and I simply could not rise from my chair. I watched the minutes click by in the top corner of my computer screen. Late. Very late now. I watched the sun sink. And I never explained my absence except to email Benjamin the next morning. *So sorry, was not feeling well.* I imagine that afternoon they won him over with story after story of my surliness, my unexplained aloofness, and now he had firsthand proof. Now he is on their side. Now he thinks I am an Owie.

I have always wanted to explain to Benjamin about that day. How I wanted to go to his party. How the email thread thwarted me. But I have a feeling he'd just blink. *What?*

So I tell him, "Yes, I have a plane to catch now."

"That's too bad." He looks genuinely sorry.

"Well, if you won't stay, at least take some home with you," he says, handing me a cellophane bag of their baking atrocities.

"I believe Eleanor made those," he says, seeing me eye the gingerbread men. "Aren't they just adorable?"

I stare at the gingerbread man's leering face. His warped limbs. His icing eyes capable of anything. "Very."

I take the cookie bag, because to say *No, thank you,* to explain, requires words and my throat is still burning. I walk away from Benjamin like I have somewhere to be. Like I'm late. I make my way out the front door with my head down and nearly collide with a wall of flesh.

I look up.

The Lion.

"Samantha, I wondered if we could have a word in my office?"

22

Shut the door, please." He sits behind his desk, rearranging his papers, not looking at me. "Have a seat."

I take the seat opposite him. Still in my coat. Clutching my cellophane bag of cookies. Swaying slightly from the wine.

He looks taller, trimmer. His mane glows in the office light. More tattoos of trees climb his forearms. More crows peering from their inky branches, watching me with white eyes.

"Samantha, we need to talk."

He looks at me, then at the cookie bag in my fist. I haven't been in his office since those awkward monthly meetings last winter, so formal and stilted compared to the off-campus ones we had in fall. Languorous Moroccan teas at the Middle Eastern place. Lunch in the basement pub, sometimes dinner. A drink. Two drinks. Three drinks, why not? And then—

He raped you? Drugged you? Tied you to a chair?

No.

Asked you to suck him off?

No.

Showed you his cock, surely?

No.

Please don't tell me he put a hand on your knee or I'll scream.

He said he liked my tights. And my bangs. He complimented my perfume once. He asked me if it had an amber base note.

And?

I said it didn't. And then I said maybe it did, I didn't know.

And?

"What was that, Samantha?"

"Nothing," I mumble now.

"So. How's your semester been?" he asks me.

"Good." I nod. "Really wonderful."

He raises an eyebrow. I shared my Fosco nickname with him one drunk night and he laughed so hard he nearly projectiled his wine into my face. "You enjoyed Ursula's Workshop, then?"

"Yes. Very much."

He nods. Another lie.

"How's your writing going, Samantha?"

"Pretty well."

"I'm concerned that you haven't checked in with me this semester. Have you been working on your thesis?"

I think of my notebook full of eyes and swirls and fragments.

"Of course."

"Ursula says she hasn't really seen anything from it this semester."

I feel myself get hot. "I've sort of changed directions."

"I see."

Silence. I lower my eyes to his desk. Dizzy. I'm getting dizzy.

"Well, can you send me some of this . . . new direction?"

"It's in the drafting phase still," I say to his desk.

"The drafting phase," he repeats.

I glance up at him, expecting to meet anger, disappointment, concern. Instead, no expression. His face is literal negative space.

"Look, Samantha, I never thought I'd say this but I'm actually beginning to worry about you."

"Worry about me?"

"About you graduating."

"Oh."

"You've really only got a few months left here. I know it may seem like a lot of time now, but it actually moves very quickly."

I gaze at his black band T-shirt—an industrial German one we both like. The graphic features a large-busted woman getting strangled by a horned monster. The woman looks, of course, as if she is in ecstasy. They always do.

"Samantha, is there something you want to tell me?"

Yes. I don't understand what's happened between us. Why don't we talk anymore? Why are you so cold with me now? Like I'm a stranger to you suddenly. Like I'm an embarrassment. Like you're ashamed. Is it because of that weird night we pretend never happened?

"No."

"Because if you want to talk to me about something, I'm here."

Liar. "Okay. Thank you."

He sighs. "You know, Samantha. I brought you here. To Warren. Because I liked your work. I liked you."

Past tense. I nod.

"Such imagination. Such inventiveness. Such a great voice." He looks at the space on his desk where the plastic wolverine figurine used to be, which I stole from his office last winter and which he knows I stole. Slipped it in my pocket when he stepped outside to photocopy some form. When I told the story to Ava, she was so proud of me I gave it to her.

"Look, Samantha, if I don't get some writing from you by the end of the winter break, we're going to have to have a serious talk. Do you understand?"

I wait for his icy face to crack, for his voice to melt, resume the friendly contours of the person I knew last fall, for him to tell me something softly, something kind. Nothing. Just doing his job. Checking in. What more could I possibly expect?

"I understand."

Satisfied, he begins to pack up.

"So. Going home for the holidays?" He glances up at me, waiting. He knows, of course, about my father hiding out, my mother being dead. We both know I'm not going anywhere.

"Yes. I have a plane to catch, actually."

He gives me a slight smile. "Have a good trip."

23

Back at my apartment, I fall into bed, flushed but shivering. I thought I might find Ava waiting outside my apartment door. But of course, the hallway was empty of all but the salt-stained monster Crocs of the perverted giant. A swamp of Walmart bags surrounding his half-open door—the yellow-face logos smiling daggers at me.

I recall passing the Bunnies just now in the hall, glutted with Christmas cookies and their own Bunny love, which is probably only stronger now that they have witnessed my failure. Glowing with the happy knowledge that they all have places to go. *Samantha, I wonder what home means to you?*

As I lie here, suddenly so tired, I imagine them leaving. Hopping back to the various states they came from. Purses of the softest leather slung over their camel-coated shoulders. Sleek little suitcases being wheeled in the snow by kid-gloved hands. Blowing air kisses to each other as they slip into airport-bound taxis. Cashmere scarves getting tangled as they faux-hug good-bye. *Good-bye, Bunny. Wait. No. Not good-bye! Let's taxi pool to the airport! Should we? Can we, please? Because I just can't bear to be away from you, Bunny! Because I'm not ready to say good-bye to you yet! I'm going to miss you so, so much! Text me every day, okay? I'll text you too.*

They will not text me. I have proven I am not one of them, that I am capable only of making bunnies hop away.

Fuck them, Ava would say.

It makes me smile for a second. Until I realize Ava isn't going to text me either.

I turn off my phone, close my eyes.

When I wake up, the sky is dark and blowing snow. I am burning, I am freezing. My limbs are stiff. My throat is a red, pulsing fist in my neck. Chills all through my body. Water. I need water but the sink's far away. I can't bring myself to rise from my bed, which feels like it's breathing beneath me. I feel it rise and fall as though we're adrift. I reach for my phone. No texts, no missed calls. What did I expect?

Outside, the snow's falling sideways.

Everyone's long gone now, they must be. The Bunnies. Jonah probably. Even the Lion is probably on a plane back to whatever craggy, mist-covered isle he comes from. And Ava? Definitely gone. Maybe gone farther than the Lion by now. And I let her go, let her leave, just sat there in a kitten dress, watching her say, *I'm leaving*. Gave her no words to come back by, no words to come back for. Just sat there with my mouth open, all my words still inside.

I feel the fist in my throat tighten. Burning, pounding head. Singing chills, skipping heart. Which I deserve.

Absolutely.

*

Nights pass into days pass into nights.

Every time I open my eyes, it is darker outside, colder. The city earns all the names I came up with for it, and as I lie shivering in bed, I come up with more. RancidAquariumLand. Jailville. BlackSkyGrayEarth. ZombieCity. Outside is actual hell and the internet confirms this. I watch weathermen making apocalyptic gestures at maps. Behind them, footage of blowing snow, icy unplowed roads. News of violence escalates. My in-box floods, as it did last summer, with alarming crime-alert messages from campus security. Shooting in the early evening. Sodomy in the morning. Decapitation at 3:30 in the afternoon. I wonder when is a nonbeheading time to go out and buy ginger ale.

I close my eyes. I dream of cold medicine. Dark green as forests. Chilled to mind-nullifying perfection in my fridge that is not empty, it's full of beautiful, bubbling things like the amberest ginger ale. Right there on the shelf, not at all a mirage. I dream of water that comes from mountains, from pure, cold-sweet streams. Poured into a tall clear glass like a vase. A magical hand bringing it to me. Setting the glass on the floor here by my head. A water-chilled palm laid softly on my face. I close my eyes the better to feel its cool, tender touch. Whose hand? Whose touch? Ava's? *You don't deserve that hand, Bunny, we've been over this.* Father? *Father has his own problems. Father is farther away than the sink.* Mother? *Never again but don't go down that road.* Jonah? *Can't drag poor Jonah into this, don't deserve that hand either.* One of the Bunnies? Maybe before but not anymore. *Forget about whether you like them or hate them. Ship's sailed either way, Bunny. Thanks to your embarrassingly unmagical mind that can't even make one fucking bunny boy, that can only make a bunny hop away. So. No Bunny hands for you, Bunny. Sorry-not-sorry.* The Lion? *God, no.*

No hands left.

Better just lie here. Alone on the breathing bed. In this room that is too hot then too cold then too hot, depends entirely on the whims of the radiator god. Chills singing through my body now like an aria. Listen to the opera girl in the apartment above sing along even though I know she is long gone for the holidays. Promise myself not to look at the Bunnies' holiday photos on the various social media. Stare at pics upon pics of them donning chunky sweaters of a wool so soft I can see the lamb being shaved. Slouched in the depths of couches like velvety seas beside blazing fireplaces, tastefully decorated trees, the similarly attired people who spawned them in the background. Posing in aerodynamic snowsuits at the foot of absurdly majestic mountains, wielding glinty pink poles.

And then their captions:

Mulled wine and Mariah Carey's Christmas yes please ☺
#amwriting
oops i just ate a fuckton of spice cookies sorry-not-sorry ☺
#amwriting
WHEN YOU ARE SO EXCITED FOR SANTA YOU ALMOST PEE ☺
#amwriting
Elf porn's hot
#realtalk #amwriting

Each post followed by mile-long threads of comments, *OMG, Bunny you are SO CRAY! OMG I miss you!!! Come here! You come here, Bunny! No you fucking come here, please!*

Kill me now, Ava would say. She would feel no shameful tugs of longing to wear their camel coats (*boring*). To don their fur-lined gloves, their knitted hats (*I'd rather be fucking cold*). No awful itch in her mesh fingers to steal their soft purses. To slip into their creamy skins and live there. To lie in their just-right princess beds with the clean white cloud sheets and dream their bland dreams. To be welcomed through their pillar-flanked doors by their Wonder Bread mothers and fathers. Who are alive. Who are not in debt. Who are not hiding in the mountains of Mexico among the emaciated dogs and the sunbaked dust. Who are not wanted for fraud or corruption.

What's home to you, Samantha? I wonder what's home to you.

Ava. Ava's home. I need to get there. I get out of bed even though I'm shivering and when I step outside, the air is so cold it takes my breath away. But I can't remember the way to her house. All the twists and turns she would take, there were so fucking many. Cutting through gardens. Cutting through alleys. Did we cross a river? I cross three just in case. Brave all the streets I am normally too scared to walk down alone. Cars roar past, sometimes slowing down ominously. I ignore them. I keep going the way I used to when I would follow her back to her place in the dark. *Just follow me.* Keeping my head down, scurrying like prey from some unknown but imminent beast, what shape it will take I have no idea.

Why the hell are you walking so fast? Ava would ask me.

I don't know. I just feel like it, I guess.

Even though I couldn't see her face, I could feel her smiling in the dark.

Okay, Bunny, she'd say. Then she would start to walk slowly just to piss me off. Stop to look at a tree or the moon. *What a moon. Don't you think?*

I wander for what feels like hours, days, weeks. My eyes hunting the blurred, shifty streets for any sight of her familiar house. For the flowers dying outside it. For the raccoons on the roof. Shouldn't I know where it is? Didn't I live there? Maybe she took it all with her when she left. Packed it in her snakeskin suitcase along with her holey fishnets and her lucky magpie feather and her lady-shaped flask with the missing eye. So I'd never find it again. She was that disappointed in me. I picture her folding up the walls of her house like a sweater. All folded up and carried away.

I roam past the city, to the ocean. She isn't in the ocean. Or the sky. Or in this dumpster. Or behind this tree.

I skulk back to my apartment, which I have no trouble finding, despite how far I roamed and how much the city spins and tilts. I sit at my desk chair telling myself I will write, I must write, now is the time to write. Instead I stare through the window at the bricks. I see a crew-cutted old man through the window of an apartment across the way, also sitting at his desk chair. He sits very, very still. Hours pass, and he does not rise from this chair or even move. Perhaps he is dead.

I crawl back into bed, defeated. Stare at my phone. A home-screen pic of five fuzzy Bunnies in a snuggly heap. It used to be a picture of me and Ava on her roof, cheek to cheek, unsmiling but soul happy. When did I change it? I can't even remember is the saddest thing.

I text her *where are you?* Then erase it.

did you really leave? Erase. *im so sorry for everything i have not bin in my right*—Erase.

I know i havent been the best Erase.

i have been the shittiest Erase.

Erase erase erase erase.

Leave it be. Leave her be. You don't deserve her.

When I open my eyes, she's here. Standing in the middle of my stupid room that she is too tall for. Bearing a basket of cold, bright cherries, where did she get them? A peach ginger smoothie from the yuppy juice bar.

"I'm sorry I kept deserting you," I tell her. "I don't know what came over me."

Shhh, she says. She puts her cold hand on my freezing-burning forehead and though her hand is terribly cold, it feels wonderful. It is exactly the hand I have dreamed of, the hand I have longed for.

"I thought you were leaving," I tell her.

Then she's air.

She becomes air and I scream.

I wake up drenched in sweat. Nothing here but the stale empty air, the weak white light coming into my bedroom, the maniacal laughter of the perverted giant in the next room.

24

Christmas Eve morning. Fever finally broken. I'm shopping at Cheapo's, a store where the despair is auditory in the afterlife Muzak. Old people creaking through the grim endless aisles of canned crap, produce pyramids gleaming eerily under too-bright lights. The bananas here will never be edible—they will remain green before immediately turning black. Even the apples looked shined up in a way I do not trust, like overly rouged circus animals being trotted out into the ring. My cart is half full of the ramen I will have tonight and then tomorrow.

God this is depressing, Ava says. *And boring. Aren't you bored?*

It's what I can afford, I tell her. Because even if she's not here, I might as well talk to her all the same.

Afford? Come on, Smackie. Spare me the violins, please.

I'm not like you, okay? I can't be fucking interesting in every fucking aspect of my life. I can't make something out of nothing.

But in my head, she only finds this amusing. Looks at me with a wry smile that is both pleased at my outburst but also pitying.

Fine, I'll go to the expensive store, okay? I'll go to Forestier's. Is that what you want?

Only if you steal something wonderful for yourself.

*

At Forestier's, the air smells richly of slaughtered pines and roasted fowl. I am greeted by an abundance of summer flowers when I walk in the door, though it is winter. *Well?* I say to Ava. *Happy now?* But she's deserted me. And why would she be happy? She hates this place more than Cheapo's, I remember. So why am I here again? I look at the forests of kale, the organic raspberries, the designer apples and pomegranates, the exotic trail mix selections in never-ending bulk, the aisles upon aisles of cold-pressed juice in every color of the rich-girl rainbow. *Yes, why?* it is all saying to me. Suddenly I am the weird, sad circus vegetable. And it's the absurdly priced organic produce that is staring at me with something like horror.

I wander through the aisles for I don't know how long. Maybe hours. Staring longingly at everything. Expensive cocoa. Fancy pasta sauce. A package of dried chanterelles. Pomegranate seeds. Not putting anything in my basket. Getting lost. Where is just fucking bread anyway? I have to get out of here. I have to buy something first. I go to grab something like ramen, and I hear pop music suddenly come on loud. A voice singing softly along behind. *Roam if you want to.*

I look up. He's standing by the fancy mushrooms. Same weathered black trench coat. Same dark disheveled hair framing a sharp, wolfish face. Wild eyes that seem to smile. At me. The man from the bus.

There's a chewed-off baguette sticking out of his pocket

and a package of chanterelles in his all too human fist. Seeing me, he stops in midswipe. He waves. *Hi.*

I wave. *Hi.*

Then he continues to blatantly steal, while whistling the B-52s. Fancy pasta sauce. Cocoa, extra dark, extra pressed. A box of marrons glacés—the ones my father bought us when we spent a Christmas in France. *Aren't they heaven?*

I watch him shove it all into the dark bowels of his coat, wink at me, and turn away. I follow him, though he's walking quickly now, weaving his whistling way through the aisles. Stealing his way through the pickled fish. Scottish smoked salmon, don't mind if I do. A selection of the finest goat cheeses, please. Circling the olive bar like a vulture. He gets the bright green ones only. *These are the only ones worth eating, Samantha,* my father told me. *French. Lemony. Subtle.*

"Well, hello, Samantha."

Fosco. In her drapey Decembral velvets. Her operatic head tilted to one side. Leaning against the glass case full of artfully arranged meat as though the world of it is hers to plunder.

"Ursula. Hello. Sorry, I was—"

"I thought I saw you wandering around here," she says, smiling. "Looking lost."

"No, I—yes, well, this store is a bit . . ." I scan the aisle but he's gone, I've lost him.

"Disorienting?" she fills in. She gives me a sad smile that is the full-grown version of what the Duchess merely aspires to with her bitchy lip curl. "I suppose it can be. So. Still in town?" Concern furrowing her brows.

"Yes."

"I didn't know you had family here. . . ."

"I don't."

Silence after this admission. A nod of the head. Ah yes, the one with the troubles. Disgraced father. Dead mother. Something like that. So sad. I feel her sizing me up with a gaze that I know she believes pierces right through to the throbbing core of things. She takes in the empty shopping basket. My worn coat. The tears in the pockets.

"So what are your plans for the holidays?"

Think of a lie, think of a lie. Lie lie lie.

"I—"

But she's looking at me as if she already knows. Can see me twirling ramen with a warped fork in front of illegally downloaded television that keeps freezing due to a bad connection. Watering a sad rosemary bush I've strung with Christmas lights.

"I hope you're not planning on spending it *alone*? Are you?"

The way she says *alone* makes it sound like a cave. Like some hideous, dark cave whose oozing walls are teeming with all the unpleasant things of this world, and I am crawling willingly, brazenly, into this awful space of my own free will. Shoveling the vermin I find scuttling across the floor into my mouth for sustenance.

I tell her, no, of course not. Not *alone*. But her smile says how easily she has punctured my sad girl lie.

And then I see him again. Behind her now. Standing by the tower of gleaming pomegranates. He locks eyes with me over Fosco's shoulder, just as he is tucking a pomegranate into the inner pocket of his long black coat. Smiles at me. Waves again, wiggling his fingers.

"Samantha, you must come over. David and I are having a little Yuletide feast."

Over her shoulder, I watch as he puts more pomegranates in his pocket. Two. Three. How is he fitting them in there?

Shhh, he gestures, index finger pressed against his lips. Then he starts stealing from the bulk. Shoveling crystalized ginger and dried mango and omega-3 chocolate cherry trail mix into his pockets by the fistfuls. Eyes on me the whole time. I smile in spite of myself.

"Samantha," she takes me by the shoulders and stands directly in front of me, obscuring my view of him, "is that a yes?"

I tell her thank you so much but really I couldn't possibly, I couldn't impose. But she won't take no for an answer, absolutely not, Samantha. Because it would be her pleasure, don't I see that? Her finger pads are pressing themselves into my shoulder flesh. She's completely eclipsed my view of him. An itch in my fingers to move her. To seize her by her own shoulders and physically shove her out of the way.

"Really and truly our pleasure," she is saying. "And you won't be alone. Some other students who are still in town will be there too." And then she leans in and says in a pointed whisper, "You're not the only one in this boat, Samantha."

All over her face is *Aren't you grateful I ran into you like this? Gratitude, please. Gratitude?* She isn't going to release me from her grip until I say yes.

"Thank you, Ursula. That's a very kind offer. I'm grateful."

"So you'll be there?"

"I'll be there."

"Wonderful." She releases me at last, but it's too late. The produce aisle is empty of all but the usual thin people in black sportswear, dumping beautiful things into their brimming-over carts without a second look.

25

World music swelling from unseen speakers. Celtic fused with Zimbabwean, or so she informs me when I inquire for the sole purpose of making conversation. It's lovely, I say, and my lie echoes uncomfortably in her enormous living room. Larger than Cupcake's or Creepy Doll's, larger than even the Duchess's. African masks scowl at me from her very white walls. The odd painting of a clitoris posing as a flower or a flame in the manner of O'Keeffe but probably her own masterpieces.

If Ava were here, she would say *Run. Break a window if you have to.*

Or she would just look at me and the look would say all the thoughts of my whole soul back to me and I would feel comforted. I would be able to bear the pipes and steel drums with a smile.

She might even to say to Fosco, *What a compelling music choice,* with an absolutely straight face.

"Thank you, Samantha. I *did* think it would be more compelling than just your usual carols," she confides.

"So much more compelling," I agree and then I think: *I said that out loud?* I am drinking the wine she handed me at the door too fast, way too fast. *Slow the fuck down, Samantha.*

“I’ve always wanted to go to Zimbabwe,” I hear myself saying now. What is wrong with me?

“Have you, Samantha?” Fosco says, with something like newfound respect.

I nod. “Oh yes. So . . . ,” but I can’t finish my sentence. All possible adjectives with which I could describe this country about which I know little leave me. “Vast,” I say at last.

She shows me into the living room where “several students” turns out to be just Jonah, sitting on the center of her white suede couch in his half-zipped parka. I’ve never been so relieved to see him. There’s also a gaunt teenage girl in a black ball gown—*my daughter, Persephone, have you met?*—sitting with her legs thrown over the armrest of a lounge chair, frowning at a phone covered in manga stickers. Her face says that the poor graduate students her mother has insisted on sheltering like so many lame chicks have murdered her Yule.

“Hey, Samantha,” Jonah says when he sees me. “I didn’t know you were here for the holidays.” He holds a napkin with a skewered shrimp on it in the palm of one hand and waves happily at me with the other.

Why can’t you be happy? Why do you always assume the worst about every situation? my mother is asking me in my head, as she often used to. But I am happy to see Jonah. From his shaggy hair to his parka to his smell of cigarettes so comforting and potent that for a second I want to smoke him.

“Hey Jonah, I didn’t know you were here either.”

“Serendipitous,” Fosco offers, smiling.

Now I’m sitting on her couch, staring at jars upon jars of

vagina-pink roses arranged to look like balls. *Because I must have my roses around me always,* I imagine her saying to the florist, her peers, her students, but then I feel guilty for this thought. *She invited you, you ungrateful cunt. This is her Yule after all. She didn't have to have you over for canapés and catered Indian.* I smile at her and her husband, Silky, who has just joined us. He is a lanky man with Eraserhead hair who has garnered a million grants and residencies in crumbling castles and villas all over Europe, to write cryptic little poems in a language he calls *Tree.*

The poets, of course, worship him. I haven't had much to do with him apart from small talk once or twice at receptions. *Hello, Sasha. And how are you coming along, Sarah?* I never correct him.

They sit on the other side of the coffee table laden with the flower balls and several canapé trays that they keep holding out, offering, *canapé? Canapé? Have you tried a canapé, Samantha?*

"Yes. it was wonderful, thank you." Wonderful? Really?

"Have another?"

"I'm good for now, thanks."

I take another large sip of wine under the naked glare of Persephone.

"I'll take a couple," Jonah says.

"Take two, by all means, Jonah. Take three, before the other students arrive and they're all gone!"

Nod from Silky. Scoff from Persephone. The audible rearrangement of her limbs meant to signal her profound irritation. Jonah is oblivious.

"Thanks. They're pretty awesome. I could probably eat a hundred of them, I guess."

"I'm so glad."

We all watch him chew contentedly. Then swallow. Then chew again. If we could watch him digest, we would. She keeps repeating that she is so glad we came. That we're all here. Together. Quite a few more students should be joining us too, any minute now. No one joins us. Instead, Persephone leaves with the muttered promise that she'll be back down later for dinner. I look out the window at the storybook street. The Duchess lives across the way, with her golden-haired dogs. None of the other Bunnies can afford to live here, though the street is called Friendship. *That's because this is a street full of assholes,* Ava would say whenever we passed the sign. I was hoping she'd call me today. But when the phone rang it was my father. At first, I let it ring and ring. Braced myself for the sound of his faraway, broken-up voice, for what we might talk about. Other, happier Christmases. The weather here versus the weather there. The appalling price of everything. Not my mother, never my mother. If he was drunk, he might describe to me his Black Sea spa that never was or will be. The splendor of the saltwater baths. The healing caves of steam. The suites themselves like actual dreams, *you would think you were dreaming, Samantha. And yet it would feel like home,* he'd add. Very important for a place to feel that way.

Instead, when I picked up the phone at last, he told me how I used to be afraid of wind in the grass when I was three. *I took you to a park and you were playing just fine, just fine, and then a wind came and made the grass ripple a little, you know? And when you saw that, you screamed like hell and ran. Just bolted right out of the park, crying the whole way. It scared the shit out of me, Sam, I'll be honest. Seeing you run and scream like that at grass?*

I didn't say anything. Just listened to the static. The sound of him breathing. He'd told me this story many times before. He always ended it the same way.

I was worried for a bit, I'll admit it now. About you. We both were. But you turned out okay. In the end? Didn't you?

Meanwhile Jonah is telling them "I mean, if I didn't end up coming to Warren, I'd probably be passed out in the snow somewhere on schnapps or horse tranquilizers right now. Probably both." He smiles at our hosts.

How interesting, says Fosco. Hearing this admission from Jonah, she lightly presses her own heart area as though it were really swelling under there, behind her boob. The Duchess often does this too. She is currently in a place that looks like Costa Rica, posting pictures of herself in bell-sleeved tunics, doing just that gesture before bloody suns, volcanoes, in what looks like an enchanted forest. The last time I checked, she'd posted a closed-eyed picture of her face pressed fervently into the muzzle of a very white horse. In the throes of my fever, I had a terrible wish that all that beauty would kill her. That the horse would mistake her head for a small fruit. Or that when she was riding him, he'd shake her off like a bug.

"In fact, I might even be dead," Jonah finishes.

A grave exchange of looks between Fosco and Silky.

"And where would you be, Samantha?" Silky asks, turning to me.

It's all over his face. How he is hoping for a horror story.

I suppose I could tell him one. That my father works for a sideshow, a gang of freaks. How before I came to Warren, I was head freak because of my height. If I had gone home for Christmas, home being a tent beneath an underpass of a Utah highway, he'd force me to do the bit where I eat glass. Or the one where I eat crickets. You'd be surprised how much they taste like salad.

I would be dead too, I could tell them. Probably. Definitely. Or at least seriously, seriously maimed. Emotionally broken by loneliness. My lifeless body hanging from my broken light fixture until the smell of my rot alerts the pervert down the hall. *But thanks to you, kind sir and madam, thanks to this invitation to sit here in this living room teeming with the scent of lavender on fire, in the cacophony of a music worse than silence, I am saved, reborn.* I imagine falling to my knees. Clutching Silky by his mauve-toned slacks.

Instead I say, "I just wanted to focus on my writing."

"Dedicated," Silky offers.

"Yes, very," Fosco says.

I take a big sip of the wine I am still drinking way too fast. An unseen man to my right keeps pouring it into my glass as though by magic.

"And how are you feeling about your semesters?"

It's a throwaway question, a limp hand extended. But Jonah takes it seriously.

"My semester? Good. I mean pretty okay. I took all these classes I didn't have to take because I figured, you know, I'm at Warren. I might as well learn as much as I can. Also, they all sounded so interesting I couldn't decide so I just sat in on them all."

"That was very ambitious, Jonah."

"It was dumb too. They're really hard classes like math and robot science. This school is intense. Everyone's so smart. I sort of thought I was going to kill myself for a little while."

"How lovely," Fosco says, refilling everyone's wineglass. "Of course, if it got in the way of your writing, that would be terrible. . . ."

"Oh, I'm still writing. Maybe too much."

"*Too much*? Jonah, that's wonderful."

"I don't know, I think it really might be too much."

"Now remind me what is it you're working on?" As if she had ever remembered it enough to forget.

"This long poem about Alaska. I thought it was going be two pages but it's like ninety pages so far. I just keep writing it so I guess that's good but it's also a bit scary because I can't stop."

"Well, when inspiration strikes. When the muses are speaking."

"Maybe but I literally can't stop. It might go on forever. I'm actually sort of freaked out."

"So wonderful. Samantha, how did you feel about Workshop this semester?"

"Workshop?"

I have a vision of a *Top Gun*–era Tom Cruise with a harelip. His beautiful head exploding. The hail of bone, the shower of blood, the terrible brain rain from which I no longer bothered to take cover thanks to the magic Tic Tacs. And then his lovely eyeball landing in my kitten lap, blue-green as my dream of the sea, winking at me like a hard-won cat's-eye. Afterward, to stop me from screaming, because there was no amount of Tic Tacs that could stop me from screaming, Cupcake showed me her walk-in closet. *Look, Bunny*. All her bell-skirted dresses arranged in a neat little line like fascists, organized by color to create a rainbow.

"Great," I say. "Amazingly well. I'm really happy here."

But *Amazingly well* is not enough, I can tell. She wants what Ava and I call Trauma Porn. *Give me something, you whore. Don't make me regret that I pity-invited you at the grocery store.*

She raises her eyebrows. "Really?"

"Oh, yes." What would we do, Fosco, without your feigned interest in our horror stories? Your attempt to unleash them from us through prompts involving tarot cards, hand puppets, and bits of soapstone?

"Well, that's quite a relief to hear, Samantha, I must say. I know you were having some . . . *difficulty* with the women in your department." She's referring to last winter, when I sat in her office full of wind chimes, requesting, no begging, to be excused from Workshop for the semester. I told her I'd do double the work, I'd do triple the work, I'd—

May I ask why, Samantha?

I told her I worked better independently. I also had a really strong sense of my project at the moment. Workshop would only confuse me. Lead me astray. All manner of lies, which, to her credit, she didn't buy for a second.

Samantha, she sighed, *Workshop is an integral part of the Process. Workshop never "confuses" us, rather it opens us up, helps us grow, leads us in new and difficult and exciting directions. My Workshop in particular, I think you'll find. Have you ever considered that perhaps your project would benefit from being led astray? Productive disorientation?*

She smiled at me, her office caftan shimmering. Her ego was bound up in all this, I saw. I'd have to take another tactic.

It's not Workshop itself so much as my cohort.

You mean the other girls?

Yes. And then I felt like I was four. A ridiculous, pouting child tattling to the teacher.

I mean, they're perfectly nice and smart and I love their work, I lied. *They're just a bit of a . . . a clique. And that's fine. Totally fine. It's just I'm not really part of it. And I'm the only other person in the class. So. It makes things . . . weird.*

I see.

She said she would see what she could do. But in the end, "after careful consideration" she made me return to Workshop. Gave a speech in the next class about how her practice as a teacher, as a writer, was inclusive; she liked to think she brought people together. And she eyed me the whole time as if to say, *See? See how I'm laying the groundwork?*

And the Bunnies looked from her to me and I swore they knew. And I wanted to die. And I stared at her hands folded over her thirty-year-old handwritten lecture notes, the capelet on her shoulders, the dry ice that in my mind is always smoking around her self-satisfied person. And so the name Fosco was born.

But now, of course, this is my thesis semester. No more Workshop. I can just lie and say everything is fine.

"Oh, that's all been straightened out. We're all one big happy family now." I smile. "In fact, I've actually been experimenting with different mediums of expression lately."

Ah, her face says. "Well. Warren is the place for that sort of experimentation. That deep, personal work."

Over her shoulder, a tall, broad-shouldered boy in a catering uniform appears to pour her more wine. He looks at me with his Barbie blue eyes, smiles with his warped lips.

"Is something wrong, Samantha?" Her concerned expression. His leering one beside her. *Hello. I know you. You made me, remember?*

"Yes."

"Yes? What's wrong?"

They don't remember, girl, Caroline said when we spotted one behind the counter of the Snuggery. *They don't. Seriously. They're really infantile in some ways. Relax. Have another mini muffin.*

"Samantha?"

The bunny boy is still staring at me. *Sometimes they find their way back,* Creepy Doll told me once. *A lot of them end up getting jobs, believe it or not. Under the table, obvi. Violent? Sometimes they get violent, I guess. I don't know. Whatevs, girl. Should we go to Trader Joe's and get more cookie butter? I need it, like, for my soul.*

"Fine. I'm fine," I say, looking into my wineglass.

"Well," Fosco says. "I'm glad you're finally taking advantage of this place to broaden your horizons, your creative wingspan, so to speak."

She holds out her glass and he pours, wearing white gloves that I know conceal flawed hands. Was I there when we conjured him? Hard to tell. Despite all the Bunnies' nuanced conjuring talk, the boys all look more or less the same. But this one's looking at me like he knows me. *Tell me everything, Samantha.*

"I'm definitely broadening it."

"Wonderful. You know, Samantha, yours is the first all-female cohort we've ever had at Warren. You could say you young women are all pioneers of sorts."

Behind her the bunny boy blinks at me. *Samantha, I will hunt for you.*

"Such *nice* young women too. We get spoiled here at Warren, really. We get the cream of the crop."

"The cream," I agree. "Absolutely."

"I always say your cohort is your life-support system while you're here."

"I say that too."

"You need them as much as you need your solitude. Perhaps even more than your solitude. Too much solitude, Samantha, can just lead to the worst kind of paranoia and navel-gazing."

"Exactly."

"Learning from each other, growing with each other, on the other hand."

I think of us sitting in Creepy Doll's bloody attic, and I picture us learning and growing with each other and I start laughing. Laughing and laughing and laughing. Jonah laughs with me even though he has no idea what I'm laughing at. The bunny boy laughs too.

Fosco looks at me like I've lost my mind.

I'm sorry, I say, but I can't stop, the laughter keeps coming. It's irrepressible. It's the same laughter I heard from Ava at the *Demitasse* when she first saw the Bunnies, threw her head back and just laughed and laughed. And I couldn't believe that she couldn't stop.

"What's so funny? Did I miss something?"

But I can't even answer her for the laughter bubbling out of my own throat. Laughter is a rabbit hole and I'm falling, falling like Alice. There is no way up or out. The only way is down, down, down. The only way is to keep falling. Succumb. I shake with it. Ava's laughter. Suddenly I miss her so much I want to cry. Tears, real tears, stream out of my eyes.

"Samantha?" Jonah says, reaching out and touching my arm. We're alone in the living room. I can hear Fosco and Silky speaking hushed words to one another in the kitchen.

"I have some drugs if you want them," Jonah says to me. "Not crack or anything. Pills. Just legal stuff. They'll still make you feel better probably. Relaxed." He hands me a small, cloudy plastic bag of variously colored pills. They look like the shiny backs of poisonous bugs.

He's still cupping a holiday napkin with shrimp tails on it. His hair has been combed to look what he imagines to be festive or presentable or both.

"Jonah, I'm so sorry."

"For what? It's nice to hang out with you again." He smiles.

Under the parka, I see, he's wearing a button-down shirt and a tie featuring a graphic of Edvard Munch's *The Scream.*

Jonah's formal outfit, which he's worn to every school event.

"I should go."

"I can drive you."

"No, you should probably stay here. It's bad enough that I'm leaving early. I don't want to draw you away too."

"Okay. Hey, did you ever find that book?"

"What book?"

"That one you were looking for the other day, remember?"

Ava's face through the diner glass. *I'm leaving.*

"I really should go."

"Leaving already, Samantha?" Fosco coming in from the kitchen.

They all insist that I stay. At least for dinner. It's Christmas, after all.

"No, I should head home." Her eyes say, *Oh Samantha. What could that possibly, possibly mean?*

26

Outside, the sun is weak and high in the sky. Snow gently falling. I see The Duchess's house not too far off. A fantasy of breaking in consumes me briefly. I could set fire to all the diamond proems. Dishevel her artfully arranged stacks of Latin American novels. Lick all the probiotics and kombucha in her fridge. I think of my apartment, back in the opposite direction. Cold. Fridge empty. I polished off the last of my New England needle wine before I left. Across the street, I see the bus stop where I watched him disappear into the bus that disappeared into the dark.

A bus approaches as if on cue.

"Excuse me, where does this bus go?"

The driver just looks down at me with his one eye.

"All over. Where are you headed?"

"Um. I forget the name of the street," I lie. "I'll know it when I see it, though."

He looks at me, unphased. Your funeral, lady.

I use change, not my Warren card. I'm not going to give him the satisfaction. And I don't want to stand out, make myself a target. *What do you mean, target?* Ava asked me once. And I explained: *They think we all have money and probably I'd have no time to explain that I'm not like other Warren students.*

Her face said *that's exactly what makes you like other Warren students.*

I look around now at the Ava-less bus, sparsely populated with the deeply dismal. They sit on the duct-taped seats with legs splayed, heads turned toward the grime-covered windows, grim faces looking dazed and subdued by the blue bus light and the dark outside. I walk down the aisle, keeping my head down. Sit across from a very old woman in a windbreaker who at first looks to me a little like my dead grandmother, at least in the face. I'm comforted. There is my grandmother sort of. Wearing the clothes of a slightly insane person. Tattoo on her throat of a spider in a web. Reading a ripped-up medical poster about schizophrenia aloud.

SCHIZOPHRENIA: *Do You Have the Symptoms??*

She reads each symptom on the list, going, "Oh I have that, oh I have that." Making sounds of delighted surprise. Like it's a recipe she's reading and she's tickled to discover that—

"—she already has all the ingredients in her fridge. No need to go shopping."

Whispered into the nape of my neck, blowing softly into the small hairs there, taking the words right out of—not my mouth, but my mind. I turn. He's in the ripped-up seat behind me. Headphones around his neck blaring "Your Silent Face."

Black trench-coated frame slouched coolly. His chaotic hair falling into his eyes, each its own cloud of glittering gray smoke. Smiling at me like we're friends.

"So. Did you ever find your bunny, Samantha?"

In the blue light of the bus, I stare at his gaunt, wolfish face. His eyes are fixed on me, waiting.

"You said it died," I say in a small voice.

"Did I?" He shrugs. Turns to the window, even though there is nothing to see but grime. I notice a tattoo of a black ax on his neck. Pinpricks all down the back of my neck like little stabbing stars. He looks back at me. Eyes that are profoundly every color and no color at all.

"So where are your friends?"

"Friends?"

When he looks at me, I feel my rib cage open like a pair of French doors. Everything that keeps me alive suddenly bared and there for the taking.

"They're not my friends. I hate them." The words leave my mouth in twisted smoke.

He smiles. Light on green leaves. Me looking up at the fast-moving clouds, the damp grass on my back. The smell of wet budding flowers all around me. I'm fifteen.

"So where are those girls who aren't your friends, Samantha?"

A club in my old town. My back against chipped bricks. A stranger's white spikes in my fist. Frankenstein forehead but a red pillow of a mouth. He was wearing a silver shirt that gleamed in the dark of the bar like an aquarium fish. The bass of a New Wave song pounding in my heart. His mouth a clove-smoky tunnel into which I was falling and falling.

"It's Christmas break. They went home for the holidays."

"All on the same plane? The same burning plane that is spiraling out of the sky as we speak?"

When he smiles this time, I see the drummer of a black metal band who once rattled my soul's spine.

"Different planes. Different places," I say.

"What a shame," he says.

He pulls a silver flask from his coat pocket and drinks, then offers it to me. Shakes it at me when I hesitate. I take it from him and drink. Green fire hatches in my gut. I try to hand it back to him, but he stops me.

"You keep that. You look like you need it."

"But what about you?"

"I'm high on love, Samantha."

Cherry blossoms falling. Rob Valencia convulsing on the stage floor. A fishmonger I once had sex with whose eyes said *I know the insides of everything.*

He leans forward now, so close I can feel his cold breath on my face. Forests. Freshly killed things. The smell of wet white sage. He reaches a hand out toward my face. He might try to kill me. That's fine. But he just grazes my cheek gently. When I open my eyes, he's showing me his palm, dusted with gold glitter from when the Bunnies painted my face like a faery princess. It's been on my skin for god knows how long.

He smears the glitter across his own cheek and smiles at

me. Even with glitter on his face, he remains all of the not-cute things of this world in one man. And then it hits me. I feel it like a sudden singing in my skin, a blaze in my blood, an opening up of my heart itself. *Are you my—*

"Home," he says. And just then, the bus stops. He gets up. Slips his headphones back on and walks down the aisle toward the door, whistling.

27

I follow him in the dark. Him moving ahead with a wolfish prowl, me several steps behind. I think he's going to turn around and say, *what the fuck do you think you're doing*? But he's letting me follow him, it seems. Turning around slightly every now and then to see if I'm still behind him. Maybe smiling to himself a little. I can't tell.

He walks farther and farther ahead but never so far that I lose him entirely. Because there are so few streetlights in this town, sometimes he dissolves into the dark for a while and I get scared that I've lost him forever. But then there's a circle of light again and I see his distant shape up ahead. Taller than a redwood. Dark hair turning white with snow.

We turn this way and that, this way and that. Through a woodlot, a parking lot. Through alternately nice and shit parts of town I've never seen. Cutting through people's gardens where I watch him break off a branch of holly here, a branch of pine there. I pace outside a greenhouse while I watch him clip the delicate snow-white flowers that grow inside. He gathers it all into a spiky bouquet, then moves on, walking more quickly now. Down between the line of houses and into a never-ending alley where for sure I think I lose him because the world goes black, black, black, but at last I see the alley open to a street up ahead, his silhouette turning onto . . .

. . . a row of abandoned-looking houses. Junk-filled front yards. A black cat sitting primly on the steps of a shuttered store.

Jesus where the hell are we? *But I've been here before. Haven't I been here before?*

He slows his pace at last, swinging his bouquet, running his palm over the snowy spokes of all the fences we pass. *Stop doing that!* my mother would scream whenever she caught me. *You'll get a disease for god's sake. Do you know how filthy?* But I could never resist.

I'm about to reach out my hand to do the same when I see he's stopped suddenly up ahead.

He's standing on the snowy front lawn of a small, two-story brick house.

Why are we stopping here? What are we doing?

I look at the house. My chest tightens. Red front door. Flowers still dead in their pots. The whole foundation leaning a little to the left—*just like being in Amsterdam*, she used to say. *If you close your eyes you can even hear the bicycle bells, the live sex shows.* The roof where we danced now covered in snow.

I didn't recognize the route, a different one than Ava used to take.

"What are we doing here?" I ask, turning back to him. He's vanished. Just vacant snowy street as far as I can see. Just me standing here alone in front of her brick house.

I run up to the red door. Try the ice-cold knob, locked.

Knock, no answer. I pound on the door until my fists burn. Try the knob again, which instantly comes off in my hand. "Ava, Ava, Ava," I shout until I'm hoarse. I want to call his name too, but I realize now I don't know it.

Forever. Forever is how long I've been standing here in the cruddy snow outside her house, the frozen knob of her front door in my hand. Staring up at her vacant windows. Watching, waiting for any signs of life or light. But all is dark and dead within. Like she doesn't live here. Never lived here. Like maybe no one has in a long, long time.

No sign of the man anywhere, as though I dreamed him. Nothing but empty dark all around.

Give up, the dark says. *Give up, give up, give up. Go away. Go away and be a bunny, Bunny. Hop, hop, hop along. Isn't that what you wanted?*

I didn't know what I wanted.

Too late, the dark says. *Too late now.*

I hear a scratching sound from above and look up. Raccoons regarding me curiously from the roof—*my priests,* Ava called them. *I've confessed everything to them. Not that I want to burden them. But raccoons, you know, they can handle it. They love trash, rot, all the bottom things. You should try them sometime, Smackie.*

I watch them scatter and disappear. All but the little one we used to cheer on in the hour between the dog and the wolf as he made his careful way down the drainpipe. The small raccoon is standing still in the snowy eaves gutter. Looking down at me.

Tell her I'm sorry. Tell her I should have never left. I fucked up. I miss her. So much.

I watch him turn and disappear down the side of the house. Shut my eyes.

"Smackie, is that you?"

A small yellow square that lights up the whole night. Her feathery-haired silhouette standing there like it's been standing there the whole time.

"Jesus. How long have you been standing out here?"

Forever and ever. But I say, Oh, just like a minute or so.

"Loser. Didn't I give you a key ages ago?"

Part Three

28

In some ways it's as though I never left. As though I was always here, lying on her dark silk cushions, staring up at the tapestry of one-eyed birds perched among the twisting vines, holding her Drink Me flask filled with mulled wine in honor of the season. My feet sinking into the faux-fur rug that caresses my heels like so many soft grasses. In this living room that smells like a thousand old frankincense sticks, always a new one burning. The scent of her rain perfume lingering in the rooms like a thread I can't help but follow. The turntable playing tango or some weird French sixties stuff that sounds exactly like the music you dream of but can never find. The lady-shaped lamps lit all around us—more than ever before, it seems, were there always this many? The red velvet curtains parted. In the window, the serious moonlight shines in a way that it never shines where I live.

That's because the moon hates where you live.

We lie by a fireplace that I don't remember being here before. Strung with Christmas lights. Taller than both of us. A great mouth full of high, leaping flames. Was this always here?

Shhh. Come closer. You're freezing for fuck's sake.

She takes my hands in hers, still gloved in black mesh like

it's a gothic prom in 1985. Her pale hair surrounded by flames like live snakes.

"I thought you left," I say.

"I thought you left."

"Me? But you were the one who—"

"Actually, I thought you were dead."

"Dead?"

"Your soul anyway. Murdered. By that little-girl cult. I even lit a candle for you." She gestures toward the windowsill. I stare at the tall, blue flickery candle all bleedy with wax, then at her face. Dead serious under her fishnet veil. She hates me.

"How could I fucking hate you?"

She reaches across and strokes my cheek with her hand, rubbing the pad of her index finger against the tip of my nose. Shows me her gloved fingers covered in glitter sparkles. And I remember him. Smiling at me in the blue light of the bus. The glitter on the whorls of his finger pads. How I followed him here. Watched him walk right up to her house, then disappear into the dark.

I try to ask Ava if she knows him but she just says, "*Shhh*. Go to sleep now."

When she says this, I feel the immense heaviness of my limbs. How long I have been dragging them. My eyes close and close and close.

So then Ava says I sleep for like a thousand years. Sleeping Beauty among her briars has nothing on me. But I do not sleep peacefully, my eyelids prettily fluttering, my lips parted but silent, the soft yielding O of my mouth awaiting the lips of my blandly heroic prince. Instead, I wake up damp and sweating, the Bunny braids that still restrain my hair strangling me, my throat raw from what I will later find out were my own night screams. I wake to a white window, snow falling like bright, quick fish. A woman in a red dragon robe sits at the foot of my bed. She's holding a tall glass of coffee like a vase and a cigarette, which she's ashing into the crotch of a crystal mermaid. She looks concerned.

"How did you sleep?" she asks me.

"Good, I think."

"You were screaming a lot."

"I was?"

"The neighbors must have thought I was taking a chainsaw to someone. Or else having the most wondrous fuck of my life." She grins. Then looks worried. Really worried. "What the fuck did those girls do to you, anyway? Never mind. Let's not talk about it right now. I'm just glad you're home."

"Home," I repeat, and the word is like the fresh Chinese sweet buns we will eat at her rickety table, the green tea we will drink. It is the table and the chairs and us sitting in them together, smoking and tipping our ashes into the same crumb-crusted plate. "Me too."

And just like that, we go back. To how it was before. A winter like last summer. The days, weeks, months stretching out endlessly before us. Her drawing her beautifully monstrous worlds. Me writing, finally writing, I don't know how it's happening but—

"Don't overthink it, Smackie."

Sitting across from one another at her kitchen table. Each with our own black notebook. Sharing an endless cigarette, an ever-smoking cup of gunpowder tea. The oven, which we keep feeding random bakeable objects—sweet potatoes, avocados, bananas—like sticks to a fire to keep warm in her frozen kitchen. When it gets very cold, we just open the oven door.

"Are we poisoning ourselves?"

"Probably."

At night, we cook dinner together drunk on whatever's in her Drink Me flask, careening through her kitchen like it's a tossing ship. How she affords alcohol and food when she doesn't seem to be working these days is a mystery to me, but she just says, *I have my ways.* After dinner, we dance together on her lake-colored rug. Swaying to our own inner tango music, what we can remember from class. We learned so many dance moves.

Do you remember any of them?

Not really.

Me neither.

But we practice the ones we remember until we collapse. Her mesh palms pressed hard into my cheeks so I have no choice but to stare right into her different-colored eyes.

She's saying, *Are you sure you're not dead? Are you sure, are you sure, are you sure?*

I nod. Yes. I'm not dead. Although the truth is I am not entirely sure. Today was so wonderful. Probably this is heaven. The night is a waterfall of music and lights. The night is a rabbit hole into which we enter, hand in mesh hand. The night is a dark earth I could dig my hands into forever. The night becomes a page of literature that I would, at sixteen, press against my heart. The night is a—

But she isn't listening. She's telling me once again about how she thought they stole my soul. Tore it apart with their little bonobo hands. Fumigated my heart with their grassy perfume. Braided my hair so tightly my skull nearly exploded from the pressure. She thought I was lying in an alley somewhere in a sparkling heap, my face painted like a fairy kitty, my limbs covered in gold stars, that they'd sewn bunny ears or a tiara or both into my infected scalp. Rubbed out my memory of her with a cupcake eraser. Not just my memory of her but of myself, all the things she loved.

She paints this picture until I start drunk-crying.

Well. This is what she pictured. "Do you know how that *was* for me?"

I shake my head. It feels so light now without the braids, I could shake it forever. She unbraided it the day after I arrived like she was dismantling a bomb. All those elaborate knots and twists I had somehow become numb to. We did it in front of her bathroom mirror, her unleashing one impossibly tight braid after another, while I drowned my pain in Drink Me.

My hair still stands suspended all around my head, like a dark kinked cloud.

Fuck clouds, Ava says. *What you have now is a fierce black mane.*

Now she lets go of my face, slumps against the wall next to me, and slides down. I slide down with her until we're both sitting with our backs against the warm, oozing brick beside her fireplace. Spray-painted on the wall before us are pleas for Cthulhu to *come back, come back, please!* And in the same hand, but different paint *Lonely I am so lonely*. Ava guesses it's from the previous tenants, probably misfit art school dropouts like her. She didn't have the heart to paint over it.

Outside, a light snow is falling.

"I'm sorry," I say. "For everything."

She reaches a hand toward me, and I think she's going to stroke my shoulder, tell me it's okay. Instead, she holds up a long, thin braid that was apparently hiding in my hair cloud, that she must have missed in her dismantling. It looks like the tail of a rat. It's long lost whatever ribbon or bow or glittery ouchless elastic they used to secure it.

"I blame Them, she says. *And* that school." She turns to me. "We just should go blow it up."

"We should," I agree.

She looks at me drunkenly.

"We should? Really? Do you *really* want to, though?"

She worries I'm still under mind control from the bonobos. Bunnies. Whatever. Same difference. Anyway, it's important that I exercise agency, free will. All day she makes me practice with even the littlest things. At the zoo, at the thrift store, in the anarchy bookstore, in the tunnels and cafés. I, Samantha Heather Mackey, want to stare for hours at the island fox in his sad, synthetic zoo tree. I do not want to see the monkey exhibit. I want to see the penguin parade that starts at noon, once I am assured yet again that their participation is entirely voluntary. I want her to steal for me that silver skull ring. I prefer green tea today. The Chinese sweet bun I want from the bakery is red bean.

But when I tried on a black coat I'd picked out for myself at the thrift store—*because it's fucking cold and you need a coat,* Ava said—came out from behind the curtain in it, looked at myself in the mirror, at Ava waiting expectantly behind me, I said, *Looks great, Love it,* only to satisfy her. The truth is I saw nothing. The tall watery form of a stranger with a black cloud for hair. A woman blurred around the edges. The Dead.

29

January, February, March. The winter is a torrent of snow. Falling slow and fat. Falling quick and bright. The sun if it rises at all is a weak white flame. Ava says she's never seen a winter like this. It's fucking insane but sort of nice. Now that I don't have to go to class, Warren becomes a faraway country where I can't believe I ever lived. The Bunnies a distant memory. My phone is dead silent and for once I love the sound. *Like we're dead, you're right,* Ava smiles. *And this is the afterlife.* She clinks her glass of Scotch against mine.

My hair starts to feel like my hair again. Loses its tight kinks. Falls in my face uncombed. All around me, what she calls the old bitch curtain. My scalp no longer screams from being pulled in absurd twists. *Hold still, Bunny,* Cupcake would say. *If it's in your eyes all the time, then we can't see your face.* My fingernails, upon which they painted countless little warped flowers and rainbows, are bare but for the odd mint- or sky-blue-colored chip. The remaining bits of permanent glitter whisker leave my face at last. I'm still screaming in my dreams, according to Ava. Odd things. About cupcakes. Twisted lips. About an ax. *Don't tell me,* she says. *I don't want to know.*

And when I wake up her name leaves my lips in a cold,

vaporous cloud. I panic. Run through the cold hallway of her apartment, calling her name. Sometimes I can't find her right away, and my heart starts to pound, I get breathless. But she's always there. Lying curled on the carpet, her head curled into her chest, her limbs folded into themselves like an origami crane. *I've never cared for beds.* Or else she's awake, putting a sweet potato in the oven. Making Vietnamese coffee, which drips from the little metal hat into long glass mugs. Sitting at the table, drawing a picture of us battling our many enemies. She looks up at me and smiles.

"Morning, Sunshine."

"Morning."

I don't ask her, *what about your job*? She doesn't ask me, *shouldn't you be at school*? Not that she would. And anyway, final thesis semester. *Though we do expect you girls to check in now and then, be visible, attend events, Demitasses, readings, be active citizens of the rich Warren community because the learning doesn't stop in the classroom.* Fuck that. Instead, I join Ava at the table. I write. And for the first time in so long, it comes. It not only comes, it's easy. I can't believe how easy. As easy as being here with her. It's joyous. It's frightening. It might very well be terrible. I don't care. At least it's back, the thing that I thought I lost or killed or that left me in disgust. Not gone or dead after all but here, just like she is now. Right here with me across the table.

We work and fuck around and eat and dance all day until at last we drop before the fire. We close our eyes and listen to the folk singer woman sing about loneliness and squirrels. The one who disappeared one afternoon, just walked right out of her own life, and never came back. We listen like her lonesome dove voice is a bath in which we are sinking.

No sign of him. The man from the bus. My bunny? I start to think I dreamed him. Maybe took one of Jonah's pills when I left Fosco's. Conjured my own white rabbit to lead me back to her. There are moments when I'm tempted to ask her, *Have you ever seen a man with a tattoo of an ax on his neck hanging around? Tall? In a black trench coat? Bearing a bouquet of twigs?* But something stops me. I open my mouth and close it again. I look around this room, this house, this world of just her and me, and lean my head against her shoulder. Close my eyes. Let the night become the dawn. Let the snow outside fall and fall like it will bury us. Please bury us. It would be totally fine by me.

Then one night, there's a creaking sound above our heads. Coming from the ceiling.

What was that noise?

I look over at Ava. Who shrugs. I expect her to tease me and say it's Cthulhu, but she says, "Oh. Probably just Max."

"Max?"

"My lodger. He moved upstairs after you left."

"Upstairs? Here? Why haven't I—?"

"He's gone all day and comes home late. Hope we haven't been too loud."

"Loud?" What kind of loud?

"Speak of the devil," Ava says.

*

And then. And then he's standing in the living room doorframe like he was always here. Grinning at me just like he did in the blue light of the bus. His ax tattoo gleaming blackly at me from his neck tendon. His hair a dark, dapper chaos. His eyes like smoke.

So it wasn't a dream.

Nope, his eyes say. Not a dream. Definitely not a dream. As if to prove it, Ava goes to him and he kisses her. Deeply. Intimately. In a way that tells me they've kissed before. At last, he pulls away and looks at me. His unscarred mouth slashed by her Lady Danger lipstick. His long arms loosely holding her body like he's oh so familiar with its contours.

"Hello, Samantha."

30

I really don't know what my face is conveying as I stare at him. Leaning against the doorframe like he is not at all the spawn of my wildly wavering emotions and one furred little fist. But a human man, always was. And not just any human man, a cool one. Sexy. Scary-sexy. Whose name apparently is Max. A cool, sexy man named Max who, with his smoky eyes and his tall, slouching grace and his ripped-up black clothes full of pins, makes leaning against a doorframe his own. His army-coated arm still around Ava who is saying, "Oh, do you two know each other?"

"No," I say quickly just as he says, "Yes."

Ava looks at me. Then at him. Then at me. Well, which is it?

"We've seen each other around," he says. Casually, oh so casually. I notice his fingernails are painted silver. Filed into sharp points. "Haven't we, Samantha?"

Suddenly I feel my phone begin to buzz in my pocket. For the first time in weeks.

He smiles at me.

"You," is all I can bring myself to say.

Ava's looking at me like, *what the fuck is wrong with you*?

"Don't mind Smackie. She's been through a rough time. Sort of a long story."

He nods sympathetically, like he understands. Then he walks toward me, growing taller and taller as he comes closer. His long, thorny shadow falling over my body. Darkening the entire corner where I am sitting with my hands pressed against the floor.

He crouches down before me so we are eye to smoke-encircled eye. Rib cage opening. A buzzing all through my body. He takes my hand. Brings it to his human lips. Kisses it. Lightly, so lightly.

Then, just like that, he drops it. Reaches out and ruffles my hair like I'm a dog.

"I should be off, my love," he says, turning to Ava.

My love? My love?

I'm high on love, Samantha, he said that night, on the bus.

I look down at the imprint of Ava's lips he's left on the back of my hand. And then I see the way he's staring at her. The way I once stared at light dancing through the leaves of a tree. I was lying beneath it, the leafy shadows shivering over me, all that golden-green light over me. He looks at her like this while she, seemingly oblivious, casually suggests he come home—home!—early tonight so we can all hang out. Maybe have drinks?

"Wouldn't miss it," he says. He'll even bring dinner.

"Already dead this time, please," Ava says.

He grins, promises. But his eyes and his mouth curve say *oh who knows what I am capable of?* I watch them exchange secret smiles, enjoying what must be a private joke. Just between them.

And then he kisses her again. So deeply and for so long, I feel like a sun rises and sets and rises again as I sit there slumped against the back of the couch like my legs don't work, watching them. When they part at last, there's no lipstick left on her lips, her mouth surrounded by a pale pink ring. The same ring that's around his mouth when he turns to me and says, "See you around, Samantha."

He goes out the door, leaving behind him the smell of forests, and underneath that, a vital animal scent that reminds me. As if I could forget.

I pull out my phone, which has been buzzing all this time. Four missed calls. Four texts. Each of them just one word, one all-too-familiar word, long. Followed by a question mark/exclamation, a tulip and a ghost, a pointed period, nothing at all.

And then one more now:

Bunny where are you?

31

Rabbit cooked four different ways, his specialty. He hopes we enjoy it.

"Enjoy it?" Ava interrupts. "It's a fucking mouth opera."

"Mouth opera," he repeats. "I like that."

By candlelight, I watch him rip the bunny flesh and bone with his human hands as though he bears no connection at all to that animal. Did the Darlings eat bunnies? I never saw them eat anything but Pixy Stix. I watch him tear at the bunny meat with his straight, white teeth. Wash it all down with the dark red wine he brought home, which I'm sure he must have stolen. All the while staring at Ava. She is cherry blossoms falling. She is serious moonlight. She is shivering green leaves.

Meanwhile, his animal shadow climbs and climbs the walls. Horned and furred and fanged. Do bunnies have horned shadows? Not any that I've seen. How can Ava not see it? But she doesn't. At all. She looks at him from across the table, chin on her lacy palm, cigarette turning to ash between her fingers, like he's Jacques Brel or maybe even Lux Interior, about to sing her a song about Amsterdam or getting fucked up. Believes him when he tells her that he too wishes to blow up Warren. He too has a soft spot for The Cramps, Scott Walker, sixties

French pop, the scores of Mancini. Oh, and he just loves to dance. Tango especially.

Responsibility is what I feel. Ethical-moral obligations. Because you simply can't sit back and allow your best friend to date an animal-man of your own creation and say nothing. You can't. And say nothing? That would be just wrong. On so many levels. I have to say something. I have to say—

"More wine, Samantha?"

"Yes, please."

He's trying to get me drunk, that's obvious. I watch him pour and pour and pour. Smile at me. So mannered. So cavalier. Maybe he isn't mine. That's still a possibility? Because bunnies do not eat other bunnies. Bunnies do not ever drink wine. Bunnies do not have eyes like smoke and wolfish faces full of knives. He must not be mine. But that gleam in his eye says otherwise, that faint smirk too. He knows and I know and that's why every time I look at him I have to look away. Looking at him is like looking into a black mirror, is like being inside my own dreammare.

Dinner with him and Ava is in fact like an extended déjà vu. I know exactly when he's going to lean forward in his chair and look at her with an intensity that makes me flush. Or when he's going to lean back, nod, and then agree with whatever she just said. When he's going to say *Yes, Exactly, Me too, Oh, I feel the same way*.

My phone buzzes in my lap, as it has all day. Why, after weeks of silence? What could they possibly want?

Bunny haven't seen you around campus lately! Come out for cocktails, please

Bunny oh no r u still sick? Can I bring you soup? Juice? Text anytime!

bunny where are u?

?

"What's that noise, is that your phone, Samantha?"

"No."

I know exactly how long he's going to laugh at the joke she just told—hahaha she is *so* funny—before he makes one of his own. A dumb one. I'm embarrassed by it, though probably it's one I would tell. She'll never laugh. You lose, I think.

But Ava does laugh. Hahaha. *You think you're funny. Doesn't he, Samantha?*

"Yeah."

I know exactly when his ax tattoo is going to catch the candlelight and shimmer blackly at me from across the table. Reminding me he might be dangerous. Reminding me I must be vigilant. Reminding me—

"Samantha, you haven't touched your rabbit," he says.

"Haven't I?" I stare down at my plate. He's given me the head of the one he roasted whole. A gift from the chef. I stare deep into its unseeing eye. *Samantha, you have to tell her.*

"Ground control to Samantha," Ava says. "Everything okay?"

"What? Fine, yes."

"Just in your own world again?"

I smile. Yes. That's all it is.

"Samantha's a writer," she says to Max, who looks at me over the hunk of thigh he's just ripped from the animal's side. As if he didn't already know.

"Is she? How about that. So what do you write, Samantha?"

The thing about him that frightens me the most is his features don't stay fixed, they shift. Sometimes he is the street busker I watched eat fire in Edinburgh. Sometimes the silver-shirted dark wave boy with the white spikes and the clove-smoky kiss.

"Smackie?"

The lone wolf I would visit at the zoo as a teenager with Alice. I'd stare at his lean body sitting still beneath a wind-warped tree and think if he went free what would happen? *Everything,* Alice would say, exhilarated.

"Smackie."

The Czech cab driver who I thought was going to pull over and kill me. I was so convinced of my imminent death at his hands I prayed all the way home. My childhood best friend Brian of the wheat-colored hair and the gentle voice and the quiet intelligence my mother proclaimed positively freaky for a five-year-old. He promised me he would marry me when we grew up. We even had a pretend wedding before he moved away. I wore a white sundress, threw a bouquet of twigs and dandelions over my shoulder. Whatever happened to Brian? He exists in my memory as sunlight on a white-blond cowlick.

"Samantha!"

"Sorry, what?"

"Max asked you a question," Ava says.

I look at Max, who is holding his wineglass by its stem, his features having shifted again, how does she not notice? He is now the picture of smiling, gentlemanly patience, the perfect boyfriend who is interested, genuinely interested in the lives of his girlfriend's friends.

"I just asked what do you write? Ghost stories?" he offers. "Dark romance?" Wry grin.

I tell him it's hard to explain.

He nods. Sure it is. It must be very hard to explain.

Well, he's so sorry we haven't met sooner, he says. But he's been busy, Samantha, terribly busy. Literally he's had to be in four different places at once.

"Max is a performance artist," Ava says. "He's been working on this huge project all winter. At your school actually."

"*My* school?"

She misinterprets my look of horror. "I know. *Blegh.* But apparently it's highly subversive. A real fuck you to the institution, which you know I'm all for. I told him, just watch you don't get your soul stolen by the bonobos."

"Bunnies," I automatically correct, then instantly regret it, because he looks up. At me. His smile a question that already knows the answer.

"Bunnies?" he repeats. And I'm reminded of when he said it that first night. The word in his mouth. Needing salt, but good. Definitely. He holds up the hunk of red-wine-soused rabbit flesh skewered on his fork. Waves it around.

Ava laughs. Such a card, he is. "I wish. Just these cultish girls Samantha was involved with for a while. They tried to eat her soul like a placenta."

"I don't know that I would—" I start to say, blushing.

"Like a fucking placenta," she repeats, not looking at me.

He looks from me to Ava and whistles. "Wow," he says. Slips the forkful of bunny meat into his mouth. Chews thoughtfully. Shakes his head. "They sound *jusht* awful."

"They are," Ava and I say quietly.

"Like they should be destroyed slowly."

"They should," I whisper before I can even think.

Ava looks at us both, appalled. "*Destroyed?* Why even bother? Fuck *them*."

"Exactly," he and I say at the same time. "*Fuck* them."

I watch him lick his knife with his very long tongue. I feel a lick of fear up the inside of my thigh. Both thighs. "What are you doing at my school?"

He looks at me, feigning surprise, genuinely amused by my question, as though I've aimed a toy gun at him from across the table.

"Oh, I don't like to talk about my work, Samantha. Ruins the thrill of the reveal. Surely you understand."

"Samantha's the same way about her writing," Ava says, patting my arm.

He stops sawing at what looks like an ear stump and smiles at Ava. "Really?"

"Are you kidding? She's so secretive about it," Ava says.

"I am not *so* secretive," I mumble.

"You should see her. Scribbling in that notebook. Covering the page with her hand like it's a test in junior high." She smiles at me. "It's kind of sweet."

Max grins at me from across the table.

"That's because she's writing about you," he says.

I feel my chest catch fire. A redness spreading that I know, even in this dark room, is going to betray me. I can feel Ava looking at me. Samantha, is this true? But I can't face her.

I keep my gaze fixed on Max, his scary-handsome, yet oh so innocently smiling face. I attempt telepathy. A warning. *Traitor.* But he's either oblivious or doesn't care. Clearly I don't have the sort of power over him that the Bunnies had over their Hybrids, their Darlings, even their Drafts. *Stay! Sit! Fetch me fro-yo! Lie here, beside me, good Darling.*

"I'd write about you too," he continues to Ava. "If I were a writer."

"Fuck off," she tells him softly but she looks touched. Really touched.

"I would. You're the most exciting and wonderful thing that's ever happened to me."

The way he says it, so sincere. Like it came from his own brain and not page three of my secret notebook, which is shoved under my bed.

She tells him to shut up, but I know she doesn't mean it. Her shut up is *Continue, please.* Much to my horror and fascination, he does.

He leans forward and takes her hand. But for his monstrous shadow on the wall, he is the embodiment of the edgy but romantic soul. Sid Vicious when Nancy was his sun.

"Being with you," he says to Ava, "is like being in literature. I have no idea where you'll lead me next. But I'm excited. My life could change. And I'm not alone anymore."

I die inside when he says this. Recall the words, which I

wrote down in another, older notebook. Scrawled it ecstatically on the lonely campus green when I was hungover after one of our first day- and nightlong escapades. After I met her at 11:00 in the morning and she took my hand and didn't let go until the next sunrise. I might have whispered it to the flying-hare statue, the leaves falling in my never-yet-braided hair. *I met a friend.* To hear my words from his mouth now. The shame. The melodrama. The lonely, sweaty hopeful need. I ask for the floorboards to open up and swallow me. I look down at them and pray. They're covered in dust because Ava never dusts and neither do I and apparently neither does he.

What could she possibly say to all that? Shut up? Fuck off? For real this time.

"That's sweet," I hear her say. I look at her. She's gazing down at her plate, empty of everything but a couple of gnawed bones. Ava never eats much, really. She smokes over untouched plates and then leaves them for me to finish later, her ash sprinkled over the top like salt. But her plate's gleaming now as if she licked it clean. And she's blushing. All the way down to her neck.

"It's true," he responds almost immediately. Exuding intensity like a scent. That foresty smell he brings with him into every room like a wind gust, a shadow. "Isn't it, Samantha?"

He reaches out and grabs the last crust of bread, which I was tempted by, and chugs the wine from the neck of the bottle. Then he hands it to Ava, who does the same. She hands it to me and I tip it back but there's only one drop left.

*

After we've finished the last bottle, he revisits the subject of tango, his very favorite dance. Wait, it's her favorite too? Both of you? Well, fuck. How wild. How crazy. How serendipitous, isn't it, Samantha?

Ava suggests we roll up the rug. "Oh, come on, Smackie. I'll even be Diego for you."

And he says, "Diego? Who's Diego?"

"Just this clichéd man Smackie and I invented to dance with. I mean, really we were dancing with each all other along. Weren't we?"

"Yes."

He smiles. "How sweet. Show me."

When Ava and I danced together before, where did we look? Did we look at each other? I can't seem to remember. I only know that now we look a little away from each other. I try to smile into that nothing space, like that is where she is actually standing. Except now there isn't nothing. There is Max. Leaning against the doorframe in his scary-sexy way, a handsome, evil tree. He is smoking and holding a tumbler full of dark amber whisky. Casting come hither scents, weird shadows. Watching us intently. Not us. Ava. He's watching Ava.

"I think I'm pretty tired," I say, breaking away from her. "I better turn in."

But I don't turn in. I stay seated, watch them turn and turn and turn before the fire, which never ceases to burn. I bring his still-smoking cigarette to my lips. Drink his whisky, which tastes like an actual bonfire by the North Sea. Watch their souls entangle like squid tentacles. I am horrified. I am mesmerized. I am embarrassed in ways I cannot explain. I am also increasingly drunk and I can't stop looking. At the way he looks at her. The way she looks at him. I drink the bonfire he pours and pours for me. Ignoring my now endlessly buzzing phone.

Bunny this isn't funny. You've fucking disappeared.

Bunny r u dead?? Did the gross apt where u liv kill u??? If ur not dead, pls text me!

Hey! Where the fuck R U?

S, haven't seen you around campus of late. I'm concerned. We should reconnect. Soon.

The world is going soft around the edges as I watch him turn and turn Ava. Even when the music stops, they're still turning. It hits me then, even though I already knew.

They're fucking. Of course they are.

32

Of course we are," she says the next day. "What are you, twelve?"

We're sitting on her roof, the sky a gray slate expanse hanging over us. She looks at me, wanting to know, really wanting to know if I'm twelve. Because this is the age of a person who whisper-asks a grown woman the question, "So are you guys, you know . . . ?"

Fucking? she finished.

And the word apparently looked like it hurt my face. Don't look so fucking horrified, she says. I say I don't look horrified and she says well, I should see my face. Which she *can* see thanks to my bonobo hair. My bitch curtain is still not in full swing. So she is free to look into both my eyes. To see how violently my lip is jerking while I try to appear calm, chill, casual. Not at all shocked or pleased or horrified to learn that Max, unlike the dickless bunny boys, is capable of sex. With my best friend.

How was your sleep, Samantha? he asked this morning, not waiting for an answer before he kissed me on the nose and then kissed Ava on the mouth, the neck, the ear, the shoulder, the mouth again, the other ear, the neck again. And then he was gone. Wherever he goes. Where does he go, anyway?

I don't know. Your school, I guess? To work on his project. He says it's site specific, whatever that means.

I'm really so anxious for you to see it, Samantha, he whispered to me on his way out the door. *Once it's finished, of course.*

But where in my school exactly? I asked Ava.

How should I know? I don't keep tabs on him. This isn't a Bonobo House!

I look down at the patches of green poking through the snow on the ground below. The wet, dripping trees full of bright buds. Because apparently, somehow, it is now spring. The air smells sweet, bloomy, like plants having sex. My brain is cottony as Ava tells me all about how they hooked up. Back when she thought I was dead or bonobo feed. And she was a wreck, lonely as hell, but trying to forget me because I was just a ghost of myself anyhow. Then he just showed up, asking about the spare room, even though she didn't advertise it. Just appeared out of nowhere, really. This anarchist with *the* best music taste. And such a serious artist too. Not that she knows what he is doing exactly. He's being very mysterious about it. And serious. Like someone else she knows. Whatever. She's certain it's blazing. And he's an amazing cook, well, I saw that with my own eyes last night, didn't I?

"Yeah," I nod. Nodding is a strange thing when you think about it. How your head just bobs and bobs on your neck.

"What is up with you, Smackie?"

"Nothing's up with me. What could be up with me?"

"You're being. I don't know. Weird."

"Weird? I'm not weird." I shake my head. Not weird at all.

Not me. "I'm just . . . you know, *concerned.*" I can't even look at her when I say this. Instead, I look at the raccoon priests who obviously want me to speak up. *Because you should just tell her, Samantha,* they pronounce. *Because he's obviously not what he says he is, right? She should know.* But would she even believe me? Would anyone?

"Concerned," she repeats, like it's a highly suspect word. Which it is. But I plow ahead anyway.

"He just seems kind of . . . intense."

She smiles suddenly like I've just conjured him before her on the roof.

"I like that," she says. "He's . . ."

"What?" I prompt. Try not to sound too eager.

She looks around like there's glitter in the air, all around us that I can't see. That I'll never be able to see because I don't have those kinds of eyes. But it's fucking there.

"What?"

"Sexy," she says at last, letting out a shapeless cloud of smoke. I watch it rise and disappear among the treetops.

"Ava, I have to tell you something."

"Tell me."

Don't tell her. You'll fucking lose her forever if you tell her.

Ava looks at me a long time. She kisses me on the forehead. "Don't worry, Smackie. I still love you most of all."

The room upstairs is where he lives now apparently. I enter, telling myself I'm not snooping. This did used to be my room after all. Anyway, he left the door open. Sort of. Not locked, anyway. Basically inviting me. *Come in, Samantha. Come see.*

I scan the room now . . . looking for . . . I don't know what I'm looking for. Everything is pretty much as I left it. A few new things. A stack of small, white Chinese take-out cartons. Empty. A cheap rainbow speaker that twirls and changes color as it plays "Bring On the Dancing Horses" by Echo & the Bunnymen. Apart from these, no real evidence that anyone has ever lived here but me. No real evidence that anyone has lived here at all. The bed looks like it's never been slept in. The books I left here still climb the walls, untouched. I walk over to the worn, black writing desk sitting in the corner by the window that was a present from Ava. *A room of one's own, all that jazz.* She even carved an *S* into the corner with her knife. So that it knew it was mine. Still, most days we just ended up working across from one another at her kitchen table. *She* was working. I was picking at my own damage, just shark-circling the thin black notebook, looking for a way in. A notebook like this one, in fact. Just like this one sitting right here in the middle of the desk.

Like it wants to be found. It wants to be picked up. Opened.

My heart sinks when I see my own handwriting. A few pages of seething observations and sad scrawl. Some random quotes not worth remembering. Lists. So many lists. The words *I don't know* surrounded by tangled vines and lidless eyes. I hate my handwriting. The barely legible, fevered script slanting so severely it looks like it could keel over any minute, then veering off the line entirely and tumbling into the margins in little suicidal clusters. So many words scratched out. Whole paragraphs with x's through them. Even the lists look dogged by uncertainty. But as I flip back now, I see there's something new on the first page. Beneath a long tender quote about loneliness I must have copied out from somewhere a while back that means nothing to me now. Some new text in shimmering black ink. A list. Written in a different hand. That is my hand and is not my hand. More erect. Cocksure. Not ever wondering *Is this right? Am I wrong?*

I stare at this list.

Samantha_Mackey@warren.edu praisexenu

Caroline_Anderson@warren.edu Iluvcorgies

Kira_Stone@warren.edu Unicornsplease

Victoria_Fielding@warren.edu bloodmilkforgogol

Eleanor_Brown@warren.edu ledaswanned

Ursula_Radcliffe@warren.edu 7SeAwiTcH7

Alan_Reid @warren.edu fleshmarketclose

Heat creeps up my neck. I drop the notebook as though it bit me. Jesus fucking Christ. My breath stops. I look down at the *S* carved into the desk corner, my heart pounding in my ears. Try opening the desk drawer. Locked. Locked? Did these drawers lock before?

A buzzing sound makes me jump.

On the bed is a phone I didn't see. I pick it up. The screen is covered with unread texts from various numbers.

Icarus, you burn me.

Byron, oops! That hatching duck emoji was for someone else.

Hope I'm not distracting you from your work ☺ Just haven't seen you in a bit so . . .

Text back when you can ☺

I miss our tete-a-tetes ☺

A LOT ☹

PS. The scars look so pretty now I'd love to show you xoxo

(it's Caroline btw. 🐰)

Tristan! Not sure if you're getting these???

My phone's been SO weird lately ☹

Pls help I'm lost in a thick, thick wood and

I'm afraid that I am not afraid of wolves!

😿

Hud. u make me hot. cum over

This last one is followed by a picture of her naked torso, reclined on a bearskin rug. Her blue-white body cut off at the neck like—

"—the archetypal persecuted heroine. But you can just picture the half smile, half frown on her face?"

I scream. He's standing in front of me. Right in front of me. Close. So close I can smell both the forest and the animal. Leaning casually against the wall, casually cornering me at the same time.

"You found my phone," he says.

Smoky gaze betraying nothing. Inscrutable smile.

"Oh, I don't know about *inscrutable,* Samantha," he says, taking the phone easily from my open palm. Almost like I handed it to him. Dark electricity when his fingers brush against my hand. Rib cage opening the way it does, I've learned, whenever he touches me. But I will not be manipulated or distracted or manipulated. Instead, I look up, right into his eyes whose many swimmy colors drown me (*Is it me drowning you, Samantha, or did you wade in here of your own free will, your pockets full of black stones?*), and I say: "What the fuck is going on?"

Now his lovely brow furrows. His smoky gaze clears into innocent surprise. "Going on?"

"Those texts!"

"What about them?"

"What about them? What *about* them?" I say, like where do I even fucking begin. But then I find I can't begin, I can't put into words what I want to know. Which is so much.

He smiles at me like I'm sweet. My sputtering mouth, open and ready to accuse him, endears me to him in ways I don't understand.

"Samantha," he says and reaches out and tenderly musses my hair cloud. He places his cool forest palms on either side of my burning face. It feels so wonderful a sigh escapes my lips and I can't take it back even though I want to, I want answers.

Instead he asks me a question: "Shouldn't you be heading off to school now?"

"School? What are you talking about?"

He lets go of my face. Reaches into his pocket. I brace myself for a knife, a spiked club of some sort. But it's only my own cracked phone in its cheap purple case. "Must have taken yours by mistake." An obvious lie. "Here."

I just stand there. Staring at it.

"Go on," he says, waggling it at me the way he waggled the flask that night on the bus.

I see the screen is open to my school in-box. To an email.

> Dear All,
>
> Please arrive at the Cave at 5:00 pm today for an Emergency Mandatory Workshop as discussed. Please be prompt. Please arrive with your ears and eyes open. Please be prepared to Tap the Wound.
>
> Blessings,
>
> Ursula

"Whoa," he says, reading over my shoulder, looking fake surprised. "Sounds serious. Guess you'd better be off."

He musses my hair again, letting the bitch curtain fall so that once again I can only see the world with one eye. "You know, the Wound isn't going to Tap itself, Samantha."

33

No idea. I have no idea what I'm going to encounter in the Cave. I enter the room, holding my breath. Bracing myself for the sight of them after so long. Playing their texts over and over in my head, but not daring to imagine what they might mean, what the hell is going on. I open the door, readying myself for any and all possibilities, readying myself for—

The usual square of tables, empty for now. Fosco smiling at me in her iridescent smock. Not one scarf out of place.

"Samantha," she calls from inside the dark of the Cave. Looking actually genuinely pleased to see me. "There's no need to run. Relax. Breathe. You're not just on time, you're actually a little early." *For once* says her smile.

She puts her hand on mine. Whispers even though we're alone. "I really appreciated your email, by the way."

"My email?" I recall her email address and password, scrawled on the page in his confident hand.

"Samantha, there's no shame in transparency. In a cry for help. Other teachers might have found it . . . oh . . . weak, I suppose. I thought it was candid. Brave. And so did your wonderful peers, who are eager to help. Such a wonderful group, so supportive of each other."

She squeezes my hand very tightly.

"We think we are alone. We think we are so special. We are deeply mistaken. Now as per your email, I *know* you don't have any work to share with us today. Not to worry. It's absolutely nothing to be ashamed of. For you, today will just be about listening. About watching and perhaps offering some feedback. *If* you feel so compelled. How does that sound?"

She's looking at me with such magnanimous triumph that I'm tempted to undo his lie, tell her that actually I do have work for once, lots of work I could share. Instead, I nod.

"Great. Thank you for . . . understanding."

"Are you sure you're all right, Samantha? You're trembling."

I'm about to mumble something about maybe having caught a chill on the way over, when behind us, I hear a noise. The patter of steps approaching. I hold my breath. Prepare myself by force of habit for the onslaught of grassy perfume, high sugary voices, the verbal and physical affection so intense that it borders on violence. But I smell nothing. I hear nothing apart from soft, clicking steps.

Then I see Caroline emerging from the dark. By herself. Smiling.

"Hello, Ursula. Hello, Samantha."

Pale lavender dress. White cardigan. Clutching a small white box fiercely with both hands. The kind you get for Chinese takeout. The kind you find in his room.

My heart begins to pound in my ears as she sits down in the chair facing me. Staring at me. Mistily. Her expression soft and dreamy like a heroine in a black-and-white film, the camera lens smeared thickly with Vaseline.

"Samantha, it's so good to see you," she says. Her voice sounds very far away. Like it's dreaming elsewhere. Floating amid smiling clouds. I notice that her white cardigan has anthropomorphic cupcakes for buttons. Have I seen her in it before? With her cardigan and lavender dress and her freshly bobbed hair, dyed what looks in the dark to be a very pale blond, she has never looked more like her namesake. Or a child of the corn.

"I like your hair," I say.

She touches it dreamily as if she isn't sure it's still there. Then smiles at me in a way that makes my skin shiver. "Thank you. I'm still getting used to it."

"An interesting side effect of the Process," Fosco observes. She recounts how these sorts of transformations are common during the final thesis semester. When we all leave the maternal embrace of the Cave and retreat to our own individual dark spaces—to spin the pain and fear and shame that lives there into so much literary gold. Genitals get impaled with pins. Hair gets chopped off with hacksaws, sometimes ripped from the root. Genders become fluid, orientations shift, white people suddenly discover other races in their lineage. And then, of course, some take it too far. One poor young man chopped off an ear. That was . . . unfortunate, but also indicative. Of the deeper Transformation required by the Work. The Work does not come without Cost.

Caroline just sits there, humming to herself, a warped version of "Summertime," ignoring Fosco's dog jumping on her shins until it gives up and skulks away. I see now that her hair is actually dyed a very pale shade of purple.

"I'm surprised to see you here alone," Fosco says to Caroline. "Normally you all arrive in one big group."

Caroline smiles politely but says nothing. She stares down at her white box. Nods as though it's telling her a secret. Then looks up at me. "Samantha, I overheard you saying you had a chill."

Did I say that out loud?

"Perhaps you'd like my cardigan?" she continues. She begins to take it off. That's when I see the words *EAT ME* carved all over her chest and arms with a razor. The scars look fresh, blood barely congealed in the Ms and Es. And yet she is smiling as she shakes her little white cupcake cardigan at me. I don't want it? Am I sure? All right, well. If I change my mind. She hangs it on the back of the chair. Then gazes back at me, pleased. The look on my face is its own reward.

"Do you like it?" As though she's asking me about a treat she baked, a scarf she knitted. "It's part of a performance piece I'm working on. A collaboration. I thought I'd involve the Body more viscerally."

"Lovely," Fosco says, looking completely unphased, like she's praising a child's drawing of a cat or a rainbow. "Isn't that lovely, Samantha?"

"Lovely."

"I *knew you'd* appreciate it, Samantha." Her misty smile makes my skin crawl right out of the room. She lowers her gaze to the white box she's clutching so fiercely I think it's going to break apart in her hands, then back up at me again. Mistier still.

"Samantha, I sent you some texts. . . ."

Bunny this isn't funny.

"Did you?"

You've fucking disappeared.

"Yes, a number of times."

"Sorry. My phone is—"

"I see." But I can tell by her face she knows I'm lying. "Well. I'm just glad you're all right. I was worried." The mist thickens, the clouds in her voice darken. The red scars on her white skin wink and shimmer. "Maybe we could go for coffee or something," she continues. "Catch up sometime. . . ."

The corner of her lip jerks up into a little ticking smile. I realize now she's wearing lipstick, a very pale shade of rose, and not her usual colorless balm. *Lipstick is for whores, Bunny.*

"Sure," I lie.

She smiles, looking so relieved I almost feel sorry for her.

"*When?*" she presses. "When are you—"

But there's the sound of footsteps again and she falls silent. Stares at her box. Ignoring the heels heading toward us. Stridently announcing themselves with each step. Not a diminutive click but a resounding clack. Until she's here. Kira. Also alone. Kira who is never alone. Kira who is always clutching the forearm of some person like she is lost in a fairy-tale forest. Kira who is wearing a dark red velvet babydoll dress with its own red velvet hood. Kira who is also clutching a white box. Kira who does not scream with joy at the sight of her dear friend,

Caroline, who is looking at Kira's exposed, shapely legs in their spiderwebby tights like they're a pair of snakes. Kira who does not envelop her friend Caroline in an organ-crushing hug or even sit by her. Who instead looks at Caroline's fresh torso scars and rolls her eyes, then takes the seat beside me.

"Sam," she says in a voice that is not babyishly high or breathy but deep. Fathoms deep. Her true voice. She places a hand on mine and smiles at me with her blue-black lips. "Long time no see."

Completely ignoring Caroline. Caroline completely ignoring her. Both of them completely ignoring Fosco's dog, who is turning mad, frothing circles in the center of the room, desperate to get their attention.

"So, Sam, tell me," Kira says, rubbing my hand. Voice deeper still, a well with no bottom. "How are you?"

She's wonderful, by the way, she says. The Work (secret smile) has been going so well.

Something else about her is different. No cat ears. Her long, loose red hair is that of a witchy-princess wandering the mists of Avalon.

I glance at Caroline, who is staring at me now with what I can only describe as quiet desperation. What the hell has happened to you bitches? Why aren't you hugging? Why aren't you collectively cooing around someone's memory of a cat?

"Samantha," Kira says, her tiger eyes boring into my skull. She asks where I've been hiding these days. She says she sent me some texts.

Bunny r u dead?

I open my mouth to say something and instead I gasp. We all do. Because in stomps Victoria, her hair looking spectacularly unbrushed, her red lipstick a diagonal slash across her face. She is dressed in a soiled wifebeater and a dirty crinoline, like a jewelry box ballerina come to life and gone off the rails. Her sour garbage smell takes our breath away as she drops loudly into a chair. In her soiled lap sits, of course, a white box, smudged with gray fingerprints. Beyond a soft *hi* to Fosco and a not unkind smile at me, she says nothing to anyone. Just hums softly to herself, while Fosco's dog whines at her foot. Stroking the box provocatively with her fingers, caked in dirt like she's spent all morning clawing at mud. Her whole face is a grinning *fuck you* to no one in particular.

"Victoria. You seem in quite good spirits," Ursula observes.

"Oh, I am. Such good spirits."

She's looking at me now. They all are. Still smiling. Ignoring each other. Sitting exactly one chair apart. Three white boxes in their laps ticking like bombs.

Ursula looks around the room like this is all to be expected in the final semester, at this time in the Process. Speaking of which, maybe we should get started since—

Then the sound I have been fearing most. The step of a boot of softest suede. Expensively wrinkled like the skin of a Shar-Pei. The white moon of her face coming out of the dark. Looking . . .

. . . flustered, apologetic. And frail. Pale, very pale. Is it her skin or the fact that she's wearing black? A long caftan that goes up to her neck like a nun's habit. Her hair is pulled back severely like someone is trying to hang her by it.

"Eleanor, you're late."

I watch her features become warped by confusion, panic. Both firsts. A sick joy spreads through me as she apologizes (another first), then quietly protests: "But . . . you sent out an email saying you weren't starting until 5:11."

"My email said 5:00. Why would anyone request a meeting at 5:11?"

Eleanor cowers a little, looks even more confused by this.

I imagine his human fingers clacking on laptop keys as he composed first in my pleading voice to Fosco, then in the voice of Fosco to Eleanor, all the while humming to himself.

"But—"

"We can discuss this more after class, Eleanor. For now, why don't you take a seat and let's get going, shall we?"

She opens her mouth, then looks at me and closes it. Better not to piss off KareKare, who is really the only one on the faculty who has anything kind to say about her diamond proems. I watch her sit down slowly. In the highly uncharacteristic corner seat. Poking out of her black purse, I see the corner of a small white box. Seeing me looking at it, she tucks the bag under her chair.

"Now, I understand you all have work to share with me today. Except Samantha, of course." I don't bother correcting her.

"Of course," they say, almost in unison. Still not looking at one another. Still smiling to themselves. Dreamily. Smugly. Or, in Eleanor's case, tensely. As though they're each cradling a secret, both wondrous and dangerous. I feel fear. Shimmering fear.

"Well. Who'd like to start?"

"I will." From all of them at the same time. Fosco looks pleased. So eager!

"All right, well, why don't we make this easy and just go in the order in which you arrived. Caroline, let's start with you."

Caroline stands up. Jagged scars gleaming in the spotlight shining down on her.

"This is called 'Peeled,'" she says quietly. "Honestly, I don't quite know what it is yet. Sort of a poem, I guess. . . . I don't normally write poems, but." She bites on her lavender grin. "I was inspired." Her hands are shaking a little as she grips the page.

"Anyway, I really think this could be the beginning of something."

An audible snort from Victoria. I can feel Kira side-eyeing me but I keep my gaze fixed on Caroline, who looks down at her trembling page lovingly as though it is his face. She begins to read as if under a spell.

A man is standing in her living room holding a razor.

Did he break in or did she let him in? So muses the unnamed heroine of "Peeled," who is very obviously Caroline. Thus begins her psychosexual obsession with/possession by a demonic rake named Byron. Tea is stirred suggestively. The *clink clink* of a spoon in its cup has a trance-inducing effect.

And then.

And then I recall Caroline's face when she shaved that

cinnamon stick at Smut Salon. Her head tilted back in a restrained performance of ecstasy. Eyelids fluttering open and closed like she was possessed. Did he carve those words into her peaches-and-cream flesh or did she, while he merely leaned back on her couch and observed, encouraged, supervised with eyes like smoking tar, asking softly what good is it to be left with no trace, to be wounded without the pleasure of a scar?

Silence when she lowers the page. No one claps. No one says, *So good, Bunny.* No one hugs her. There's a pointed cough from Fosco. I hear the word *slut* leave what I am certain is Eleanor's closed lips.

Caroline sits down looking pleased and purged. She opens her white box. Inside is a monstrous cupcake with purple icing the same shade as her hair. I see his face when he offered it to her, the gallant gentleman knowing just the thoughtful confection. She begins to eat the cupcake as if she's starving. Shoveling big chunks in her mouth with her cut-up hands.

"Does anyone have feedback for Caroline?"

Silence save the choked-back laughter of Victoria. The squeak of Kira's pen as it makes the note: *Bitch.* Eleanor is staring murderously at the floor.

"Interesting," Ursula murmurs, surveying the room, then observes how sometimes the silence itself speaks.

"Yes," Caroline says. Her voice still among the smiling clouds. Whatever. This is precisely the reaction she expected. We can all go fuck ourselves. She shovels more cupcake into her mouth.

Purple icing on either corner of her rose lips. Her scars sweating beneath the lights.

Meanwhile, Fosco offers some feedback platitudes. A *departure.* Pregnant pause. *Quite a departure for you, Caroline. This dark . . . romance that you've given us.* Second pregnant pause. Condescending smile.

Normally Fosco adores Caroline's pieces, fragmented narratives involving anxious young women who clearly have never had jobs, who instead brood through afternoonish times of day, think quirky thoughts, bake, and are wistful.

"But of course, it's fine to depart, Caroline. To get lost now and again."

"Lost? But—"

"Because this is why we're here, isn't it? The Process can be tricky, elusive."

Suddenly, Caroline's eyes shine with tears. "I think it's the beginning of something," she whispers. Her face turns pitifully to Ursula, but Ursula has already turned away.

"Who's next?"

No one raises a hand. I gaze deeply down at my desk, at the grains in the wood, trying to hide what I tell myself is strictly my own horror, trying to hide the ticlike smile that I seem to be smiling in spite of myself, that surely must be hysterical. The three white boxes continue to gleam dreadfully in my eye corners no matter where I look. A dread that won't stop winking at me. Nudging. *Psst. Not at all curious, Samantha?* I hear Max's voice saying in my head. *Not even a little curious to know what's inside?*

"I'll go," says Kira, who is holding her bundle of pages like it is an executioner's list. She can't wait to read the names.

"Kira, wonderful."

I watch as she opens her white box. A doll. Wearing a velvet dress. Glassy tiger eyes that stare at me. Cherry mouth smiling. *Enjoying yourself so far, Samantha?*

"This is called 'Wolf Meets Girl,'" Kira says. "It's sort of a fairy tale but totally reenvisioned. I think it's the beginning of something." An audible sniff from Caroline. Victoria makes a fart sound with her mouth. Eleanor now has her eyes closed tight as fists.

"Slut!" Cupcake hisses before Kira's even done, her tale of a lovely redheaded mute whose delicate spirit has been too-long smothered by wicked sisters, and has now been released from her silent prison by a wolfish stranger with the gift of tongues. He is just beginning to speak in a low voice of her fierce depths, to count the many ways she is magic while she counts the many colors of his eyes. Agate. Jade. Periwinkle. Puce. But Caroline has run crying out of the room. Silence. No one moves. I don't know whether to laugh or to cry or to scream. Instead I stare at the doll who is still staring at me. Smiling inscrutably. Kira opens her mouth to continue but Fosco expertly cuts her off, an absolute first. "Thank you, Kira. I believe we have the *gist.*"

A pause so pregnant it delivers, consumes its own spawn, then grows big with child again. "You've given us *more* than enough to discuss, I think." She looks at us all in her probing, intensely gynecological way. *Well?*

"I hated it." This from Caroline, now emerging out of the dark. Her mouth still covered in the icing that so exactly matches her hair. "It's so *derivative.*"

"Derivative, Caroline? That's quite a—"

"Stealing! From the fairy-tale canon. Which is so wrong and so typical of her."

"It's called *literary appropriation,* hello?" Kira says, stroking her doll's blood-colored hair.

Caroline snorts. "It's theft. Narrative theft."

"Say more about that," Fosco urges.

Caroline shakes her head. "I can't." Tears in her eyes. She eats more of the cupcake.

"Anyone else? Victoria, yes, let's hear from you."

"I didn't *hate* it," Victoria says, arms casually crossed. "I just thought it was lame, stupid, and utterly uninteresting."

Fosco frowns. Looks troubled. There'll be no cruelty in the Womb that doesn't come from herself, from Mother. "Can you be more specific?"

"No," she spits, looking Kira up and down. "It's a general impression."

"Samantha? Eleanor?"

I stare at the glassy eyes of the doll that accuse me. Accuse me or acknowledge me?

I look away. "I'm still processing."

"I must say, Samantha, once more I'm right where you are today. I'm processing too." She puts her hands together as though she's praying for us.

"Well, who would—"

"I will," Victoria interjects. She stands and empties her white box onto her desk.

Words tumble out and scatter onto the desk and the floor. A. The. This. Because.

Megalomaniacal. Penis. Dove.

Magnetic poetry. I close my eyes. See him handing over the little bag of words with total seriousness.

Victoria holds up a single wrinkled page. "So this is a vignette."

"Surprise, surprise," Kira whispers to me.

"Excuse me?" Victoria says. "What did you fucking say? What did you whisper-whisper over there like a little bitch?"

"I didn't say anything at all, did I, Samantha?"

Kira turns to me for backup, doing her look of innocent surprise.

An experimental pornographer/garbageman named Hud. An existential ballerina. What happens between them in the dumpster is an obliteration of the flesh conveyed in a sound poetry of grunts. Punctuated by the odd magnetic word. Thigh. Ooze. Genesis.

After she's finished, Victoria drops back into her seat like a marionette suddenly abandoned by its puppeteer. She looks like she puked up soup all over us and she is daring us to like it or hate it. She couldn't care less. She begins to arrange the words with her fingers oh so tenderly. The laugh-scream-cry that has been rising in my throat at last threatens to erupt, and I'm forced to hide my face behind my hands.

"Thoughts, anyone?"

"Liar," Caroline growls. "You're a liar. And you're a terrible fucking writer. *Blood clock? Mind moon?* I'm sorry but *what* does that even mean?"

"Caroline!" Fosco chides.

"It's not *my* fault if you don't *get* it, Caroline."

"Yes, it is!"

"May *I* say something?" Kira actually raises her hand.

"Of course."

"Whenever I read one of Victoria's vignettes, I always feel so dumb because I can hardly understand them at all. And then I blame myself. I think, Kira, this must be just *too* brilliant for you to grasp. Surely *you* must have missed something. Even though there's always been this small voice inside of me that says, *Um, what the fuck is this, please? This makes no sense. This is coy and this is willfully obscure and no one but Victoria will ever get this.* I would in fact need to live inside Victoria's spoiled, fragmented, lazy, pretentious little mind to get it. And who apart from us, apart from *me*, is going to be willing to do that? To work all night with a Victoria Decoder? Who would even care to? And then I feel like screaming JUST SAY IT. TELL ME WHAT HAPPENED. TELL ME WHAT THE FUCK THIS MEANS AND WHAT YOU DID WITH HIM EXACTLY."

A silence so profound it's noise. White noise. Beneath which I hear laughter. His laughter. Behind a human fist whose fingernails he's painted all the colors of the rainbow.

"I guess what I'm saying," Kira continues, more quietly, "is that I understand now. I should have trusted myself as a reader.

My instincts as a reader are so, so valuable. And I'm grateful to Victoria for illuminating that for me. For teaching me about who I am as a reader. Thank you so much for that, Victoria."

Victoria gives her a wide smile. And under the table she spreads her legs, revealing bruises all the way up her thighs.

"You're so, so welcome, Kira."

Beside me, Kira swallows a gasp.

"I hate you," Caroline whispers. Closing her eyes as though she has a headache. It's unclear who she's saying it to.

"I agree," Kira whispers, her gaze still on the thigh bruises like someone struck.

"What is your take on all this, Samantha?"

Now they're all looking at me, sort of pleadingly. I think of Max. Casting his huge shadow over each of them in turn. Playing the sadist, the sly god, the garbageman. Sitting in their living rooms, in their bedrooms, smiling at each of them like he's The Bachelor. Holding a red rose between his pointed fingernails. Holding their hands. Handing them each a small white box. *This is you.* And then I feel like I've fingered their various underwear, am deeply, unbearably familiar with the colors and cuts, the hand-feel, that I know all the songs on their Spotify sex playlists. That I held the razor blade over Caroline's peach-fuzzed skin, mine are the teeth sinking into Victoria's thigh flesh. I kicked their stuffed ponies off their sleigh beds, caused their nightstand novels to topple over, their bottles of melatonin and Valium to spill to the floor, their jelly-bean-colored vibrators to roll around in the little drawer, beginning to collect dust at last. And after, mine was the hand that turned out the unicorn-shaped light. The breeze coming from their open bedroom windows cooling my skin as I replayed their various humiliations, a triumphant smile on my untorn lip.

I feel sick. Hideously sick.

"Well, this is so wonderful," Fosco says, taking up my silence like a fallen torch. "These sorts of difficult conversations. So *illuminating*, so valuable. How they open us up. The Wound is tapped and it bleeds. I must say, though, I'm a little concerned by the androcentric leanings in today's pieces so far. Did you notice that, Samantha?"

"Yes."

"As female storytellers, writing at this level, at this institution, we must be mindful of this. Do we really want to enforce the narrative that we're 'saved' by a *boy*? Illuminated by a *boy*? Ravished by a *boy*? The same *boy*, it seems? Who says the same things to save and ravish and illuminate us? Do we really want *that* to be the Work? The fruit to come out of our time here at Warren? One would hope the Work wouldn't just be the stuff of slumber parties. Samantha, wouldn't you agree?"

They stare at me. Kira stroking her doll, Caroline among the now frowning clouds, Victoria still smirking and trying for bored but clearly pissed. Well, Samantha?

I look over at Eleanor, who has been silent all this time, holding the still-closed box in her hands, watching me over it, a caveman enemy over a flame. The diamond-etched proem sits in her black lap containing god knows what.

"I think I need to hear from everyone," I hear myself say.

Eleanor looks at me and I feel her soul hiss.

"Now Eleanor, I *hope* you're not writing about a *boy* too," Fosco says.

Eleanor suddenly smiles. "Of course not, Ursula. I'd never be that stupid. But as it turns out I brought the wrong story," she says looking at me. "My mistake."

"Eleanor, that's highly unlike you."

"I know it is. I'm sorry. It'll never happen again."

34

When I get home, I find him in the backyard leaning against the fence, smoking, wearing Kira's cat ears. He's staring at the patchy corner of lawn where he has talked of planting something. God knows what. He smiles when he sees me, raises his whisky glass. Oh so casual. Maintaining his cool-man slouch. I think of the way my black metal drummer boyfriend would saunter over to me after his gigs, his fake-blood-splattered lab coat heavy with sweat, his corpse paint running down his eyes. Dying to know. Too cool to ask.

"So. How was Workshop, Samantha?"

I stare at his mouth that has spoken so many lies. Hands that might have touched god knows what parts of their pink-and-white bodies.

"Illuminating," I say.

"Illuminating," he murmurs, taking a thoughtful drag of his cigarette. *Huh.* Not the adjective he was hoping for exactly but—

"What did you do to them?" I blurt out.

He looks at me. Confused. Disappointed. Frankly, a little irritated.

The smoke slowly escapes his mouth. Blows right into my face.

"You have to tell me."

He stares at me, at my attempt to look authoritative, the desperate pleading it conceals, then snorts and looks away. Shakes his head. Takes another drag. Defiant this time.

"I can't just *give* it away like that, Samantha. I wanted to leave it open. To interpretation."

He smiles slightly at the word *interpretation*, recalling perhaps key moments in his own genius.

"You need to tell me what you did. You need to tell me exactly."

"*Do* I?"

He's pissed now. *And not a little hurt, Samantha.* I am his audience of one, do I not realize that? The work he put into this thing, the planning. He was expecting, frankly, for me to be blown away. Instead, here I am asking for little annoying details and worse: explanations.

"I mean, why bother if I'm just going to *tell you exactly*. Where's the fun in that? Why bother making art at all?"

"I never asked you to make . . ." and then I trail off.

He moves in closer to me, raises his brows. *What was that?*

I bite my lower lip, feeling myself flush.

He laughs, throwing his head back so the moonlight catches his neck, and when I look up, I can see the entirety of the black ax from the handle to the blade. When at last he stops, he looks at me tenderly. With something like love. Oh, Samantha.

I lower my gaze to my shoes, the mud they stand in.

"Do you realize they're all in love with you?" I say this softly, accusingly. I accuse the mud.

I look up at him.

He shrugs. "Good for them," he mumbles. This isn't interesting to him, this news. Inevitable casualties of the Process, the Work. Can't make an omelet, etc.

"But they're acting like they're . . . possessed."

He smiles dreamily. "They're free now . . . from each other anyway."

"They're dangerous, you know," I say, recalling their shining faces warped with intensity and rage in Workshop today. Our old Workshops in the attic. With the ax.

"I'm afraid," he says softly. "Truly."

"I'm serious."

"So am I. Look into my eyes. See how scared?"

"Did you sleep with them?"

He makes a face. "Ew."

"Did you woo them?"

"*Woo*?" he repeats. Ugh. "I can promise you I didn't *woo*."

"Did you *hurt* them?"

God, this question bores him. *Come on, Samantha. You* saw *the scars yourself. The bruises, the bites, the hair, the voice like a void, hello?*

But he plays along. "What am I, Samantha? A monster?"

Yes. And I've unleashed you upon the world.

I brush his hair away from his eyes because it's driving me crazy not to see them. It's what Caroline used to do to me. She braided my bitch curtain away from my face, pulling it onto the top of my head in a twisty crown. *There you go, Bunny.* But just as I'm unveiling his one forever hidden eye, he beats my hand away instinctively. Hisses at me like a big cat. When he sees me get scared, he smiles.

He cups my face in his ungloved hands. They will not charm me into submission, these real human hands on my face. I can feel the lines on the palms and everything. I close my eyes instinctively at their warmth. At their lightness.

"Samantha," he says. "Did you or did you not enjoy it?"

Watching them humiliate themselves and each other? Scream at each other? Hug only their own pink and white, scarred and bruised, sugar-bloated bodies? Read especially terrible work that they must have written in some sort of love trance? A work and a love that mocked them? Watch them get admonished by Fosco?

He nods my head gently for me while I say, No. I did not. At all enjoy myself.

"What about Ava?" I ask.

He lets go of my face. Becomes Mr. Intensely Sincere. Christian Slater with the bomb in his trench coat pocket. Christian Slater with the baboon heart.

"What about Ava?" he says.

"Wouldn't she be upset if she knew?"

"If she knew what, exactly, Samantha?" He looks at me until I blush.

"What are you guys whispering about down there?" Ava yells. She's on the roof among her raccoon priests. Deep in her Drink Me.

He looks up at her like she is the sun. All he's missing is a bouquet of twigs. A soft filter. The sky to open and let fall upon his head a spotlit movie rain that will drip from his hair onto his eyelashes, slide in rivulets down his knifey cheeks. Is he crying or is it the rain? We'll never know. And anyway, listen to the love song swelling all around us.

I'm looking at him from across the dinner table. Max. Tristan. Byron. Hud. Icarus. Whatever the fuck his name is. Watching him dish the gamy stew I will devour tonight in spite of myself. Watching him pour me a blackish wine. Perhaps this is the only child I'll ever have. Mine and not mine. Complete with his own unknowable will. *Is it so unknowable, Samantha?* he seems to say to me with the side of his face, though he's turned toward Ava, always toward Ava. Does she truly know how beautiful she is? he is asking her for the millionth time.

Shut up, I hear her say, but her shut up is *Don't shut up*. *Ever, please.* He tells her things I never thought of telling her. I hear all my own scratched-out lines on his lips. Things I whispered to the hare statue, to the trees, on the way home in the morning from hanging out. Full of the beginnings of stories. Things far too lame to ever say out loud. He says them all in a voice I know I've heard before. Low. Sure. Always smiling inside of itself. You never know if it's serious or not.

"I'm serious."

She swoons. Opens for him like a flower in the morning. Hides her already veiled face behind a lace black glove. My friend. My dearest friend. Warn her. I have to warn her. I drink more black wine and my eyes grow heavy as I watch his shadow consume us. Wanting to ask him questions. What do you want? With me? With my friend? With my enemies? Are you actually born of that hideous runt that hopped away under my gaze in the Duchess's living room, leaving too-large prints in the snow, far too large for a bunny? Or are you born of another animal? A monster of my own making? But my lips remain shut. I drink more wine. I follow them into the living room. I watch them dance.

Drinking Ava's Campari and soda. Bringing her half-smoked cigarette to my lips. Looking at her, his face lights up in a way that makes my soul embarrassed. It is so nakedly in love. Is hers that way? Hers is more like a slowly unfurling fist. It might unfurl all the way. Or not. We'll see.

I watch their bodies come together and fall away as the music dictates. I watch them kiss. I watch their lips open up for each other. Something inside of me opens and opens too. Opens so wide I feel like everything inside could fly out. I'm afraid and exhilarated all at once.

Between their bodies, in the window, I see my own face reflected. Cheeks flushed with Ava's cocktail. So dreamy and happy. A smile of such pure bliss on my lips. I look like Jonah when he is deep in his poetry cloud where nothing can touch him.

There's another face that appears in the pane. This one is on the outside looking in. Like it was always there and I'm just seeing it now. The Duchess. Looking at me looking at Ava and Max. She's smiling too. But it's another kind of smile. Infuriated. Glutted with knowledge. Readying itself for revenge.

I scream.

"Samantha?! Are you okay?" This from Ava, who rushes to my side.

I point to the window, which Max goes to check. But she's disappeared into the dark.

There's nothing there anymore but dark. Just a moon, shining like it never shines where I live. *That's because the moon hates where you live, remember?*

She was there, though. I'm certain of it. "It was her."

"Who? Who was there?" Ava asks.

"Nothing, no one. It was just a dream. Probably. Or a hallucination. I've had a long day. Maybe I should go to sleep."

"Yes," Max says, "maybe you should."

You're sick, is the text I get moments later.

We're on the roof, Ava and I, watching him below us in the garden. Hunched over that patch of damp green he's been contemplating. It's warm enough to start at last, he said this morning, staring out the window. Nefariously, I thought.

Start what? I asked, imagining the worst.

Planting, he answered.

Planting what?

Seeds.

Visions of him pouring arsenic into the earth. Setting all the grass and weeds ablaze. Putting a spell on the lawn so that it grows tall and tangled and buries us. If I'm truly being honest I have no idea what his intentions are with the lawn or anything else.

My intentions? he repeated, when I asked him—confronted him!—the other night, drunk, the living room spinning all around us. *It's not the living room spinning, Samantha, it's you.* We were dancing together, which we almost never do. Because it's a shitshow. Because we kill each other's feet. Because when he goes left, I go left. When I go right, he goes right. *A fucking shit-show,* Ava observed from the couch. *You guys could make money doing this. They would have eaten this up at my alma mater.*

It was clear my use of the word *intentions* amused him terribly. He let out a great honking laugh. *My INTENTIONS. MY intentions.*

Well? I said. I was not at all amused. I needed to know. Desperately. I looked into his eyes, which I wished would stop changing color for one fucking second.

But he looked amused even by this, my desperation.

I don't know, Samantha, he said, *what are they?*

It has been eerily silent for the past few days. No texts from the Bunnies. No tulip. No troll. No hatchet. No open-armed ghost. No phone calls. Just one email from the Lion, Fosco cc'd. Subject line: *Checking in.* Followed by ellipses. The message was brief. *I'm afraid we need to have a chat at this point. 7 at the Cave tonight, please.* No sign off. Not even an icy *Best.* But the white space that follows his message says everything I know he must be thinking. That I'm the one who is supposed to get in touch with him about my thesis. That it's my job, not his, hello?

"Blow it off," Ava says now, lighting a cigarette and passing the Drink Me.

"I can't."

"Well, give him a big fuck you from me. Tell him no one I love gets fucked with and lives."

"You love me?"

"What a question. Of course. No one loves you like me." She smiles at me. She means it. With her whole soul. It is holding itself open like a hand, palm up.

Ava, I love you.

"Ava, Max isn't real." As the words leave my lips, I stare straight ahead at the dripping trees.

"What do you mean he isn't *real*?"

I take a breath. "I mean, I made him."

She laughs.

"I'm serious," I whisper.

"You *made* him," she repeats.

I nod. "Yes. From a bunny." Closing my eyes. It's all too terrible.

"You *made* him from a bunny."

I nod again. "Don't hate me," I plead. "Please don't hate me."

"Samantha, look at me. What the fuck are you talking about?"

So I tell her. Everything. About the Bunnies. About the boys. About "Workshop." What happened after she went away. How I made this boy only I didn't know it at first because he didn't seem like a bunny boy. At all. He was so different from the others. He was actually so real seeming, I didn't know he was a bunny myself. Until later. And by then, he'd already hooked up with her. I tell her he loves her because I love her. But I tell her he's also fucking with the Bunnies. To get back at them. Not because he loves them or anything. He hates them. Because I hate them. Which makes sense. Anyway, I think he's stopped now. Fucking with them. I'm not sure. They might still be in love with him. They might be pissed. Definitely they are pissed. Probably plotting something. Look, it's all very unclear. This question of intentions. This question of what everyone wants, of where this is all leading in the end. All I know is we could all be in very grave danger. And it's all my fault.

I tell her this with my eyes on the trees, branches brimming with pale green buds. I don't dare look at Max, who is still down there in the garden, shoveling. I can hear his spade turning the earth.

Ava's not saying anything. Is she dead? Did I kill her with my words? No, I hear her breathing quietly beside me, smoking. Her pulse making her rain scent bloom. But I can't bear to look at her.

"Well," I ask, after another excruciating stretch of silence, still looking at the trees drip-dripping away, "aren't you going to say something?"

"About what?" she says. Her tone is flat. Frighteningly flat.

"About what I just told you?"

She looks at Max, his broad, treelike frame bent at his task. His ripped arms gripping the spade, shoveling. Probably even his sweat is foresty.

"I think you're a brilliant artist. And I applaud your work."

She looks at me and I see there's a laugh brimming there under her straight face.

"What? Ava, no, this is real, what I'm telling you. It's real. I mean, I know it sounds insane. . . ." I trail off, hearing the manic quality of my own voice.

I turn to look at her, but she's looking down at Max. He isn't hunched over. He's standing up. Looking up at her from where he stands below. He waves at us. At her.

We both watch him wave. Dark hair covering one eye. Earnest face. Waving and waving and waving. His hand high above his head.

She looks at him, then back at me. She looks at me for so long and so intently I want to look away but I don't. Then something in her expression shifts. The laughing lightness fades. And something terrible dawns in her eyes. "Samantha—"

"I'm sorry," I say quickly, cutting her off. "I don't know where I came up with that story. Crazy. I guess I'm still pretty messed up." I shake my head. Look at her.

The shift is still there, in her face. The lightness doesn't come back. She's staring at me in a way I can't bear. I turn away from her, letting the bitch curtain fall.

"You should get going. To your meeting," she says.

No more talk of blowing it off. I start to climb down the ladder, clumsy under her gaze, then suddenly I am possessed by a terrible feeling. I stop and turn around and slip and almost fall and kill myself.

She's still sitting there, no longer watching me, but watching him.

"Ava."

"What?"

"Nothing," I say. But I don't move. Can't bring myself to leave her, even though the shingles are crackling beneath my feet and I feel myself starting to slip again.

"You'll still be here?" I ask. "When I come back?"

She smiles. "Of course I'll still be here. Where would I go?"

35

Hello?" I call out in the Cave. But all I hear is the echo of my own voice bouncing off the drippy walls. Darker than usual. No womblike warmth about it today. Didn't he say 7:00? But there are no clocks in the Cave. There are no lights in the Cave. Even the door I came in by has already blended into the black.

"Hello?" I call out again.

Nothing.

"Alan?"

No answer. Just my echo. Calling and calling his name.

Probably fucking with you. He likes to fuck with you, remember?

Waiting for him, looking for his shape in the dark, I feel my heart starts to pound. The silence and the dark gather into his quiet judgment. Into his pedagogical and psychosexual strategy. Into his sleek silhouette. That appeared in the alley that spring night at the party. That night where nothing happened, nothing at all happened. That came out of the dark like a dream when I was so drunk the sky and earth had crashed into one another. *Cuntscapades!* I'd screamed then stormed away from Jonah, down the alley, into the tilted night. And there he was, standing where the alley meets the street, leaning against the bricks as though I wrote him there, wearing a T-shirt of a monster devouring a girl, black branches climbing his bare arms. Standing absolutely still while the alley rocked like a ship.

"Samantha," says a velvety voice now. Male. Lilting. Thistle and heather swaying gently on a crag.

Hearing it in the dark, I shiver, though I tell myself I should be relieved.

"Alan," I say, putting the relief in my voice, my echo revealing the tremor. "You're here."

I look around but there's nothing but black.

"I'm here, Samantha." Patience eternal. "Where are you?"

Visions of leaving the alley with him. Getting into the passenger seat of his car. Watching him drive us somewhere. *Where are we going?* I didn't care to ask. Then, at a stoplight that he nearly missed, that he had to drunkenly slam on his brakes to catch, I saw the Bunnies through his passenger window. They'd moved their drunken hug-fest to some bistro terrace near campus that sold champagne by the glass. Though I kept staring straight ahead, right through the windshield at the eternal red light, I saw them see me in his car. See us. I kept my chin up, my stare straight. *Think whatever you want, think the worst, I dare you.* I glanced at him out of my eye corner. He was looking straight ahead at the windshield too, literally looking as straight ahead as you can look. And I knew that he'd seen them too. That he'd seen them see us. And then suddenly it was all wrong. Me sitting in his car. Us together. My crossed legs in lace tights full of holes, my heels dangling from my feet, my wildly swaying mind, the way the sky and the earth were at such odd angles with each other, the terrible glimpse I caught of my face, its expression, in his side-view mirror. All wrong. And him. Beside me in the driver's seat. Trying to appear sober. Waiting calmly for the light to change. He was all wrong too.

"Samantha," says the voice again now. Velvety. Closer. Though I see nothing in the black but the black.

"Where are you?" I ask.

I barely remember getting to his apartment that night. Dimly recall stumbling up some dark spiral staircase that seemed to wind up and up forever. Sitting across from him in his ever-spinning living room. Our slurred talk skipping from one book to the next, from one topic to the next, like we were on a jerky fast-forward. Telling myself it was just like all those other times we'd talked and wasn't this nice to finally be talking again. Except this time I was doing all the talking. Except this time I spoke loudly, like I wanted to be overheard by someone outside. Speaking my words with such exactitude. Like the names of things and people and books weren't slipping from my lips, spilling onto his floor like wine. As though it weren't all wrong. Him watching me, saying nothing at all. Like I was a play he was already deeply familiar with—had seen many productions of—was frankly slightly bored by at this point, but there were some good parts coming potentially, depends. Depends entirely on the production. I said I was glad we were talking again, even though I was the only one talking. Talking into a silence so loud it felt like a live thing in the room. That seemed to be growing, gathering shape and shadow, no matter how much I kept talking like everything was fine.

Until all my words had spilled to the floor. I was too drunk to pick them up. *So leave them there.*

I recall staring down at his polished floor, my head full of blood, my heart beating in my ears, silence now roaring unbearably around me.

And then, embarrassingly, I began to cry. Tell him everything. Embarrassing things. Shameful things. Anything to change how silent it was and the kind of silent it was. How much I hated the Bunnies. How much they hated me. My loneliness all winter. My worry that I'd disappointed him somehow. How blocked I was. My shifting, lonely life before I came here, my father falling off the map, even my mother. I sobbed like a child except I was a grown woman slurring these words into her lace thighs. Expecting at any moment for his silence to lift, the room to stand still, lighten, and right itself, a hand to reach out, a voice to offer some words of comfort and kindness. But he just kept drinking, kept watching. Didn't speak, didn't touch. No arm around my shoulder. No hand on my knee. No cock against my thigh. No mouth on my neck or breath in my ear. The absence of his voice and touch so palpable it acquired physical weight.

I scan the Cave again now for his silhouette. Still nothing, nothing but black, nothing-black.

"*Here,* Samantha. Right here." Alan's brogue again, growing impatient.

"I'm sorry, I . . . can't really see. . . ."

In the stories I tried to write about that night later, something happens in that silence. Rather than us getting up, walking down his dark hallway, him turning to go up the stairs, me stumbling out his front door. I fill it with something. Something like sex. An insinuation of violence. A pass made. A line crossed. Something, not nothing. Definitely not nothing. Because it's the only way to explain how neither of us could look one another in the eye for the remaining weeks of the year. The weird shame and hurt that would well up in me whenever I saw him pretend not to see me, or even worse, when he would just curtly nod. How we never hung out after that in a room with a closed door. How I left that night. Wondering what the hell just happened. Knowing nothing happened, knowing too that everything had changed. How empty and emptied I felt walking away with all my words still on his floor. Wanting so badly to pick them back up. Take it all back. Wipe away the night, my dumb tears, my endless tumbling out of words. *I never meant to give this to you.* How alone now. Truly alone I was, making my shuffling way through the dark, the ground seeming to give beneath my feet, the dark of the street and the dark of the sky, one big dark. So lost I somehow wound up at the pond instead of home. *Where you met me,* Ava reminds me. *See, Smackie? Sometimes being lost is a fucking wonderful thing.*

"Are you lost, Samantha?" Alan says, softly now. "We're right here."

We?

"Yes, Samantha," says another voice. Female this time. Familiar too. "Right here." Fosco.

"Ursula? I didn't expect—"

"Samantha, just walk toward our mouth sounds, please," says Fosco.

Mouth sounds?

"Yes, precisely," says Alan. "Or, um, keep talking and we'll find you."

Run, says a voice inside my head. *Right now. Run as fast as you—*

Then I feel a hand cup my mouth in the dark. Gloved. Leather. I am suffocated by the sweet smell of muffin mix on fire. Like a baking project gone terribly wrong. I try to scream, but the hand holds me fast. A suited arm wraps around my chest like a snake and another hand cups the nape of my neck. Now I scream through the leather hand. Bite the fingers hard. A high-pitched wail behind me like a shrieking girl. And then the hand cupping the back of my neck tightens its grip. And suddenly all is bright darkness forever and ever.

A figure before me. Two figures. Because of how the light is or the dark is, I can't see their faces, I can't see their bodies. Only their shapes. Both large. One stocky, one slim. Stocky and Slim. *Who are you?* I want to ask them but my mouth doesn't work, it seems. Focus. Focusfocusfocusfocusfocus. But keeping my eyes open is such heavy, hard work, *why*? Because of drugs. The knowledge courses through me like heavy, sweet syrup. Drip. Drip.

The figures are seated. Smiling even, I think. At me. That's nice. Maybe they're nice. They are waiting, it seems. Waiting so patiently. For what, I wonder? And then I grow afraid.

Uh-oh. Scary, says my brain. *I had better leave. Bye-bye time.* I am about to wave to the figures and say *bye-bye it was so nice to meet you, figures,* but I find I cannot lift my hand, I cannot move. I am seated too. Tied to a hard chair. Bound. *Bound, bound, bound.* Though I am terrified, the thought is pleasant, like a buoyant red balloon sailing through a bright blue sky. I watch it sail dreamily through the cloudless air thinking, *I have been here before in my mind, watching this red balloon,* and then somewhere in the air there is screaming. My screaming. A voice inside saying, *Fucking run.*

"What was that, Samantha? I'm sorry, I couldn't quite make that out," says one of the figures. Stocky. Wild hair sprouting from his head like mange. His voice says *Trust me.*

Who are you? I want to ask, but my lips aren't moving right. Nothing but gurgling comes out.

"Samantha, I'm afraid that's unacceptable. You'll have to speak more clearly." This from Slim, who I see now has long silver-and-black hair like the scary lady from fairy tales, what's she called again? The witch. I know that voice. I know both voices. Where? Where do I know them?

"This is *your* committee meeting, Samantha, after all, and we have much to discuss."

"So much to discuss, Samantha."

Committee meeting! Discuss! Relief floods me. Alan and Ursula. I could weep.

I move to hug them but my hands are tied. Seeing me attempt this, they lean forward, I presume to untie me so that we can all hug. But no, they just lean in so that I may see their faces in the dim red light. Their warped features. Their zombie skin. Their lips twisted and ripped on one side only. Jutting from their heads, the beginnings of a pair of long, gray, twitching ears.

I try to scream, but nothing comes. No sound from my dead mouth.

They look at me curiously with their wrong-color eyes, and I feel the wild black animal gaze of the Duchess upon me. *Hello there, Samantha.*

"Are you ready to discuss or not, Samantha? Can we begin, please?" Bunny Lion says with his ripped lips. His hands encased in the all too familiar black leather gloves *because hands are hard, Bunny*. His lumpy body shrouded in a dark blue suit cut to hide all his deformities and imperfections in design. *Because bodies are hard too*. He looks like they made him in five minutes.

More silent screaming comes out of me. I am deep in the eye of the Bunny drug I know too well.

"Samantha, perhaps *you* would like to get us started." This from Bunny Fosco. Ensconced in hissing scarves. Eyes like violet voids behind which loom the anime glare of Caroline, looking like she wants to eat me and yet I am not cooked entirely to her liking, *oh, dear*. She holds a small ax lightly in her hands as if it's a bundle of burning sage. Here to purify the room.

"No? Then I suppose I will start even though this is YOUR meeting, Samantha. Are you ready?"

I watch her open a black book that reads *My Sad Girl Novel by Samantha Mackey* on the cover.

Under the title is a picture of a female stick figure frown-pouting and crossing her stick arms.

"I've been perusing your work, Samantha. And I must say, Samantha, I'm so disappointed."

"Me too. So disappointed. *So*," Bunny Lion says. "I mean, I was like 'intrigued' at first." He air quotes with his gloved fingers.

"Oh, we were all 'intrigued' at *first*. Maybe even dazzled. Smitten by a certain grittiness, a certain dark charm."

"Sure, all of that," Bunny Lion agrees. "But now?" He shrugs his misshapen shoulders. "Ew. Is what I think." He looks at Bunny Fosco, who nods gravely.

They both turn their hideous heads to me. Gray faces pensive, probing.

"Samantha, it isn't giving itself to us. It's being . . . *coy*," she spits.

"Willfully withholding," Bunny Lion says. "Unnecessarily inaccessible. Not delivering on its premise."

"And it was a dazzling premise. Who could deny that?"

"Not me."

They both look at me hungrily. I think of Rob Valencia gazing at my corsage like he wanted to eat it. His mouth full of orchid. They're looking at me like my face is an orchid.

They move in closer, licking their lips.

"Samantha, I must say I'm so concerned about your heroine," says Bunny Fosco.

"So concerned. So," adds Bunny Lion.

"Although we could hardly call her a heroine, could we? I mean, could we even call her that, Samantha?" Her bunny ear stumps twitch like antennae. "She's quite *passive,* Samantha, isn't she?" She tilts her hideous gray head.

I try to protest but I feel something soft filling my mouth. The same softness binding my hands. A gag. Has it been there all along?

"Things just *happen* to her, don't they, Samantha?"

My lips make a burbling noise around the soft gag, which seems to be growing larger and larger in my mouth. It feels alive, this softness filling my mouth, binding my wrists. Animal. There is the scent of decomposing animal all around me. Cloaked in a muffiny sweetness that barely conceals the rot.

I feel all eight of their eyes upon me as the drug spreads through my body. The velvet swaddling of the brain, of all motor function, the syrupy heaviness coursing through my limbs. Why can't I think my way out of this? But my brain has been overrun by prancing pink ponies baring their teeth.

"When is she going to be *empowered,* Samantha? Hmm? Exercise *agency*? When is she going to assume *responsibility* for all the shit she's stirred up?"

"When," he growls, "is she going to stop having her warped little threesome where she doesn't even get to fuck anyone is what I want to know."

Bunny Fosco nods sadly, like yes, oh, yes, that's right. "Her 'friend' or whatever. Ada, isn't it? Whatever."

"Whatever," Bunny Lion says, rolling his eyes.

Fosco leans forward, her warped face so close to mine I can feel her zombie breath on my skin.

"Still," she murmurs. "It's sad, I suppose. What happens to her in the end."

What happens? What happens to her in the end?

She comes closer still, searching my face with something like tender hunger. I sense her turning Kira's ax in her gloved hands while the soft alive thing fills and fills my mouth, pushing against the roof, pressing down on my tongue.

"Samantha, do you know what a book should be? Every Great Book, that is? Certainly a thesis at Warren?"

She holds up the ax to my throat. Brushes the blade gently against my sweating neck, like a kitten scratching.

"Well, Samantha?"

Let me go. Stop it. Please, I burble-drool.

"Very good, Samantha, an ax. A book should be like an ax."

"*For the frozen sea within us,*" finishes Bunny Lion.

She presses the blade a little deeper into my neck. *No,* I sigh through the velvet swaddle. I try to untie my hands but I can't find them to untie them, they're gone. *Hands are hard, Bunny.*

They watch me wriggle uselessly. Sigh fake-sadly.

"Samantha, after reading this, we're starting to worry you're not Warren material."

"And we should know, Samantha. I mean, we teach here."

"We should never have let you in, Samantha. You weren't ready."

"So not ready."

"But even though you're an asshole," Bunny Fosco starts in, "we still want to help you. We really do. So we're giving you a gift, Samantha. Because we're so nice. Something to look at and ponder and consider."

"A token. A writing prompt. A surprise," Bunny Lion says. "It'll be waiting for you when you get home."

"*If* she gets home. I mean . . . should we even let her go home?"

They appear to consider this. Hmm.

They're going to kill me. They're going to fucking kill me.

No. I shake and shake and shake my head, which is nodding, nodding.

Bunny Fosco gets up from her chair; so does Bunny Lion. She holds up the ax while his leather hand reaches out and grazes the side of my face. Gently, so gently. He reaches around to the back of my neck. He's going to kiss me now. He's going to kill me now. Instead he finds that place on the nape and squeezes and all is darkness again.

36

Hey." I open my eyes to bright overhead lights. I'm lying bound and gagged on the floor of the Cave in a turned-over chair. My soul empty of prancing ponies, my brain no longer giggling mulch. A janitor is standing over me with a giant broom in his hand, looking bored. He blinks at my ribbon restraints like he's seen this sort of thing before.

"All right. Time to move it along, miss."

He nudges my side with the handle of his broom.

"Please untie me," I try to shout through the gag. White feathers spill from my mouth like snow.

He watches them fall from my lips, unphased. "What's that now?"

"Can you untie me, please?" I try again.

He shrugs. Reaches down and mutteringly unties the ribbons around my wrists and ankles, which slip off *pretty easily, lady*.

"Thank you," I gasp, releasing more white feathers. "You saved me. They were trying to kill me."

He shakes his head. "You kids and your conceptual art."

"No, you don't understand, they were *really* trying to . . ."

One last feather bit floats from my mouth and hangs in the air between us. He looks at the feather with boredom. Watches it float down to the ground along with the other feathers, the pile of ribbons, which he will now have to sweep up. He sighs.

"The real world, lady. It's out there. Do you even know that? You're going to have to get back to it sometime."

A low red moon shining down on me. Ran all the way from Warren. Faster and faster as the Bunny drugs left my body. Believing I was followed. Taking side and roundabout streets. Dodging my invisible yet inevitable pursuers. A sick feeling inside, like a panicked black animal scurrying around in my gut.

We're giving you a gift, Samantha. Because we're so nice.

It'll be waiting for you when you get home.

As I approach Ava's, I see the front window's wide open. Not unusual. She likes a breeze. *The breeze is my lover, Smackie,* she tells me all the time. *Meet my lover, the breeze. It speaks to me with a Scottish accent. It cools my legs and feet.* A rosy glow from inside, music faintly playing. I catch her scent of wet leaf, green tea hanging here and there in the sweet spring air.

Relief floods through me. She's still here. Of course she's still here.

Where would I even go?

"Ava," I say as I come in.

Inside, all the lady-shaped lamps are lit. Ditto her candles and Christmas lights. A record playing "La Vie en Rose." The smell of a thousand long-burned-away incense sticks. A new one burning somewhere. Birds in the tapestry above her bed, each regarding me with its one eye.

I call her name as I walk through the rooms, as I climb the stairs.

"Max? Ava? Max?"

I reach the top of the stairs. And then I freeze.

You've read books that say things like "Time stood still"? I always thought it was bullshit. But it does. It can. It can stand as still as I am standing, here in the kicked-down doorway. It can stand as still as the blood-spattered walls and the broken window. It can be as still as the giant dead swan with the ax in its back lying in the middle of the room, its white wings extended as though poised for flight, a pool of dark blood oozing from its giant body. As still as Max sitting beside it in the blood pool that seems to be spreading. As still as my own lips, which do not scream even as my body fills with something dark and fluid and burning.

I stare at the long, lifeless white neck. The glinty blade cleaving the white feathers. It's a dream, I tell myself, the ground beneath my feet swelling and sinking, as I float on the dark red water.

"Max," I say and I hear the great crack in my voice, right down the middle of his name. "What is this? What happened?" But he doesn't answer me. His whole body is turned away, hunched over the swan, oblivious. His head hangs. Hair in his eyes. He is absolutely still.

I look back at the white bird, the blood spreading around my feet. Feel myself sink to my knees. The blood is dark and so terribly warm around my legs.

"Max." I reach out and shake him by his shoulders. Was he always this frail? Were his shoulders always this thin, this insubstantial?

"What is this? What have you done?" I say, the great crack in my voice spreading like a crack in a mirror.

His head still hangs down, his neck slack.

This has to be a dream. Surely, just a dream. Ava will wake me any minute and tell me so. But Ava isn't here. Somehow I know this.

"Max."

"She told me to go."

"What?"

"After you left. She told me to go. She said she wanted to be alone."

"What are you talking about?"

"She never asked me to leave before. I didn't understand what I'd said or done. She just said, *go.* So I left. Walked away, gave her some space. But then I had this feeling. This sick, sick feeling. So I ran back here."

He's still staring at the swan. Whose white body is burning my vision. Whose white body is so very still.

"Max, please. I don't understand what's happening. Tell me what's happening."

I turn his shoulders around to face me and it's like propping up a toy you want to play with, a sad cheap doll who refuses to go along with the story. I shake him and I shake him and I shake him while I say and say his name and still his head hangs down. I recall my mother shaking me like this. How many times she shook me like this when I was a child, when I was a teen. *Samantha. Please. Listen to me. Stop this, okay? This has to stop. You need to stop pretending.*

A sick feeling. A sick, sick feeling.

With my hands, I raise his head up to meet my gaze.

"Max." His face in my hands is so smooth and small and light. My palms tingle.

"Please. Tell me. Where's Ava?"

But even as I ask I know the answer. The answer is the dark chill rising in me. The answer is in his face, which is staring at the swan with such love. Like she is cherry blossoms falling. Serious moonlight. Light shivering on green leaves. The answer is my mother's voice suddenly flooding my ears, calling my name wearily, worriedly, scoldingly, *Samantha.* The answer is in the scent of green tea and wet leaf still hanging here and there in the air faintly, so faintly, rising from the body like a wish made. The answer is the white feathers still being blown softly, so softly, around the room by the breeze from the open window. Blowing softly through her hair like white feathers whenever they caught the light. *The breeze is my lover, Smackie. Meet my lover, the breeze.* Blowing softly through her hair like white feathers, blowing around her face the last time she smiled at me with love, always with love.

The answer is my own heart. Which is caving in.

A bench by the pond's edge. Last spring. Early morning. I'm sitting here watching a swan turn circles in the sludge. Just left the Lion's house. Didn't intend to come here. But you know when your feet just walk you to a place? Black clothes sticking to my body. Hands empty and open at my sides. Empty and emptied. Alone, alone, alone. Watching the swan, alone too, morning light on its white feathers as it glides along the dark water like a dream, I wish it was all a dream. Wish I could erase the night. Fill it with something else. Someone.

Someone's sitting here beside me on the bench. Suddenly there.

A woman. Right beside me on the bench. Smiling like we're already deep friends.

Hey, do you have a light?

Black silk dress, black mesh gloves. Eyes a different color, one blue one brown, gazing at me through a fishnet veil. Platinum hair like white feathers when they catch the light.

When I hand her the lighter, she smiles, thanks me.

I watch her light up and smoke. I could watch her smoke forever.

Samantha, says someone, calling my name from far, far away. Fuck off. Go away whoever you are. I want to talk to this woman, smoking beside me, smiling beside me, tilting her head up to the light.

"You look familiar," I say to her. "Have we met before?"

She turns to me. Her smile is like light on my face. Light shivering on green leaves.

"I think maybe we have."

Something in her voice. A certain music in it. Very specific. Instantly familiar. Do you know the music I mean? Like it's not just a sound but a place. A place I think I've been before. Where I could live forever. There is air and light in it. There are windows and doors. It is inside and it is outside. It's a hand. Soft. Firm. Open. Have I held it before?

I look out at the pond now. Empty. Just lily pads floating on a still surface.

Samantha!

Now we're on the roof, she and I, dancing. Tango music playing softly to drown out the Mexican music next door. It's the hour between the dog and the wolf. We've consumed so much of a cocktail that is probably poison, but fuck it, what a way to go. Rocking in each other's arms. Between us, a beautiful man we made of air. And we're laughing, because we're a shitshow at the leading and following thing. But fuck that too. Because I'm so, so happy. Here. With you. I'm afraid to even close my eyes in case—

Samantha!

My mother. Standing in the garden below. Looking up at me on the roof. Arms crossed. Shaking her head. What is she doing here?

Samantha, listen to me, please. You need to stop. Stop letting your imagination run away with you. Whatever. She's said to this to me before. All my life.

I always nodded *yes. Okay. Listening. Stopping.* But I wasn't listening, I wasn't stopping. Because we were already running away again, me and my imagination. We were holding hands on the edge of the cliff by the North Sea, we were high, high up in a redwood tree, we were on a train to Paris, we were blue-lipped in the river trying to swim to India. Or we were just fucking running. Down a steep and endless hill, she and I, holding hands. She was a great girl-shaped forest. She was a thing on fire. Her hand was leaves and smoke and snow and flesh all at once. We were running away together down a curving dirt road, through a dipping valley of grass, by a rushing mud-colored river, into an even greater forest, or we were just running who knows where? No idea. Didn't care. But I was excited. My life could change. And I wasn't alone anymore.

And now? Now we are tangoing on the roof.

She reaches out and brushes my hair away from my face with her hand of black mesh.

"Tell me the story of how we met, Smackie," she's asking me again.

Her touch is as cool as water on my skin. I close my eyes, press against her as we dance.

"I think it was early morning."

Though my eyes are closed, I can feel her nodding. *Yes.*

"I think I was sitting by the pond. On a bench, alone."

Yes.

"I came to watch the swan on the water—"

"Except there was no swan that morning, remember?" she fills in.

I open my eyes to look at her. Still smiling light on my face. Hair like white feathers.

Samantha, my mother says now, sadly, shaking and shaking her head. Looking up, up, up at where I'm tangoing in the blue hour with a woman I conjured from a swan. Like I'm a cat that has scrambled up yet another tall tree from which I now refuse to come down. But this time it's different. Her face says, this is different. This is the tallest one I've ever climbed. This is the farthest I've ever traveled from the ground. This is the deepest I've ever retreated into the golden-green leaves she knows I love so. She shakes her head at me from where she stands on the firm ground, to where I am wavering high, high in the branches. Dancing on my rickety roof. I look at this woman swaying in my arms. Slightly taller than I am. Who feels as real as the earth itself. Not something I conjured out of loneliness and a bird circling a pond. Because how could I not have known?

You're real, I tell this woman. *Aren't you?*

She looks at me as if considering this. Then she smiles. Reaches out with a hand of flesh and fire and snow and air. Strokes my hair. *Smackie.* I close my eyes.

And then she's gone.

The roof and the evening light are gone.

I'm in a pool of blood staring at a swan with an ax in its back. The room is dark and empty. No bed. No chair. No carpet. No curtains. No music. No lamps. Just a floor of an abandoned house and the moon coming in red and full through a barred window with a crack in the glass. Just me and Max on a concrete floor covered with dark blood. More blood than is possible to come out of a bird.

I look at the bird's long snakelike neck. Dark glassy eyes wide open. The smell of green tea, wet leaf hangs in the room so faintly now.

I stare at bare walls, at the single suitcase on the floor, my dark clothes tumbling out of it like a spilled secret, my musty sleeping bag in the corner, my open notebook facedown on top of it. A lady-shaped lamp I rescued from the dorm dumpster beside a coffee mug I stole from the English department lounge that says A Room of One's Own.

"Ava." My voice echoes in the unfinished room. Off the cheaply insulated walls of wood. Nothing but rusted pipes and beams and hanging wire above my head.

I look at Max beside me, swimming in his anarchy trench coat. I stare at his face. The knives and the wolf have fallen away like so much costume makeup. His features no longer shift, no longer recall transcendent moments or former lovers. His face is simply my face. Undisguised at last. Familiar as mud. Punched in with grief. Rage. Suddenly, I want to kill him. This thing I made out of hate and love and air and one fucking animal. There's an ax right there. The handle slightly curved, cherry colored. And then I know it wasn't him. I see it now, the pinky white hand that clutched it. Small and delicately fingered, trained in piano. Calloused from violin. Nails painted the color of natural poisons. I can picture it. See her spindly egret arms raised above the silver crown of her head. The Duchess, growing taller in that moment. Stretching into the monstrous thing she truly is beneath her fairy clothes, the ax poised and wavering over Ava's turned back.

Ava's back.

Ava.

Before I can even move, before I can even think, Max reaches out, takes the ax from her back, and charges out of the room.

37

I follow him in the predawn dark. A man carrying a bloodied ax in his fist, walking the streets with singular intention. Walking, I know exactly where, to exactly which lacquered front door. His destination is in my blood. His intention is in my heart.

You would think someone would stop him. You would think someone would stop me chasing a man with a bloodied ax. But no one does. We may as well be invisible as we make our way from the west side to the east side, him charging ahead always, me running after. A blood-splotched pair racing through a city that for once I am relieved has barely any streetlights. Me calling his name. Him not answering. I don't think he even hears me over the rage and sorrow in his own heart. Or if he does, no time for that. No fucking time or eye for anything but the task at hand. And what is the task at hand? *You know.*

I didn't realize how tall or broad he was, truly. I really didn't.

I didn't realize how thorny and monstrous his shadow. Really.

Until I see him standing before the ornate gate that leads to the tulip-lined path that leads to the stone steps that leads to the Duchess's front door.

Staring at her house with all the hate I have in my heart.

Staring at her house with all the loss I have in my heart.

Staring at her ridiculous house with a rage and sorrow that floods our blood, is bottomless, is far too big for her front door.

Only one thing to do, really.

Only one thing that can be done, really.

Justice. Vengeance. Very simple. Easy. We've seen them do it a thousand times, have we not? Just one swing—*one!*—and off with their—

"Max."

He turns to me as if called out of a dream. Like he's forgotten I was even there or who I am.

I look at her bland house, the mundane lawn brimming with carefully clipped bushes. Her dumb car shining in the moonlit driveway.

"We can't."

You know this. You know we can't.

I expect him to nod. Of course we can't. But he just looks at me like he doesn't understand my words, or doesn't care. *Fuck that.* He charges through the gate, the ax raised in his hand.

"Max! Stop! Please! Look, this is all my fault."

He turns back. "*What?*"

"Ava." Just saying her name breaks something in my voice, in both of us. Makes our eyes sting so that we're looking at each other through water.

"I told her about you."

"Told her about me?"

"Before I left. That's why she made you leave. It's my fault. All of this."

"What did you tell her about me?"

I hear the break in his voice as surely I heard it in mine. I recall her on the roof yesterday gazing at me, then at Max, then at me. The laughing lightness suddenly leaving her face.

"Everything. Who you are."

"Who *I* am," he repeats softly. I can hear almost a smile in his words, drowning in sorrow.

"Why? Why did you tell her, Samantha?" His voice now wavering as mine is wavering, his body swaying slightly now, as mine is swaying, as if we're about to dance. I close my eyes.

You know why.

Say it.

"Because I loved her. I loved her too."

Loved. I open my eyes and he looks at me like he's been punched. Lowers the ax. Sinks to his knees in a bed of the Duchess's dirt, her overly pruned flowers.

"Max."

But he just sits there. Looking at the mown grass.

Soft tango music playing, wafting from an open window like a scent. Reaching its fingers toward us.

"Max, please let's get out of here."

I reach down and touch his shoulder. But it's useless. He may as well be stone.

A light goes on in the living room. Through the window, I see them inside. Just their heads and necks lit golden from above, making their hair appear that same shiny nonshade.

I see a fishnet veil on Cupcake. A fishnet veil on Creepy Doll. They must have torn it in half *to share, Bunny*. Mesh gloves on the hands of Vignette, who is covering her mouth in what appears to be a laugh. And feathers. A barrette of white feathers in the tresses of the Duchess. Who is wearing a black silk dress I've seen before. Saw just yesterday. On the roof. When she looked at me for the last time with her different-colored eyes and smiled.

Of course I'll still be here. Where would I even go?

And just like that, I pick up the ax. Tuck it in my coat like I've seen Creepy Doll do a hundred times. Like it's a wallet, lip gloss, her house keys. *Whatevs, girl.* And with a steady, panther-footed grace, I walk up to her front door. Which they've left unlocked. Of course. For him.

At the sound of my heavy footsteps in the corridor they begin calling his names. *Tristan? Icarus? Byron? Hud?*

When I enter the living room with the ax tucked away in my coat, they fall silent. Look surprised, very surprised, to see me. Scared, maybe? Difficult to tell their expressions through their veils. Ava's veils. They remain seated in their semicircle on the suede couch. They appear to be having some sort of predawn cocktail party. Champagne flutes all around.

"Samantha, I must say this is a surprise."

"Such a surprise."

"What the fuck are *you* doing here?" Cupcake spits. "Where's Byron?"

Vignette just blinks at me. Adjusts her mesh gloves on her wrist. She's wearing black. They all are. Vintage-style dresses in slim cuts. Each one the lesser sister of the black silk dress that the Duchess is wearing, the one I know so well, that knocks the breath out of my lungs to see closer up. I can smell the rain and green tea perfume from here. My knees begin to buckle slightly. My vision feels seared. *This can be quick. This can be very quick. Just one swing and—*

"Samantha, we sense you're very . . . *upset*? About something? We can *only* imagine what it must be since, of course, *our* imaginations have limits, but go on, tell us. We're all ears."

The Duchess looks at me. Well? The Warren girl version of a gypsy giving me the death stare on the Paris metro. Her smile like a hate bouquet above her sea of black silk. I stare back at her from across the rattling train, my hand on the ax.

Only one thing to do, really.

Only one thing that can be done, really.

"Why? Why did you do it?"

My words hang there in the dustless air of the golden-lit room.

"What are you even talking about, Samantha?"

"Samantha, we're afraid we really have no idea what you're talking about."

They're going to make me say it.

"You killed her. I know you killed her."

They stare at me, and this time I do not look away. I stare at them until my eyes water, my hand on the ax, getting slippery in my hot fingers. But I do not dare to blink. For a moment I think they are going to hang their heads in shame. Wake from the nightmare of themselves. Become graduate students again, the sensible creatures they must once have been. Instead, they side-eye each other through their makeshift veils and then take pointed, slow sips of their champagne.

"Samantha," the Duchess says, arranging her features into a hasty origami of false sympathy. Shaking her head. "This is all just so sad, it's actually embarrassing."

"So embarrassing," says Creepy Doll.

"For you," Cupcake clarifies. "Is Byron with you, by the way?"

Vignette glares at me in a glazed way. Bored-horny. *Borny*, as she would say. Where the fuck is Hud?

"Tragically humiliating, really," the Duchess says, employing Fosco's pregnant pause. "Don't you think?" Her stolen black silk dress gleams under the golden light, so ill fitting.

"How could you?" I say. But my voice doesn't sound like a threat, it sounds broken, torn up. A felled thing. "How could you do that to her?"

The Duchess smiles sadly. Vignette yawns. Cupcake and Creepy Doll glower at me through their veils. "*Us*?"

"What about what *you* did, Samantha?"

"Going back and forth between us and your *companion* or whatever like a little fucking waffler."

"Talk about betrayal."

"On *both* sides."

"It's no wonder your 'friend' flew away or died or got killed or whatever. Not that we can pretend to have any idea what you do in your sad little *room*, Samantha. I mean, *our* pretending only goes so far."

Smiles that see me tangoing on the roof, no longer alone. Falling for what I didn't know was my own invention. The room dissolves and then comes back into focus and then dissolves again. The soft rug I'm standing on is so thick and plush I can't feel the floor beneath. *You have to keep your eye on the bitch in the purloined dress, you have to—*

"We *did* want to tell you, girl. About your bird friend or whatever. We almost did a couple of times. But you were just *so* delusional. We thought maybe if we told you, you would have like a breakdown or pee your pants or something. We didn't know. I mean, you were just so invested in being too cool for everyone, in not being around us or even the poets or any actual people at all, you know."

The ax in my hand is slipping. My gaze is still pointed at her like a gun.

"You fucking killed her. I know you killed her."

The Duchess looks at me like she is so sorry for me, really. Truly. But not really. Not fucking really at all.

"Honestly, Samantha. Probably *you* killed her, if anything."

"And probably you don't even remember because you're just that crazy, you're just that *lost*."

The darkness of the abandoned attic comes back to me. The red moon shining through the window with the crack in the glass. Me and Max sitting in a pool of blood.

"Samantha, we're not going to pretend we know the details of whatever squatter drama you had with your little fake threesome in that abandoned house on the west side. But we *can* tell you this. Whatever *happened* in the end? We're sure it was for the best. You can really, really trust us on that. Maybe it will even . . . I don't know . . . help you *grow*."

"I mean, you have to kill your Darlings, remember?"

"I mean, they're not *real*, Samantha, remember? Oh wait, that's right. Samantha forgets."

"Conjures little bird friends . . ."

"Maybe more than friends . . ."

"Plays with them all by her lonesome and doesn't even realize. So, *so* embarrassing for you."

"And sad. Super sad. And sort of scary-crazy?"

"Not that we don't appreciate that, girl. Certainly, the crazy-scary-sad adds a certain something or other. Like that time in first year—you weren't there, obviously—when we added that weird exotic spice to a cake by mistake? What was the name of that weird spice? I can't even remember. And for a minute we were like, *oh my god, amazing more please*? But then we tried to add more. And we were like, *No, definitely not*. There's a reason why this spice is only available in certain ethnic stores. In the end, it turns out you just need like an eighth of a teaspoon of that shit. Every now and then. That's all."

She gives me the full hate bouquet of her smile. Every fuck you flower. She knows full well that I'm gripping an ax in my coat. She's not stupid, she fucking invented this game, remember? She knows my every murderous thought, rising and falling like white feathers in a wild breeze. But whatevs. She sips her champagne slowly, savoring it under my wavering gun gaze. Because I'll never actually go through it, *will you, Samantha? Killing us? Real people? Wouldn't that be going just a little too far, even for you?*

"Samantha, we *so* love how you love to go to that edge."

"But it's one thing to go to the edge. It's another thing to fall off entirely, isn't it?"

"Where not even your 'friends' can bring you back?"

"Or like, real people."

"I mean, Samantha, if *you* can't tell the difference between reality and illusion, we can't help you."

"We really can't, girl."

"A *true* artist knows the difference. I remember learning that that's actually the difference between an actual artist and, like, an insane person, you know? We learned that in high school. At least, we learned it in mine."

"Samantha, honestly?" the Duchess continues. "I think if you look deep and hard inside yourself, you'll finally see. I think you'll see that this was all for the best in the end."

"Totally for the best, girl."

"I mean, we were always like *'you do you,'* but still. This had to end sometime, didn't it? I mean, you're about to go into the *real* world, aren't you, Samantha? You can't be having these sorts of . . . attachments."

It hits me then. There are no bunny boys languishing in the corners of her living room. The room is pristine, corners empty even of dust. No evidence. No sippy cups on the coffee table or Pixy Stix dust or half-chewed freesia petals on the floor. No whining rising from the basement through the floorboards like heat that at first would give me nightmares, made me want to go down there—*No, Bunny, don't. Leave them there*—that eventually I learned not to hear, like white noise. None of it. Just them. And me. In a regular rich-girl living room. Beige as fuck. And all around us the regular dawn beginning to break. Finger by pink finger.

I can't kill them.

I really can't.

The Duchess's smile shifts. Victorious, knowing my thoughts so instantly. No, wait. Not victorious, dreamy. She suddenly looks like she's gaping at a dream. They all do. A lightness breaks across their half-veiled faces. Like a rainbow just appeared over my shoulder.

I turn. Max. His silhouette outside the living-room window, lighting a cigarette. His beautiful knifelike face lit up by the flame. And then darkness again. Just the red cherry of his cigarette. Moving away.

"Tristan!"

"Byron!"

"Hud!"

"Icarus!"

They rise like a black wave. Rush past me out of the living room like they're on fire.

I find them all standing on the Duchess's stone front steps in a ringlike huddle. Standing absolutely still. Holding each other's hands like friends might, but really just holding each other back. They appear frozen. Transfixed. Their lips parted. Staring down at Max, who's standing in the misty front yard smoking, still in shadow. He could be looking at all of them, at one of them, at none of them.

Hard to say.

Very hard to say in this early misty light.

All a matter of perspective.

A collective sigh suddenly leaves their lips like a spring breeze. I watch them gaze down dreamily, hungrily at the man with the cigarette held loose but firm between his fingers. As if he's holding a bouquet of wildflowers, a razor blade, a blue orchid, a boom box playing your favorite song in the rain.

For you.

Just for you.

He brings the cigarette to his smiling, unripped lips.

And then they storm him. A mad rush down the stairs across the yard to where he's standing. Pushing past each other. Pulling each other back by the hair, by the neck. Tripping each other in their black heels. A single squid monster of pink flesh and black silk whose tentacles have turned on each other. Cupcake reaches him first and wraps her arms around his chest and closes her eyes and just starts screaming. Meanwhile Vignette grabs him by the leg and Creepy Doll by the opposite arm. *No, you don't, bitch,* they growl in perfect synchronicity. Then a rabbity grunt bursts forth from the Duchess as she jumps up and grabs him by the neck like she's going to rip his head off.

For a second, I'm frozen. Frozen as they were just a moment

ago. Transfixed, watching them. Pulling at his body, making shrieking noises of want that are terrible to hear. *He's mine, no he's mine, no he's fucking mine, you cunt, let go, we talked about this! He's fucking mine, mine, mine, mine.* Even the Duchess is now squealing like a pig. If I weren't seeing it with my own eyes, I wouldn't believe it. The froth. The straight white teeth bared. The hissy screaming. The inhuman sounds issuing from their meticulously painted mouths. Mouths that have cited countless philosophers and critics in grandly appointed auditoriums. I watch them tug at him with a fury that no doubt they put into their graduate school applications. An endlessly entitled fury that will drive them toward the shiny pretty things of this world and not stop until they have claimed them.

Max, meanwhile, is impassive, allowing this to happen, allowing his redwood body to be pulled in four screamingly opposing directions by rabid dolls come to life, cigarette still between his lips. Despite their violent tugging, they don't appear to be doing much damage. At all. He stands there like a patient dad letting a bunch of toddlers climb him like a tree.

Is he smiling? Maybe.

Hard to say.

Very hard to say in this shifting light, in the shadows of her blooming trees.

But he's looking at me, that I know. I can feel tingling on either side of my face. Down the back of my neck. Rib cage opening.

Get ready.

For what?

But the knowledge is already burning in my chest like a pilot light. Just need a spark to set it ablaze.

No, I tell him.

He suddenly sinks to his knees as if felled, as if hurt.

"NO!" I shout.

They all freeze. Look at me.

Not at me, but at the ax I'm now holding in my hands. Shaking because my own hands are shaking. Slippery because my own hands are slippery.

The girls freeze, but don't let go of him.

I look at Max. Who is staring straight at me, his gaze like foresty hands on my face, opening my heart itself. *Do it.*

He tilts his head back, exposing his neck, letting it catch the fiery light in the sky, and I see the ax tattoo shining blackly at me like it first did in the blue light of the bus, like it did from the very beginning.

No.

Yes, Samantha.

No, I can't, please.

Do it.

I look at all of my dreams and nightmares distilled into one man-shaped shape. All the love and hate I have in my heart plus one fucking bunny. His horned shadow swallowing her front lawn now, as the sun begins to rise behind him. Do bunnies have horned shadows?

I raise the ax over my head. They cling to him, screaming at me to *stop, please fucking stop!*

He smiles. *Trust me.*

I take aim and strike. Ax to ax. The blade hits something terribly soft. I hear an awful crack. My whole body thrums with it.

I hear them start to scream. I open my eyes. The boy they are fighting for isn't a boy anymore. Where there once was a black coat and human skin, there are hooved limbs, a smooth tawny hide, thorny antlers growing out of what used to be a human head. Large dark eyes like smoke. A stag. Kicking them away with its powerful, beautiful legs. Knocking them over with a shake of its grand antlered head.

It's a glorious sight. To watch it strike with its furious legs and shake its elegant head *no, no, no, no* until they're all felled, knocked off their heels, and they're lying on the wet dirt in their torn black silk, whimpering softly like their own bunny boys in the basement.

Then and only then does the creature stop. Rise to its full, majestic height. Stand exactly where it stood when I locked eyes with it here last winter, when it passed through her snowy front yard like a dream.

He looks at me once with his eyes of smoke. Then saunters away into the trees. I watch it disappear into the leaves and the mist, the long shadows.

Something heavy is in my hand. The handle of an ax.

I drop it.

38

Graduation at Warren, as I'm sure you know, is legendary. Really quite something, a spectacle. Champagne overflowing from glass flutes. All the shelled creatures of the deep on ice. Clouds of billowing tulle. Clusters of white tents on the blooming, budding green. And in each tent, a host of gowned assholes about to be ceremoniously released into the world, one by grinning one.

Silky calls each of us to the podium. Reads out the awards we have won. Shakes our right hands while he pretends to give us a fake diploma we pretend to take with our left. When my name is called, I walk to the stage trying to remember all of this. But when he holds out the diploma, I forget that it's fake, meant solely for the purposes of ceremony, and I try to take it from Silky, who holds fast to it and says through his teeth, *Remember, remember the email*? I don't remember, I just think, *Fine. You can have it.*

As I stand there, I look for Ava in the crowd, a reflex. Something I find myself still doing, something I can't seem to help. No black silk. No belligerent cigarette dangling from blue-red lips. No different-colored eyes gazing at me through a fishnet veil. I try to leave the podium, but Silky keeps my hand clasped in his fist, his face still fixed into a smile for invisible cameras. There are no cameras, I want to tell him. There is no one to capture this momentous occasion for me. But I don't grab him by his tie and hiss this in his ear despite the overwhelming temptation. I just walk back to my hard white chair. Try very hard not to look to my left. Where they're sitting on the opposite side of the tent. In the front row for easy access because of all the injuries. Sitting in a straight line, chairs exactly as far apart as they ought to be, no closer. Between them they have three broken legs, two broken arms, six shattered ribs, and two sprained ankles. The Duchess is wearing a neck brace.

Book arts accident, I heard they told everyone. In the press room. So sad. *We were just these innocent girls in the night trying to make something beautiful. We nearly died. We very nearly did, didn't we?*

When it's over, I stand among tent pillars wrapped with billowing tulle, watching people clink glasses and tell each other congratulations, congratulations, with well-bred smiles. The faculty patiently deliver the same camera-perfect smile over and over for each acolyte with an iPhone. Little trays of food architecture go floating by. Flutes of champagne, don't mind if I do each time. Staring at all the perfect light she hated. The stately trees she hated. Overhearing all the talk of grand summer plans, at which she would roll and roll her eyes. If I close my eyes, I can almost feel her black silk shoulder against mine. Can almost hear what she might say under her breath. *Can we get the hell out of here? You know I only come here for you.*

"Samantha, there you are."

Under the white tent, the low afternoon light on his face, he looks spectacularly unfrightening. Just a man. Not much older or taller than I am. Awkward, like I am. His expression well meaning under his untamed mane of hair. He saw me standing alone. He just wanted to say hi and congratulations.

"Not taking part in any of the revelry? The picture-taking?" he asks me. His voice is open, familiar, almost kind, bringing back with it the light, the leaves of that first fall. When he was what I needed most—a friendly face, someone to talk to, someone who believed in me.

I feel my eyes well up inexplicably, stupidly, and I look down at my shoes, the wet grass they stand in. Then I look up at him. If he sees that I've cried, he pretends not to notice.

"Maybe later," I tell him.

He nods, smiles as if he understands. Awkward pause. Very awkward.

"By the way, I enjoyed your thesis," he offers suddenly, like a benediction.

"You did?"

"Yes, very much. It was . . ." He trails off, searching for the right word.

Last year, I would have been on my hind legs waiting for this word like a starved dog. Head cocked. Panting for this biscuit of adjectives that would make me or break me. That could make me or break me. This afternoon, I just wait.

"Different. From what I expected. From what you came in with. Anyway, I liked it."

"Thank you."

"I really do think your writing is going to take you places, Samantha. I think it will bring you great things. I always have."

He smiles again. Another silence. I fill it with nothing. I fill it with absolutely nothing as we both turn away and allow ourselves to be absorbed in other clusters.

Or not so much absorbed in my case, as gently seized. By an arm draped in silk. Ursula in her spring iridescence looking pleased as punch with herself and not a little drunk. She stands at the helm of a ring of broken girls. Four crooked pink-and-white bodies. Four drugged faces that twitch when they try to fake-smile. At me.

Hello, Samantha.

I do not return their smiles.

After they got kicked to the ground, after the stag sauntered off into the trees, I walked away, leaving the ax on the wet lawn, leaving them lying there in the dawn mist. Back at my apartment, I waited for the police to call. For the dean to call. For their lawyers to call and tell me they'd see me in court, thank you. Nobody called. I was free to sit and stare out the window, my hands open and empty at my sides, sometimes seeing my own reflection, sometimes the bricks and sliver of sky beyond, sometimes both, for as long as I liked. Forever, even.

Except I didn't. Eventually, I went back to the house. Her house. Our house. My house. Gathered my half-filled notebooks off the attic floor. Went up on the roof where we danced. Finished the story. Looking up every now and then at the tree he must have planted in the corner of the garden. Where I buried her.

"I was *just* about to congratulate my girls," Ursula says now, "my *pioneers,* and then I realized: we couldn't have a proper toast without Samantha, could we?"

Of course not, they murmur politely. Voices reduced to whispers, limply holding up flutes of champagne with their bandaged hands.

"Congratulations," they actually say to me, quietly, very quietly. Like they didn't murder my soul mate. Like I didn't summon a demonic animal man to destroy their souls. Like we're actually just five young women graduating from an arts program. Warren's first all-female cohort. *Such trailblazers we are, yes?*

I do not say congratulations. I do not raise my glass of champagne in this fake toast. Instead I just watch the four of them sip under my gaze. Sips that look like they hurt. And I ask them, "So what happened to you guys again?"

"Book arts accident," Caroline whispers, her pastel cardigan failing to cover the faded EAT MEs on her chest. She's redyed her bob a golden blond, but like the cardigan, it doesn't fully cover the evidence. The sickly pale purple still shows through here and there, like a trick of the light.

"Book arts accident," I repeat. "Who would have thought book arts could do *so* much damage."

They glare at me. Or try to. It's hard for them. Very hard with all the Tic Tac painkillers taking away their edges. Leaving them suspended and floating, possibly forever, in the mist, in the rainbow sky.

"That's what I was just *saying*, Samantha," Ursula chimes in. "Not that we haven't had our little mishaps here and there over the years, of course. Of course we have. But this." She shakes her head.

"I guess sometimes you can just go too far," I offer like a pearl of wisdom. "And you know, when you go too far, not even your friends can bring you back."

"What sort of project were you girls working on, exactly, anyway?" Ursula asks. She looks at them all, wondering, waiting. Eyebrows raised in maternal concern.

They look panicked. Begin to breathe with their mouths. Side-eye is weakly attempted. Hive-minded telepathy attempted too, perhaps, through the pink mist. They even look at me, to me, for a moment.

Suddenly, Eleanor drops her crutch. It lands at my feet, the handle pointed at me like a plea.

I look at it lying there in the grass.

I drink my champagne down and walk away, leaving them there under the tented green. I throw the empty flute over my shoulder and I don't look back. I walk out of the tent into the slanting afternoon light that hurts my eyes, passing through the billowing white tulle for the last time. It caresses my shoulder like so much black silk.

There's a swan on the water today. Apart from that, nothing's changed since the last time I came here. The bench is empty. It gives dangerously when I sit down. Smoking the first of what will surely be five million cigarettes.

The noises of graduation are now distant behind me. The

white gauze undulating in the breeze. The flowering green littered with rich-people party detritus. The camera-clicking mothers. The ever-nodding fathers with their hands in their pockets, looking a little lost even though they are not lost. The glaring siblings. The gowned graduates glowing beneath their tilted caps, waiting to get their picture taken by the gates, by the buildings she never entered except once, for my sake.

You know I only come here for you.

All of it's behind me now. Leaving me. Like my spilled words on the floor of the Lion's living room. *So leave them there.* I stare at the swan gliding along the surface of the water. What did I imagine? That she would be here?

"Samantha! Hey!"

Jonah is coming toward me in a cap and gown, waving. He must have walked in the general ceremony, the only one among our cohort to have done so.

He smiles as he approaches, trailing smoke from a cigarette between his fingers, holding what must be just a cup of water in his fist.

I smile back. Wave.

"I was looking all over for you, Samantha! I was worried you'd already left."

"Still here. You really went all out with that cap and gown."

He grins. "Yeah."

"Was it fun to walk?"

"Honestly, it was actually just a lot of standing around. But hey, I took some pictures of you walking up to the podium earlier."

"You did?"

"Yeah, of course I did. You're my friend. Hey, what's wrong?"

I look down at the ground so he can't see my face.

"Nothing."

"Are you sure?"

"Yes. Just I'm happy. I'm happy that you are. My friend."

"Do you want to see the pictures?"

"Sure."

He holds up his phone for us to look at them. "Here's a good one. You're hanging on to that fake diploma pretty tight, though. It's actually kind of funny, look."

"Yeah."

"Don't worry, I almost forgot it was fake too, but then Eric reminded me just before I went up there."

He waves at Eric and the other poets who are still standing at the edge of the tent. Four men in black with varying degrees of facial hair who seem to do everything, even blink, in eerie tandem. Their synchronized look of naked contempt actually makes a noise. But Jonah just keeps waving. Completely oblivious. Or maybe he isn't so oblivious after all. Maybe he knows and he just doesn't give a fuck. How would that be?

He smiles at me. His eyes don't shift shades. His eyes are one color.

"So where are you heading now anyway?" he asks me.

"Honestly, I have no idea. I mean, the future is a question mark, isn't it? I might stay here for a while but then . . . I don't know."

His smile shifts, and he nudges my side. "I meant tonight. Where are you heading tonight?"

"Oh. Probably just going home." Our place. "Sit on the roof and celebrate with the raccoon priests."

Watch the dog become the wolf. Feel the wind cupping my face like the foresty palms of his hands. Stare at that patch of dirt in the corner of the garden where a flowering tree is now blooming.

"Raccoon priests, huh? Sounds cool."

The swan moves closer to us now, skirting the pond's edge. I think of that spring morning, just before dawn. How she appeared at my side on the bench. How I felt so suddenly alive with possibility. Saw in her a wondrous world, an open hand, a person I knew in my bones would be someone I'd love. How I had no idea. How the not knowing was the most wonderful and terrible thing. I gaze at the swan floating by the bank. Maybe I could do it again. Imagine her back. Live on the roofs and trees of my mind with another her beside me forever. Take her mesh hand in mine and this time never let go.

I watch it float away into the shivering shade.

"You could come with me," I say to Jonah. "If you want."

I lower my gaze to the mud.

"Sure, Samantha," says the mud, "I'd love to."